Enid Blyton

THE WIZARD'S UMBRELLA
STORY COLLECTION

Hodder
Children's
Books

HODDER CHILDREN'S BOOKS

This book includes stories from *Sunny Stories for Little Folk*, *Enid Blyton's Sunny Stories*, *Sunny Stories* and *Round the Clock Stories*
Previously published as *The Chimney Corner Collection* in 2011 by Egmont
This edition published in 2016 by Hodder and Stoughton

1 3 5 7 9 10 8 6 4 2

Text and illustrations copyright © Hodder and Stoughton
Enid Blyton's signature is a Registered Trademark of Hodder and Stoughton

A CIP catalogue record for this book is available from the British Library.

ISBN 978-1-444-93009-2

Typeset in ConcordeBE by
Avon DataSet Ltd, Bidford on Avon, Warwickshire
Printed and bound in Great Britain by Clays Ltd, St Ives plc

The paper and board used in this book are made from wood
from responsible sources.

Hodder Children's Books
An imprint of
Hachette Children's Group
Part of Hodder and Stoughton
Carmelite House
50 Victoria Embankment
London EC4Y 0DZ

An Hachette UK Company
www.hachette.co.uk
www.hachettechildrens.co.uk

CONTENTS

Winkle-Pip Walks Out

Once upon a time Winkle-Pip the gnome did a good turn to the Tappetty Witch, and she was very grateful.

'I will give you something,' she said. 'Would you like a wishing-suit?'

'Ooh, yes!' cried Winkle-Pip, delighted. 'That would be lovely.'

So the Tappetty Witch gave Winkle-Pip a wishing-suit. It was made of yellow silk, spotted with red, and had big pockets in it.

'Now,' said the witch to Winkle-Pip, 'whenever you wear this suit, your wishes will come true – but there is one thing you must do, Winkle.'

'What's that?' asked Winkle-Pip.

'Once each year you must go out into the world of boys and girls and grant wishes to six of them,' said the witch. 'Now don't forget that, Winkle, or the magic will go out of your wishing-suit.'

1

Winkle-Pip promised not to forget, and off he went home, with the wishing-suit wrapped up in brown paper, tucked safely under his arm.

Now the next day Winkle-Pip's old Aunt Maria was coming to see him. She always liked a very good tea, and often grumbled because Winkle-Pip, who was not a very good cook, sometimes gave her burnt cakes, or jam sandwich that hadn't risen well, and was all wet and heavy.

So the gnome decided to use his wishing-suit the next day, and give his aunt a wonderful surprise. He put it on in the morning and looked at himself in the glass – and he looked very nice indeed. He thought he would try the wish-magic, so he put his hands in his pockets and spoke aloud.

'I wish for a fine feathered cap to go with my suit!' he said.

Hey presto! A yellow hat with a red feather came from nowhere, and landed with a thud on his big head.

'Ho!' said Winkle-Pip, pleased. 'That's a real beauty.'

He looked round his kitchen. It was not very clean, and none of the breakfast dishes had been washed up. The curtains looked dirty too, and Winkle-Pip remembered that his Aunt Maria had

said he really should wash them.

'Now for a bit of fun!' said Winkle, and he put his hands in his pockets again.

'Kitchen, tidy yourself, for that is my wish!' he said, loudly.

At once things began to stir and hum. The tap ran water, and the dishes jumped about in the bowl and washed themselves. The cloth jumped out of the pail under the sink, and rubbed itself hard on the soap. Then it began to wash the kitchen floor far more quickly than Winkle-Pip had ever been able to do.

The brush leapt out of its corner and swept the rugs, which were really very dirty indeed. The pan held itself ready for the sweepings, and when it was full it ran outside to the dustbin, and emptied itself there.

You should have seen the kitchen when everything had quieted down again! How it shone and glittered! Even the saucepans had joined in and had let themselves be scrubbed well in the sink. It was marvellous.

'Now for the curtains!' said Winkle-Pip, and he put his hands in his pockets again. 'I wish you to make yourselves clean!' he called.

The curtains didn't need to be told twice. They sprang off their hooks and rushed to the sink. The tap ran and filled the basin with hot water. The soap made a lather, and then those curtains jumped themselves up and down in the water until every speck of dirt had run from them and they were as white as snow! Then they flew to the mangle, which squeezed the water from them. Then out to the line in the yard they went, and the pegs pegged them there in the wind. The wind blew its hardest, and in a few minutes they flew back into the kitchen once more. The iron had already put itself on the stove to heat, and as soon as the curtains appeared and laid themselves flat on the table, the iron jumped over to them and ironed them out beautifully.

Then back to their hooks they flew, and hung themselves up at the windows. How lovely they looked!

'Wonderful!' cried Winkle-Pip in delight. 'My, I

wonder what my old Aunt Maria will say!'

Then he began to think about food.

'I think I'll have a big chocolate cake, a jelly with sliced pears in it, a dozen little ginger cakes, some ham sandwiches, some fresh lettuce and radishes, and some raspberries and cream,' decided Winkle. 'That would make a simply glorious tea!'

So he wished for all those – and you should just have seen his kitchen coming to life again. It didn't take the magic very long to make all the cakes and sandwiches he wanted, and to wash the lettuce and radishes that suddenly flew in from the garden.

'Splendid!' cried the gnome, clapping his hands with joy. 'Won't my Aunt Maria stare to see all this?'

In the afternoon his old aunt came – and as soon as she opened the kitchen door, how she stared! She looked at the snowy sink, she looked at the spotless floor. She stared at the clean curtains, and she stared at the shining saucepans. Then she gazed at the lovely tea spread out on the table.

'Well!' she cried in astonishment. 'What a marvellous change, Winkle-Pip. How hard you must have worked! I am really very, very pleased with you.'

She gave the gnome a loud kiss, and he blushed very red.

'It's my wishing-suit, Aunt,' he said, for he was a truthful little gnome. He told her all about it and she was full of surprise.

'Well, you be sure to take great care of it,' she said, eating a big piece of chocolate cake. 'And whatever you do, Winkle-Pip, don't forget to go out into the world of boys and girls and find six of them to grant wishes to – or you'll lose the wishing-magic as sure as eggs are eggs.'

Winkle-Pip *did* enjoy his wishing-suit! He granted wishes to all his friends – and you may be sure that everyone wanted to be his friend when they knew about his new magic suit! Then a time came when he knew that he must go out into our world, for the magic in his suit began to weaken.

So one day Winkle-Pip put on his suit of yellow

silk and his fine feathered cap, and walked to the end of Fairyland.

'How pleased all the boys and girls will be to see me!' he said. 'And how glad they will be to have their wishes granted. I am sure they don't see fairy folk very often, and they will go mad with joy to find me walking up to them.'

'Don't be too sure,' said his friend, the green pixie, who had walked to the gates of Fairyland with him. 'I have heard that boys and girls nowadays don't believe in fairies, and are much too busy with their wireless-sets and their Meccanos to want to listen to tales about us. They might not believe in you!'

'Rubbish!' said Winkle. He shook hands with the green pixie and walked out into our world. He looked all around him and wondered which way to go.

'I'll go eastwards,' he thought. 'It looks as if there might be a town over there.'

So off he went, and after a few miles he came to a little market town. He went along, peeping into the windows of the houses as he passed by, and at last he saw a nursery. A little boy and girl were playing with a beautiful dolls' house, and they were talking about it.

'You know, this dolls' house is very old-fashioned,'

said the little boy. 'It's got oil-lamps, instead of electric light. It's a silly dolls' house, I think.'

'Well, I'm sure Grandpa won't have electric light put into it for us,' said the little girl. 'I do so wish he would. That would be fine!'

'Ha!' thought Winkle-Pip. 'Here's a chance for me to give them a wish.'

So he jumped into the window, and walked quietly up behind the children. 'Would you like electric light in that dolls' house?' he asked. 'You have only to wish for it, whilst I am here, and you shall have it.'

The children looked round in surprise.

'Of course I'd like it,' said the girl. 'I wish I *could* have electric light all over the house!'

In a second the magic had worked, and the dolls' house was lit up with tiny electric lights from top to bottom! How the children gasped to see such a wonderful sight. They found that there were tiny switches beside each door, and when they snapped these on and off the lights went on or out. They began to play with them in great excitement.

Meanwhile the gnome stood behind them, waiting for a word of thanks. The children seemed quite to have forgotten him. He was terribly hurt, and at last he crept out of the window, without even saying good-bye.

'Fancy not thanking me for granting their wish!' he thought, mournfully. 'Well, that was a nasty surprise for me! I thought the children would be delighted to talk to me too.'

Winkle-Pip went on again, and after a while he came across two boys hunting in the grass for something they had lost.

'Where *can* that shilling have gone?' he heard one of them say. 'Oh, I do wish we could find it, for we shall get into such trouble for losing it, when we get home.'

Up went Winkle-Pip to them. 'I can grant you your wish,' he said. 'I am a gnome, and have my wishing-suit on.'

The two boys looked at him.

'Don't be silly,' said one. 'You know quite well that there are no such things as gnomes – and as for wishing-suits, well, you *must* think us stupid to believe in things like that! You couldn't possibly grant us a wish!'

Winkle-Pip went very red. He stuck his hands in his pockets and looked at the two boys.

'Do you really want to find that shilling?' he asked.

'Yes, rather!' said the boys. 'We wish we could, for we shall get whipped for coming home without it.'

No sooner had they wished than the silver shilling rose up from where it had been hidden in the grass, and flew into Winkle-Pip's hand.

'Here it is,' he said to the boys, and gave it to them. But were they pleased? No, not a bit of it!

'You had it all the time!' they cried, for they had not seen it fly into the gnome's hand. 'You have played a trick on us! We will beat you.'

They set upon the poor gnome and he had to run for his life. He sat down on the first gate he came to and rubbed his bruises.

'Well!' he thought miserably. 'That's two wishes granted and not a word of thanks for either of them. What is the world coming to, I wonder? Is there any politeness or gratitude left?'

After a while he went on again, and soon he heard the sound of sobbing. He peeped round the corner and saw a little girl sitting on the steps of a small house, crying bitterly.

'What's the matter?' asked Winkle-Pip, his kind heart touched by her loud sobs. At first the little girl didn't answer, but just frowned at him. Then suddenly from the house there came a voice.

'Now stop that silly crying, Mary! You deserved to be smacked. It was very naughty of you to break your poor dolly like that, just out of temper.'

'I shall break her again if I like!' shouted the naughty little girl, jumping to her feet and stamping hard. The gnome was terribly shocked.

'You shouldn't talk like that,' he said. 'Why, do you know, I came to give you a wish, and –'

'Silly creature, silly creature!' screamed the bad-tempered child, making an ugly face at him. 'I wish you'd go away, that's what I wish! I wish you'd run to the other end of the town; then I wouldn't see you any more!'

Well, of course, her wish had to come true and poor Winkle-Pip found himself scurrying off to the other end of the town in a mighty hurry. He was soon very much out of breath, but not until he was right at the other end of the little town did his feet stop running.

'My goodness!' said Winkle-Pip, sinking down on the grass by the road-side. 'What a horrid day I'm having! What nasty children there are nowadays! Three more wishes to give away – and, dear me, I do wish I'd finished, for I'm not enjoying it at all.'

As Winkle-Pip sat there, two children came by, a boy and a girl.

'Hallo, funny-face,' said the boy, rudely. 'Wherever do you come from?'

'I come from Fairyland,' said the gnome. 'I am a gnome, as I should think you could guess.'

'Pooh!' said the boy, 'what rubbish to talk like that! There are no gnomes or fairies.'

'Of course not,' said the little girl.

'Well, there *are*,' said Winkle-Pip, 'and, what's more, I'm rather a special gnome. I've come into your world to-day to give wishes to six children. I've wasted three wishes, and I'm beginning to think there are no children worth bothering about nowadays.'

'What, do you mean you can grant wishes to us?' asked the boy. 'I don't believe it! Well, I'll try, anyway, and we'll see if what you say is true! I wish for a banana, a pear, and a pineapple to come and sit on your head!'

Whee-ee-ee-ee-eesh! Through the air came flying a large banana, very ripe, a big pear, and a spiky pineapple. Plonk! They all fell on poor Winkle-Pip's head and he groaned in dismay. The children stared in amazement and began to laugh. Then they looked rather scared.

'Ooh!' said the boy. 'He must be a gnome, after all, because our wish came true!'

Winkle-Pip was so angry that he couldn't think what to say. The children gave him one more look and then took to their heels and fled, afraid of what the gnome might do to them in revenge.

Poor Winkle-Pip! He was so distressed and so hurt to think that children could play him such a mean trick when he had offered them a wish, that he hardly knew what to do. He tried his best to get the fruit off his head, but it was so firmly stuck there that it would not move.

'Oh dear! oh dear!' wept the gnome. 'I shall have to let it all stay there, because I can't have

any wishes for myself till I have given away the six wishes to boys and girls.'

Presently there came by a little girl carrying a heavy load of wood. She stopped when she saw the gnome, and looked at him in surprise.

'Why are you carrying all those things on your head?' she asked. 'Aren't they dreadfully heavy?'

'Yes,' said the gnome with a sigh. 'But I can't very well help it.' Then he told the little girl all his story, and she was very sorry for him.

'I do wish I could get it off for you,' she said. 'If I had a wish, I would wish that, and the fruit would fly away.'

No sooner had she spoken these words than her wish came true! Off flew the banana, off went the pear, and off jumped the pineapple. They all disappeared with a click, and the gnome shook his head about in joy.

'Hurrah!' he said. 'They've gone. Oh, you nice little girl, I'm so glad you wished that wish. You're the only unselfish child I have met in my journeys to-day.'

'And you're the first person who has ever called me unselfish,' said the little girl, with a sigh. 'I live with my stepmother, and she is always telling me I am lazy and selfish. I do try so hard not to be.'

'Poor child,' said Winkle-Pip, thinking it was a dreadful shame to make a little girl carry such a heavy load of wood. 'Have you no kind father?'

'No,' said the little girl. 'I have an aunt though,

but since we moved she doesn't know where my stepmother and I live. My stepmother didn't like her because she was kind to me, and wanted me to live with her. She said I was nothing but a little servant to my stepmother, and so I am. I wouldn't mind that a bit, if only she would love me and be kind to me.'

Winkle-Pip was nearly in tears when he heard this sad story. 'I do wish I could help you,' he said. 'What a pity your kind aunt isn't here to take you to her home and love you.'

'I do wish she was,' said the little girl, lifting the bundle of wood on to her shoulder again – and then she gave a loud cry of delight and dropped it. Winkle-Pip cried out too, for, what do you think? – hurrying towards them was the kindest, plumpest woman you could possibly imagine!

'Auntie! Auntie!' cried the little girl. 'I was just wishing you were here!'

'Of course,' said Winkle-Pip to himself with a smile, 'that's the sixth wish! I'd quite forgotten there was still another one to give. Well, I'm very, very glad that this little girl has got the last wish. She used up one wish to set me free from that banana, pear, and pineapple, and she deserves to have one for herself, bless her kind heart!'

'Where have you come from, Auntie?' asked the little girl, hugging the smiling woman round the neck. 'Oh, I *have* missed you so!'

'I've come to fetch you home with me,' said her aunt, kissing her. 'I've had such a time trying to find out where your stepmother took you to. I don't quite know how I got here, but still, here I am, and you're coming straight home with me, and I'm going to look after you and love you.'

'But what about my stepmother?' asked the child.

'Oh, I'll go and see her for you,' said the gnome, with a grin. 'I'll tell her what I think of her. You go

home with your aunt and have a lovely time. I'll take your wood back for you.'

So the little girl went off happily, with her aunt holding her tightly by the hand. Winkle-Pip shouldered the bundle of wood and ran off to the little cottage that the child had pointed out to him.

An ugly, bad-tempered-looking woman opened the door, and frowned when she saw Winkle-Pip.

'I've brought you the wood that your little stepdaughter was bringing,' said the gnome. 'She has gone to live with her auntie.'

'Oh, she has, has she?' said the woman, picking up a broom. 'Well, I'm sure *you've* had something to do with that, you interfering little creature! I'll give you such a drubbing!'

She ran at the little gnome, but he stuck his hands into his pockets, and wished quickly.

'I've given away six wishes!' he said. 'Now my wishing suit is full of magic for me again – so I wish myself back in Fairyland once more!'

Whee-ee-ee-eesh! He was swept up into the air, and vanished before the angry woman's eyes. She turned pale with fright, and ran inside her cottage and banged the door. She was so terrified that she never once tried to find out where her stepdaughter had gone.

As for Winkle-Pip, he was delighted to get home again.

Over a cup of cocoa he told the green pixie all his adventures, and they both agreed that he had had a most exciting day.

It will soon be time for Winkle-Pip to walk out into our world again – so be careful if you meet him, and do try to use your wish in the best way you can.

Trit-Trot the Pony

There was once a brown pony called Trit-Trot. It belonged to old Mrs. Kennedy, and she used it for pulling her little pony-cart along when she went shopping. But, as she didn't go shopping very often, Trit-Trot spent a good deal of time alone in the field.

Every day, as he went to and from school, a boy called Billy stopped to speak to the pony. 'Hallo, Trit-Trot!' he would say. 'How are you to-day? Found any nice grass to eat? I'll bring you my apple-core to munch when I've eaten the apple at school this morning.'

He always remembered to do as he said, and Trit-Trot liked Billy very much. He thought he was the nicest boy he had ever met. Some of the boys that came by were not so nice.

'There's Leonard – he once threw a stone at me,' thought the brown pony, as he ate the grass. 'And there's that nasty big boy called Harry – he has tried to catch me and ride me heaps of times. I wouldn't at all mind giving him a ride – but he always has a big stick to hit me with, and I won't have that! Ah – Billy's the nicest. Always a kind word for a lonely little pony, and sometimes a juicy carrot, and apple – or even a lump of sugar saved from his breakfast cocoa! He really is a friend to have. I wish I could do something to pay him back for his kindness.'

Now one day, when Billy was standing on the field-gate talking to Trit-Trot, the big boy called Harry came along.

'Hallo, Billy!' he said. 'Got any money to-day? There's some fine new marbles in the toy-shop.'

'I've got three pennies and a ha'penny,' said Billy. 'But I'm saving them up for my mother's birthday.'

'Well, lend them to me till Saturday, and I'll get the marbles,' said Harry.

'No,' said Billy. 'I lent you a penny last month, and you never gave it back to me.'

'What! You won't lend me the money to get the marbles!' cried Harry, angrily. 'We'll see about that. I can easily get them away from a little shrimp like you!'

And before Billy could shout or say a word, Harry had him down off the gate, and had taken the little purse from his pocket. He emptied the money out, put it loose into his own pocket, and threw the purse back to Billy. It wasn't a bit of good Billy trying to get his money back. Harry was far too big and fierce to fight.

Harry went off whistling. Billy stared after him, angry and miserable. Trit-Trot the pony watched from surprised brown eyes. Billy turned to him and stroked his long nose.

'It's too bad,' he said. 'I shan't get that money back. I know I shan't. It took me three-and-a-half weeks to save it.'

Trit-Trot was sorry. He didn't like Harry any more than Billy did. He suddenly left the gate and ran down the field. At the end of it there was a gap that he could just squeeze through. Trit-Trot squashed his fat little brown body through it, and then stood waiting for Harry to come by. Ah – there he was, whistling merrily. Harry stopped when he saw Trit-Trot. 'Hallo!' he said. 'You've got out of the field. Give me a ride, will you? Come on!' Usually Trit-Trot ran away when Harry came near – but now he stood still, and let Harry get on to his back. 'Gee-up!' said Harry, and hit the pony with the stick he always carried.

The pony trotted off to the opposite side of the road, where there was a muddy patch. He suddenly stopped still, gave himself a jerk and off went Harry, landing in the mud with a bump and a splash. Trit-Trot neighed. Then he bent down his big head, and took hold of Harry's belt with his strong teeth. Harry screamed. He half-thought the pony was going to eat him! But Trit-Trot had another idea in his mind! He carried the wriggling boy down the lane to the field-gate, where Billy was still standing.

'Hrrrumph!' said Trit-Trot, still holding Harry tightly by his belt.

'Trit-Trot! You've caught Harry – and brought him to me!' cried Billy, with a laugh, for really Harry looked very funny. 'I suppose you thought I could get back my money if you held him like that for me. Well – I can!'

And Billy quickly took back the money Harry had taken from him, and put it safely in his purse. Then Trit-Trot dropped Harry on to the ground and looked at Billy, asking him with big brown eyes to open the gate and let him into his field once more.

Harry jumped to his feet and fled down the lane at top speed. He was afraid Trit-Trot would go after him and grab him again. He disappeared round the bend and Billy gave a sigh of relief!

'Thank you, Trit-Trot,' he said. 'You really are a good friend! I'm sure Mother won't believe me when she hears what you did!'

'Hrrrrumph!' said Trit-Trot, rubbing his nose against Billy's arm. Billy knew what that meant quite well – he was saying: 'I've paid you back for your kindness!' And he certainly had, hadn't he?

The Magic Walking-stick

Tell-Tale Tippy was a pixie that nobody liked, and his name will tell you why. He told a hundred tales a day about other people – horrid, sneaky tales – and made all his friends very unhappy.

'Can't we do something to stop Tippy from telling tales?' asked Gobo the elf. 'He would be quite nice if only he hadn't that nasty habit.'

But it wasn't a bit of use – scolding and coaxing made no difference to Tippy. He just went on telling tales.

'Gobo went shopping with a hole in his stocking this morning!' he told everybody.

'Pippit hasn't got enough money to pay his chocolate bill this week!' he whispered.

'Silverwing hasn't been asked to Tiptoe's party,' he said. Wasn't he mean? It is so horrid to tell tales and, really, Tippy had a new tale to tell almost every minute, so sharp were his little green eyes, and so long was the nose that he poked into everyone's business.

Aha! But he did it once too often, as you will see!

When the Enchanter Too-Tall came to Tippy's village to see his old Aunt Mickle-Muckle, Tippy was delighted – because, you see, Mrs. Mickle-Muckle lived next door to Tippy, and he could spy on all that the Enchanter did.

Now Too-Tall the Enchanter had a habit of getting up very early in the morning, and walking in the garden in his dressing-gown to get the fresh, cool air. Tippy heard him and crept to the window.

There, down below in Mrs. Mickle-Muckle's little garden, was Too-Tall the Enchanter, his mass of curly hair blowing in the morning breeze.

And, as Tippy watched, what do you think happened? Why, the enchanter's hair all blew away in the wind, every single bit of it! And Tippy saw that he was quite bald.

'Ooh! He wears a wig! He wears a wig!' said the peeping pixie. 'I never knew that before! Why, he is as bald as a pea! Oh look! His curly wig has blown into the big rose-bush!'

Too-Tall the Enchanter was horrified when his wig blew off. He looked round hurriedly to see if anyone was about who might see his bald head, but he couldn't spy Tippy, who was safely behind his curtain. Quickly he ran to the rose-bush and pulled out his wig, which had settled down right in the middle of it. He scratched his hands on the prickles and said, very loudly, 'Oh, bother! *Bother!* BOTHER!'

Then he put his wig on his head again, rather crooked, and went indoors.

Tippy rubbed his hands in glee. What a lovely tale he would have to tell everyone that morning! He dressed very quickly, had his breakfast, put on his pointed cap, and went out. The first person he met was Gobo the elf, and he ran up to him.

'Gobo, listen! Too-Tall the Enchanter is as bald as a pea! His hair is a wig! It blew off this morning and he said "Bother! *Bother!* BOTHER!"'

'Ooh!' said Gobo, surprised. 'But really, Tippy, you shouldn't tell tales, you know. You've been told ever so often. Too-Tall would be awfully cross if he knew you had told about his bald head.'

'Pooh! He'll never know,' said Tippy, and he ran off to tell Skippy-Wee the brownie, who was just coming out of his cottage.

'Skippy-Wee! Listen! Too-Tall the Enchanter is as bald as a pea! His hair is a wig! It blew off this morning and he said "Bother! *Bother!* BOTHER!"'

'Ooh!' said Skippy-Wee, with wide-open eyes. 'Fancy that! I always thought he had such curly hair – but, Tippy, Too-Tall would be very angry if he knew you were telling tales about what you saw.'

'Pooh! He'll never know,' said Tippy, and ran off to tell his news to someone else.

Well, he told his tale to forty-two different people that morning, and once of them happened to go to tea with Mrs. Mickle-Muckle's old gardener that afternoon. As soon as the gardener heard the tale he went straight to Mrs. Mickle-Muckle and asked her if it were true that her nephew, the great enchanter, hadn't a single hair on his head.

'Ooh my, who told you that?' said Mrs. Mickle-Muckle. 'Well, as far as I know, Too-Tall's hair is his own. I never knew he wore a wig.'

Now it so happened that the enchanter's sharp ears heard every word of this, and he went red right down to his collar. Oh, dear! He hadn't wanted

anyone to know that he wore a wig – and now it seemed that all the village knew it! He had lost his hair because of a powerful spell that went wrong, and he had had a curly wig made just exactly like the hair he had lost – and he hadn't told a single person about it!

'Who's been telling tales?' he wondered, with a frown. 'Well, I'll find out.'

He took a large silver ball and set it on the table in front of him. Then he stroked it with a peacock's feather and sang in a low voice a little magic spell. At the end of it he struck the ball with the feather and said loudly:

'Now let the face of the tell-tale appear!'

And, gracious goodness, what a very strange and peculiar thing! In the silver ball came a misty face, and as the enchanter stared at it, it came clearer and clearer, and there at last was Tell-Tale Tippy's face!

'What is your name?' asked the enchanter.

31

'Tippy,' said the face in the silver ball.

'Where do you live?' asked the enchanter, sternly.

'Next door,' answered the face. Then the enchanter struck the ball with the peacock's feather and the face gradually grew misty and then vanished. Too-Tall put the ball on to a shelf and sat down to think.

Oho! So it was that nasty little Tippy next door who had seen his wig blow off that morning and had told everyone about it! The horrid little tell-tale! His aunt, Mrs. Mickle-Muckle, had often told him what a tell-tale Tippy was – and, really, it was about time that pixie was punished.

The next day Too-Tall the Enchanter went to a shop that sold walking-sticks. He bought one with a crook handle and took it home. It was a really beautiful stick, bright red with a yellow crook, and round the neck of the stick was a silver collar. If you twisted the crook the handle came right off. It was really a very fine stick indeed.

Too-Tall took it home to his aunt's. He unscrewed the handle, and put a funny little blue spell into the neck of the stick. Then he put on the handle once more, screwed it up, hung the stick over his arm, and went next door to see Tippy.

Tippy opened the door himself, and wasn't he

surprised to see Too-Tall! He began to shake at the knees, because he knew that he had been telling tales about the enchanter's wig. But Too-Tall didn't frown, and he didn't scold – no, he simply bowed politely, and held out the bright-red stick to Tippy.

'I hear you are a tale-teller,' he said. 'Pray accept this stick from me – it is one that all tale-tellers should use!'

Tippy was almost scared out of his life! He knew that the stick must be a magic one, and he was afraid to take it – but he was also afraid to refuse it! So he just stood there, trembling, his mouth opening and shutting like a goldfish, not knowing what to do.

The enchanter stood the stick in Tippy's umbrella-stand, and walked back to his aunt's cottage. Tippy stood in the hall, very much afraid of the stick. But it seemed quite harmless. It didn't do anything, or say anything, so suddenly Tippy made a face at it.

'Pooh!' he said. 'You needn't think I'm afraid of you! I shan't take you out with me, and I shan't take any notice of you at all – so you won't be able to do anything to me, you silly old stick!'

The stick stood still and said nothing. And just then there came another knock at the door. Tippy opened it, and outside stood Gobo the elf.

'Oh, Tippy,' he said, 'I've brought back the book you lent me. Thank you very much.'

'Oh, thanks,' said Tippy. 'I say – do you see that blot of ink on the cover? Well, Skippy-Wee did that when I lent him the book. Wasn't it careless of him?'

'Oh, don't tell tales,' began Gobo – and then he stopped in surprise! The red-and-yellow stick had jumped out of its stand and was whipping Tippy!

And all the time it cried out loudly: 'Tell-Tale Tippy! Tell-Tale Tippy!'

Tippy howled in pain and ran into the kitchen, but the stick followed him there, and not until he said he was sorry he had told tales did it stop hitting him and go quietly to its stand.

'Ooh my, Tippy, you'd better be careful!' said Gobo the elf. 'That stick will make you black and blue if you tell any more tales. I say! Won't everyone laugh when they hear about your stick?'

'Oh, don't tell anyone; please, don't tell anyone!' begged Tippy. 'They would laugh at me so.'

'Well, you are always telling tales about other people,' said Gobo. 'Why shouldn't I tell tales about *you*, Tippy?' And out he went, laughing to himself.

Tippy frowned hard at the magic stick. Then he suddenly ran at it, grabbed it from the stand, and flung it out of the back door into the garden. He slammed the door, and cried out: 'Stay there, you miserable thing!'

He put the kettle on to make some cocoa, for he really felt quite ill – and then he heard a tap-tap-tapping upstairs. The tap-tap-tap came all the way down the stairs, and, goodness me, when Tippy looked out into the hall, there was the magic stick back in the umbrella-stand again! It had crept in at one of the bedroom windows and gone back to the stand by itself.

After he had had a drink of hot cocoa, Tippy thought he had better go and do some shopping. So he put on his pointed cap and out he went – but as he passed through the hall the stick jumped from the hall-stand and quietly hooked itself on Tippy's arm! He didn't notice it, and went walking on with the stick beside him.

Soon he met Mrs. Cuddle, the balloon woman, and he stopped to speak to her.

'Do you know,' he said, 'I heard that Mrs. Hallo,

who lives in Lemon Cottage, stole two of your balloons the other day when you weren't looking.'

With a leap the magic stick jerked itself off Tippy's arm, and before the surprised pixie could get away it began to whip him soundly again, crying out loudly all the time, 'Tell-Tale Tippy! Tell-Tale Tippy!'

In a trice a crowd collected, and, dear me, how delighted everyone was to see Tippy being soundly whipped for telling tales! They clapped their hands and cheered, for there wasn't a single person there that Tippy hadn't told tales about. Tippy fought the stick, but it was too quick for him, and at last the weeping pixie took to his heels and ran as fast as he could back to his cottage. The magic stick flew after him and neatly hooked itself on to his arm again – and when at last the pixie got home he found that he had brought the stick with him!

'I'll punish you for beating me in front of everyone!' wept Tippy, angrily. 'I'll burn you, see if I don't!'

He went out into the garden and made a big bonfire. Then he fetched the stick and threw it into the middle. The flames roared up and Tippy rubbed his hands in glee. Hurrah! Now the stick was done for!

He ran indoors to change his tunic, for he was to go to dinner with his Aunt Wumple, who lived at the other end of the village. He put on his best yellow silk tunic and his finest green knickerbockers. Then he sat down to read a book until it was time to go.

He didn't hear a tap-tap-tapping coming across the floor – but suddenly he felt something brushing against him – and, oh, my goodness me, it was the magic stick again! It wasn't burnt, but it had got all black and sooty in the fire, and when it brushed against Tippy's fine clothes it made them black and dirty.

'Go away, go away!' yelled Tippy, angrily. 'I thought you were burnt! Look what a mess you have made of my clean clothes!'

The stick wouldn't go away. It wiped itself all up and down Tippy till it was clean – and you should have seen him when it had finished! He was covered with sooty marks and looked a real little sweep!

He was ready to cry with rage. 'All right!' he said. 'You wait, you miserable stick. I'll drown you!'

He caught up the magic stick and ran to his well with it. Plonk! Splash! He threw it into the water far below and then left it there to drown.

'Ho!' he thought, as he changed into some clean

clothes, 'that's the end of that nasty stick!'

He hurried off to his Aunt Wumple's, and stayed with her until it was dark. Then he ran back home again, and undressed to go to bed, for it was late. He soon fell asleep, and began to snore.

Suddenly he woke with a jump! Whatever was that noise? He sat up. Something was squeezing itself in at the window, which was just a little bit open. Then, oh, dear me – tap-tap-tap, he heard across the wooden floor, and something crept close beside him under the bedclothes.

'Let me get close to you, I am cold and wet,' said the voice of the magic stick. 'I have struggled all the day to escape from the well, and I am tired and cold.'

The wet stick pressed itself against Tippy, and he shivered. He got as far away from it as he could, but it crept after him. He didn't dare to push it away in case it began to whip him again. So all night long he and the magic stick lay shivering together, and Tippy was as scared a little pixie as you'd find anywhere.

In the morning he dressed very solemnly, and thought hard. He couldn't burn that stick – he couldn't drown it – perhaps he could chop it into pieces and use it for firewood. So he fetched his chopper, and laid the stick on the chopping-block. Chop! Chop! Chop! It wasn't a bit of good, the stick was as hard as iron. Every time he chopped it it flew up and hit him on the nose, and soon Tippy threw down the chopper in despair.

'It's no good, Tippy,' said the stick, hopping to the umbrella-stand. 'You can't get rid of me. You must just put up with me, that's all.'

So Tippy had to make up his mind to make the best of that magic stick. It went with him everywhere, and if he slipped out alone, it hopped after him and hooked itself on his arm. Every time he told a tale about someone the stick whipped him soundly and cried out loudly: 'Tell-Tale Tippy! Tell-Tale Tippy!'

And soon Tippy thought twice before he told tales! If his tongue began to tell a tale, he felt the stick jerk on his arm, and he quickly made the tale a nice one, in case the stick should start to beat him again.

'Have you heard that Gobo–?' he would begin, and feel the stick jerk, ready to beat him if the tale was an unkind one – and quickly he would alter his tale. 'Have you heard that Gobo gave a nice rocking-horse to the gardener's little boy? Wasn't it kind of him?'

Then the stick would rest quietly on his arm, and Tippy would be glad. But, dear me, how hard it was to remember to tell only nice things about his friends. For so many years he had been a nasty little tale teller that he found it very difficult to stop. He had many a whipping before he learnt his lesson.

Then the day came when he knew that he would never, never tell tales again. He had grown to be a kind-hearted, generous little pixie, and although the magic stick still hung on to his arm whenever

41

he went out, it no longer whipped him, for it never
had any need to do so.

One morning, when Tippy was in the village
shopping, the stick jerked itself off his arm, and
went tap-tap-tapping down the street, all by itself.

'Where are you going?' shouted Tippy.

'Oh, I'm off to seek my fortune!' called back the
stick. 'You do not need me now. You are no longer
a tale-teller!'

'Well, come back to me and be just an ordinary
walking-stick!' shouted Tippy. 'I've grown quite
fond of you, stick!'

'No, no!' called back the stick. 'I am a magic

stick. I could never be an ordinary one. Good-bye, Tippy, don't miss me too much. I'm off to find another tale-teller!'

And with that it tapped away over the hill and was lost to sight. It didn't go back to Too-Tall the Enchanter (who, you will be glad to know, grew all his hair again through using his Aunt Mickle-Muckle's hair-cream) and it never went back to Tippy's village any more.

It is probably still tap-tap-tapping through the world, waiting to hear someone tell an unkind tale about somebody else – and then it will hook itself on to his arm, and wait until it can give him a good beating! So do be careful, won't you, not to tell tales about anyone, because you never know when that magic stick might be tap-tap-tapping somewhere near by!

The Snoozy Gnome

Have you heard of the Snoozy Gnome? His real name was Tippit, but he was always called Snoozy. He was the sleepiest, yawniest fellow that ever lived! He could go to sleep at any time – even whilst running to catch a bus!

Now one day Snoozy's village was tremendously excited. The Prince of Heyho was coming for the day, and so the gnomes decided to give a fancy dress party in his honour.

'It shall be at five o'clock in the afternoon, so that even the tiniest gnome can come,' said Mister Big-Nose, the chief gnome. 'Now all go home, please, and think out some really good fancy dresses for the party!'

Snoozy went home and sat down to think. 'I shall be a bear!' he decided excitedly. 'I can wear my bearskin rug, and pull the head right over my head. I will pin it tightly round me – and dear me, how astonished everyone will be! That will be a fine fancy dress!'

When the day came, Snoozy took up his bearskin rug and tried it on his back. He crawled about with the bear-head over his head, and the rug over his back. He really looked fine – just like a real bear!

'It's a bit big round my neck,' thought Snoozy. 'I must alter that. Let me see – what is the time? Oh, only two o'clock. I've got heaps of time till five.'

He got out a big needle and a strong thread and sat down to make the neck of the bearskin a little smaller. It was a hot afternoon and Snoozy rested his head against a soft cushion. He was very comfortable.

'Aaaaaah!' he yawned. 'My goodness, I'd like a nap. I do feel sleepy!'

He looked at the clock again. 'I think I'd have time just for 10 minutes' snooze,' he decided. 'Then I shall be all fresh for the party!'

So he lay back and fell asleep. The time went on – three o'clock, four o'clock, five o'clock! And still Snoozy slept on! He dreamed pleasant dreams. He was as warm as toast, and his armchair was very comfortable. Oh, what a lovely snooze!

Time went on – six o'clock, seven o'clock, eight o'clock, nine o'clock. Snoozy, aren't you *ever* going to wake up? The party is over – everyone has gone home and Mister Big-Nose is wondering why Snoozy didn't go to the party like everyone else!

Ten o'clock, eleven o'clock, midnight! Everywhere was quite dark and silent. Snoozy slept on, dreaming pleasantly. The clock ticked out the minutes in the darkness – but when the hands reached five minutes past four in the early morning, the clock stopped. It had to be wound up every night and as Snoozy had been asleep the evening before, it hadn't been wound up as usual.

After that there was no more ticking, and no more chiming! But the time went on – five o'clock, six o'clock, seven o'clock, eight o'clock! The sun was up, and most of the folk of the village. And at last Snoozy stirred in his armchair and stretched out his arms. He yawned widely – and opened his eyes. He looked round the room – and then he remembered the fancy dress party! My goodness!

'What's the time?' said Snoozy, and looked at the clock. 'Five minutes past four! Gracious goodness, and the party is at five! I must hurry. I have had a longer snooze than I meant to have. Dear, dear, now I *shall* have a rush!'

You see, Snoozy hadn't any idea at all that he had slept all the night through. He simply thought he had slept till five minutes past four the day before – and he thought it was yesterday, not today! Poor old Snoozy! He didn't think of looking at the sun to see whereabouts in the sky it was, for, like most sleepy-headed people, he was rather stupid – and though the sun shone in at the wrong window, he still thought it was the afternoon!

'I shan't have time to alter the bearskin now,' said Snoozy to himself. 'Can't be bothered! My, how hungry I am! I shall eat quite twenty cakes at the party, and I believe I could manage two or three jellies, and as for sausage-rolls, aha, give me fifteen of those, and you won't see them again!'

He put on the bearskin rug and pinned it tightly all round him. Then he pulled the bear-head over his own head, and pinned it well round his neck. He could hardly breathe, but he didn't mind. He was pleased to think he had such a fine fancy dress!

'Now, off we go!' said Snoozy and, crawling on all fours, he went out of his front door and down the street. As he went, he growled, because he thought that would make people look round and say: 'Oh, look! Here's someone in a wonderful fancy dress!'

But the party was over long ago – and the folk of the village were hurrying to do their morning shopping. When they saw the life-like bear walking down the street, growling, they were frightened.

'Oh, oh!' they cried. 'Look at that monster! He came out of Snoozy's house – he must have eaten him! Run, run!'

'Get a gun and shoot him!' cried Mister Big-Nose, meeting the bear round a corner, and getting the fright of his life.

Now Snoozy could NOT understand all this. So he stood up on his hind paws and shouted – or tried to shout through the bear head: 'I'm going to the party. Don't be frightened of me!'

But all that came out of the bear-head was something that sounded like: 'Ah-wah-wah-wah-wah-wah-wah! Wah-wah-wah-wah-wah-wah-wah! It was really very difficult to speak with a big bear-head over his face, and Snoozy tried his best to talk clearly.

'Oh! It's growling at us! It's a *fierce* bear!' shouted everyone in terror. 'Listen to it jabbering!'

Poor Snoozy was now quite puzzled. How stupid people were! Couldn't they even *guess* that it was a fancy dress? He shouted again, trying to say: 'I tell you, I'm going to the fancy dress party! Don't you UNDERSTAND?'

But all that came out was something like:

'Ah-who-wah, sh-wsh-wah-woo-wah-woowoowoo-wah! Wah-woo – YAH-HAY-YAH!'

'Oh! It's getting fiercer!' yelled the frightened people. Mister Big-Nose, fetch a gun! Oh, get a spear! Oh, where's a great big stick to knock it on the head! It'll eat us!'

Snoozy was now quite frightened. A gun! A spear! A stick to knock him on the head! Really, was everyone quite mad? Wasn't he telling them he was going to the party?

'I think I'd better go to the Town Hall, where the party is to be held, and then when people see me going up the steps, they will know I'm just someone in fancy dress,' said Snoozy to himself. So he dropped down on all fours again and padded off to the Town Hall. Behind him came crowds of people, talking, pointing, and all ready to run away at once if the bear so much as turned his head.

But he didn't. He went right on to the Town Hall. He padded up the steps and into the big hall where three gnomes were busily sweeping up all the mess from the party the day before.

Snoozy stopped and looked in astonishment. '*Where* was the party?' he wondered. 'No tea – no balloons – no people there – no nothing!'

He spoke to the three servants, who had been

so busy with their work that they hadn't noticed the bear padding in. Snoozy said: 'Where is the PARTY?'

But all the three servants heard was: 'Wah-wah-wah-wah.'

'Ooooooh!' they screeched in fright, when they saw the bear. 'Ooooooh! A wild bear! Growling at us! Chase him out, chase him out!'

So, to Snoozy's great surprise and anger, the three little gnomes rushed at him and chased him out of the Town Hall! Yes, they really did, and it was very brave of them for they really and truly thought he was a wild bear from the woods.

'Don't! Don't!' yelled poor Snoozy. But as it sounded like 'Woof! Woof!' it didn't help him much.

Down the steps of the Town Hall went Snoozy. The three gnomes ran down after him and chased him into a very large puddle.

Snoozy was terribly upset. He sat in the puddle and cried loudly: 'Boo-hoo-hoo! Boo-hoo-hoo!'

And this time the noise he made was really like someone weeping, and all the villagers stopped and looked at one another.

'The bear is crying!' they said. 'The bear is crying! Poor thing! Perhaps he has come with a message to someone. Ask him, Big-Nose!'

'Where was the party?' he wondered.

51

So Mister Big-Nose stepped forward and spoke to the bear. 'Why have you come?' he said. 'Do you want to speak to someone?'

'No,' said Snoozy, and it sounded like 'Woof!'

Big-Nose shook his head. 'We can't understand what you say,' he said.

Just then a small, sharp-eyed gnome gave a shout and pointed to the bear's neck. 'He's got a safety-pin there!' he cried. 'Do you think it is hurting him?'

'Where?' said Big-Nose, astonished. When he saw the safety-pin, he was very sorry for the bear. 'Someone has put the pin there,' he said. 'Poor thing! Perhaps he came to ask us to get it out.'

He undid the pin – and to his enormous surprise, the bear's head dropped sideways, and out of it came Snoozy's own head, very hot, very rumpled, and with tears pouring down his cheeks!

'SNOOZY! It's SNOOZY!' cried everyone in the greatest astonishment. 'What *are* you doing in a bearskin, Snoozy?'

'I c-c-came to the fancy dress p-p-party!' wept Snoozy. 'But I couldn't find it.'

But that was *yesterday*, Snoozy!' said Big-Nose. 'We wondered why you didn't come.'

'Yesterday!' said Snoozy. 'But I thought it was to be on Wednesday, not Tuesday.'

'Today is Thursday,' said Big-Nose. 'What have you been doing Snoozy? Have you been asleep or something – and slept all round the clock? This is Thursday morning. What did you think it was?'

'Why, I thought it was Wednesday afternoon! And I came out dressed in my bearskin rug to go to the party. And now I've missed the party. Oh, why did I take that snooze! I must have slept all the afternoon and all the night – and my clock stopped at five past four, and I thought that was the real time!'

Everyone began to laugh. It was really such a joke. 'Snoozy came to the party the day after!' said one gnome to another. 'Poor old Snoozy! What *will* he do next! Ho, ho! Perhaps he won't be quite so snoozy next time!'

Snoozy went home, carrying the bearskin over his shoulder. He was very unhappy. He got himself some bread and jam; for he was very hungry, and then he sat down to eat it. But so many tears ran down his nose into the jam that they made it taste quite salty, and he didn't enjoy his breakfast at all.

'That's the last time I snooze!' said the gnome. 'Never again!'

But it takes more than one lesson to cure a snoozer. Before a week was out, Snoozy was napping again – what a sleepy-head he is!

The Three Strange Travellers

Once upon a time there was a billy-goat who drew a little goat-carriage on the sea-sands. He took children quite a long ride for a penny. But one day, when he was getting old, he became lame. He limped with his right front foot, and he could no longer draw the goat-carriage along at a fine pace.

'You are no use to me now,' said his master, a cross and selfish old man. 'I shall buy a new goat.'

The old billy-goat bleated sadly. What would he do if his master no longer needed him?

'You can go loose on the common,' said the old man. 'Don't come to me for a home, for I don't want you any longer.'

Poor Billy-goat! He was very unhappy. He looked at his little goat-carriage for the last time, and then he limped off to the common. The winter was coming on, and he hoped he would not freeze to death. He had always lived in a cosy shed in the winter-time – but now he would have no home.

He hadn't gone very far across the common when he heard a loud quacking behind him.

'Quack! Stop, I say! Hey, stop a minute! Quack!'

Billy-goat turned round. He saw a duck waddling along as fast as it could, quacking loudly.

'What's the matter?' asked Billy.

'Matter enough!' said the duck, quite out of breath. 'Do you mind if I walk with you? There are people after me who will kill me if they find me.'

'Mercy on us!' said the goat, startled. 'Why do they want to kill you?'

'Well,' said the duck indignantly, 'I don't lay as many eggs as I did, and my master says I'm no use now, so he wants to eat me for his dinner. And I have served him well for many many months, laying delicious eggs, far nicer than any hen's!'

'Dear me,' said Billy-goat, 'you and I seem to have the same kind of master. Maybe they are brothers. Well, Duck, walk with me. I am seeking my fortune, and would be glad of company.'

The two walked on together, the goat limping and the duck waddling. When they reached the end of the common they came to a farm.

'Do not go too near,' said the duck. 'I don't wish to be caught. Do you?'

'No,' said the goat. 'Listen! What's that?'

They stood still and heard a great barking. Suddenly a little dog squeezed itself under a near-by gate and came running towards them. The duck got behind the goat in fright, and the goat stood with his horns lowered in case the dog should attack him.

'Don't be afraid of me,' panted the dog. 'I am running away. My master has beaten me because I let a fox get two chickens last night. But what could I do? I was chained up and I could not get at the fox. I barked loudly, but my master was too fast asleep to hear me. And now he blames me for the fox's theft!'

'You are to be pitied,' said the goat. 'We too have had bad masters. Come with us, and we will keep together and look after ourselves. Maybe we shall find better masters.'

'I will come,' said the dog. 'I am getting old, you know, and I cannot see as well as I used to do. I think my master wants to get rid of me and have a younger dog. Ah me, there is no kindness in the world these days!'

The three animals journeyed on together. They ate what they could find. The billy-goat munched

the green grass, the duck swam on each pond she came to and hunted about for food in the mud at the bottom. The dog sometimes found a bit of bread or a hunk of meat thrown by the wayside.

They walked for miles and miles. Often the goat and the dog gave the duck rides on their backs, for she waddled so slowly, and soon got tired. At night they found a sheltered place beneath a bush, or beside a haystack, and slept there in a heap, the duck safely in the middle.

They became very fond of one another, and vowed that they would never separate. But as the days grew colder the three creatures became anxious.

'When the ponds are frozen I shall find no food,' said the duck.

'And I shall not be able to eat grass when the ground is covered with snow,' said the goat. 'I shall freeze to death at night, for I have always been used to a shed in the winter.'

'And I have been used to a warm kennel,' said the dog. 'What shall we do?'

They could think of no plan, so they wandered on. Then one afternoon a great storm blew up. Oh, my, what a wind! The snow came down softly everywhere, but the blizzard was so strong that even the soft snowflakes stung the dog's eyes and made the duck and the goat blink.

'We shall be lost altogether in this dreadful storm!' barked the dog. 'We must find shelter.'

The goat and the duck followed him. He put his nose to the ground and ran off. He went up a little hill, and at last came to a small cottage. There was a light in one of the windows.

'Somebody lives here,' said the dog. 'Let us knock at the door and ask for shelter.'

So the goat tapped the door with his hoof.

He bleated as he did so, the dog whined, and the duck quacked.

Inside the cottage was an old woman with a red shawl round her shoulders. She was darning a hole in a stocking and thinking about the dreadful storm. Suddenly she heard the tap-tap-tapping at her door.

'Bless us!' she cried, in a fright. 'There's someone there! Shall I open the door or not? It may be a robber come through the storm to rob me of the gold pieces I have hidden so carefully in my old stocking under the mattress! No, I dare not open the door!'

As she sat trembling she heard the dog whining. Then she heard the bleating of the goat and the anxious quacking of the duck.

'Well, well!' she said in astonishment. 'It sounds for all the world like a dog, a goat, and a duck! But how do they come to my door like this? Do they

need shelter from this terrible storm, poor things? Well, I have no shed to put them in, so they must come in here with me.'

She got up and went to the door. She undid the bolt and opened the door a crack. When she saw the trembling goat, the shivering dog, and the frightened duck, her kind heart melted at once and she opened the door wide.

'Poor lost creatures!' she said. 'Come in, come in. You shall have warmth and shelter whilst this storm lasts. Then I've no doubt you will want to go back to your homes.'

The three animals gladly came in to the warmth. The dog at once lay down on the hearth-rug, the goat stood near by, and the duck lay down in a corner, put her head under her wing and fell fast asleep, for she was very tired.

The old woman didn't know what to make of the three creatures. They seemed to know onc another so well, and by the way they bleated, barked, and quacked to one another they could talk as well as she could.

The goat was very thin, and the dog was skinny too. As for the duck, when the old woman felt her, she was nothing but feathers and bone!

'The poor creatures!' said the kind old dame.

'They are starving! I will give them a good meal to eat – they will feel all the better for it.'

So she began to cook a meal of all the household scraps she had – bits of meat, vegetables, potatoes, bread, all sorts. How good it smelt! Even the duck in the corner stuck out her head from under her wing to have a good sniff.

The old woman took the big saucepan off the fire and stood it on the window-sill to cool. Then she ladled the warm food out into three dishes and put one in front of each animal.

'There, my dears,' she said, 'eat that and be happy tonight.'

Well, the three animals could hardly believe their eyes to see such a feast! They gobbled up the food and left not a single scrap. Then the goat rubbed his head gently against the old dame's knee, the dog licked her hand, and the duck laid its head on her shoe. Then they all curled up in a heap together, and fell asleep. The old dame went to her bed and slept too.

In the morning the storm was over, but the countryside was covered with snow. The animals did not want to leave the warm cottage, but the old woman opened the door.

'Now you must find your way home,' she said.

She did not know that they had no homes. She thought they had lost their way in the storm, and that now they would be glad to go out and find their way back to their homes.

The animals were sad. They took leave of the kind woman, and wished they could tell her that they would like to stay; but she could not understand their language. They went out into the snow, and wondered where to go next.

'Let us go down the hill,' said the goat. 'See, there are some haystacks, and we may be able to find some food and shelter under the stacks tonight.'

So down the hill they went. But they could not find any food. They crouched under the haystack that evening, and tried to get warm. As they lay there, quite still, they heard the sound of soft footsteps in the snow. Then they heard voices.

'The old woman has a great hoard of gold,' said one voice. 'We will go to her cottage tonight, when she is in bed, and steal it.'

'Very well,' said the second voice. 'I will meet you there, and we will share the gold. She has no dog to bark or bite.'

The animals listened in horror. Why, it must be the kind old woman these horrid men were speaking of! How could they save her from the robbers?

'We must go back to the cottage,' said the dog. 'Somehow we must creep in and wait for these robbers. Then we will set on them and give them the fright of their lives!'

So the three limped, walked, and waddled all the way up the hill until they came to the little cottage. The old woman was going to bed. The goat peeped in at the window and saw her blow her candle out.

'She has left this window a little bit open,' he said to the dog. 'Can you jump in and open the door for me and the duck?'

'Yes,' said the dog, 'I can do that. I often saw my master open the farm doors. I know how to do it.'

He squeezed in through the window and went to the door. He pulled at the latch. The door was not bolted, so the goat and the duck came in at once. They could hear the old dame snoring.

'What shall we do when the robbers come?' asked the duck excitedly.

'I have a plan,' said the goat. 'You, duck, shall first of all frighten the robbers by quacking at the top of your very loud voice. You, dog, shall fly at the legs of the first robber, and I will lower my head and butt the second one right in the middle. Ha! what a fright we will give them!'

The three animals were so excited that they could hardly keep still. The duck flew up on the table and stood there. The dog hid behind the door. The goat stood ready on the hearth-rug, for he wanted a good run when he butted the second robber.

Presently the dog's sharp ears told him that the two robbers were outside. He warned the others and they got ready to do their parts. The robbers pushed the door open.

At that moment the duck opened her beak and quacked. How she quacked! Quack! Quack! Quack! Quack! Quack!

Then the dog flew at the legs of the first robber and bit them. And he growled. GRRRRRRRRRRRRRR!

What a terrible growl it was!

Then the goat ran at the second robber and butted him so hard in the middle that he sat down suddenly and lost all his breath.

The duck was so excited that she wanted to join in the fun. So she flew to the robbers and pecked their noses hard. Peck! Peck!

The robbers were frightened almost out of their lives. They couldn't think what was happening! There was such a terrible noise going on, and something was biting, hitting, and pecking them from top to toe. How they wished they had never come near the cottage!

As soon as they could they got to their feet and ran. The duck flew after them and pecked their ankles. The dog tore pieces out of their trousers. The goat limped as fast as he could and butted them down the hill. My, what a set-to it was!

The two robbers fell into a ditch and covered themselves with mud.

'That old woman is a witch!' cried one.

'Yes, she pinched my ears!' said the other. 'And she bit my legs!'

'Ho, and she punched me in the middle so that I lost all my breath!' said the first.

'And all the time she made such a noise!' cried the second, trying to clamber out of the ditch. 'She said: "Whack! Whack! Whack!"'

'Yes, and she cried: "Cuff! Cuff! Cuff!" too!' said the first. 'And how she chased us down the hill!'

The three animals laughed till the tears came into their eyes when they heard the robbers talking like this.

'They thought my "Quack, quack, quack!" was "Whack, whack, whack!"' said the duck in delight.

'And they thought my "Wuff, wuff, wuff!" was "Cuff, cuff, cuff!"' said the dog, jumping about joyfully. 'What a joke! How we frightened them!'

'Let us go back and see if the old dame is all right,' said the goat. 'She woke when the duck began to quack.'

Back they all went to the cottage, and found the old dame sitting up in bed, trembling, with a candle lighted by her side. When she saw the three animals she could hardly believe her eyes.

'So it was you who set upon those robbers and chased them away!' she said. 'You dear, kind, clever creatures! Why, I thought you had gone to your homes!'

The goat went up to the bed and put his front paws there. The dog put his nose on the quilt. The duck flew up on the bed-rail and flapped her wings.

'Wuff!' said the dog, meaning: 'We want to stay with you!'

'Bleat!' said the goat, and meant the same thing.

'Quack!' said the duck, and she meant the same thing too.

And this time the old dame understood them, and she smiled joyfully.

'So you want to stay here?' she said. 'Well, you shall. I'm all alone and I want company. It's wintertime and I expect you need shelter, so you shall all live with me. I shall always be grateful to you for chasing away those robbers.'

Well, those three animals soon settled down with the old woman. The duck laid an egg for her breakfast each day. The dog lay on the door-mat and guarded the cottage for her each night. The goat was troubled because he could do nothing for his kind mistress.

But one day he found how well he could help her. She had to go to the woods to get firewood. She took with her a little cart to bring it back, and this she had to pull herself, for she had no pony.

But the goat stood himself in the shafts and bleated. The old woman saw that he wanted her to tie the cart to him so that he might pull the wood home for her, and she was delighted. Every day after that the goat took the cart to the woods for his mistress, and very happy they were together.

As for the robbers, they have never dared to come back. They went a hundred miles away, and told the people there a marvellous story of an old witch who cried: 'Whack! Cuff! Whack! Cuff!' and could bite, pinch, and punch all at once. But nobody believed them.

The old dame and the dog, goat, and duck still live together very happily. Their house is called 'Windy Cottage,' so if ever you pass by, go in and see them all. The old dame will love to tell you the story of how they came to live together!

The Secret Cave

The adventure of the Secret Cave really began on the day when we all went out on the cliff to fly our new kite. I am Roger, and Joan and William are my sister and brother. William's the eldest, and Joan and I are twins.

We live in a house near the sea, but it is very lonely because there is no other house anywhere near us, except the big house on the cliff, and that is empty. We often wished it was full of children so that we could play with them, but as it wasn't we had to be content to play by ourselves.

Mummy and Daddy were going away for a month on a sea-trip, and they were leaving that very day. We were all feeling very sad about it, because home is a funny sort of place without Mummy. But it was holiday time, and our governess had gone, so there was only old Sarah to look after us, and we thought we'd have quite a good time really.

Mummy gave us a glorious new kite just as she said good-bye, and told us to go and fly it as soon as they had gone; then we shouldn't feel so bad about everything. So when the car had disappeared down the hill, we took our new kite and went out on the windy cliff.

William soon got it up in the air, and it flew like a bird. But suddenly the wind dropped and the kite gave a great dip downwards. William pulled hard at it, but it wasn't any good. Down and down it went, and at last disappeared behind some trees.

'Bother!' we said. 'Let's go and look for it.'

We raced over the cliff till we came to the clump of stunted trees behind which our kite had gone. Then we found that the string disappeared over the high wall that surrounded the big house on the cliff.

'The kite must have fallen in the garden,' said William. 'What shall we do?'

'Go and knock at the front door and ask for it,' said Joan. 'There might be a caretaker there.'

So we ran round to the front gate and went up the long drive. We soon came to the front door. It was a big wooden one with a large knocker. William knocked hard and we heard the sound go echoing through the house.

Nobody came, so we each of us knocked in turn, very loudly indeed. After we had waited for about five minutes without anyone opening the door, we decided that the house must be quite empty, without a caretaker or anyone at all.

'Well, how are we to get our kite?' I asked.

'The only thing to do is to climb over the wall,' said William. 'We can't ask anyone's permission because there isn't anyone to ask. Come on. We can't lose our lovely kite.'

So we ran down the drive again and made our way to the back of the garden wall, which stood high above our heads. William managed to climb up it first, and then jumped down on the other side.

'Come on, you others,' he called. 'It's all right. Oh, wait a minute, though. I've got an idea. Stand away from the wall, both of you. I've found a box here, and I'm going to throw it over. You can stand on it, and then you will easily be able to climb up the wall.'

William threw over the box. Then we stood on it and just managed to reach the top. We jumped down, and there we all were in the deserted garden of the house on the cliff.

It was a very wild place, for no one had bothered about it for years. Everything was overgrown, and the paths were covered with green moss that was like velvet to walk on. I don't know why, but we felt at first as if we ought to talk in whispers.

'Where's our kite?' said Joan. 'Look, William, there's the string. Let's follow it and we shall soon find the kite.'

So we followed the string, and it led us over a stretch of long grass that had once been a big lawn, down a thick shrubbery, and past some greenhouses whose glass was all broken.

Then William gave a shout.

'There it is!' he said, and he pointed to where a little shed stood hidden away in a dark corner. We all looked at it, and, sure enough, there was the kite perched up on the roof. It didn't take us long to pull it down, and we found that one of the sticks that ran across it was broken, so we couldn't fly it any more that day. We were sorry about that, and we wondered what we should do for the rest of the morning.

'Why can't we stay here and explore the garden?' asked Joan. 'We shouldn't do any harm, and it would be great fun.'

'All right, we will,' said William, who always decides everything because he is the eldest.

So we began exploring, and it really was fun. Then it suddenly began to rain, and as we none of us had our mackintoshes with us we got wet.

'We must shelter somewhere,' said William. 'Sarah will be very cross if we go home soaked through.'

'Well, what about that little shed, where we found the kite?' I asked. 'That would do nicely.'

So we raced to the shed, but the door was locked, so we couldn't get in.

'How about a window?' cried Joan. 'Here's one with the latch broken. Push it, William. Oh, good, it's open and we can climb in. What an adventure we're having!'

We all climbed in. I went to the door, and what do you think? The key was *inside*!

'Well, if that isn't a curious thing,' said William, looking at it. 'If you lock a door from the inside you usually lock yourself in too. But there's nobody here. It's a mystery!'

But we soon forgot about the key in our excitement over the shed. It really was a lovely little place. There was a funny old chair with a crooked leg that William felt sure he could mend if he had his tools. There was a battered old table in one corner, and two small stools, one with a leg off. Along one side of the shed was a shelf, very dusty and dirty.

'I say! Wouldn't this shed make a perfectly lovely little house for us to play in on rainy days?' suddenly said William. 'We could clean it up and mend the stool and chair.'

'Oh, William, do let's!' said Joan, clapping her hands in delight. 'I've got some pretty orange stuff Mummy gave me, and I can make it into little curtains for the two windows. We can bring a pail and a scrubbing-brush and clean the whole place up beautifully.'

'And we can use the shelf for storing things on,' I said. 'We can bring apples and biscuits here, and some of our books to read. Oh, what fun! But we must keep it a secret, or perhaps Sarah would stop us.'

'Well, we mustn't do any harm anywhere,' said William. 'After all, it isn't *our* shed, but I'm sure if the man who owns it, whoever he is, knew that we were going to clean it up and make it nice, he would only be too glad to let us. Now the rain's stopped – we must run home or we shall be late for dinner.'

We took our broken kite and raced home. We didn't need to climb over the wall again, because we found a dear little door in the wall with the key inside. So we opened the door, slipped out, locked it again, and William took the key away in his pocket in case tramps found it.

We were so excited at dinner-time that Sarah got cross with us and threatened to send us to bed half an hour earlier if we didn't eat our food properly.

At last dinner was over and we ran out into our own garden to decide what we should take to the house on the cliff.

'Let's borrow the gardener's barrow,' said William. 'We can put heaps of things in that and wheel it easily.'

So we got the barrow and piled the things into it. Joan found the orange stuff and put that in, and popped her work-basket in too. I found a very old carpet that nobody used in the attic, and I put that in. William took his tools, and we went and asked Cook if she could give us anything to eat.

She was very nice, and gave us three slices of cake, a bottle of lemonade, and a bag of raisins. Then we had a great stroke of luck, because the gardener told us we could pick the apples off one of the trees and keep them for ourselves.

You can guess we had soon picked about fifty

or sixty and put them into a basket. That went into the barrow too, and then it really was almost as much as we could manage to wheel it along.

'We can easily come back for our books and anything else we can think of,' said William. So off we went, all helping to push. At last we came to the little door in the wall and William unlocked it. We went through the garden until we came to our dear little shed.

'Oh, we ought to have brought something to clean it up with,' said Joan. 'Never mind, William. Empty these things out on to a newspaper in the corner, and we'll go back for a pail and a scrubbing-brush and soap.'

Back we went, and at last after two or three more journeys we really had got everything we could think of that day. Then we had a lovely time cleaning up the shed. The floor was laid with big white flagstones, and they looked lovely when we had scrubbed them clean. We washed the shelf and all the bits of furniture too, and soon the shed looked fine.

That was all we had time to do that day, but early the next morning we were back again, as you can guess. Joan made the little curtains and tied them back with a piece of old hair-ribbon. They did look nice. William and I mended the stool and the chair and arranged the things we had brought.

Cook had given us half a jar of strawberry jam and a pot of honey, and we had bought some biscuits and nuts. Our books went up on the shelf, and the apples stood in a corner in their basket.

'Well, it really looks quite homey,' said Joan, jumping round the shed joyfully. 'What fun we shall have here. Don't my little curtains look nice, and isn't the carpet fine? Our feet would have been very cold on those bare flagstones.'

Well, I can't tell you how we enjoyed our time in that little shed. Every day that it rained we went there, and as it was a very wet summer we spent most of our time there. We ate our biscuits and apples, read our books and did puzzles, and Sarah thought we were as good as gold, though she didn't know at all where we went every day. She thought we were down by the sea, I think.

But the most exciting part of our adventure hadn't come yet. I must tell you about it now.

We had been using the shed for about three weeks when William lost a sixpence. It rolled on to the floor and disappeared. We turned back the carpet to look for it.

'There's a flagstone here that seems rather loose,' said William. 'Perhaps the sixpence has gone down the crack.'

'It *is* loose!' said Joan. 'Why, I can almost lift it!'

'I believe we *could* lift it,' said William. We slipped a thin iron bar in one of the cracks, and then suddenly the stone rose up! It came quite easily, and stood upright, balanced on one side.

And where it had been was a big black hole, with stone steps leading down!

What do you think of that? We were all so astonished that we simply knelt there and stared and stared.

'Why, it's a secret passage!' said William at last. 'What about exploring it?'

'Do you think it's safe?' asked Joan.

'Oh, I should think so,' said William. 'We can take our electric torches with us. This passage explains the key left inside the door. Someone must have gone to this shed, locked it from the inside, and then gone down the passage somewhere. It must lead out to some place or other. Oh, what an adventure!'

We got our torches from the shelf, and then, with William leading, we all climbed down the steps. They soon ended and we found ourselves in a narrow passage that led downwards fairly steeply.

'Do you know, I believe this passage leads to the sea-shore,' said William suddenly. 'I think it is going right through the cliff, and will come out to one of those rocky caves we have sometimes seen from a boat.'

And we found that William was right. For the passage, always sloping downwards, suddenly opened out into a small dark cave. William couldn't see at first whether or not there was any way out of it besides the way we had come, and then he suddenly found it! It was just a small opening low down at one end, so small that a man would have found it quite difficult to squeeze through.

We squeezed through easily enough, of course, and then we found ourselves in a very big wide cave, lit by daylight. The thunder of breaking waves seemed very near, and as we made our way to the big opening where the daylight streamed through we saw the rough sea just outside it.

'You were right, William,' I said. 'That passage from our shed led right through the cliff down to this cave that is open to the sea. Look! When we stand on this ledge the waves almost reach our feet. I shouldn't be surprised if in very rough weather the sea washes right into the cave.'

'I don't think so,' said William, turning round to look. 'You see, the floor slopes upwards fairly steeply. Oh my! Just look there!'

We turned to see what he was exclaiming at, and what do you think? The floor of the cave was strewn with boxes of all sizes and shapes!

'Why, perhaps it's a smugglers' cave!' we cried. We rushed to the boxes, but all except two were fast locked. In the two unlocked ones were many clothes – very old-fashioned ones they were, too.

'Well, this *is* a find!' said William. 'I say, what about dressing up in these clothes and giving Sarah a surprise?'

We thought that would be lovely, so we quickly turned out the clothes and found some to fit us. Joan had a lovely frock right down to her ankles, and I had a funny little tunic sort of suit, and so did William. We put them on in the little shed because it was lighter there.

'Now, are we all ready?' said William. 'Well,

come along then. We'll give Sarah the surprise of her life, and then we'll take her and the gardener to see our wonderful find.'

We danced through the door of the shed – and oh, my gracious goodness, didn't we get a shock?

Two gentlemen were walking up the moss-grown path by the shed! They saw us just at the same moment as we saw them, and we all stopped quite still and stared at one another.

One of the gentlemen looked as if he simply couldn't believe his eyes. He took off his glasses

and cleaned them, and then he put them on again. But we were still there, and at last he spoke to us.

'Am I dreaming – or am I back in the days of long ago?' he said. 'Are you children of nowadays, or little long-ago ghosts?'

'We're quite real,' said William. 'We're only dressed up.'

'Well, that's a relief,' said the man. 'But what are you doing here? This garden belongs to my house.'

'Oh, are you the man who owns the house?' asked William.

'Yes,' he answered, 'and this gentleman is

perhaps going to buy it from me. I'm too poor to keep it as it should be kept, you see. But you still haven't told me what you are doing here.'

Well, of course, we had to confess everything then. We told him how we had found the dear little shed by accident, and made it a sort of a home. And then we told him of our great find that afternoon.

'What!' he cried. 'Do you really mean to say you've found the secret passage to the cave? Why, it's been lost for years and years, and no one knew the secret. I lived here when I was a boy, but I never found it either, though I looked everywhere.'

Of course we had to show the way down to the cave, and when he saw the boxes lying there he turned so pale that Joan asked him if he was going to faint.

'No,' he said. 'But I'm going to tell you a little story, and you will understand then why I feel rather strange.'

And this is the story he told us.

'Many, many years ago,' he began, 'my family lived in France. There came a time when they were unjustly accused as traitors, and were forced to fly from the country. They packed up all their belongings and put them on board a ship to be brought to this country, where they had a house.

This was the house. It had a secret passage from the shed to the sea, and the idea was to land at night with their belongings and go up through the passage unseen. They meant to live in the house until the trouble had blown over and they could go about here in safety, or return to France.'

'And did they?' asked William.

'No. Just as all the luggage had been safely put on board and the family were saying good-bye to their friends on shore, some men came galloping up and took them prisoners. The ship hurriedly put off without them and sailed safely to this place. The luggage was dumped down in this cave and the ship went back towards France. But, so the story goes, a storm came, and the whole crew were drowned. As for the family, some died in prison, and none of them ever came back to this house except one. He had been a small boy at the time and had no idea where the secret passage was, and though he searched everywhere he could not find it. So he gave it up and decided that all the family belongings were lost for ever.'

'And are these what he was looking for?' I asked.

'They are,' said the man. 'And, thanks to you, they are found again. Well, well, what an excitement! Now perhaps I shan't have to sell my own house.

I might even be able to come and live here again with my family.'

'Have you got any children?' asked William.

'Yes, six,' said the man.

Well, we all gave a shout at that! Fancy having six children near to play with, when you've never had any at all! It seemed too good to be true.

But it *was* true! Mr. Carnot, for that was the man's name, found that the boxes did contain all his old family treasures, and by selling some he had more than enough money to live at his old home once again with his family. I can tell you it was a most exciting day when they all arrived.

Daddy and Mummy could hardly believe all we had to tell them when they came home, but when Mr. Carnot took them into our shed and down the passage to the cave, they soon knew it was true.

And now we have heaps of playmates. They are Billy, Anne, Marjorie, Jeanne, Laurence, and the baby. We often use the secret passage, and sometimes we even row to the cave in a boat, just like the sailors did all those many years ago.

The Proud Little Dog

There was once a dog called Prince, and he lived with Dame Tiptap. She was very proud of him when he first came to her as a puppy, because his father and mother and his two grandmothers and two grandfathers had all won prizes.

Dame Tiptap gave Prince a beautiful basket of his own, lined with red flannel to keep him warm. She bought him a very expensive collar. She went to a pottery shop and had a special dish made for him, with his name 'Prince' round the bowl.

Prince thought himself very grand indeed. He looked at the old dog kennel out in the yard, and thought to himself, 'Ha! That may be good enough for ordinary dogs, but a dog like me sleeps by the fire, in a red-lined basket! I'm a prince among dogs!'

So, as he grew, he became very vain and proud. He looked down on the other dogs. He would not have a cat in the garden. He even chased away the birds that came for crumbs!

'Any crumbs in this garden belong to *me*!' said Prince.

'Fibber! They are put out for us!' chirruped the sparrow on the roof. 'Besides – what do *you* want with crumbs? Don't you have a big dinner?'

Prince did not like his mistress to have friends to the house. He growled at them. He even showed his teeth. Dame Tiptap did not like it.

She scolded him. 'This won't do, Prince. If you behave like that to my friends, I shall put you out into the kitchen when they come!'

'If you do a thing like that, I'll run away!' growled Prince, rudely.

'The trouble is, you're spoilt,' said Dame Tiptap. 'Now just you listen to me. Mistress Twinkle is coming to tea today. If you dare to bark or growl or show your teeth – out into the kitchen you go!'

Well, Prince *did* bark – and he did growl – and he did show his teeth! So out into the kitchen he went, and the door was shut firmly. He was very angry indeed, especially as he could smell muffins toasting in the sitting-room, and he liked them very much.

'I won't be treated like this!' growled Prince crossly. 'I shall run away! That will teach Dame

Tiptap her manners. She'll miss me. She'll have no one to guard the house. Ha, ha!'

He ran out of the back-door, down the path and away into the fields. He was a very good-looking dog, and he held up his head and kept his tail well up as he went. It was no wonder that a passing farmer looked at him closely and thought he would be a fine dog to steal!

'He's a valuable dog, anyone can see that,' said the farmer and he whistled to Prince. Prince ran up at once – and the man slipped some rope through his collar and led him away.

'I'll tie him up for a few days and then sell him,' thought the farmer. 'Now come on, dog – don't drag behind like that.'

Poor Prince. He was taken to the farm-house and tied up tightly at the back. He was frightened and unhappy.

Dame Tiptap did not know where he had gone. 'Foolish dog!' she said. 'He has run away, as he said. Well, if he cares so little for his home and mistress, it is not much use worrying about him. Now I can have a cat of my own. I never dared to have one before. I'll tell Mistress Twinkle I will take the lovely black cat she has offered me – the one with eyes as green as cucumbers. She's a beauty, and will catch my mice for me.'

So the next day Green-Eyes came to live with kind Dame Tiptap. She settled down in Prince's basket by the fire, delighted to find such a good home. At night she hunted mice, and Dame Tiptap was very pleased with her.

Then somebody gave Dame Tiptap a canary in a cage to sing to her in the mornings. She hung it up in the window, and told Green-Eyes never to jump at the cage. It was lovely to hear the little bird singing every morning.

A week went by – and one morning, what a surprise for Dame Tiptap! In Green-Eyes' basket were four beautiful kittens.

'Well, well, look at that now!' said Dame TipTap, delighted. 'I've always loved kittens. Now we've got four! What fun we shall have when they run about!'

Now after some time Prince bit through the ropes that tied him, and ran home as fast as he could. He had had very little food. He had a cold. He was homesick and miserable. How he looked forward to his warm basket by the fire, a good dinner in the dish marked with his own name, and a great fussing from Dame Tiptap! He ran through the back door and into the sitting-room, to find his basket and his mistress. But what was this? A big, green-eyed cat glared at him from a basketful of kittens, and then, with one leap, the cat was on Prince, and was scratching him with ten sharp claws!

'Woof, woof!' yelped Prince, and tore back to the kitchen. He heard the canary singing loudly in the window.

'Who's this bad dog, naughty dog? After him, Green-Eyes, after him! Trilla, trilla, trilla!'

Dame Tiptap went into the kitchen. 'So you have come back again, Prince!' she said. 'I thought you had run away and would never come back. You were so cross and bad-tempered because I had my friends here. I thought you would go to live with someone who was all alone. Surely you do not want to live with me again?'

'Woof, I do, I do, woof!' said poor Prince, feeling very sad and frightened. 'Let me have my lovely basket, and my beautiful dish, Mistress. I will be a good dog now.'

'I'm glad to hear that,' said Dame Tiptap. 'You can certainly live here if you wish, because it is your home. But your basket belongs to Green-Eyes now, and to her darling kittens, and Green-Eyes has your dish to feed from. But, if you like, you can

So now Prince sometimes lies by the fire
and warms himself.

have the kennel in the yard, and the old dish out of the scullery. Keep out of the house, though, Prince, because if you don't I am sure Green-Eyes will fly at you!'

So poor Prince had to live in the yard and eat from the old scullery dish. He did not dare to go into the house. When he tried to, one cold afternoon, because he badly wanted a warm fire and a nice pat, Green-Eyes flew at him and scratched him all the way down his long nose.

'You keep out!' hissed Green-Eyes. 'This is *my* house, not yours! You belong to the yard. I don't like dogs. I'll let you live here if you keep to the yard. Mistress has got me and my four kittens, and a singing canary. She can easily do without a vain little dog like you!'

Prince knew that was true. He lost his pride and his bad temper. He grew used to the kennel in the yard. He gave Dame Tiptap a great welcome whenever she came to see him. He greeted her friends with licks and yelps of joy.

'Quite a different dog!' said everyone. 'Perhaps when Green-Eyes' four kittens go to new homes she will make friends with him.'

The kittens went to new homes when they were eight weeks old. Green-Eyes no longer felt fierce and protective, anxious to save her kittens from a snapping dog.

Prince spoke to her humbly one day. 'It's very cold out here. Couldn't I come in for a few minutes? I won't lie in your basket.'

'All right. But mind – any nonsense and *out you go again*!'

So now Prince sometimes lies by the fire and warms himself, whilst Green-Eyes purrs in the basket nearby. Dame Tiptap knits and smiles to herself. She thinks that Prince will end up being quite a nice, sensible dog after all!

Prince lies there and stares at Green-Eyes – and he thinks to himself: 'It seems to me that Green-Eyes is mistress of this house now! Oh for the old days when Dame Tiptap was mistress and I could do what I liked!'

But it was he himself who changed his good luck to bad, wasn't it?

The Little Bully

Once upon a time, not so very long ago, there was a small boy called Henry. Although he wasn't very big, he was strong, and he loved to tease all the boys and girls who went to school with him. What he loved most to do was to pinch. How he pinched! He had strong hands, and he could pinch so hard that he could make a big bruise come in half a second. Another trick he played was pricking people with a pin. He used to keep a pin in his coat, and when a small boy or girl was sitting quietly beside him, reading or working, he would slyly take out his pin and prick them.

So you can guess how all the children hated him. They tried pinching him back, but that was no good because he could always pinch harder than anybody. They didn't like telling their teacher, because that was telling tales.

'He's a nasty little bully,' said the boys and girls.

'We hope one day he will be properly punished.'

Well, that day came, as you will see – but very strangely.

It happened that there was a Sunday-school treat, and the children were to go to the seaside for a whole day. They were most excited. They were to go by train, and to take their lunch with them. They would have tea all together in the tea-rooms by the sea. How they hoped it would be fine!

When the day came, the sun shone out of a deep-blue sky, and all the children were wild with excitement. They crowded into the train and sat down – but nobody wanted to sit next to Henry because he always pinched hard when he was excited. Still, someone had to, because there wasn't room for him to have a carriage all to himself. So Rosie and Margery sat by him, and hoped he would be nice and not bully them.

But, goodness me, how he pinched them! There was no teacher in his carriage, so he pinched Rosie and Margery black and blue, and when the other children shouted at him he took out his pin and vowed he would prick anyone who came near him. Rosie cried and Margery scowled, and, in Henry's carriage, it was a miserable journey down to the sea.

When they arrived at the seaside out jumped

all the children with a shout of joy. Down to the sands they raced, hand in hand – but nobody took Henry's hand. Nobody went near him. Nobody played with him. Nobody would help him to dig a castle.

Henry was angry. He went to a sandy corner near a rocky pool and sat down by himself. He took out his lunch and looked at it. It was a good lunch. There were two hard-boiled eggs, six jam sandwiches, three pieces of bread and butter, a ginger cake, and a bar of chocolate. He would

eat it all by himself. He wouldn't offer anyone anything!

Just as he was beginning on the eggs, he heard a hoarse voice near him. 'Good morning! I am *so* pleased to meet a boy like you.' Henry turned round and stared in fright. Whatever do you think he saw?

Henry saw a monster crab walking sideways out of the pool. His eyes were on the ends of short stalks and looked most odd. He held out his front claw to Henry. Henry put out his hand to shake the crab's claw, but to his surprise and anger the crab opened his pincers and nipped his hand so hard that the little boy yelled.

'You horrid thing!' he wept, nursing his pinched hand. 'Pinching me like that!'

'But surely you are a pincher, like me?' said the big crab in surprise. 'I love pinching, and so do you. Would you like to pinch me back?'

Henry looked at the crab's hard shell and knew quite well that he could never hurt the crab. Besides, if he tried, it might pinch him again, very hard.

'Ah, here is my good cousin,' said the crab pleasantly, and, to Henry's horror, he saw a large sandy lobster crawling heavily out of the pool. Before the little boy could stop him the lobster took his hand in his great pincer-like claws and pinched it so hard that Henry yelled in pain.

'Stop, stop! You are breaking my hand!' he cried.

The lobster waved its stalked eyes about and

seemed surprised. 'But aren't you a pincher like myself?' he asked in a deep voice. 'Come, come, you are making fun of me!'

He slyly pinched Henry on his fat legs, and the little boy yelled again. Then he stared at the pool in surprise, for out came sandy-coloured shrimps and prawns, more crabs, and another large lobster. The shrimps and prawns had long, needle-like feelers in front of their heads and they pricked Henry with these, just for fun. The crabs surrounded him so that he couldn't get away, and, dear me! poor Henry was soon black and blue with their pinching, and howled every time a shrimp or prawn pricked him.

'Don't you like it?' said all the creatures in surprise. 'Why, we were told you would love to see us because you were a champion pincher and pricker yourself. Come, come – join in the fun!'

Henry leapt to his feet, crying loudly. His lunch rolled into the pool, and when the crabs and lobsters saw it they ran to it and began to feast eagerly. Henry saw that they had forgotten him for a time, and he turned and ran for his life, tears streaming down his cheeks.

He found another corner, far from the water, and sat down to think. He was pinched black and blue and pricked all over. He had lost his lunch, and he had been very much frightened. As he sat thinking, his cheeks became red and he hung his head.

'They only did to me what I keep doing to the other children,' he thought. 'But how it hurt! And how I hated those crabs and lobsters! I suppose the other children hate me too. Well, I jolly well shan't pinch or prick any more.'

And he didn't, though nobody knew why. Henry never told anyone about his seaside adventure, but he had learnt his lesson. I wish all pinchers could learn it, don't you?

The Six Little Motor-Cars

Henry had six little motor-cars, all different. One was a car, one was a lorry, one was a milk-van, one was a bus, one was a racer and the last was a butcher's van.

They were very old, quite four years old. But they all had their wheels, and they all ran well along the nursery floor. It was only their paint that had gone.

The car had once been blue, and the lorry had been brown. The milk-van had been bright yellow, and the bus red. The racer had been green and the butcher's van a brilliant orange. Now all the little cars were grey, without a single bit of their bright colours left.

But Henry still played with them, and loved them. He got them out every week and ran them over the floor, hooting loudly as if he were the six cars. He put them away carefully and didn't tread on them at all.

'How you do love your little cars, Henry!' said his mother. 'They are getting very old. But you must keep them carefully because I haven't any money to buy you nice little cars like that again for a long time!'

Now one day Thomas and his mother came to tea. He was younger than Henry, and he loved cars even more than Henry did. He had one of his own, quite a big one – but he had no little ones at all. So, when he saw Henry's cars in the toy-cupboard he gave a squeal of delight.

'Oh! Look at those cars! Can we play with them?'

It was nice to have someone else playing at cars, hooting and running them forward and back. The two boys built streets with their bricks and put up posts for traffic lights. It really was great fun.

And then, when Thomas had to go home, he wanted to take the cars with him! His mother shook her head and said no, he couldn't.

'They belong to Henry,' she said. 'You have played with them all afternoon. Now you must leave them.'

Thomas began to scream. Henry looked at him in disgust. Fancy a boy behaving like that! Why, only babies yelled.

'Oh dear!' said Thomas's mother. 'Don't scream, Thomas. You know, Mrs. Hill, he has been very unwell, and I have had to give him his own way a lot. The doctor says it is very bad for him to scream. Now do be sensible, Thomas.'

But Thomas was not going to be sensible. He screamed till he was purple in the face.

'Henry,' said Henry's mother, 'will you lend Thomas your cars just for to-night? You can have them back again tomorrow.'

Thomas stopped screaming to hear what Henry would say.

'No,' said Henry firmly. 'I've never lent my cars to anyone. They are too precious.'

'Henry, be unselfish,' said his mother. 'Do it to please me. Poor Thomas is so unhappy.'

Henry looked at his mother. 'Well, Mummy,' he said, 'I'll lend him them because I want to please you, not because Thomas is unhappy. I think he's naughty, and I don't want him to come to tea again.'

Thomas stopped screaming. He looked rather ashamed, but he let his mother put the six cars into his pockets. Henry was sad. He felt sure they would come back broken, with some of the wheels missing. He was sad all that evening. His mother was sorry.

'Henry, I'm glad to have such a kind little boy,' she said, when she put him to bed. 'You make me very happy.'

Well, Henry was glad about that, but he hadn't made himself happy at all! He thought about his precious cars a great deal, and wondered if Thomas was taking care of them.

Next morning Thomas arrived at the front door, with his father this time, not his mother. In his hand he carried a big box. Henry wondered if all his cars were in it.

Thomas came upstairs with his father and the box. 'Now, Thomas, what have you got to say to Henry?' said his father

'Henry, here are your cars,' said Thomas, talking as if he were ashamed of himself. 'I'm sorry I screamed for them. Daddy was very angry when he knew.'

'It's all right,' said Henry, taking the box. He didn't like to open it in case he found some of the cars were broken.

'Do open the box,' said Thomas. So Henry did open it – and how he stared! Every single one of those little cars had been given a fresh coat of bright paint! There they were in the box, red, orange, blue, green, brown and yellow! They looked marvellous.

'I did that in return for your kindness,' said Thomas's father. 'And you will find a nice traffic-light indicator there too. Thomas took money from his money-box and bought it. He's rather ashamed of himself, you see. I'm not surprised you don't want him to come to tea again with you.'

'Oh, but I *do!*' cried Henry, quite changing his mind. 'I *do!* We had a lovely time yesterday with the cars. Oh, aren't they fine now! As good as new.

Better! And look at this lovely traffic light. You can really change the colours.'

Thomas came to tea with Henry the next week and the two of them played the whole afternoon with the cars, streets made of bricks and the traffic light. And when it was time for Thomas to go home, did he yell and scream for the cars? Not he!

He went home with his mother, sad to leave the cars, but making up his mind never to behave like a baby again.

Henry's mother watched him putting away the little cars.

'It's a funny thing, Henry,' she said, 'but whenever anyone does something to please somebody else, it always comes back to them. You pleased *me* – and now Thomas and his father have pleased *you!* I didn't reward you – but they did!'

It's a pity everyone doesn't know that, isn't it? Kindness always comes back somehow.

The Unkind Children

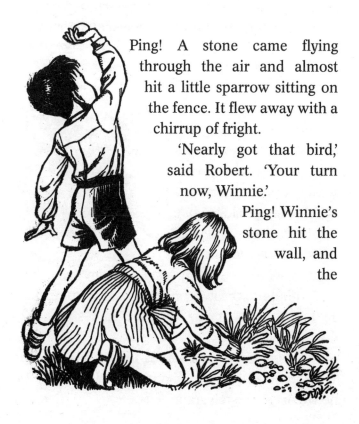

Ping! A stone came flying through the air and almost hit a little sparrow sitting on the fence. It flew away with a chirrup of fright.

'Nearly got that bird,' said Robert. 'Your turn now, Winnie.'

Ping! Winnie's stone hit the wall, and the

next-door cat, who was lying asleep there, leapt off with a loud yell.

'Those unkind children again!' she said.

Soon every bird and animal nearby was warned that Winnie and Robert were throwing stones again. Not a single one would go near. They all hated the two unkind children who loved to throw stones at any living thing.

'Nothing to throw stones at!' said Winnie. 'Let's go for a walk. Maybe we shall find some birds down the lane.'

Off they went, their hands full of small stones. They kept a sharp look-out for any bird in the hedge or on the telegraph wires.

They came to a low wall that ran round a garden. Winnie stopped and pulled Robert's arm.

'Look – what a funny bird! Do you see it?' Robert looked. He saw a very odd-looking bird indeed. It was on a level with the wall. It was red, with yellow wings and a bright green tail.

'See if you can hit it!' said Winnie. Robert took a stone, and aimed it carefully. It struck the bird full on the back!

'Good shot!' said Winnie.

And then a dreadful thing happened! Somebody stood up from behind the wall – somebody wearing a hat which was trimmed with the red and yellow bird! The bird hung sideways from the hat now, looking very strange.

'Oooh! It was a bird in a hat!' said Winnie, frightened. A big woman glared at the two children. She wore a red cloak, the bird-trimmed hat, and big spectacles on her nose.

'Come here!' she rapped out. 'It's time you were taught a lesson! I'm Mrs. Do-the-Same-to-You! Maybe you've heard of me?'

The children hadn't, but they didn't like the sound of her at all. They turned to run away. But in a trice Mrs. Do-the-Same-to-You was over the wall and was holding them firmly by their arms. She had a big bag with her. She opened it and popped the two unkind children into it. It wasn't a bit of good struggling. They couldn't get out.

Mrs. Do-the-Same-to-You took them to her cottage in the middle of the wood. She shook the children out of her bag on to the grass. Bump! They fell out and yelled.

She took a whistle from her pocket and blew on it. At once a small army of brownies, not much bigger than dolls, came running from the wood.

'These are the Brownie King's pea-shooters,' she said to the children. 'They don't get enough practice at shooting peas at people. You don't seem to mind hitting others with stones, so I don't expect you'll mind if you are shot at with peas! It will be excellent practice for the pea-shooters.'

The children didn't like the sound of this at all. They could see no way of escape, because there was a high wall round the garden, and Mrs. Do-the-Same-to-You stood by the only gate. They tried to run behind a bush.

The brownie pea-shooters all had little blow-pipes and bags of hard, dried peas. Quick as lightning, they slipped peas into their mouths and blew them hard out of the blow-pipes or pea-shooters.

Ping! The first one hit Winnie on the nose.

Ping! Another one hit Robert on the ear.

Ping! Ping! Ping! Three peas hit the children hard on hand, knee and neck. They yelled.

'This is good sport!' cried the little brownies. 'Are you sure it's all right for us to practise on these children, Mrs. Do-the-Same-to-You?'

'Oh, quite,' she said. 'I found them throwing stones at birds. They can't object to you shooting peas at them! After all, you are doing much the same thing, but using peas instead of stones.'

'Stop! Stop!' cried the children. 'The peas hurt. They sting! Oh, stop!'

'Well, don't stones hurt, too?' asked Mrs. Do-the-Same-to-You. 'Perhaps you would rather the pea-shooters shot stones?'

'Oh no, oh no!' cried Winnie. 'Stones would be worse. Oh, let us go! That pea nearly went into my eye.'

Ping! Ping! Ping! Ping! The little pea-shooters were having a fine time. The children dodged here and there, they tried to hide behind trees and bushes, they ran to corners, but always the brownies followed them, blowing hard peas at them and hardly ever missing. Soon the children were covered with red spots where the peas had hit them, and they began to feel very sorry for themselves indeed.

Mrs. Do-the-Same-to-You went indoors to put her kettle on to boil. As soon as Robert saw that she had left the gate, he took Winnie's hand and dragged her there. In a trice he had it open and the two children shot through it.

After them poured the delighted brownies, shooting peas as hard as they could! They chased Winnie and Robert all the way to the edge of the wood. Ping, ping, ping, ping, went the peas. You should have heard the children yell!

They got home at last, tears running down their faces. They rubbed the red places that the peas had hit.

'Horrid little brownies!' sobbed Winnie.

'Unkind little creatures!' wept Robert.

'How dare they, how dare they?' cried Winnie. 'Just look at all the places on my face, hands and knees! I'm hurting all over!'

'Wait till I see that nasty Mrs. Do-the-Same-to-You!' yelled Robert. 'I'll tell her what I think of her! I'll throw a big stone at her!'

But when he met her, he didn't say a word and he didn't throw a stone. In fact, neither he nor Winnie have ever thrown a stone at anything again. They know now how it hurts to have something hitting you hard. They still have little red spots where those peas struck them.

I don't feel a bit sorry for them, do you?

The Little Paper-Folk

One very wet afternoon Jimmy and Susan thought they would borrow two pairs of Nurse's scissors and cut out pictures from a book. Nurse said they might, so they found the scissors, took two old books from the newspaper-rack in the dining-room, and went to the nursery to cut out.

'I'm going to cut out these motor-cars,' said Jimmy. 'They're fine ones, all in colour. Look, Susan.'

'Yes,' said Susan. 'Well, I shall cut out some people. See, there's an old woman carrying a basket, and a tall man in a pointed hat, and a little man in a dressing-gown. I shall cut out lots of people.'

Jimmy soon cut out his motor-cars. There were three – one red, one green, and one blue. Then he thought he would cut out smaller things. There was a poker, a pair of tongs, and a coal-shovel on one page, so he cut those out. Then he found a page of boxes of chocolates, all with their lids open to show the chocolates inside. They did look delicious.

'I shall cut out these boxes of chocolates,' he said to Susan. 'Oh, what a nice lot of little people you have cut out! Stand them up against something, Susan. They will look real then.'

Susan stood them up. There was the old woman, the tall man, the little man in a dressing-gown, a black imp, and a fat boy bowling a hoop. She stood them all up against a book.

'We've cut out lots of things,' she said, 'cars and people, fire-irons, and boxes of chocolates. Oh, Jimmy, wouldn't it be lovely if those chocolates were real?'

'Let's take everything we've cut out to the big window-sill,' said Jimmy, gathering up his paper cars and other things. 'We'll stand the cars up and the people too. They will look fine.'

So they went to the window-sill, behind the big blue curtain, and began to stand up all their paper things.

'I wish, I wish we were as small as these little people,' said Susan. 'Then we could play with them and see what they are really like.'

Well, I don't quite know how it happened, but there must have been some magic about that day, for no sooner had Susan wished her wish than it came true!

Yes, it really did! She and Jimmy grew smaller and smaller and they felt very much out of breath, for it all happened so quickly. But when at last they stopped growing small, they found themselves on the window-sill with the paper people and cars. And the paper people were alive!

They smiled at Susan and Jimmy, and came to shake hands with them. Their hands were funny – all flat and papery – and when the old woman turned round Jimmy saw that she hadn't a proper back – there were printed letters all over her!

'That's the other side of the page she was cut out of!' whispered Jimmy, as he saw Susan's look of surprise. 'There was a story the other side, and that's part of it. Isn't it strange?'

'We are glad you cut out such lovely boxes of chocolates for us,' said the man in the pointed hat, picking up a box and looking at it.

'And I'm glad you cut out my hoop for me,' said the little fat boy. He raised his stick to trundle his hoop, but, alas, it would not roll properly, because Susan's scissors had cut right through the hoop in one little place.

The boy was cross. 'The hoop won't roll properly,'

he said, frowning. 'You were careless when you cut it out! I don't like you after all!'

'Don't take any notice of him,' said the little man in the dressing-gown. 'He's a bad-natured boy. I am pleased with the way you cut out my dressing-gown. Look, even my girdle is well cut out, so that I can tie it round me.'

The man in the pointed hat picked up a box of chocolates and offered them to Susan.

But she couldn't get her fingers into the box! You see, it was only a painted box, so of course the chocolates couldn't be taken out. She was so disappointed.

'I can't take out any of the chocolates,' she said, trying hard.

The black imp she had cut out came and looked at the box. He put up his little black hand, and, to Susan's surprise, he picked out a handful of the chocolates and ran off with thcm.

'I expect he can do it because he's made of paper like the chocolates,' whispered Jimmy. 'Anyway, they'd taste horrid, I'm sure!'

'Let's go for a ride in these cars,' cried the old woman with the basket. They ran to the cars. The tall man took the wheel of the red car and the old lady climbed in beside him. That left the imp all alone with the green car, and he looked as black as thunder.

'I can't drive a car,' he said. 'One of you children must get in with me and drive me along. I'm not going to be left out!'

'I don't want to get in that car with you,' said Jimmy. 'You look so black and dirty.'

'You nasty boy!' cried the imp, in a rage. 'Get into the car at once. How dare you insult one of the paper-folk!'

To Jimmy's surprise all the other paper-folk sided with the black imp. They shouted angrily to the children:

'Get in and drive him! Get in and drive him! You wouldn't eat our chocolates, and now you are too grand to drive our car!'

The children felt quite scared. Jimmy went to the green car and tried to get in. But of course he couldn't, because it was only paper. He tried and tried, but his leg simply slid down the paper to the ground.

The imp was sitting at the back, watching. He frowned at Jimmy, and cried out crossly:

'You're only pretending not to be able to get in. You're only pretending! Why can't you get in? You're the same as us, aren't you, and *we* got in!'

'Well, we're *not* the same as you, so there!' said Jimmy, losing his temper. 'You're only made of paper – you haven't even got proper backs! We're real. You're just cut-out people; and your cars are cut-out cars, so of course we can't get into them! Don't be so silly!'

Well, when the paper-folk heard Jimmy saying that, they were all as hurt and angry as could be. They climbed out of the cars and looked all round them for something to fight the children with. They suddenly saw the poker, the tongs, and the shovel that Jimmy had cut out, lying on the ground by the boxes of chocolates.

The tall man picked up the poker, and the man in the dressing-gown picked up the tongs. The imp snatched up the shovel. The old woman took her basket, and the boy took his hoop-stick to fight with, and together all the paper-folk rushed angrily at the scared children.

'Don't be frightened, Susan,' said Jimmy. 'They're only paper.'

'But we haven't anything to fight them with,' cried Susan, looking round on the window-sill.

'Let's blow them with our breath,' shouted Jimmy. 'They are only paper, you know.'

So, much to the cut-out people's surprise, as

soon as they were close to the children Jimmy and Susan blew hard at them with all their breath.

'Wheeeeeeeeeeeeeew!' went the children together, and the paper-folk were all blown over flat! What a surprise for them! They picked themselves up again and rushed at the children once more.

'Wheeeeeeeeeeeeeew!' blew Jimmy and

Susan, and once again the paper-folk were blown down flat – and, oh my, the fat boy was blown right over the edge of the window-sill on to the floor below. How the paper-folk screamed to see him go!

'I shan't have much breath left soon,' whispered Jimmy to Susan. 'Whatever shall we do?'

'I wish we could grow to our own size again,' wailed Susan, who had had quite enough of being small.

Well, she had only to wish that for it to become true, for there was still a little magic floating about in the air. Just as the paper-folk were rushing at them again the children shot up tall, and the cut-out people cried out in surprise.

In a trice the children were their own size, and at that moment they heard Nurse's voice.

'Wherever are you? Jimmy! Susan! I've been looking for you everywhere!'

'Here we are, Nurse,' said Jimmy, peeping round the window-curtain.

'But you weren't there a minute ago, Jimmy, for I looked to see,' said Nurse in astonishment. 'There were only a few bits of paper blowing about on the window-sill. Now, where have you been hiding?'

'Truly we were there, Nurse,' said Jimmy, and

he and Susan told her of their adventure with the paper-folk.

But Nurse laughed and wouldn't believe it. 'Don't make up such silly tales,' she said. 'Fighting with paper-folk indeed! Whoever heard such nonsense?'

'Well, Nurse, look!' cried Susan, suddenly. 'Here's that nasty little fat boy on the floor, with his hoop. Jimmy blew him over the edge of the window-sill. That just proves we are telling the truth.'

It did, didn't it? The children and Nurse looked

at the paper-boy on the floor, and at the other paper-folk who were all lying quietly on the window-sill.

'I should paste them fast into your scrap-book,' said Nurse. 'Then they won't do any more mischief!'

So that's where the paper-folk are now – in the middle of the scrap-book, pasted down tightly. You can see them there any time you go to tea with Jimmy and Susan!

The Tiresome Poker

Once when Sleeky the pixie went by Dame Ricky's cottage, he heard her talking to Mother Goody over the fence.

'My dear!' said Dame Ricky. 'I *was* in a way this morning, I can tell you! When I went to light the kitchen fire, I found I hadn't a bit of firewood in the house. It was my baking day, too.'

'You should have borrowed some firewood from me!' said Mother Goody.

'Well, I would, my dear,' said Dame Ricky, 'but I suddenly remembered that old magic poker that belonged to my grandmother – you know, the poker with the red knob at the top. I always used to use it to light my fires – and then it got rather tiresome and talkative and I put it away.'

'Dear me! I haven't heard of the magic poker before,' said Mother Goody. 'Tell me about it. How does it light a fire?'

'Oh, you just stick it into the empty fireplace and put a few coals on top,' said Dame Ricky. 'Then you say, "Poker, light up!" and in half a minute there's a wonderful fire burning away!'

'Well, well,' said Mother Goody, surprised. 'That's a useful poker to be sure!'

Now Sleeky the pixie heard all this and he couldn't help feeling a bit excited. And that afternoon, when Dame Ricky had gone shopping, Sleeky slipped along to her house and looked into her kitchen.

There, standing by the fireplace was a big poker with a red knob at the end. 'That's the one!' said Sleeky, pleased. 'I'll borrow you for a few days – but I shan't tell Dame Ricky!'

He ran off with the poker. He thought he would try to light his fire with it, because it had gone out twice that day. He put the poker into his fireplace and piled coals on top.

'Poker, light up!' said Sleeky. And the poker made a sizzling noise as if it were getting hot, and then the coals burst into flame. A beautiful fire burnt in the fireplace, as hot as could be!

'How marvellous!' said Sleeky, very pleased. He took the poker out, and stood it by the fireplace. It sizzled for a little while and then made no more noise.

Soon Hallo the brownie came in to see Sleeky. He looked at the roaring fire.

'Fine fire, that!' said Hallo, rubbing his hands together.

'Yes, I'm good at getting a hot fire going,' said Sleeky.

'So am I,' said a sharp voice from somewhere. 'But I don't know what Dame Ricky will say when she knows what you've done.'

Sleeky looked all round in alarm. Hallo looked most astonished. 'What have you been doing to make Dame Ricky cross?' he asked.

'Nothing at all,' said Sleeky.

'Fibber! Story-teller!' said the voice again, and the poker jiggled itself a little.

'It's the poker talking!' cried Hallo, and he shot out of the house at once. Sleeky glared at the poker in a rage.

'How dare you interfere when I am talking to my friends?' he cried.

'I shall say what I like, when I like, and how I like,' said the poker, banging itself against the wall. 'I'm a very old and wise poker.'

'You're not. You're silly and stupid and interfering,' said Sleeky. 'If you're not careful I'll take you back to Dame Ricky and tell her you came here all by yourself.'

'Naughty little story-teller!' said the poker in a shocked voice. 'Yes – you must take me back to Dame Ricky, and see what *I'll* tell her! My goodness me – what a lovely spanking you will get!'

Sleeky stared at the poker in alarm and anger. What could you do with a poker like that? No wonder Dame Ricky said it was a tiresome poker, and put it away!

There was a knock at the door. In came Snibble the goblin.

'Hallo, Sleeky,' said Snibble. 'Could you possibly spare me a box of matches? I'd like some to light my fire, and I haven't any.'

'Neither have I,' said Sleeky. And then he had a

fine idea. 'But I've got a magic poker here – take it and use that, if you like.'

The poker did a real dance of rage in the fireplace. 'Lending me here, there, and everywhere!' it cried. 'Who do you think I am? Look on the stove over there, Snibble, and you'll find matches all right. Sleeky is a mean old story-teller, and a naughty little thief, too!'

'Is that – is that – can it be – the *poker* talking?' said Snibble, scared as could be.

Sleeky nodded. 'It's a dreadful poker,' he said gloomily. 'It just interferes in everything. Talks all the time, and says the most dreadful things. Do take it, Snibble, please do.'

'No, thank you,' said Snibble, and he went away in such a hurry that he forgot all about the matches. The poker laughed loudly and jiggled itself in a most annoying manner.

'Stop fidgeting,' ordered Sleeky.

The poker jiggled all the more, and even began to whistle. Sleeky got angrier and angrier. He suddenly got up, ran over to the poker, took it into his hand and threw it right out of the window!

Oh, goodness gracious! It hit Mister Slow-Foot on the shoulder, and he looked round in surprise and anger.

'Who did that? Who did that?'
he shouted. Sleeky hid behind the
window curtains. He was afraid of
Mister Slow-Foot. The poker stood
up on its one leg and spoke politely
to Slow-Foot.

'It was Sleeky who threw me at
you. He's a bad pixie.'

Mr. Slow-Foot went to Sleeky's
house and in half a minute you might have heard
a sound of smacking and crying, for although
Slow-Foot was slow of foot, he was mighty quick
of hand!

Sleeky sat crying in a chair by the fire. He wiped
his eyes and said to himself: 'Well, anyway, that

horrible poker is gone. I hope it won't tell tales of me to Dame Ricky.'

There was a knock at the door. Tap-tap-tap! Tap-tap-tap!

'Come in!' shouted Sleeky, wiping the last tears away. But nobody came in. 'COME IN!' yelled Sleeky, getting cross.

Tap-tap-tap! Tap-tap-tap! Sleeky got annoyed and went to the door. He opened it – and oh dear, in hopped that poker on its one steel leg, as lively as could be!

'Thanks!' said the poker. 'Couldn't reach the handle myself. Well – I'm back, you see. You don't look very pleased to see me!'

It went back to its place by the fire. Sleeky glared at it. 'Pleased to see you!' he cried. 'I should just think I'm not! Go out! I will NOT have you in my house.'

'I'm sorry about that,' said the poker, leaning back against the wall. 'I mean to stay, you see.'

Well, that poker meant what it said. No matter how Sleeky begged it, scolded it, even cried tears to it, it just said the same thing.

'I mean to stay!'

And oh, what a nuisance it was all that day! How it chattered and talked! What dreadful things it said!

'Sleeky, you'd better get rid of that poker,' said Feefo, when he came in for a few minutes. 'No one will come and see you if you let it stand there and say cheeky things.'

When Sleeky was alone after tea he sat and stared at the poker. How could he get rid of it? Ah – he would put it into the dust-bin – and then the dustman would take it away to-morrow. That would be fine!

He waited until the poker seemed to be asleep. Then he quickly took hold of it, rushed out into the yard and threw it into the dust-bin! Clang! The lid went on – the poker was a prisoner among the tea-leaves and the cinders!

'That's finished *you!*' said Sleeky, fiercely, as he heard the poker begin to jiggle against the lid. 'You can't get out of there! You won't annoy me any more with your tiresome ways!'

But Sleeky was wrong. Just wait and see what that tiresome poker did!

That evening Higgle the brownie came in to have supper with Sleeky. Sleeky liked Higgle. He was a generous fellow, and always brought a present of some kind with him. This evening he brought four sausage rolls, which smelt most delicious.

The two of them sat down to eat the sausage rolls, with pickles, bread and coffee. Just as they were in the middle of the meal there came a tapping at the window.

Tap-tap-tap! Tap-tap-tap!

Well, of course, Sleeky knew quite well what was making that noise – the poker! He had just heard a crash – that was the dust-bin lid falling on the ground – and now came the tap-tap-tap. Bother that poker! It wanted to come indoors

again. Well, Sleeky was quite determined to take no notice of it.

Tap-tap-tap! Tap-tap-tap!

'Sleeky, what's that noise?' asked Higgle.

'Tree against the window, I expect,' said Sleeky. 'Take no notice.'

Tap-tap-tap! Tap-tap-tap!

'Funny sort of tree,' said Higgle, puzzled.

'Let me in!' suddenly yelled the poker.

'That tree wants to come in!' said Higgle, in astonishment.

'Take no notice,' said Sleeky, in a rage. But it wasn't a bit of good taking no notice – because the poker suddenly tapped so hard that it broke the window.

CRASH! Down came the glass in tiny bits, and Higgle and Sleeky almost jumped out of their skins! The poker hopped in and went to the fire. It was shivering.

'Mean creature!' it said to Sleeky. 'Putting me in the dust-bin with tea-leaves and things! I'm cold. I'm going to stand here and tell you exactly what I think of you. You're a nasty, mean fellow, and I don't like you a bit. You're a horrid...'

Higgle stared in horror at the magic poker, feeling quite frightened. Sleeky was so angry that

he nearly burst with rage. He jumped up and ran to the poker. He picked it up and shouted:

'Ho, so you think you'll stand there and be rude to me, do you? Well, you won't! I'll put you into the village pond! It's deep – and cold – and wet! Ho, ho – you'll be sorry you ever came back to me when you go splash into the pond!'

And out he went into the night with the poker. Higgle sat and stared – and then he felt a bit frightened and got up to put on his coat. He went home, wondering how in the world Sleeky had got hold of such a peculiar poker.

Sleeky went to the village pond. The poker wriggled about in his hand for all it was worth, trying to get away, but it couldn't. And into the pond it went, flying high into the air, and then down, down, down into the cold water, splash! It disappeared. It was gone.

'Good!' said Sleeky. 'That's the end of you!'

The pixie went home. He finished up the sausage rolls and pickles, and then he went to bed. He got himself a hot-water bottle, because he was cold. He was soon fast asleep.

In the middle of the night he woke up very suddenly. What could that noise be? He could hear funny footsteps coming down the lane. Tip-tap, tip-tap, tip-tap! Sleeky sat up in bed and listened.

'Oh my, oh my, I hope it isn't that horrid, nasty poker!' he groaned. 'Oh, I really couldn't bear it. Oh, what ever shall I do?'

Tip-tap, tip-tap! The noise came nearer and nearer. It came to Sleeky's gate. It stopped there. The gate creaked as it opened.

Tip-tap, tip-tap! The noise came up the garden-path. Then there came a rapping on the door below.

'Well, knock all you like, I'll not let you in!' said Sleeky fiercely. 'Wake everyone up if you like – but I'll NOT LET YOU IN!'

The poker stopped knocking after a while. It went to the broken window. It got in through there, and Sleeky heard it land with a bump on the floor.

'Well, maybe the horrid thing will put itself by the fire and stay quiet,' thought the pixie, lying down again.

But after a bit Sleeky heard the poker grumbling away to itself downstairs.

'The fire's out! It's cold as ice in this kitchen. I'm wet and shivering! Oooooooooosh! I shall catch such a cold. A-tish-oo!'

Then there came the noise of the poker coming upstairs. Tip-tap, tip-tap, tip-tap! Quick as lightning Sleeky jumped out of bed and shut his door. Then back to bed he went again, grinning to himself. The poker got to the door. It knocked on it.

Tap-tap-tap! Sleeky pretended to snore. The poker knocked again, more loudly. TAP-TAP-TAP!

Sleeky snored again. The poker shouted angrily. 'You're not asleep. I know you're not. I heard you get out of bed just now. If you don't open the door to me I'll go downstairs and break all your cups

and saucers, dishes and glasses. Yes, I will, I will!'

'You wicked poker!' cried Sleeky, in a rage, quite forgetting to be asleep.

'I'm going downstairs to break the cups to begin with,' said the poker and tip-tapped down a few steps. But Sleeky leapt out of bed at once and opened the door.

'Don't you dare to do a thing like that!' he shouted. 'Just don't you dare!'

The poker hopped up the stairs again and into the bedroom. Sleeky sulkily got into bed. The poker hopped over to the bed and tried to get in between the sheets.

'Look here! What are you doing?' cried Sleeky. 'Get out of my bed, you nasty, wet, cold thing!'

'Well, who made me cold and wet?' said the poker, getting right into bed. 'You did! Now you can just warm me up. Let me cuddle close to you. Oooooh – that's better.'

'You're sticking into me,' said Sleeky, pushing the poker away. 'You're hurting me. You're all wet. Get away.'

But Sleeky might as well have talked to the moon for all the notice that poker took! It just stuck itself well into Sleeky and warmed itself on him. After a bit the pixie simply couldn't bear it.

He got out of bed, found a rug, and went to sleep on the floor.

Then the poker was happy. It had a warm bed all to itself, and a hot-water bottle. My, it was lovely!

In the morning Sleeky was very miserable. He was stiff and cold with sleeping on the floor. The poker popped its knobbly head up and spoke to him.

'I like living with you. You've got a nice warm fire in your kitchen, and a nice warm bed at night. Go down and light the fire before I get up. Then the kitchen will be warm.'

Sleeky didn't say a word. He just felt that he couldn't do anything with a poker like that. He dressed himself and then slipped out of the

house. He went to Dame Ricky's and knocked on her door.

She opened it in surprise. 'What do you want so early in the morning, Sleeky?' she asked.

'Please, Dame Ricky, I took your poker the other day,' said Sleeky, hanging his head.

147

'Oh, so it was you, was it?' said Dame Ricky. 'I wondered who it was. Well, though it was a very naughty thing to do, I'm very, very glad you took it. I always wanted to get rid of that cheeky, talkative poker.'

'Dame Ricky, please come and take it back,' said Sleeky. 'I can't tell you how awful it has been to me. I simply can't tell you! It has broken my kitchen window. And last night it got into bed with me, all wet and cold – and I had to sleep on the floor.'

Dame Ricky began to laugh. 'Sleeky, I can't help thinking you've been well punished,' she said. 'You're a naughty little pixie, you know – a very naughty little pixie. And now, for once in a way you've met something that has got the better of you.'

'Dame Ricky, don't laugh,' said Sleeky, beginning to cry bitterly. 'Please, please come and take the poker away. I'm very unhappy about it.'

'A little unhappiness will do you a lot of good,' said Dame Ricky. 'No – I tell you I don't want the poker back. I'm glad to be rid of it. Now, you go back and get your breakfast. Take no notice of the poker, and maybe it will get tired of talking.'

Poor Sleeky! He went back home very sad. The poker was still in bed. It yelled out to Sleeky to light the kitchen fire at once. But Sleeky didn't. He

got himself a quick breakfast and then he went to Higgle's.

'Higgle, you said the other day that if I wanted some work to do you'd give me a job in your shop,' he said. 'Well, I do want some work to do – work that will take me out of my house all day long. So will you give me that job?'

'Certainly,' said Higgle. 'It will be very good for you to have a job. Start to-day if you like!'

So Sleeky started his job that very day – and the poker didn't have a kitchen fire to warm itself by after all. What a time it gave poor Sleeky when he got home that night!

'You won't get a fire at all,' said Sleeky fiercely. 'I'm going to be at work all day long, so there! You'd better go and find somebody else to annoy, you nasty, horrid thing!'

Well, well – it's done Sleeky good to have work to do. As for that poker, it's making up its mind to move somewhere where there's a good fire every day. Tell me if it comes to you, won't you!

The Enchanted Table

Once upon a time there was a strange table. It was perfectly round, and had four strong legs ending in feet like a lion's – paws with claws. Round its edge there was carved a circle of tiny animals – mice, cats, dogs, weasels, rats, pigs, and others.

For many years this table stood in the kitchen of a tailor named Snip, and no one knew of its magic powers. Mrs. Snip laid a white cloth on it each meal time and spread it with food and drink. Once a week she polished it. All the little Snip children sat round it three times a day and, dear me, how they kicked it with their fidgety feet! How they stained it when they spilt their tea! How they marked it with their knives, pens and pencils!

One day an old man came to see Snip the tailor. Mrs. Snip asked him into the kitchen for a cup of tea, and he suddenly saw the table, with its edge of carved animals and its four paws for feet. His eyes opened wide, and he gasped for breath.

'That table!' he cried. 'It's magic! Didn't you know?'

'How is it magic?' asked Mrs. Snip, not believing him at all.

'Look!' cried the old man. He went up to the table and ran his fingers round the carved animals. He pressed first a mouse, then a cat, then a pig, then a weasel, muttering a few strange words as he did so. Then he tapped each of the four paw-like feet with his right hand.

'Mercy on us!' cried Mrs. Snip, in horror and surprise. 'Look at that! Why, it's alive!'

'Wait!' said the old man, in excitement. 'Let me show what it can do now!'

He went to the table and put his hands on the middle of it. Then, knocking three times sharply, he said: 'Bacon and sausages! New bread! Hot cocoa!'

And, would you believe it, a dish of bacon and sausages, a loaf of new bread, and a jug of hot cocoa suddenly appeared on that strange table!

Mrs. Snip couldn't believe her eyes! She sat down on a chair and opened and shut her mouth like a fish, trying to say something. At last she called the tailor in from the shop.

When she told him what had happened he was amazed.

The old man knocked three times on the table again and said: 'Two pineapples! Stewed mushrooms!'

Immediately two large pineapples arrived, and a heap of stewed mushrooms planted themselves in the middle of the dish of bacon and sausages. They smelt very nice.

'Can we eat these things?' asked Mr. Snip at last.

'Of course,' said the old man. They all sat down and began to eat. My, how delicious everything was! The table kept quite still, except that once it held out a paw to the fire, and frightened the tailor so much that he swallowed a whole sausage at once and nearly choked.

'This table is worth a lot of money,' said the old man. 'You should sell it, Snip. It's hundreds of years old, and was made by the gnome Brinnen, in a cave in the heart of a mountain. How did you come to have it?'

'Oh, it belonged to my father, and to his father, and to *his* father; in fact, it has been in our family for ages,' said the tailor. 'But I didn't know it was magic.'

'I expect someone forgot how to set the spell working,' said the old man. 'Look, I'll show you what I did. First you press *this* animal – then you press *this* one – and then *this* – and *this* – and all the time you say some magic words, which I will whisper into your ear for fear someone hears them.'

He whispered. The tailor listened in delight.

'And then,' said the old man, 'just put your hands in the middle of the table – so – and think what food you want. Then rap smartly three times on the top of the table and call out for what you'd like!'

'Marvellous!' said the tailor, rubbing his hands together. 'Wonderful! But I shan't sell my table, friend. No, it has been in my family so long that I could not part with it. I will keep it and let it provide food for me and my family.'

'Well, treat it kindly,' said the old man, putting on his hat to go. 'It has feelings, you know. Treat it kindly. It likes a good home. And don't forget to say those magic words once a week.'

'Come and dine with us each Sunday,' said the tailor. 'If it hadn't been for you we should never have found out the magic.'

Well, at first all the tailor's children and friends couldn't say enough about that marvellous table. They simply delighted in rapping on it and ordering meals. It didn't matter what they asked for it came. Even when Amelia Snip, the eldest child, rapped and asked for ice-cream pickles they appeared on the table in an instant.

What parties the Snips gave! Roasted chickens, legs of pork, suet puddings, mince pies, apple tarts, sugar biscuits, six different sorts of cheese – everything was there and nobody ever went short.

The table seemed quite content, except that it would keep walking over to the fire, and sometimes it stroked someone's leg, and made that guest jump nearly out of his skin.

But one day the table became impatient. Six

little Snip children sat round it, and they were very fidgety. Amelia kicked one table-leg. Albert kicked another. Harriet spilt her lemonade over it and made it sticky. Paul cut a tiny hole in it with his new penknife. Susan scratched it with her finger-nails. And Bobbo swung his legs up high and kicked the underneath of the table very hard indeed.

The table suddenly lost its temper. It lifted up a paw and smacked Bobbo hard on his bare leg.

'Ooh!' cried Bobbo, slipping down from his chair in a hurry. 'Horrid table! It slapped me!'

'How dare you slap my brother!' cried Amelia, and kicked the table-leg hard. It immediately lifted up its paw, put out its claws, and scratched her like a cat!

'Ow!' cried Amelia, and she ran to the shop, howling. Soon the tailor and his wife came back with her, and the tailor scolded the table.

But instead of listening humbly, the table put up a big paw and slapped Mr. Snip! Then it got up and walked over to the fire.

'How many times have I told you that you are *not* to stand so close to the fire?' scolded Mrs. Snip. 'No one can sit at you if you do that. It's too hot.'

The table ran up to Mrs. Snip and with two of its great paws it pushed her into a chair. Then it shook one of its paws at her crossly and went back to the fire again. Mrs. Snip was very angry.

'Ho!' she said. 'So that's how you're feeling, is it? Well, I'll give you some work to do.'

She went over to it and rapped smartly on the top three times, calling out: 'Roast beef! Roast pork! Roast mutton! Steak-and-kidney pie! Suet roll! Jam sandwich! Currant cake! Plum pudding!' and so on and so on, everything she could think of! The table soon groaned under the weight of all the food she called for, and its four legs almost bent under their burden.

'There!' said the tailor's wife. 'That will punish you for your spitefulness!'

But the table had had enough of the Snip family. It had never liked them, for they were mean and selfish. So it made up its mind to go away from the house and never to come back.

It walked slowly to the door, groaning again under the weight of all its dishes. Mrs. Snip and the tailor guessed what it was trying to do, and they rushed at it to push it back. The table rose up on two of its legs and began to punch with its other two.

Crash! Smash! Bang! Splosh! Every dish on the table slid off to the floor! There lay meat, pudding, pie, cakes, everything, and a whole heap of broken china. My, what a mess!

The table was pleased to be rid of its burden. It capered about and gave Mr. Snip a punch on the nose. The tailor was frightened and angry. He really didn't know how to fight a fierce table like this. He tried to get hold of the two legs, but suddenly great claws shot out of the table's paws and scratched him on the hand.

Then the table slapped Mrs. Snip and smacked Amelia and Paul hard. Then it squeezed itself out of the door and ran away down the street. It went on all-fours as soon as it left the house, and was so pleased with itself that it capered about in a very extraordinary way, making everyone run to their windows and doors in amazement.

Well, of course, the news soon went round that the marvellous magic table was loose in the land. Everyone secretly hoped to get it, and everyone was on the look-out for it. But the table was artful. It hid when the evening came and thought hard what it wanted to do.

'I will put myself into a museum,' said the table to itself. 'A museum is a place where all sorts of interesting and marvellous things are kept for people to wonder at and admire. I will find a museum and go there. Perhaps no one will notice that I have come, and I shall have peace for a while.'

It wandered out into the street again, and went to the next town. It was a big one, and the table felt sure it would have a museum. So it had – but the door was shut.

The table looked round the building to see if a window was open. Sure enough there was one, but rather high up. However, the table cared nothing for that. It climbed up a rain-pipe with all its four paws, and squeezed itself in at the window. Then it clambered down the wall inside and looked about for somewhere to stand.

Not far away was a big four-poster bed, a square table, and two solid-looking chairs. They had all belonged to some famous man. The table thought it might as well go and stand with these things, so off it went, and arranged itself in front of the chairs. Then it went comfortably to sleep.

But in the morning it was, of course, discovered at once! The museum-keeper saw it first, and perhaps he would not have known it was the lost magic table if the table had not suddenly scratched one of its legs with a paw, nearly making the poor man faint with amazement.

'It's the enchanted table!' he cried, and ran off to spread the news.

Soon the room was quite full of people, all staring and exclaiming, wondering how in the world the table had got into their museum. Then of course began the rapping and the commanding of all kinds of food to appear. The table sighed. It was getting very tired of bearing the weight of so many heavy dishes. It was surprised to think that people seemed so often hungry.

It didn't like being in the museum after all. It was dreadfully cold; there was no fire there, as there had been at the tailor's, and a terrible draught blew along the floor. The table shivered so much that all the dishes on it shook and shivered too.

That afternoon a message arrived from the King himself. He wanted the marvellous table in his palace. It would save him such a lot of money in feasts, he thought, and it would bring him quite a lot of fame.

The table heard the people talking to the messenger, and it felt quite pleased. It would be warmer in the palace, at any rate. It got up and walked to the door. The people ran away as it came near, for they had heard how it had fought the tailor's family and defeated them.

But the table didn't want to fight. It just wanted to get somewhere nice and warm. The museum-keeper tried to shut the door to stop it from going out, but the table pushed him over, and went out, doing a jig to keep itself warm. It meant to walk to the palace.

Everyone thought that it was going to run away again, and men, women, and children followed it to see what it was going to do. They were filled with surprise to see it mounting the palace steps one by one, and entering the palace doors!

'It's gone to see the King!' they cried.

The table walked into the palace, and no one tried to stop it, for all the footmen and soldiers were too surprised to move. The table went into the King's study, and found the King there, writing a letter.

'Who is it. Who is it?' asked His Majesty crossly, not looking up. 'How many times have I said that people must knock before they interrupt me?'

The table went up to the King and bowed so low that it knocked its carved edge on the floor. Then it stood up and saluted with one of its paws.

The King looked up – and in a trice he sprang from his chair and ran to the other side of the room in fright, for he had never seen a table like that before.

The table went over to the fire to warm itself. Soon the King recovered from his fright and called his servants.

'Here is that wonderful table,' he said. 'Take it into my dining-hall, and send out invitations to all

the kings, queens, princes, and princesses living near to come and feast to-night. Tell them they shall each have what they like to eat and drink.'

The table went into the gold-and-silver dining-hall, and thought it was very grand indeed, but cold. It pointed one of its paws at the empty grate, but as nobody imagined that a table could feel cold, no notice was taken at all. So the table contented itself with doing a little dance to warm itself whenever it began to shiver, and this amused all the servants very much.

When the time for the feast drew near, the footmen laid a wonderful golden cloth on the table-top. Then they set out golden plates and dishes, golden spoons and forks, and golden-handled knives. How they glittered and shone!

No food was put there, not even bread. No, the table was to supply that.

Soon all the guests arrived, and how they stared to see such an empty table! 'Nothing but a vase of flowers!' whispered King Piff to Queen Puff.

'Take your seats,' said the King, smiling. 'I have brought you here to-night to see my new magic table, as enchanted and as bewitched as any table can be! Behold!'

He rapped three times smartly on the table.

'A dish of crusty rolls! Some slices of new-made toast!' he cried.

Before his guests' wondering eyes these things appeared, and the King bowed a little as if he were a conjurer performing tricks.

'Now, Queen Puff,' he said, 'kindly say what you would like for your dinner, and I will see that it comes. Rap three times on the table before saying.'

Queen Puff did as she was told. 'Celery soup, stewed shark's fin, roast chicken, roast beef, cauliflower, potatoes, and plum pudding!' she said, all in one breath. 'Oh, and ginger-beer to drink!'

One by one all the guests wished for the dinner they wanted and marvelled to see everything appear on the table in a trice, all steaming hot and beautifully cooked. They sat and ate, lost in wonder. Then King Piff had an idea.

'I say,' he said to the King who had invited him, 'won't it give you – er – gold, for instance?'

Everybody there listened breathlessly, for one and all they loved gold, and wanted as much as they could get.

'Well,' said the King, 'I've never tried anything but food. Perhaps it would spoil the magic of the table if we did. We'd better not.'

'Pooh! You mean to try when we're not here, so that you can get as much gold as you want for yourself!'

'Yes, you old miser!' cried Prince Bong, and everyone began to talk at once. The King was horrified to hear himself called such names, and he threatened to call in his soldiers and have everyone arrested.

No one listened to him. They were all rapping hard on the poor table, crying out such things as: 'A bag of gold! A sack of gold! Twenty diamonds! Six rubies! A box of jewels! Twenty sacks of gold! A hundred bars of gold!'

The poor table began to tremble. It had never been asked for such things before, and had always been able to give what was demanded. But the magic in it was not strong enough for gold and jewels. It tried its best, but all it could give the excited people were sacks of cabbages, bags of apples, and bars of chocolate!

'Wicked table!' cried Prince Bong, and drew his sword to slash it. 'Horrible table!' cried Queen Puff, and slapped it hard. But that was too much for the frightened table. It jumped up on two legs and began to fight for itself.

Down slid all the dishes, glasses, plates, and knives! The King found a roast chicken in his lap, and Queen Puff was splashed from head to foot with hot gravy. Prince Bong howled when a large

ham fell on his toe, and altogether there was a fine to-do.

The table hit out. Slap! That was for the King. Slosh! That was for Prince Bong. Punch! That was for King Piff. Scratch! That was for Queen Puff. Oh, the table soon began to enjoy itself mightily!

But, oh my, the King was calling for his soldiers, and the table could not hope to fight against guns. It suddenly ran down the dining-hall, jumped right over the heads of the astonished soldiers, and disappeared out of the door. How it ran!

'After it, after it!' yelled the King, who did not mean to lose the magic table if he could help it. But the table had vanished into the darkness.

It stumbled on and on, grieving that it could find no place where it would be treated properly. All it wanted was a room with a warm fire, a good polish once each week, and no kicking.

At last it came to a funny-looking shop, lighted inside with one dim lamp. The table peeped in. What a funny collection of things there was there! Old-fashioned furniture, suits of armour, rugs from far countries, lovely vases, old glasses, beaten-brass trays, strange, dusty pictures – oh, I couldn't tell you all there was.

It was a shop kept by an old man who sold strange things, Outside hung a sign on which was written the word 'Antiques.' The table did not know what that meant. All it knew was that there was a fire at the end of the shop, and that everything looked dusty and old – surely a table could hide here and never be discovered!

It crept in at the door. There was the old man, reading a book as old as himself, and the table hoped he would not look up as it walked softly among the dusty furniture.

'Who's there? Who's there?' said the old man, still not looking up. 'Wait a minute – I must just finish my page, and I'll serve you.'

The table squashed itself into a corner by the fire. It put up one of its paws and pulled down an embroidered cloth from the wall to cover itself. Then it heaved a sigh and stood quite still, enjoying the fire.

When the old man had finished his page he looked up – but there was no one in his shop. How strange!

'I felt sure I heard someone!' he said, rubbing his chin and looking all round, but he could see no one. So he went back to his book, and the table sidled a bit nearer the fire.

From that day to this no one has ever heard of that enchanted table. There it stands, happy and forgotten, in the old furniture shop, warming itself by the fire. If ever you see a round table with little animals carved round its edge, and with four big paws for feet, buy it. It is sure to be the long-lost enchanted table. But *do* be careful how you treat it, won't you?

The Boy Who Boasted

Sammy was always getting into trouble with the other children because he boasted. I expect you know children who boast, and I'm quite sure you don't like them a bit.

'I've got a bigger kite than anyone in the village,' Sammy would say. 'And it flies higher than anybody else's! Ho, you should just see it!'

Then, when George brought his new engine to school to show everyone, Sammy boasted again.

'Pooh! That's only a clockwork engine. You should see mine at home. It goes by electricity!'

'Don't boast,' said George, feeling suddenly that his engine wasn't so nice as he had thought it was.

But Sammy couldn't seem to stop boasting. 'I can run faster than any boy at school!' he boasted to his father. 'I can do more sums in half an hour than anyone else. I can write better than anyone in my class.'

'Well, it's a pity your school reports aren't better then,' said his father. 'Stop boasting about what you can do, and *do* something for a change. Then I might believe you.'

Now Sammy might have gone on boasting for the rest of his life if something hadn't happened. It's a good thing it did happen, because though it's bad enough to hear a child boasting, it's ten times worse to hear a grown-up doing the same thing. I'll tell you what happened.

One day Sammy was going home from school when he picked up a most peculiar pocket-knife. It was bright yellow, with blue ends, and when Sammy opened the blades, he saw that they were made of green steel. He stood and stared at the knife, wondering who had lost it.

And because he was an honest boy, he looked round to see if he could find the owner. Not far off was someone as small as himself and he was hunting everywhere on the ground.

'Hi, boy!' shouted Sammy. 'Have you lost a knife, because I've found one?'

The little fellow looked up – and Sammy couldn't quite make him out. He was as small as a boy and yet he looked more like a grown-up. He was dressed a bit strangely, too, in a green tunic and long stockings, and he wore a pointed hat on his head with a bell at the tip.

'Oh,' said the little fellow, 'have you found my knife? Thank you! My name is Smink. What's yours?'

'Sammy,' said Sammy. 'That's a funny-looking knife. I've got one at home. It's better than yours –

much sharper. It can cut through wood like butter!'

'Oh, mine's sharper than that,' said Smink. 'It can cut through a tree-trunk like butter!'

'Fibber!' said Sammy. 'You're boasting.'

'Well, so are you,' said Smink. 'But I'm telling the truth and you're not. Look!'

And, to Sammy's enormous surprise, Smink went up to a birch tree, drew his knife right through the trunk, and cut the tree in half! Crash! It fell to the ground.

Sammy was startled. 'Gracious!' he said. 'That knife of yours certainly *is* sharp. But you'll get into trouble if you cut trees down like that.'

'I was only showing you,' said Smink. He lifted the little tree up again and set it on its trunk. He took a tube of sticky stuff from his pocket and rubbed some on the tree and its trunk. Then it stood upright, looking quite itself again.

'It'll grow all right again,' said Smink. 'That is Growing-Glue I used. Stronger than any glue you've ever used, I'm sure!'

'Well, at home I've got a tube of glue that will stick all kinds of broken things,' said Sammy, beginning to boast again. 'It will stick legs on to tables, and backs on to chairs, and …'

'Fibber,' said Smink. 'You haven't any glue strong

enough to do that. Now this glue of mine is so strong it would even stick your feet to the ground.'

'You're boasting,' said Sammy. 'I shan't listen to you.'

'All right, I'll prove it,' said Smink – and quick as lightning, he tipped Sammy over so that he fell to the ground, and then Smink dabbed a little glue on the sole of each shoe. Sammy jumped to his feet in a rage, meaning to slap Smink – but, dear me, the little fellow had spoken the truth – Sammy's feet *were* stuck to the ground. He couldn't move a step.

'Oh, oh, my feet won't move!' he shouted in a temper. 'Take your glue away.'

'Can't,' said Smink with a grin. 'You'll have to get out of your shoes and leave them behind.'

And that's just what poor Sammy had to do! He slipped his feet out of his shoes and ran at Smink in his stockinged feet.

'I'm the strongest boy in my class!' he shouted. 'So look out for yourself!'

But Smink was off like the wind. 'It won't help you to run away,' panted Sammy. 'I can run faster than any boy in my school. I'll soon catch you.'

'Well, I can run faster than any boy alive!' yelled Smink. And he certainly could. There was no doubt about that at all – he went like the wind. Sammy couldn't possibly catch him. Smink sat down on a grassy bank and let Sammy catch him up that way.

'Now I warn you – don't hit me,' said Smink, 'because although you may think you can slap harder than anyone in your village, I can smack harder than any boy anywhere. So be careful.'

But Sammy wasn't careful! He gave Smink a slap – and Smink at once jumped up and smacked Sammy so hard that he fell down to the ground and rolled over three times!

'Oooh!' he said, sitting up. 'What hit me then?'

'I did,' said Smink. 'Don't say I didn't warn you.'

'I'll tell my mother and father about you,' said Sammy, beginning to cry. 'And you'll be sorry then, because my father and mother are big and strong and they will punish you hard.'

'Well, my mother and father are big and strong too,' said Smink. 'There they are, walking over there. Would you like to see what they do to horrid boys like you?'

Sammy looked to where Smink pointed – and to his surprise, saw two very tall, rather fierce-looking people walking through the wood. They were so tall that Sammy half-wondered if they could be giants! He decided at once that he didn't want to have anything to do with them.

'Don't call them,' he said hurriedly to Smink. 'I can see how big and strong they are without them coming any nearer. Where do you live?'

'In this wood,' said Smink. 'Where do you?'

'In the village,' said Sammy. 'And our house is the biggest one there, and it has the best garden too. And we've got a pond. You should just see it.'

'I live in a castle,' said Smink. 'Our garden is so big that we keep fifty gardeners. And our pond is a lake with a steamer on it.'

'Oh, you really are a most dreadful fibber,' said Sammy, quite shocked.

'I'll slap you again if you call me a fibber,' said Smink. 'I don't boast like you. What I say is always true. Come with me and I'll show you.'

He dragged Sammy off by the arm – and in a few

minutes, to Sammy's enormous astonishment, they came to a great wooden gate let into a high wall. Smink pushed it open – and there, set in the most beautiful grounds, was a real, proper castle with towers and all! And working in the garden were so many gardeners that Sammy felt there might even be more than fifty!

'Oooh! There's the lake,' he said. 'And it really has got a steamer on it. Goodness, aren't you lucky? Have you got a bicycle or a tricycle to ride? I've got a wonderful tricycle. I'm sure it's the best

in the world. Its bell rings so loudly that everyone gets out of the way at once.'

'I'll show you *my* tricycle,' said Smink, and he went to a nearby shed. He opened the door and wheeled out a most marvellous tricycle!

'It's made of gold,' said Smink, and he got on it. 'Out of the way, boy.'

He rode straight at Sammy, ringing the bell – and my word, the noise that bell made! It was like a hundred church bells clanging together at once. Sammy put his hands to his ears and fled out of the way of the swift tricycle.

'Stop ringing the bell!' he cried. 'Oh, stop! It's making me deaf.'

Smink stopped. He got off the tricycle and grinned. 'Do you want to see anything else?' he asked.

'Well, I must be getting home,' said Sammy, feeling that he had seen quite enough for one day. 'My puppy-dog will be missing me. I bet you haven't got a pup half as nice as mine. Do you know, mine's got a bark that would frighten any burglar at once, and his teeth are so big and sharp. And run – well, you should just see him! He could run you off your feet any day!'

'Well, I've got a puppy, too,' said Smink. 'And he's got a marvellous bark. And teeth! Gracious,

you should see them! They're so sharp that when he took a dislike to the lawn-mower yesterday, he just chewed it all up! And when he runs you can't see his legs, they go so fast!'

'Oh, don't boast,' said Sammy, in disgust. But Smink wasn't going to have Sammy saying that. He went to a big yard and opened a gate. He whistled – and out of the kennel there came a simply enormous puppy, gambolling round happily. He barked – and it sounded like the crash of a gun! He growled – and it was like the rumbling

of a thunderstorm! He showed his enormous teeth, and Sammy shivered. Goodness, yes – this puppy could chew up a lawn-mower and never notice it!

Sammy began to run. He was afraid of that big puppy. The puppy gambolled after him merrily. Sammy ran faster. The puppy snapped playfully at his ankles. Sammy was simply terrified. He felt certain that the puppy could chew him up just as his own puppy at home had chewed up his father's slipper.

Poor Sammy! He tore home in his stockinged feet, and felt the puppy snapping at his heels the whole way. Not until he was indoors and had slammed the door did he feel safe. He lay on the sofa, panting, his feet without any shoes, and his stockings all in holes.

He told his mother what had happened, and she found it very difficult to believe. 'Well, Sammy,' she said, 'if it's true, you'll have to remember one thing. Never boast again in case you meet another Smink. See what happens when you do!'

So I don't expect he *will* boast again. I guess Smink had a good laugh about it all, don't you?

The Disagreeable Monkey

Once upon a time six monkeys lived in a big cage together. They were all brown, they all had funny little faces, and they all had very long tails.

Five of them were good-tempered peaceable creatures, willing to share a banana with one another, or to give each other a monkey-nut. But the sixth monkey – oh, what a disagreeable fellow he was! He was the biggest of the lot, which was a pity, because if he had been *small* and disagreeable nobody would have taken much notice of him – but as he was so big, all the other monkeys were afraid of him.

He was a greedy fellow, Bula, the sixth monkey. When visitors came and poked pieces of orange, banana, or cucumber through the wires, Bula was always there first! Even when his hands and mouth were full of fruit or nut, he still snatched at the other monkeys' tit-bits.

When nobody came to give the monkeys fruit, Bula would sit in a corner, sulking. If one of the other monkeys came near him he would snarl, and perhaps chase him. Then round and round the cage they would go, and when at last Bula caught the frightened creature, he would pull handfuls of hair out of him and pinch him cruelly.

So, as you can see, he really was a horrid animal. As for the game of Pulling Tails, nobody was cleverer at it than Bula. You should have seen him creep quietly under the perch on which two or three of the others were sitting, with their long tails dangling down. He would suddenly catch hold of the tails and give them a hearty pull so that all the monkeys screeched and nearly fell off the perch with fright. But Bula never had *his* tail pulled – no, he always curled it neatly round him when he sat on a perch. He didn't let anyone have a chance of pulling it!

The other monkeys didn't know what to do about Bula. They could have been so happy without him. But the keeper came to their help, and what do you think he did? He put a big mirror in the cage one night when the monkeys were asleep! You wouldn't think that would help much, would you? – but you shall hear what happened!

When the monkeys awoke in the morning, one of them saw the mirror. He ran over to it and looked at it. To his enormous astonishment he saw another monkey there – one he had never seen before, for of course he didn't know what he himself looked like!

He ran back to the other monkeys and told them about the new monkey. Bula was still asleep, so they didn't wake him. One by one the other four monkeys crept over to the mirror and peeped in to see the new monkey.

'How cross Bula will be to see there is another monkey!' said the smallest monkey. 'He says there are too many of us already!'

'He will give the new monkey a dreadful time,' said another. 'He will pinch him and pull his tail!'

'Perhaps the new monkey will fight Bula and conquer him!' said the biggest monkey, who had once tried to fight Bula himself and had been beaten.

'Let's tell Bula there is a great big new monkey over there, ready to fight him,' said the smallest monkey, excited. 'Then he will rush over and start fighting and perhaps the new monkey will beat him. Oh my, what fun that would be!' 'Yes, let's go and tell him that,' said the biggest monkey. So off they went to wake up Bula. He was very cross.

'What do you want?' he chattered angrily. 'How dare you wake me up!'

'Oh, Bula, there is a new monkey in our cage,'

said the biggest monkey. 'He is over there. He is bigger than you, and stronger, and he will fight you and make himself our king. Then you will have to sit in a corner all day and say nothing, whilst the stranger takes your tit-bits and pulls your tail.'

Well, you should have seen the dreadful face that Bula pulled and heard the awful screech he gave when he heard this news! He was angrier than he had ever been in his life before!

He rushed off at once to where the monkeys pointed, and came to the looking-glass. He looked in and saw himself – but he didn't know that – he thought there was another monkey there!

'Ugly creature!' he cried. 'Disagreeable-looking fellow! What nasty little eyes you have! What a horrid mouth! How dare you come here? Go away at once or I will hit you on the nose!'

The other monkey looked just as angrily at Bula as Bula was looking at him. Bula shook his hairy little fist and the other monkey shook his fist too. That was too much for Bula. With a howl of rage he threw himself on the cheeky monkey – and banged his head dreadfully hard on the glass! He thought the monkey had hit him, and he was so angry that he tried to strike his enemy with both fists at once.

But the other monkey seemed to have a very

hard body! Bula's fists were quite sore with hitting against the glass – only to bang his head and bruise his hands. It was most extraordinary.

At last, tired and puzzled, Bula crept away to a corner and hung his head. He couldn't beat that monkey and he was ashamed and sad.

Then the other monkeys went to the looking-glass to praise the winner – and to their great surprise they saw there, not one monkey, but five! They couldn't understand it at all!

'What a marvellous monkey this is!' they cried. 'He can turn himself into as many monkeys as he likes. No wonder he was able to beat Bula. Oh, he is a wonderful monkey, the king of all monkeys, and we will tell him so every morning and every night.'

They do – and if they go alone, they see only one monkey there – but if they go together they see many, and they bow and scrape very humbly. As for Bula, he has never been near the looking-glass since that strange fight, and he is quite a different monkey now – for, if he looks disagreeable, the others say:

'Ho, Bula! What are you looking like that for? Be pleasant or we will tell our King Monkey to fight you again!'

And the only one who knows the secret is the keeper. Dear me, how he laughs to himself when he sees how much nicer Bula the monkey has become!

The Golden Enchanter

Once upon a time there lived in Shining Palace a great enchanter. He had thick golden hair, a golden beard, and always dressed in tunics and cloaks made of cloth-of-gold. So he was known as the Golden Enchanter.

He was very, very rich. All his plates, dishes, and cups were made of the purest gold. The very chairs he sat upon were gold, and the table where he sat for his meals was made of such heavy gold that it could never be lifted.

In his cellars were sacks upon sacks of gold, but nobody ever saw them except the Enchanter, for only he had the key to those dark cellars.

Shining Palace was very beautiful. Its walls were built of gold, and there were very many windows, all shining and glittering in the sun that shone every day on the palace. The Enchanter loved the sun. He used its golden beams in his magic, and many a bright sunbeam he had imprisoned in his heavy bars of gold.

The Golden Enchanter was generous and kind-hearted. He gave much of his gold away, and the people loved him. But other enchanters were jealous of his riches.

The Green Magician who lived on the next hill envied him very much, and tried to learn his secrets. The Hobbledy Wizard was jealous of him too, and wouldn't even speak to him when he met him. But the Golden Enchanter didn't mind. He felt sure that his gold was safe, locked up in the strong cellars.

One day there came to Shining Palace a little, lean man, whose eyes were a strange green. He asked to see the Enchanter and he was taken before him.

'Sir,' he said, bowing down to the ground, 'I have worked for Wily-One, the greatest of magicians, but he has turned me away after twenty years' service. So now I come to you to ask for work. There is not much that I do not know, for Wily-One was clever and taught me most of his secrets!'

'Wily-One was wicked,' said the Golden Enchanter sternly. 'I heard that he had been driven away.'

'That may be true,' said the green-eyed man. 'But

listen to all the things I can do, O Enchanter, and I think you will find that I may be very useful to you.'

Then, in a long string, the lean man recited all the marvellous spells he could make, and, as he listened, the Enchanter's eyes opened wide.

'I do not know how it was that Wily-One the Magician trusted you so much as to tell you all the secret spells,' he said. 'Only enchanters are supposed to know them. Well, you must have proved yourself trustworthy to him, so I will engage you to help me. Start tomorrow.'

The green-eyed man bowed again, and a strange smile came over his face. The Golden Enchanter did not notice it or he would have wondered about it, and guessed the lean man's secret. For he was no other than Wily-One, the great magician, himself! He had been driven away from his castle, and had had to wander hungry and homeless about the country.

Then he had thought that he would disguise himself and go to the Golden Enchanter to beg for work. Once he was in the Shining Palace, surely he could steal the keys to the cellar and help himself to enough gold to make him rich again.

He was delighted when the Enchanter engaged him as his chief helper. Day after day he did magic

'He wanted to sneeze, but he dared not.'

for him, made strange spells, caught sunbeams for gold, and sang magic words as he stirred the big cauldron on the fire. But he could not get permission to go down into the cellars where the sacks of gold were kept. The Enchanter kept his keys guarded carefully, and slept with them under his pillow. He thought that his new servant was very clever, but he did not like him, nor trust him.

The green-eyed servant lived in a small cottage not far from the palace. One day he found a trap-door in the floor, and lifting it up, spied a small cellar underneath.

'I will keep my potatoes there,' he said to himself, and he went down the steps. But when he got there an idea came to him that made him shiver with delight.

'I will use my magic to bore a passage from this cellar to the cellars of Shining Palace,' he thought, and he set to work. All day long he worked for the Golden Enchanter, but half the night he worked for himself, bewitching a spade to dig deep into the earth, making a tunnel through the darkness.

At last the tunnel was finished. Wily-One crept through it and came to the small hole leading right into the cellars of Shining Palace. He was delighted. He was just about to crawl through when he heard the sound of footsteps. He crouched down in fear and saw that it was the Golden Enchanter himself, dragging a new sack of gold into place. As Wily-One hid behind the crumbling wall of earth, something tickled his nose. He wanted to sneeze, but he dared not. He held his nose tightly between his finger and thumb, and made the tiniest noise imaginable.

The Golden Enchanter had very quick ears, which could even hear the grass grow in the spring-time. He heard the tiny noise and wondered what it was. He thought it must be the click of a beetle's wings. He dragged the sack into place, and then went to another cellar.

Wily-One thought that he had better not try to steal any gold that night whilst the Enchanter was about. So, very quietly he turned and crept back along the dark tunnel to his cottage. He went to bed and dreamed all night long of the large sack of gold he would have on the morrow.

The Enchanter had a great deal of work to do the next day, for there was a very fine and delicate spell he was making. It was mostly made of cobwebs and the whiskers of gooseberries, and all the windows had to be shut in case the wind should blow in and upset the spell.

The green-eyed servant was helping. His eyes

shone strangely and his cheeks were red with excitement. He kept thinking of that night, when he would once more have gold of his own and be rich. He would go far away to another country, build himself a fine castle, and be a magician once again.

The Golden Enchanter wondered why his assistant's eyes shone so green, and why his hands trembled when he carefully arranged the cobwebs in the right order.

'What's the matter with you this morning?' he asked. 'You don't seem yourself.'

'I'm all right!' said Wily-One.

'Now for goodness' sake don't sneeze or breathe too hard,' said the Enchanter, giving the last touches to the spell. 'If you do, all these cobwebs will have to be arranged again.'

But one of the gooseberry whiskers must have got up Wily-One's nose, for all of a sudden he wanted to sneeze.

He held his nose tightly between his finger and thumb and stopped the sneeze, making only the very tiniest noise, the same noise that he had made the night before in the cellar.

And the Golden Enchanter remembered the noise.

'So that's what that little noise was last night!'

he thought to himself. 'It was this green-eyed servant of mine stopping a sneeze. It wasn't a beetle's wings clicking! Oho! I shall have to look into this. Perhaps this clever servant of mine is not what he seems.'

The more he thought about it, the more the Enchanter felt sure that his servant was really a magician – and suddenly he guessed Wily-One's secret! Of course – he was Wily-One himself, disguised! Wily-One had those strange green eyes too. However could he, the Golden Enchanter, have been tricked like this?

'I'll hide in the cellars tonight and see what he is up to,' thought the Enchanter. So that night very early he hid behind his sacks and waited. Just as he had guessed the green-eyed servant crept along the tunnel, climbed into the cellar, and caught up a sack of gold!

'Hi!' shouted the Golden Enchanter. 'Put that down, you robber! I know who you are! You're Wily-One, the wicked magician who was driven away from his castle!'

Wily-One leapt through the hole and scuttled along the tunnel to his cottage. There he shut down the trapdoor and bolted it so that the Enchanter could not follow him. Then he took a magic broomstick he had once stolen from a witch, and rode away on it, taking the sack of gold with him.

But following him he saw a little bird, whom the Enchanter had ordered to chase Wily-One, for he did not like to leave his palace unguarded. He would call out his guards, bid them surround the palace whilst he was gone, and then follow the wicked magician himself. Meanwhile the little bird tracked Wily-One for him.

Wily-One landed at last in a broad field, so sleepy that he could fly no longer. Dawn was just breaking. He saw the little bird who had followed him wheel round and fly off towards Shining Palace.

'Well, by the time you come back with the Golden Enchanter I shall be gone!' he said. He looked at the sack of gold and decided that he had better bury it instead of taking it with him, for it was heavy. So he bewitched a strong stick and bade it make little holes all over the field. When that was done, he bade each piece of gold hide itself there. In a very short time the thousands of golden pieces were hidden all over the field, and there was none to be seen.

And at that moment Wily-One saw the Enchanter running towards him! He changed himself into a rabbit and ran away at top speed.

The Enchanter turned himself into a fox and a breathless race began. Just as the rabbit was almost caught Wily-One changed himself into a lark. Up and up into the sky he rose, hoping to get away from the Enchanter.

But the Enchanter turned himself into an eagle and soared swiftly after the lark. Down the sky they went, the lark trying its hardest to escape. But with a downward rush the eagle was upon it, and both dropped to the earth. As they touched the ground Wily-One turned himself into a tiny mouse, hoping to hide among the bracken. But the Enchanter turned himself into a big black cat and began to hunt the mouse here and there. Smack! It clapped its great paw on to the mouse's back, and knowing himself so nearly caught Wily-One changed swiftly into a snake and tried to bite the cat.

The Enchanter changed back into his own shape and struck the snake with a stick. It glided away and came to a deep pond. The Enchanter followed and lifted his stick again. Hey presto! Wily-One changed into a big fish and slipped silently into the water.

The Enchanter became an otter and slid into the water after him. Round and round the pond they swam, the fish twisting and turning in fear lest the otter should bite him in the neck.

Just as the otter pounced, the fish leapt into the air and changed into a brown bear. He clambered out of the water and ran to the mountains. The otter climbed out after him and changed into a bear too. He raced after his enemy, growling fiercely.

Wily-One saw a cave in a hillside and ran inside. In a trice the Golden Enchanter changed from a bear back to his own shape and laughed loudly. He took a great stone and rolled it in front of the cave, pinning it there by the most powerful magic he knew.

'Well, there you are, and there you may stay!' said he. 'I would never let a wicked magician like you free, for you do so much harm. No, here you will stay for hundreds of years and perhaps you will find time to repent.'

With that he left him and went back to Shining Palace. He did not bother to look for the stolen gold, for he had so much that he hardly missed it.

But one day he happened to pass the field where Wily-One had hidden the gold – and he stared in wonder and delight! Each little gold piece had taken root and grown! The plants had flowered in thousands all over the field and were waving their bright golden heads in the sunshine.

'I've never seen anything so beautiful in my life!'

said the Enchanter. 'I hope the seeds will spread so that the flowers may be seen by everybody!'

They did spread – they spread all over the world, and now each summer-time you may see fields full of the bright gold flowers that once grew from the stolen gold. Do you know what we call them? Yes, buttercups, of course!

As for Wily-One, he is still in the cave, and long may he remain there!

The Wizard's Umbrella

Ribby the Gnome lived in a small cottage at the end of Tiptoe Village. Nobody liked him because he was always borrowing things and never bringing them back! It was most annoying of him.

The things he borrowed most were umbrellas. I really couldn't tell you how many umbrellas Ribby had borrowed in his life – hundreds, I should think! He had borrowed Dame Twinkle's nice red one, he had taken Mr. Biscuit the Baker's old green one, he had had Pixie Dimple's little grey and pink sunshade, and many, many more.

If people came to ask for them back, he would hunt all about and then say he was very sorry but he must have lent their umbrellas to someone else – he certainly hadn't got them in his cottage now. And no one would ever know what had happened to their nice umbrellas!

Of course, Ribby the Gnome knew quite well

where they were! They were all tied up tightly together hidden in his loft. And once a month, Ribby would set out on a dark night, when nobody was about, and take with him all the borrowed umbrellas. He would go to the town of Here-we-are, a good many miles away, and then the next day he would go through the streets there, crying: 'Umbrellas for sale! Fine umbrellas!'

He would sell the whole bundle, and make quite a lot of money. Then the wicked gnome would buy himself some fine new clothes, and perhaps a new chair or some new curtains for his cottage and go home again.

Now one day it happened that Dame Twinkle went over to the town of Here-we-are, and paid a call on her cousin, Mother Tantrums. And there standing in the umbrella-stand in Mother Tantrum's hall, Dame Twinkle saw her very own nice red umbrella, that she had lent to Ribby the Gnome the month before!

She stared at it in great surprise. However did it come to be in her cousin's umbrella-stand? Surely she hadn't lent it to Mother Tantrums? No, no – she was certain, quite certain, she had lent it to Ribby the Gnome.

'What are you staring at?' asked Mother Tantrums in surprise.

'Well,' said Dame Twinkle, pointing to the red umbrella, 'it's a funny thing, Cousin Tantrums, but, you know, that's my red umbrella you've got in your umbrella-stand.'

'Nonsense!' said Mother Tantrums. 'Why, that's an umbrella I bought for a shilling from a little gnome who often comes round selling things.'

'A *shilling*!' cried Dame Twinkle in horror. 'My goodness, gracious me, I paid sixteen shillings and ninepence for it! A shilling, indeed! What next!'

'What are you talking about?' asked Mother

Tantrums, quite cross. 'It's *my* umbrella, not yours
– and a very good bargain it was, too!'

'I should think so!' said Dame Twinkle, looking
lovingly at the red umbrella, which she had been
very fond of indeed. 'Tell me, Cousin, what sort of
a gnome was this that sold you your umbrella?'

'Oh, he was short and rather fat,' said Mother
Tantrums.

'Lots of gnomes are short and fat,' said Dame
Twinkle. 'Can't you remember anything else
about him?'

'Well, he wore a bright yellow scarf round his
neck,' said Mother Tantrums, 'and his eyes were a
very light green.'

'That's Ribby the Gnome!' cried Dame Twinkle,
quite certain. 'He always wears a yellow scarf, and
his eyes are a very funny green. Oh, the wicked
scamp! I suppose he borrows our umbrellas in
order to sell them when he can! Oh, the horrid
little thief! I shall tell the wizard who lives in our
village and ask him to punish Ribby. Yes, I will! He
deserves a very nasty punishment indeed!'

So when she went back to Tiptoe Village, Dame
Twinkle went to call on the Wizard Deep-one. He
was a great friend of hers, and when he heard about
Ribby's wickedness he shook his head in horror.

'He must certainly be punished,' said the wizard, nodding his head. 'Leave it to me, Dame Twinkle. I will see to it.'

Deep-one thought for a long time, and then he smiled. Ha, he would lay a little trap for Ribby that would teach him never to borrow umbrellas again. He took a spell and with it he made a very fine umbrella indeed. It was deep blue, and for a handle it had a dog's head. It was really a marvellous umbrella.

The wizard put it into his umbrella-stand and then left his front door open wide every day so that anyone passing by could see the dog's-head umbrella quite well. He was sure that Ribby the Gnome would spy it the very first time he came walking by.

When Ribby did see the umbrella he stopped to have a good look at it. My, what a lovely umbrella! He hadn't noticed it before, so it must be a new one. See the dog's head on it, it looked almost real! Oh, if Ribby could only get *that* umbrella, he could sell it for a for a good many shillings in the town of Here-we-are. He was sure that the enchanter who lived there would be very pleased to buy it.

'Somehow or other I must get that umbrella,' thought Ribby. 'The very next time it rains I will

hurry by the wizard's house, and pop in and ask him to lend it to me! I don't expect he will, but I'll ask, anyway!'

So on the Thursday following, when a rainstorm came, Ribby hurried out of his cottage without an umbrella and ran to Deep-one's house. The front door was wide open as usual and Ribby could quite well see the dog-headed umbrella in the hall-stand. He ran up the path, and knocked at the open door.

'Who's there?' came the wizard's voice.

'It's me, Ribby the Gnome!' said the gnome.

'Please, Wizard Deep-one, could you lend me an umbrella? It's pouring with rain and I am getting so wet. I am sure I shall get a dreadful cold if someone doesn't lend me an umbrella.'

'Dear, dear, dear!' said the wizard, coming out of his parlour, and looking at the wet gnome. 'You certainly are *very* wet! Yes, I will lend you an umbrella – but mind, Ribby, let me warn you to bring it back to-morrow in case something unpleasant happens to you.'

'Oh, of course, of course,' said Ribby. 'I always return things I borrow, Wizard. You shall have it back to-morrow as sure as eggs are eggs.'

'Well, take that one from the hall-stand, Ribby,' said the wizard, pointing to the dog's-head

umbrella. Ribby took it in delight. He had got what he wanted. How easy it had been after all! He, ho, he wouldn't bring it back to-morrow, not he! He would take it to the town of Here-we-are as soon as ever he could and sell it to the enchanter there. What luck!

He opened it, said thank you to the smiling wizard, and rushed down the path with the blue umbrella. He was half afraid the wizard would call him back – but no, Deep-one let him go without a word – but he chuckled very deeply as he saw the gnome vanishing round the corner. How easily Ribby had fallen into the trap!

Of course Ribby didn't take the umbrella back next day. No, he put it up in his loft and didn't go near the wizard's house at all. If he saw the wizard in the street he would pop into a shop until he had gone by. He wasn't going to let him have his umbrella back for a moment!

Now after three weeks had gone by, and Ribby had heard nothing from the wizard about his umbrella, he decided it would be safe to go to Here-we-are and sell it.

'I expect the wizard has forgotten all about it by now,' thought Ribby. 'He is very forgetful.'

So that night Ribby packed up three other

umbrellas, and tied the wizard's dog-headed one to them very carefully. Then he put the bundle over his shoulder and set out in the darkness. Before morning came he was in the town of Here-we-are, and the folk there heard him crying out his wares in a loud voice.

210

'Umbrellas for sale! Fine umbrellas for sale! Come and buy!'

Ribby easily sold the other three umbrellas he had with him and then he made his way to the enchanter's house. The dog-headed umbrella was now the only one left.

The enchanter came to the door and looked at the umbrella that Ribby showed him. But as soon as his eye fell on it he drew back in horror.

'Buy that umbrella!' he cried. 'Not I! Why, it's alive!'

'Alive!' said Ribby, laughing scornfully. 'No, sir, it is as dead as a door-nail!'

'I tell you, that umbrella is *alive*!' said the enchanter and he slammed the door in the astonished gnome's face.

Ribby looked at the dog-headed umbrella, feeling very much puzzled – and as he looked, a very peculiar feeling came over him. The dog's head really did look alive. It wagged one ear as Ribby looked at it, and then it showed its teeth at the gnome and growled fiercely!

My goodness! Ribby was frightened almost out of his life! He dropped the umbrella on to the ground and fled away as fast as his fat little legs would carry him!

As soon as the umbrella touched the ground a very peculiar thing happened to it. It grew four legs, and the head became bigger. The body was made of the long umbrella part, and the tail was the end bit. It could even wag!

'Oh, oh, an umbrella-dog!' cried all the people of Here-we-are town and they fled away in fright. But the strange dog took no notice of anyone but Ribby the Gnome. He galloped after him, barking loudly.

His umbrella-body flapped as he went along on his stout little doggy legs, and his tongue hung out of his mouth. It was most astonishing. People looked out of their windows at it, and everyone closed their front doors with a bang in case the strange umbrella-dog should come running into their houses.

Ribby was dreadfully frightened. He ran on and on, and every now and then he looked round.

'Oh, my goodness, that umbrella-dog's still after me!' he panted. 'What shall I do? Oh, why, why, why did I borrow the wizard's umbrella? Why didn't I take it back? I might have known there would be something strange about it!'

The umbrella-dog raced on, and came so near to Ribby that it was able to snap at his twinkling

legs. Snap! The dog's sharp teeth took a piece out of Ribby's green trousers!

'Ow! Ooh! Ow!' shrieked Ribby in horror, and he shot on twice as fast, panting like a railway train going up a hill! Everybody watched from their windows and some of them laughed because it was really a very peculiar sight.

Ribby looked out for someone to open a door so that he could run in. But every single door was shut. He must just run on and on. But how much longer could he run? He was getting terribly out of breath.

The umbrella-dog was enjoying himself very much. Ho, this was better fun than being a dull old umbrella! This was seeing life! If only he could catch that nasty little running thing in front, what fun he would have!

The umbrella-dog ran a bit faster and caught up Ribby once more. This time he jumped up and bit a piece out of the gnome's lovely yellow scarf. Then he jumped again and nipped a tiny piece out of Ribby's leg.

'OW!' yelled Ribby, jumping high into the air. 'OW! You horrid cruel dog! Leave me alone! How dare you, I say? Wait till I get home and find a whip!'

The dog sat down to chew the piece he had bitten out of Ribby's yellow scarf, and the gnome ran on, hoping that the dog would forget about him.

'Oh, if only I could get home!' cried the panting gnome. 'Once I'm in my house I'm safe!'

He ran on and on, through the wood and over the common that lay between the town of Here-we-are and the village of Tiptoe. The dog did not seem to be following him. Ribby kept looking round but there was no umbrella-dog there. If only he could get home in time!

Just as he got to Tiptoe Village he heard a pattering of feet behind him. He looked round and saw the umbrella-dog just behind him. Oh, what a shock for poor Ribby!

'Look, look!' cried everyone in surprise. 'There's a mad umbrella-dog after Ribby. Run, Ribby, run!'

Poor Ribby had to run all through the village of Tiptoe to get to his cottage. The dog ran at his heels snapping every now and again, making the gnome leap high into the air with pain and fright.

'I'll never, never, never borrow an umbrella again, or anything else!' vowed the gnome, as the dog nipped his heel with his sharp teeth. 'Oh, why didn't I take the wizard's umbrella back?'

At last he was home. He rushed up the path, pushed the door open and slammed it. But, alas, the umbrella-dog had slipped in with him, and there it was in front of Ribby, sitting up and begging.

'OH, you horror!' shouted Ribby, trying to open the door and get out again. But the dog wouldn't let him. Every time Ribby put his hand on the handle of the door it jumped up and nipped him. So at last he stopped trying to open it and looked in despair at the strange dog, who was now sitting up and begging.

'Do you want something to eat?' said the gnome.

'Goodness, I shouldn't have thought an umbrella-dog could be hungry. Wait a bit. I've a nice joint of meat here, you shall have that, if only you will stop snapping at me!'

The dog ran by Ribby as he went hurriedly to his larder and opened the door. He took a joint of meat from a dish and gave it to the dog, which crunched it up hungrily.

Then began a very sorrowful time for Ribby! The dog wouldn't leave him for a moment and the gnome had never in his life known such a hungry creature.

Although its body was simply an umbrella, it ate and ate and ate. Ribby spent all his money on food for it, and in the days that came, often went hungry himself. The dog wouldn't leave his side, and when the gnome went out shopping the strange creature always went with him, much to the surprise and amusement of all the people in the village.

'Look!' they would cry. 'Look! There goes Ribby the gnome and his umbrella-dog! Where did he get it from? Why does he keep such a strange, hungry creature?'

If Ribby tried to creep off at night, or run away from the dog, it would at once start snapping and snarling at his heels, and after it had nibbled a bit out of his leg once or twice and bitten a large hole in his best coat, Ribby gave up trying to go away.

'But what shall I do?' wondered the little gnome, each night, as he looked at his empty larder. 'This dog is eating everything I have. I shall soon have no money left to buy anything.'

Ribby had had such a shock when the stolen

umbrella had turned into the umbrella-dog, that he had never once thought of borrowing anything else. He felt much too much afraid that what he borrowed would turn into something like the dog, and he really couldn't bear that!

'I suppose I'd better get some work to do,' he said to himself at last. 'But who will give me a job? Nobody likes me because I have always borrowed things and never taken them back. Oh dear, how foolish and stupid I have been.'

Then at last he thought he had better go to the Wizard Deep-one and confess to him all that had happened. Perhaps Deep-one would take away the horrid umbrella-dog and then Ribby would feel happier. So off he went to the wizard's house.

The wizard opened the door himself and when he saw Ribby with the dog he began to laugh. How he laughed! He held his sides and roared till the tears ran down his cheeks.

'What's the matter?' asked Ribby, in surprise. 'What is the joke?'

'*You* are!' cried the wizard, laughing more than ever. 'Ho, ho, Ribby, little did you think that I had made that dog-headed umbrella especially for you to borrow and that I knew exactly what was going to happen! Well, you can't say that I didn't warn

you. My only surprise is that you haven't come to me before for help. You can't have liked having such a strange umbrella-dog living with you, eating all your food, and snapping at your heels every moment! But it's a good punishment for you – you won't borrow things and not bring them back again, I'm sure!'

'I never, never will,' said Ribby, going very red. 'I am very sorry for all the wrong things I have done. Perhaps I had better keep this umbrella-dog to remind me to be honest, Wizard.'

'No, I'll have it,' said Deep-one. 'It will do to guard my house for me. I think any burglar would run for miles if he suddenly saw the umbrella-dog coming for him. And what are *you* going to do, Ribby? Have you any work?'

'No,' said Ribby, sorrowfully. 'Nobody likes me and I'm sure no one will give me any work to do in case I borrow something and don't return it, just as I used to do.'

'Well, well, well,' said the wizard, and his wrinkled eyes looked kindly at the sad little gnome. 'You have learned your lesson, Ribby, I can see. Come and be my gardener and grow my vegetables. I shall work you hard, but I shall pay you well, and I think you will be happy.'

So Ribby is now Deep-one's gardener, and he works hard from morning to night. But he is happy because everyone likes him now – and as for the umbrella-dog, he is as fond of Ribby as anyone else is and keeps at his heels all the time. And the funny thing is that Ribby likes him there!

The Little Singing Kettle

Mister Curly was a small pixie who lived all by himself in Twisty Cottage. His cottage stood at the end of the Village of Ho, and was always very neatly kept. It had blue and yellow curtains at the windows and blue and yellow flowers in the garden, so you can guess how pretty and trim it was.

Mister Curly was mean. He was the meanest pixie that ever lived, but he always pretended to be very generous indeed. If he had a bag of peppermints he never let anyone see it, but put it straight into his pocket till he got home. And if he met any of the other pixies he would pull a long face and say:

'If only I had a bag of sweets I would offer you one.'

'Never mind,' the others said. 'It's nice of you to think of it!'

And they went off, saying what a nice, generous creature Mister Curly was!

Now one day, as Mister Curly was walking home along Dimity Lane, where the trees met overhead, so that it was just like walking in a green tunnel, he saw a fellow in front of him. This was a Humpy Goblin, and he carried a great many saucepans, kettles and pans all slung down his back, round his shoulders and over his chest.

They made a great noise as he walked, but louder than the noise was the Humpy Goblin's voice. He sang all the time in a voice like a cracked bell.

'Do you want a saucepan, kettle or pan?
If you do, here's the Goblin Man!
The Humpy Goblin with his load
Of pots and pans is down the road,
Hie, hie, hie, here's the Goblin Man,
Do you want a saucepan, kettle or pan?'

Now Mister Curly badly wanted a new kettle, because his own had a hole in it and the water leaked over his stove each day, making a funny hissing noise. So he ran after the Goblin Man and called him. The Humpy Goblin turned round and

grinned. He was a cheerful fellow, always pleased to see anybody.

'I want a good little kettle, nice and cheap,' said Curly.

'I've just the one for you,' said Humpy, and he pointed to a bright little kettle on his back. Curly looked at it.

'How much is it?' he asked.

'Sixpence,' said the Goblin. This was quite cheap, but mean old Curly wasn't going to give sixpence for the kettle. He pretended to be shocked at the price, and then he gave a huge sigh.

'Oh, I'm not rich enough to pay all that,' he said sadly. 'I can only pay threepence.'

'Oh, no,' said Humpy firmly. 'Threepence isn't enough. You must pay sixpence.'

Well, they stood and talked to one another for a long time, one saying sixpence and the other saying threepence, until at last the Humpy Goblin laughed in Curly's face and walked off jingling all his kettles and pans.

'You're a mean old stick!' he called after Curly. 'I'm not going to sell you anything! Good-bye, Mister Mean!'

Off he went and soon began to sing his song again. Curly heard him.

'Do you want a saucepan, kettle or pan?
If you do, here's the Goblin Man!'

Curly stood and watched him angrily. Then he started walking, too. He had to follow the Goblin Man because that was the way home to Twisty Cottage. But he took care not to follow too close, for he was afraid that Humpy might call something rude after him.

It was a hot day and the Goblin was tired. After a while he thought he would sit down in the hedge and rest. So down he sat – and it wasn't more than a minute before he was sound asleep and snoring! Curly heard him and knew he must be asleep. A naughty thought slipped into his head.

'I wonder if I could take that kettle from him whilst he's asleep! I could leave threepence beside him to pay for it. How cross he would be when he woke up to find that I had got the kettle for threepence after all!'

He crept up to the Humpy Goblin. He certainly was sound asleep, with his mouth so wide open that it was a good thing there wasn't anything above his head that could drop into it. Curly carefully undid the little shining kettle without making even a clink of noise. Then he put three bright pennies on the grass beside the Goblin, and ran off, chuckling to himself for being so smart.

He soon reached home. He filled the little kettle with water and put it on the fire. It really was a dear little thing, and it boiled very quickly indeed, sending a spurt of steam out of the spout almost before Curly had got out the teapot to make the tea.

Just as he was sitting down to enjoy a cup of tea and a piece of cake, someone walked up his garden path and looked in at the door. It was the Humpy Goblin. When he saw that Curly had the kettle on the fire, he grinned all over his face.

'So you've got it!' he said. 'Well, much good may it do you! Kettle, listen to me! Teach Mister Curly the lesson he needs! Ho, ho, Curly, keep the kettle! I don't want it!'

Laughing and skipping, the Goblin went down the path again. Curly felt a bit uncomfortable. What was he laughing like that for?

'Oh, he just tried to frighten me and make me think something nasty would happen,' said Curly to himself. 'Silly old Goblin!'

He cleared away his cup and saucer, and filled up the kettle again. He was washing up the dirty dishes when a knock came at his door, and Dame Pitapat looked in.

'I say, Curly, could you let me have a little tea? I've emptied my tin and it's such a long way to the shops.'

Now Curly had a whole tin full, but he wasn't going to let Dame Pitapat have any. He ran to the dresser and took down a tin he knew was empty.

'Yes, certainly, Dame Pitapat,' he said, 'you shall have some of my tea. Oh, dear! The tin's empty! What a pity! You could have had half of it if only I'd had any, but I must have used it all up!'

Dame Pitapat looked at the empty tin. Then she turned to go.

'I'm sorry I bothered you, Curly,' she said. 'It was kind of you to say I could have had half, if only you'd had any tea.'

Then a funny thing happened. The little kettle

on the stove sent out a big spurt of steam and began to sing a shrill song.

'Mister Curly has plenty of tea!
He's just as mean as a pixie can be!
Look in the tin on the left of the shelf
And see what a lot he has for himself!'

Then the kettle took another breath and shouted, 'Mean old thing! Stingy old thing! Oooooh, look at him!'

Dame Pitapat was so astonished that she stood gaping for quite a minute. She couldn't think where the song came from. She had no idea it was the kettle on the stove. But Curly knew it was, and he was so angry and ashamed that he could have cried.

Dame Pitapat went to the shelf and took down the tin that stood on the left. She opened it, and sure enough, it was full to the brim of tea.

229

'Oh, look at this!' she said. 'Well, Curly, you said I could have half of any tea you had, so I shall take you at your word. Thanks very much.' She emptied half the tea out into the tin she had brought and went out of the cottage, looking round curiously to see if she could spy who had sung that song about Curly. But she didn't think of looking at the kettle, of course.

Curly was so angry with the kettle that he decided to beat it with a stick. But before he could do that someone poked his head in at the window and called him.

'Mister Curly! Will you lend me your umbrella, please? I've lost mine and it's raining.'

It was little Capers, the pixie who lived next door. He was always lending Curly things, and now he had come to borrow something himself. But Curly was in a very bad temper.

'My umbrella's lost too,' he said. 'I'm so sorry, Capers. You could have it if only I had it myself, but it's gone.'

'Oh, well, never mind,' said Capers. 'It's nice of you to say you would have lent it to me.'

Before he could go the shining kettle gave a tiny hop on the stove and began to sing again.

'Mister Curly has got an umbrella,
He's such a mean and stingy fella,
He says he hasn't got one at all
But just you go and look in the hall!'

Then it took another breath and began to shout again at the top of its steamy voice, 'Mean old thing! Stingy old thing! Oooooh, look at him!'

Capers was so surprised to hear this song that he nearly fell in at the window. He stared at Curly, who was looking as black as thunder and as red as a beetroot. Then Capers looked through the kitchen door into the tiny hall – and sure enough Curly's green umbrella stood there.

Capers jumped in at the window and fetched the umbrella. He waved it at Curly.

'You said I could have it if only you had got it!' he cried. 'Here it is, so I'll borrow it! Many thanks!'

He ran off and left Curly nearly crying with rage. The pixie caught up a stick and ran to beat the kettle – but that small kettle was far too quick for him! It rose up in the air and put itself high up on a shelf for safety. Then it poured just a drop of boiling water on to Curly's hand, which made the pixie dance and shout with pain.

'You wait till I get you!' cried Curly, shaking his stick.

Someone knocked at his front door. Curly opened it. Rag and Tag, the two gnomes, stood there smiling.

'Mister Curly, we are collecting pennies for poor Mister Tumble whose house was burnt down yesterday,' they said. 'You are so generous that we thought you would be sure to give us one.'

Curly knew that there was no money in his pockets, so he pulled them inside out quickly,

saying, 'Oh yes, you shall have whatever money I have, Rag and Tag. Goodness, there's none in this pocket – and none in that! How unfortunate! I haven't any pennies to give you, and I should have been *so* pleased to have let you have all I had.'

'Well, that's very nice of you to say so,' said Rag and Tag. 'Never mind. Thank you very much for *trying* to be generous!'

Before they could go, that little kettle was singing again, spurting out great clouds of steam as it did so!

> *'Although he says he hasn't any,*
> *Curly's got a silver penny!*
> *Look in his purse on the table there*
> *And take the money he well can spare!'*

Then, taking another breath, the kettle shouted with all its might, 'Mean old thing! Stingy old thing! Oooooh, look at him!'

Rag and Tag stared all round the kitchen to see where the voice came from, but they couldn't see anyone but Curly. It couldn't be the pixie singing, surely! No, he looked too angry and ashamed to sing anything!

The gnomes saw the purse lying on the table

and they ran for it. Inside was a silver sixpence. They took it and put it into their box.

'Well, Curly,' they said, 'you said we might have any pennies you had, if you'd had any – and you have, so we'll take this silver one. Good-bye!'

Out they went, giggling together, wondering who it was in the cottage that had given Curly away.

As for Curly, he was so angry that he caught up a jug of milk and flung it straight at the kettle, which was still high up on the shelf. Crash! The kettle hopped aside and the jug broke in a dozen pieces against the wall behind. The milk spilt and dripped on to Curly's head. Then the kettle began to laugh. How it laughed! It was a funny, wheezy laugh, but you can't think how angry it made Curly!

He took up a hammer and flung that at the kettle

too – but once more it slipped to one side, and oh, dear me, smash went a lovely big jar of plum jam up on the shelf. It all splashed down on to Curly, so what with milk and jam he was a fine sight. The kettle nearly killed itself with laughing. It almost fell off the shelf.

Curly went and washed himself under the tap. He felt frightened. What was he going to do with that awful singing kettle? He must get rid of it somehow or it would tell everyone the most dreadful tales about him.

'I'll wait till to-night,' thought Curly. 'Then, when it's asleep, I'll take it and throw it away.'

So he took no more notice of the kettle, and as no other visitors came that day the kettle was fairly quiet – except that sometimes it would suddenly shout, 'Mean old thing! Stingy old thing! Oooooooh, look at him!' Then Curly would almost jump out of his skin with fright, and glare at the kettle angrily.

At nine o'clock Curly went to bed. The kettle hopped down to the stove and went to sleep. Curly waited for a little while and then he crept out of bed. He went to the stove and took hold of the kettle. Ah, he had it now! The kettle woke up and shouted, but Curly had it by the handle. The water in it was no longer hot, so that it could not hurt Curly.

The pixie hurried outside with the kettle and went to the bottom of his garden. There was a rubbish-heap there and the pixie stuffed the struggling kettle right into the middle. He left it there and went back delighted. He climbed into bed and fell asleep.

But at midnight something woke him by tapping at the window.

'Let me in!' cried a voice. 'Let me in! I'm dirty and I want washing!'

'That's that horrid kettle!' thought Curly, in a fright. 'Well, it can go on tapping! I won't let it in!'

But the kettle tapped and tapped and at last it flung itself hard against the glass, broke it and came in through the hole! It went over to Curly's bed and stood itself there.

'Wash me!' it said. 'I'm dirty and smelly. You shouldn't have put me on that nasty rubbish-heap!'

'Get out of my nice clean bed!' cried Curly angrily. 'Look what a mess you are making!'

But the kettle wouldn't get off, and in the end the angry pixie had to get up and wash the kettle till it was clean again. Then he banged it down on the stove and left it.

Next day the kettle sang songs about him again, and Curly kept hearing it shout, 'Mean old fellow! Stingy old fellow! Ooooooh, look at him!' till he was tired of it. So many people had heard about the strange things happening in the pixie's cottage that all day long visitors came to ask for different things, and poor Curly was nearly worried out of his life.

'I'll drown that kettle in my well to-night!' he thought. So once more he took the kettle when it was asleep and threw it down the well. Splash! Ha, it wouldn't get out of there in a hurry!

But about three o'clock in the morning there came a tap-tap-tap at the window, which had now been mended. It was the kettle back again!

'Curly! Let me in! I'm c-c-c-c-cold and w-wet! Let me in!'

237

Curly was afraid his window would be broken again, so he jumped out of bed and let in the shivering kettle. To his horror it crept into bed with him and wouldn't go away!

'It was cold and wet in the well!' said the kettle. 'Warm me, Curly!'

So Curly had to warm the kettle, and how angry he was! It was so uncomfortable to sleep with a kettle, especially one that kept sticking its sharp spout into him. But he had to put up with it. In the morning he put the kettle back on the stove and started to think hard whilst he had his breakfast.

'I can't get rid of that kettle,' he said to himself. 'And while it's here it's sure to sing horrid things about me every time anyone comes to borrow something. I wonder what it would do if I let people have what they ask for? I'll try and see.'

So when Mother Homey came and begged for a bit of soap, because she had run out of it and the shops were closed that afternoon, Curly gave her a whole new piece without making any excuse at all. Mother Homey was surprised and delighted.

'Thank you so much,' she said. 'You're a kind soul, Curly.'

The kettle said nothing at all. Not a single word. As for Curly, he suddenly felt very nice inside. It was lovely to give somebody something. It made him feel warm and kind. He made up his mind to do it again if he felt nice the next time – and to see if that wretched kettle said anything.

He soon found that the kettle said never a word unless he was mean or untruthful – and he found, too, that it was lovely to be kind and to give things away; it was nice even to lend them.

'I've been horrid and nasty,' thought Curly to himself. 'I'll turn over a new leaf and try to be different. And that old kettle can say what it likes!

Anyway, it boils very quickly and makes a lovely pot of tea.'

Very soon the kettle found little to say, for Curly became kind and generous. Once or twice he forgot, but as soon as he heard the kettle beginning to speak he quickly remembered, and the kettle stopped its song.

And one day who should peep in at the door but the Humpy Goblin, grinning all over his face as usual.

'Hallo, Curly!' he said. 'How did you like the kettle? Was it cheap for threepence? I've come to take it back, if you want to get rid of it. It was a mean trick to play you, really, but I think you deserved it!'

Curly looked at the smiling Goblin. Then he took his purse from his pocket and found three pennies. He held them out to the Humpy Goblin.

'Here you are,' he said. 'You wanted sixpence for the kettle and I was mean enough to leave you only threepence. Here's the other threepence.'

'But – but – don't you want to give me back the kettle?' asked Humpy in surprise. 'I left a horrid singing spell in it.'

'Yes, I know,' said Curly. 'But I deserved it. I'm different now. I like the kettle too – we're great

friends. I try to be kind now, so the kettle doesn't sing nasty things about me. It just hums nice, friendly little songs.'

'Well, well, well, wonders will never end!' said the Goblin Man, astonished. 'Don't bother about the other threepence, Curly. I don't want it.'

'Well, if you won't take it, let me offer you a cup of tea made from water boiled in the singing kettle,' said Curly. Humpy was even more astonished to

241

hear the pixie being so kind, but he sat down at the table in delight.

Then he and Curly had a cup of tea each and a large slice of ginger cake – and they talked together and found that they liked one another very much indeed.

So now Mister Curly and the Humpy Goblin are the very greatest friends, and the little singing kettle hums its loudest when it boils water for their tea. You should just hear it!

The Little Brown Duck

On the stream that ran between the buttercup fields two wild ducks had a nest. The drake was a most beautiful fellow, dressed in blues and greens; but his mate was a little brown duck. She kept close to the nest and sat on her eggs happily. The drake swam about and quacked cheerfully to his mate every now and again.

The only person that knew about the two wild ducks was Benny. He had seen the nest one day as he was walking along the bank, but he didn't tell anyone at all. It was Benny's secret.

'I do hope no one finds the nest,' thought Benny. 'Oh, I do hope the eggs hatch out into tiny ducklings. I shall see them then. The brown duck doesn't seem to mind me looking. She knows I won't hurt her.'

The eggs hatched. Seven downy ducklings lay in the nest of reeds by the stream-side. Benny loved them. They did look so quaint with their big beaks and fluffy feathers.

Then one day the mother duck took them all for a swim. Benny was there to see them. Each little downy duckling tumbled into the water and swam hard as soon as it was there. They swam after their mother in a long line. The father duck, the drake, swam a good way ahead to make sure that the way was clear.

Benny went to see the ducks every day. They grew and they grew. Nobody knew about them until August Bank Holiday came. Then a motor-coach brought some trippers from the towns; and three big boys, wandering along by the streamside, saw the little brown duck with her brood of ducklings.

And what do you suppose they did? Well, you

will hardly believe it, but they picked up stones and began to throw them at the little duck family. The little brown duck quacked in alarm. Her ducklings swam close to her in terror. The stones fell thick and fast around. One little duckling was hit, and quacked in pain and fright.

And just then Benny came along. He was only a little boy; but when he saw those three big boys throwing stones at the little duck family, he forgot all about being small.

'Hi! Stop that!' he shouted at the top of his voice. 'How dare you! Stop throwing stones at once.'

The boys stopped. They stared round at Benny.

'Pooh! It's only a little boy,' they said, and they began to throw stones again. 'Quack, quack, quack!' said the ducks in terror.

Benny didn't know what to do. He suddenly ran at one of the big boys and butted his head against him.

The boy lost his balance and fell headlong into the stream – splash! Benny butted the next boy, and, taken by surprise, in he went too! The third boy was full of fear, for he thought his friends would be drowned, but Benny knew the water was not deep.

'If you frighten those ducks that never did you

or anyone any harm, you deserve to be frightened yourselves,' shouted Benny.

The boys climbed out, dripping wet. They were just about to catch Benny and whip him when someone called from the field gate. 'Hi! The motor-coach is going soon. Hurry, or you'll miss it.'

The boys rushed off. Benny was trembling, and he sat down on the bank. He had quite expected to be hit by all the big boys. The mother duck brought her ducklings to the rushes as soon as she saw that the big boys had gone. Benny leaned over to see them. He picked out of the water the little duckling that had been hit. Its tiny wing was bruised, but Benny thought it would heal. He put the trembling creature back.

'Quack, quack, quack!' said the mother duck gratefully. She knew quite well that Benny had helped her.

Now when Benny's birthday came, he had a great surprise. Uncle Harry gave him a beautiful sailing-ship. Benny was simply delighted.

'Now I can go down to the river and sail it every day,' he said. So down to the river he went. The little stream on which the ducks nested ran into the river, but Benny was so interested in his ship that he forgot all about the little duck family for a time. He sailed his ship every day and loved to see it bobbing up and down on the waves.

And then one afternoon a dreadful thing happened. Benny was sailing his ship on the river, when he suddenly dropped the string into the water. The wind blew the ship strongly, and it sailed away by itself into the middle of the river. Benny couldn't guide it or pull it in, because the string was gone.

'Oh, my ship, my beautiful ship,' groaned the

little boy. 'It will float away down the river and be lost, and some other boy will get it and have it. Oh, whatever shall I do?'

He looked about to see if there was anyone near who might help him; but no, not a single person was in sight. The ship was as good as lost. There it sailed, down the river; it would soon be gone.

But what was this? A little brown head poked out of the nearby rushes, and a small brown body followed. It was the little brown duck. Her babies were all grown now and had gone away to look after themselves, but the little brown duck still swam about the stream and the river she loved.

She saw Benny's boat and somehow knew how unhappy he was. She swam after the ship – how she swam! She paddled her strong legs fast, fast, faster.

'Oh! She's going after my boat. Oh, the kind, clever little duck!' cried Benny, nearly falling into the river with joy and delight. 'Oh, she's almost got it – she's up to it – good little duck, good little duck!'

The little brown duck had reached the ship. She tried to stop it going down the river, but it slipped round her and went on again. Then she caught sight of the string that drifted through the water behind it. She darted at it with her beak, and caught it. The ship stopped and came round a bit. The duck tugged at the string. The ship jerked.

'Come, little duck, come!' shouted Benny. 'Bring the string to me. Oh, you clever little duck!'

The duck swam over the water to Benny, holding the string in her mouth. The ship followed her, rocking up and down. Benny reached out as soon as the duck was near enough. He took the string gently from the little bird's beak, and pulled his precious ship in to shore.

'Thank you very much indeed,' he said to the little brown duck. 'You were a good friend to me to-day. I suppose you remembered how I saved you from those big boys some time ago.'

'Quack, quack, quack!' said the little wild duck, which meant, 'Of course I remembered. One good turn deserves another!'

Then off she swam, bobbing up and down happily.

You never know when a kindness is going to come back to you, do you?

The Pixie who Killed the Moon

There was once upon a time a silly little pixie called Big Eyes. He never stopped to think about anything at all, and he always believed every single thing he was told. When a chestnut fell down on his head one night he ran away in terror, shouting at the top of his voice:

'A star has fallen on me! A star has fallen on me!'

The other pixies, who had seen the chestnut fall, laughed at him. 'Catch it, then!' they cried. 'It is shining in your hair.'

Big Eyes leant over a pool and, sure enough, he saw a star shining, as he thought, in his hair.

He took a comb and combed all night, but he couldn't find the star. I'm not surprised, either. Are you?

Another time he heard a nightingale singing, and he wanted to take it home to live with him, but it wouldn't come. It sat in its bush and sang beautifully, and took no notice of Big Eyes.

'Build a fence round the bush!' said the other pixies. 'Then he can't get away, Big Eyes.'

So Big Eyes gathered a great deal of bracken and weaved a tight little fence all round the bush.

The nightingale watched him with great interest. 'What's that for, Big Eyes?' he asked.

'Wait and see,' said Big Eyes.

So the nightingale waited. When the fence was finished Big Eyes jumped over it and laughed.

'Ho! ho!' he cried. 'Now I've got you, my little nightingale! Come home with me and live

in my cottage. You shall have wild strawberries for breakfast, and I will polish your beak every morning for you.'

'No, not I,' said the nightingale.

'But you must,' said Big Eyes.

'Trilla – trilla – trilla!' sang the nightingale, mockingly. 'You cannot make me!'

'Yes, I can!' said Big Eyes. 'I have built a fence all round you, and you cannot escape me. I shall catch you and take you home with me.'

'Catch me, then!' cried the nightingale, and spread his wings. He flew straight up and over the fence and disappeared, singing, into the wood.

All the watching pixies laughed as Big Eyes stared in dismay.

'Why don't you think, Big Eyes?' they cried. 'You knew that a nightingale could fly! Why didn't you *think*?'

Big Eyes was upset, but he didn't try to mend his ways – not he! It was too much bother, and *he* wasn't going to try.

Now one day a child went through the wood in which Big Eyes lived. She carried a big yellow balloon, and it floated prettily behind her. Suddenly there came a great gust of wind and – puff! – the string was blown out of her hand and the balloon went sailing gaily away into the wood. It floated through the air for a long time, until it came to the place where Big Eyes was having his dinner.

It landed just by him and stayed there with its string caught in a bramble bush. Big Eyes jumped up in fright, for he had heard no noise and hadn't seen the balloon coming.

Crash! went his plate, and Big Eyes fled through the wood, howling with fright.

'What's the matter?' cried everyone.

'The moon's fallen down by me!' wept Big Eyes. 'The big yellow moon! It came whilst I was eating my dinner, and almost killed me!'

The pixies laughed loudly and went to see what it was.

'Isn't he a silly?' they said, when they saw it was only a balloon. 'He always cries before he's hurt. Let's pretend it *is* the moon, and see what he'll do!'

So they pretended it was the moon, and Big Eyes told them again and again how it had nearly fallen on his head and killed him.

'It was a shame to give you such a fright!' said the pixies. 'I should punish the moon if I were you!'

'How?' asked Big Eyes.

'Well, prick it with a pin!' said the pixies. 'That will make the moon squeal out and punish

it finely. But wait until it is asleep in the hot sun!'

So Big Eyes waited. He got a very long pin and hid himself in the bushes near by. Then, when the sun was high in the sky at mid-day and he thought the moon was sleeping, he crept up to it.

With a trembling hand he stuck the pin into the fat yellow balloon.

BANG! It burst with a tremendous pop, and Big Eyes was nearly frightened to death. All the watching pixies were, too, and tumbled head over heels in the bushes.

255

Big Eyes fled for his life. He jumped down a rabbit-hole and sat there trembling.

'Oh dear! Oh dear!' he said. 'I've killed the moon! It's burst all to nothing! I've killed the moon! What *will* the Fairy Queen say to me? Oh dear! Oh dear, dear!'

The more he thought about it the more he shivered and shook.

'I've killed it dead!' he said. 'Bang! It went like that – and all because I pricked it with a pin! How was *I* to know that would kill the moon? And now we won't be able to dance in the moonlight any more!'

All that day and all that night, and the next day, too, Big Eyes sat in his hole, sad and sorry.

'I didn't mean to,' he wept. 'It was only to punish

the moon for frightening me. I hope the Queen won't be angry!'

When the evening of the next day came poor Big Eyes determined to go to the Queen and confess what he had done.

So he crept out of his hole and made his way to the glade where the Fairy Queen held her court. She was there, and welcomed the trembling little pixie.

'What's the matter, Big Eyes?' she asked.

'Oh, Your Majesty!' wept Big Eyes. 'I've done a dreadful thing! I've killed the moon!'

'Killed the moon!' said the Queen in astonishment. 'You can't have done that, Big Eyes!'

'But I *did*!' said Big Eyes. 'I pricked it with a pin and it went BANG! – like that, and died!'

The Fairy Queen laughed. Then she took Big Eyes by the arm and pointed to a hill in the distance.

'See!' she said. 'What is that peeping over the hill yonder?'

Big Eyes looked. It was the big round moon, yellow and bright, rising slowly above the hill.

He stared in astonishment. So he hadn't killed it, after all!

'The other pixies have made fun of you instead of helping you!' said the Queen. 'They will be punished. And you, Big Eyes, you must use your brains and think. Go back to the pixie school and learn all you can. Then you will never be so silly again!'

Big Eyes was so glad to think that he hadn't really killed the moon that he went home singing all the way. And I'm sure you will be glad to know that he was never so stupid again!

Old Bufo the Toad

Old Bufo was a toad, fat, brown, and ugly. The only beautiful thing about him was his pair of bright, copper eyes. They were like two shining jewels. Bufo was not allowed in Fairyland. The fairies said he really was much too ugly. He frightened them. So Bufo lived in our world, under a big stone by the streamside. He had a little shop under his stone, and there he worked hard all day long.

What do you think he made? Guess! Yes – toadstools! He was very clever indeed at making these. First he would make a nice sturdy stump, then a pretty curved cap-like top, and then underneath he sewed dozens of tiny frills. So you can see he was a busy fellow.

Now one day the Queen of Fairyland went on a long journey. She visited the Moon. She visited the Land of Dreams. And she visited our world too. She went with six servants, and she wore no crown, for she did not want to be known as she passed here and there.

She called herself Dame Silverwings, and travelled about quite safely in her silver coach, drawn by two white mice.

One day she heard that someone was chasing after her coach to catch her. It was the wizard Tall-Hat. He had found out that Dame Silverwings was no other than the Fairy Queen herself, and he thought that it would be a fine thing to catch her and take her prisoner. He would not let her go

until he had been paid ten sacks of gold. Aha! How rich he would be!

A blackbird warned the Queen that Tall-Hat was after her. She hurried on her way – and then alas! a fog came down – and she was lost! On and on went her little white mice, dragging the carriage, but they did not know at all where they were going. When the fog cleared, they were quite lost.

The Queen stepped from her carriage. She was by a stream in a wood. No one seemed to be about at all.

'Is anyone living near here?' she called in her bird-like voice. She listened for an answer – and one came. It was the voice of Bufo, the old toad, that answered. His home was under the big stone nearby. He crawled out and croaked loudly:

'Yes – I, Bufo the toad, live here. Pray come and shelter, if you wish.'

The Queen and her six servants looked at Bufo in surprise, but when they saw his beautiful coppery eyes they trusted him and went to his stone. The Queen was surprised to see such a pretty and neat little shop under the stone – and when she saw the stools she was delighted.

'May I sit down on one of these dear little stools?' she asked. 'Oh, how nice they are! Just the right height, too! I would like to rest here awhile.'

'Then pray rest on my toadstools,' said Bufo. 'I have enough for all of you. And let me offer you each a glass of honey-dew.'

The kindly old toad fussed over his visitors and made them very welcome. The Queen was glad to rest on the quaint toadstool after her long ride.

'I am Dame Silverwings,' she said. 'Which is the quickest way to Fairyland from here?'

'Do you see this stream?' said Bufo. 'Well, on the other side lies Fairyland. There is a bridge a little farther on.'

'Oh, we shall soon be home then,' said the fairy, very pleased. But just as she said that she heard the noise of wings and, peeping from the stone, she saw to her horror the Tall-Hat Wizard himself, looking all round for her. He passed by, and she knew he had gone to the bridge to guard it so that she could not cross to Fairyland.

She began to weep. Bufo the toad could not bear to see her tears, and he begged her to tell him what was the matter. As soon as he heard about Tall-Hat guarding the bridge to Fairyland, he laughed.

'We can easily trick him,' he said. 'You shall cross the stream another way.'

'But there are no boats here,' said the Queen.

'I have something that will do just as well,' said Bufo. He took up one of his toadstools and turned it upside down. 'Look,' he said, 'if I put this into the water upside down, you can sit on the little frills and hold on to the stalk, then the toadstool will float you across the stream safely. I have seven fine toadstools I can spare for you.'

In the greatest delight the Queen and her servants hurried down to the water with the toadstools. They let them float there upside down. Then one by one they climbed on to their toadstools, waved good-bye to old Bufo, and floated to the opposite side. Once there they were safe!

Tall-Hat waited by the bridge for six weeks – and then heard that the Queen had been safely back in Fairyland all that time. How angry he was! And how Bufo the toad laughed when he heard him go by, shouting and raging! He didn't know that Bufo

was peeping at him from under his big stone.

Bufo got such a surprise when he knew that the little fairy he had helped was the Fairy Queen herself. She sent him a gold watch and chain to wear, and an order for as many toad-stools as he and his friends could make. 'They will do so nicely for our parties in the woods,' she said.

So now Bufo and his family make toadstools all day long, and stand them about in the woods for the little folk to sit on, or to use for tables at their parties. And Bufo is allowed in Fairyland, and has a grand time at the palace once a month when he goes to tea with the Queen herself. Nobody thinks

he is ugly now, for they always look at his glowing eyes. Have you seen them? You haven't? Well, just look at them next time you see an old toad hopping along.

And don't forget to look at the dear little frills Bufo puts under every toadstool, will you?

The Boy who Pulled Tails

There was once a boy called Bobby who lived with his mother and father in a small cottage by a thick forest. His father worked at a farm nearby, and Bobby often used to go with him to see the young calves or the new yellow chickens.

But animals and birds didn't like Bobby. He always pulled their tails. He just did it to tease them, and they hated it. It frightened them. Bobby didn't care – he just went on pulling them.

He pulled the tail of Whiskers, his mother's cat, too. He often caught hold of the long, shaggy tail of Bingo, his father's old dog, and made him yelp with pain. He pulled the pony's tail, and he even pulled the pretty, drooping tail of Doodle-doo, the fine cock that lived with the brown hens in the yard at the back of the cottage.

Wasn't he silly? He just did it to annoy the animals, because he wasn't really a cruel boy. He never forgot to feed his rabbit, and he always saw that the dog had plenty of water to drink. His mother was quite upset about his silly trick.

'One of these days something will happen to make you sorry you pull tails so much!' she said. 'I'm ashamed of you, Bobby.'

But Bobby only laughed and ran out of the back door, pulling the cat's tail as he went.

And then one day something *did* happen! Bobby went for a long walk and took his lunch with him in a basket. It was a lovely sunny day, and he thought he would look for wild strawberries in the forest. He followed the little path that led into the wood and whistled gaily as he went. He hunted here and there for wild strawberries but couldn't see any at all.

'Perhaps there are some further in,' he thought, and he followed another path, a winding one that led between the big, shady trees, towards the heart of the forest.

Bobby very soon found plenty of strawberries under the trees, and he ate dozens of them. They were little and very sweet. And then he suddenly saw someone else gathering them.

It was a little bent man, dressed in a green suit. His shoes were green too, and had long pointed toes. He carried a green basket and in it he put

the wild strawberries. He had a beard that reached right down to the ground.

Bobby stared at him in surprise.

'It must be a gnome!' he thought, in excitement. 'I wonder where he lives. I'll hide behind this tree and watch where he goes.'

So he hid himself and watched the busy gnome. When the little man's basket was full he set off through the trees at a jogtrot. Bobby followed, feeling most excited.

The path widened out and suddenly ran into a lane. At the far end of the lane stood a tiny cottage, with blue windows and door and cream walls. The gnome went into the cottage and shut the door.

A red wall ran round the garden, and on it sat a big black cat with red whiskers. Bobby thought he must be a gnome cat, he looked so unusual. His tail hung down over the wall, and, of course, you can guess what Bobby did.

He caught hold of the cat's long tail and pulled it!

And then a dreadful and most surprising thing happened. The tail came off! Yes, right off in Bobby's hand. The cat gave a frightened yell and

ran to the house. It jumped in at an open window, mewing loudly.

Bobby stood there with the tail in his hand, almost as frightened as the cat. Suddenly the door of the house flew open and out rushed the gnome in a fearful rage.

He danced about on the path, shouting and yelling at Bobby.

'You wicked boy! You horrid, cruel, unkind boy! You've pulled my cat's tail off!'

'I didn't mean to,' said Bobby, the tears coming into his eyes. 'Truly I didn't.'

'You're always pulling tails!' shouted the gnome, shaking his fist at Bobby. 'All sorts of animals and birds complain about you. You're a nuisance, a great big NUISANCE!'

'What shall I do with this tail?' asked Bobby. 'Can you put it back again on your cat?'

'No, I can't. Cinders, my cat, will grow a new one in a year,' said the gnome. 'The tails of gnome cats come off very easily, and you ought to have known that.'

'Well, I didn't,' said Bobby. 'I wouldn't have pulled it if I had known that.'

'You can have Cinders' tail for yourself,' suddenly said the gnome. He snatched the tail from Bobby's hand and threw it at him. It stuck on the little boy's back – and oh, my goodness me, it grew there! Bobby had a long cat's tail behind him.

The gnome began to laugh. How he laughed! He held his sides and laughed till the tears poured down his cheeks. Then he took a whistle from his pocket and blew on it. From many little cottages near poured a troop of pixies, brownies and gnomes, and when the gnome explained to them what had happened they began laughing too.

But Bobby was crying. He wanted to ask the gnome how he could get rid of the cat's tail, but everyone was laughing so loudly that he couldn't make himself heard. So he turned and ran away as fast as he could, trying to get away from the sound of the merry fairy laughter.

He came to the edge of the forest, and sat down to think about things. He tugged at the tail. It was certainly quite fast on him. He couldn't get it off, and it hurt him to pull it. What a dreadful thing! He'd have to go home like that and tell his father and mother what had happened.

He walked slowly home, the black tail swishing behind him. He was a very sad little boy. At last he reached his cottage, and went in. His mother looked up and when she saw the long black tail she cried out in astonishment:

'What's that you've got?'

Then Bobby told her, and she looked very grave.

'I told you something would happen to you one day if you went on pulling tails,' she said. 'Now the best thing you can do is to stop pulling tails and hope that your own tail will gradually go.'

So Bobby stopped pulling tails – but dear me, as soon as the cats, dogs, donkeys, horses, hens and ducks around saw that Bobby had a tail, they went nearly mad with delight. And they all gave it a good pull and tug whenever the little boy went by!

Then he knew what it felt like to have his tail pulled. It hurt him and made him jump. The dog used to lie in wait for him round corners, and pull his tail hard. The cat clawed it and the hens pecked it. It was dreadful to have a tail like that.

'I know now how all the birds and animals must have hated having their tails pulled,' thought Bobby. 'I wish I'd never been so mean. And oh, how I wish I'd never pulled that gnome-cat's tail!'

For weeks poor Bobby wore the gnome-cat's tail, and many times a day he had it pulled. He tried putting the end in one of his pockets, but it wouldn't stay there. It took itself out and waved about in the air. It wouldn't keep still, and Bobby couldn't do anything with it. He just had to put up with it.

'I'll never pull a tail again!' said Bobby, a score of times a day. 'I never will!'

'Your tail doesn't seem to be going,' said his mother anxiously. 'I thought perhaps it would gradually disappear. I'll send a note to that little gnome and tell him you have learnt your lesson. Perhaps he will make your tail go.'

So she wrote a note to tell the gnome that Bobby was a much nicer boy now, and please would he come and take the tail away. But he didn't come.

However, the next day, just as Bobby was filling up the dog's water-bowl, his tail began to twist and turn in a very peculiar manner, just as if it was trying to pull itself off. Then it suddenly shot up into the air, danced there for a moment like a short black rope and fell to the ground. Then it wriggled away like a snake and was lost to sight.

Bobby watched in amazement. He *was* glad to see it go! He ran to tell his mother and she was glad, too.

'Now mind, Bobby,' she said, 'don't you start pulling tails again, or that tail may come back.'

'Oh, Mother, I'll never, never pull a tail again in my life!' cried Bobby. And you may be sure he never did.

As for that strange tail, nobody ever saw it again, though people do say it is waiting to grow on another boy or girl some day. I hope it won't be you or me!

The Tale of Mr. Spectacles

Tippy the gnome was sharp and sly, and no one in Apple Village liked him very much. So it was not surprising that when Dame Softly said she would have a fine garden party in her grounds she did not invite Tippy the gnome. He was most upset and annoyed about it. He sat down on his little stool, and wondered how he could go to the party, and how he could punish Dame Softly for not inviting him. Then he suddenly had a good idea.

'I'll dress up and pretend to be someone who can tell people all about themselves and say what will happen to them in the future,' thought Tippy. 'No one will know I am Tippy the gnome who knows all about everybody's business – and when it comes to Dame Softly's turn – ooh! won't I tell her some horrid things!'

So on the day of the garden party Tippy dressed himself up in a fine black cloak, put on a pair of dark green spectacles, and stuck a long beard on his chin. Then he marched up to Dame Softly's and asked her if she would care to let him sit in a corner of her garden and tell people's fortunes.

'I am Mister Spectacles, the Wizard,' said Tippy. 'I will make your party a great success. I only charge a penny a time.'

'Very well,' said Dame Softly. 'You may sit over there on that seat in the corner. I will tell my guests about you, and perhaps come to have my fortune told too.'

Down sat Tippy in delight. He waited for someone to come, and very soon up came Tickles the brownie. He paid his penny. Tippy leaned forward and pretended to look at him hard through his dark spectacles. He didn't like Tickles, because the brownie had once scolded him for being mean.

'You keep bees,' said Tippy in a deep voice, 'and you sell honey.'

'Yes, I do,' said Tickles, astonished. 'Will I do well with my bees this year?'

'No,' said Tippy, enjoying himself. 'They will suddenly feel angry with you, and will all come and *sting* you, and *sting* you, and *sting* you …'

Tickles gave a yell and shot away, shouting that he would sell his bees that very day. Then

up came Pip the elf, and paid his penny. Tippy scowled at him, for Pip had once spanked him for his slyness.

'You grow roses,' said Tippy. 'You sell the roses that you grow.'

'How clever of you!' said Pip. 'Will I ever make a fortune out of them?'

'Not out of your *roses*,' said Tippy, an idea coming into his mind. 'But underneath one of them – if you like to look – there may be a box of gold.'

'Oooh!' cried Pip happily. 'I'll go and dig every one of them up and find it.'

Off he went, and Tippy grinned to think of Pip digging up all his precious roses for nothing. Then Mother Noddy came up and paid her penny to Tippy.

Tippy hated Mother Noddy, for she had always told him what a bad little gnome he was. So he looked at her through his spectacles, and said in a deep voice: 'Dear, dear me! I can see a sad thing in store for you, old dame. One of your hens will peck you to-morrow, and you will be ill for a whole year.'

Mother Noddy gave a yell and ran off shouting: 'I shall set all my hens free. They shan't peck me!'

How Tippy grinned! What a time he was having! Ah – but wait and see!

Tippy sat and waited for the next person to come. It was Dame Softly, who had not invited him to her party. Aha! Tippy would make her sorry for that!

She paid her penny and sat down. Tippy stared at her through his green spectacles, and waggled his long beard about. She felt quite uncomfortable.

'Misfortune is awaiting you,' said Tippy in a deep, solemn voice. 'Your house will catch fire very soon.'

'It's a good thing the firemen are all at my party

then,' said Dame Softly, pleased. 'They will soon put the fire out.'

'Robbers will come and steal your fine jewels,' said Tippy.

'Well, as the village policeman is also at my party, the robbers will have a bad time,' said Dame Softly, still more pleased.

'Is the policeman really here?' said Tippy, feeling suddenly alarmed. 'I didn't know that!'

'You didn't know?' said Dame Softly in surprise. 'But I thought you were Mister Spectacles, who knew everything.'

Just at that moment up came Pip the elf, sobbing

bitterly. 'I've dug up all my lovely rose-trees,' he wept, 'and there was no box of gold under any of them. I have spoilt my trees – I can't sell my roses now – oh dear, oh dear! You told me a story, Mister Spectacles! And there's poor old Tickles, he's sold his beehives and all his bees for a few pence, because you said they would sting him and sting him – and I just saw Mother Noddy letting all her hens loose into the road because you said one would peck her and make her ill for a whole year. It's a pity you ever came to this party and upset us so, especially as I've lost all my beautiful rose-trees!'

Pip began to weep bitterly. Dame Softly stared at him; then she slipped away. In a short while she brought back Mister Grab the village policeman. He sat down by Tippy and grinned.

'Well, Mister Spectacles,' he said, 'I hear you are a wonderful teller of fortunes. Just tell me mine, will you?'

'You – you are a policeman,' said Tippy, very uncomfortable indeed.

'Right, first time!' said Mister Grab. 'Now tell me the name of someone I'm going to spank this very day!'

'I d-d-don't know,' stammered Tippy.

'Dear me, I thought you could tell anyone anything he asked,' laughed Mister Grab. 'Well, tell me this – am I going to stay at this party all the time, or am I going to leave it in the middle, and if so, shall I go alone or will anyone be with me?'

'I d-d-don't know,' said poor Tippy again.

'Well, *I* can tell you *your* fortune,' said Mister Grab, suddenly, in a very stern voice. 'Your beard will come off – like that – and your spectacles will

come off – like that – and lo and behold the great fortune-teller will turn into no other than Tippy the gnome – just as sly, but not so clever as usual! And Tippy will come along with me and be spanked – and he will give Pip those pennies to buy some new rose-trees – and he will soon be sorry he played such a very – stupid – trick!'

Well – Mister Grab was a *very* good fortune-teller, because everything he said came true! Poor old Tippy!

The Goblin's Pie

There was once a very fat goblin called Roundabout. He was fat because he was greedy. The thing he liked best of all was a pie. It didn't matter what *kind* of a pie – meat-pie, chicken-pie, veal-and-ham pie, apple-pie, plum-pie, onion-pie – he liked them all.

His friend wished he wouldn't be so greedy. They really were afraid he would burst out of his clothes one day. But Roundabout took no notice of his friends. He just went on eating and eating.

He would walk miles for a pie. Yes, really! When he heard that Dame Strawberry had baked three fine strawberry-pies one day he set out to get one. Dame Strawberry lived on Tree-Top Hill miles away, but that didn't matter. Round-about walked and walked until he got there, and he arrived the day after to-morrow.

Well, of course, all the pies were eaten by

then, except for a tiny piece left in the larder. But Roundabout ate that and said it was worth walking all those miles for! Wasn't he funny?

Now one day Pinny, one of his friends, thought he would have a joke with Roundabout. He was walking out with him in the woods, and suddenly Pinny saw a big bird, a black and white magpie, sitting on a tree nearby.

'Roundabout!' said Pinny solemnly, stopping quite still. 'Shall I tell you something?'

'Yes, do,' said Roundabout, 'especially if it's about something to eat. I feel hungry.'

'That's nothing new,' said Pinny. 'Well, now listen – there's a pie up in that tree. Look!'

Pinny pointed to the tree in which the magpie sat. Round-about licked his lips and looked up at the tree. He thought that Pinny meant a real pie.

'Is it a meat-pie?' he asked.

'It's a bird-pie,' said Pinny, laughing to himself.

'I can't see it,' said Roundabout.

'Well, go and look for it,' said Pinny.

Roundabout at once went to the tree and began to climb it. He was far too fat for climbing trees and he found it very difficult. But he wouldn't give up if there was a pie anywhere about – no, not he! Up he went, panting and puffing, looking for that pie.

How he looked! He peered down into the trunk. He put his hand into every hole. He parted the leaves and looked carefully where they grew the thickest. But he couldn't find any pie.

He climbed higher up and looked there. The big magpie looked at him, puzzled. What was this fat goblin doing? Was he looking for her nest?

She began to chatter angrily at him. He looked at her in surprise.

'What's the matter?' he asked. 'Are you looking for that pie, too?'

'Pie? What pie?' asked the big bird. 'There isn't any pie here, I can tell you! This tree is mine.'

'Nonsense!' said Roundabout. 'You can't take trees for yourself like that. Tell me where that pie is.'

'I don't know *where* it is,' said the magpie crossly. 'I'm sure there isn't one in my tree. I wish you'd go away. What do you want with a pie, anyway?'

'I want to eat it,' said Roundabout. 'I'm very hungry.'

'What's the pie like?' asked the magpie, thinking that perhaps she might have a peck at it too.

'It's a bird-pie,' said Roundabout, 'and it's in this tree, I know.'

No sooner had he said that than the bird remembered that her name was magpie. She at

once thought that the goblin was looking for her or for her little ones. She was very angry indeed, and she flew at the surprised goblin.

'So you came to eat *me*, did you?' she cried in a rage. 'Take that! Peck-peck-peck! And that! Peck-peck-peck!'

Roundabout nearly fell off the branch in surprise. He held on tightly, and tried to stop the magpie from pecking him, but she was far too cross to stop.

'Peck-peck-peck!' She pecked off his round hat and threw it to the ground. She pecked off his coat and made two big holes in it. She pecked a big piece out of his trousers and pulled off both his shoes.

'Stop, stop!' cried Roundabout in a panic. 'I'll climb down at once if you'll stop pecking me. I don't care about any pie. I'll get down, truly I'll get down, and never come here again.'

The magpie gave him one more peck for luck, and then let Roundabout get down. He was in such a hurry that he fell down part of the way, and bounced like a rubber ball on the grass.

'Goodness!' he cried. 'That's the last time I go after pies.'

He found his shoes and his hat. He picked up his coat and looked at the two big holes. He stuffed a large green leaf into his trousers to hide the hole there, and then he looked about for Pinny, his friend. But Pinny had gone back to the village to tell the folk what a joke he had played on Roundabout, sending him up a tree to look for a pie to eat – when all the time there wasn't a pie at all, but only a magpie.

All the little folk came running out of the village to see the fun – and they met poor Roundabout limping back in rags, looking very sorry for himself.

'Hallo!' he said, when he saw Pinny. 'I didn't find that pie you told me about – and a very nasty bird nearly pecked me to pieces!'

'Poor Roundabout!' said Pinny. 'That bird was the pie – it was a magpie. I didn't think it would set about you like that.'

'Good gracious, was that the pie?' asked Roundabout, surprised. 'Well, no wonder it got angry when I said I wanted to eat it! That's taught me a lesson. I'll never eat a pie again!'

Roundabout kept his word for two whole days, and then, I'm sorry to say, someone sent him an apple-pie – and he ate it all up before you could say 'Jack Robinson'!

But you've only got to mention Mag-pie to make him shiver all over!

Feefo Goes to Market

Once upon a time there was a gnome called Feefo who made a lot of money out of onion puddings. He grew specially big onions in his garden, and when they were ready he made them into such delicious puddings that you could smell them for miles.

Feefo had a wife and nine children, so although he made a lot of money he never grew rich, because there was always so much to buy for his children.

One day he sold sixteen onion puddings and made so much money that he really thought he would go and have a Big Spend. So he called his wife and asked her what he should spend his money on.

'You shall each have something,' he said, rattling his money. 'Tell me what you would like.'

'Buy me two nice big frying-pans,' said his wife, beaming all over her face. 'I'd like those very much. And buy nine tin buckets and nine tin spades for the children to dig with. They are always asking for those.'

'Very well,' said Feefo. 'I will go to the town next market-day and buy all those things for you and the children. And for myself I will buy a red waste-paper basket. I have always wanted one.'

Mrs. Feefo was so delighted to think she had such a generous husband that when she had finished her washing that day she popped in next-door to her neighbour, Mother Apple, and told her all about it.

'Feefo is buying me two new frying-pans next market-day,' she said proudly. 'And he is getting the nine children a tin spade and a bucket each. What do you think of that?'

Mother Apple thought a lot about it, but she didn't say much to Mrs. Feefo. She kept it all for Father Apple when he came home that night.

'Why can't you be generous like Mr. Feefo, the gnome?' she cried. 'He is getting his nine children a tin spade and bucket each, and two frying-pans for his wife. You never buy *your* family anything like that!'

Mother Apple told Dame Tickles about it, and Dame Tickles wished that Mr. Tickles as generous as the gnome Feefo. She told him so

when he came home, and he grew quite cross. She told Mrs. Twiddle about it too, and Mrs. Twiddle told her neighbour, Mother Bun, how generous the gnome Feefo was to his wife and children; and they all of them scolded their husbands because they didn't go to the market and buy frying-pans and tin buckets and spades.

Now Father Apple, Mr. Tickles, Mr. Twiddle and Father Bun felt very cross with Feefo for being so generous.

'What does he want to go buying things like that for?' they said to one another. 'It only makes our wives and children think we are mean because we don't do the same. We ought to do something about it.'

Poor Apple, Twiddle, Tickles and Bun! Wherever they went they heard about the gnome Feefo going to market on Saturday to get frying-pans and spades and buckets. And at last they put their heads together and thought of a plan.

'We will lie in wait for him at the bottom of Breezy Hill,' they said. 'We will jump out at him and take away all the things he has bought, and then he will not be able to go home and give presents to his wife and children.'

So on Saturday they set off to Breezy Hill, after seeing Feefo the gnome walking gaily off to market, jingling his money in his pocket.

'It is hot,' said Father Bun. 'Let's go and sit on the top of the hill where there is a breeze. We shall easily see Feefo coming and can get down to the bottom long before he is at the top.'

So up the hill they went and sat down in a ring on the top. Twiddle smoked his pipe, Bun chewed a grass, and the other two just sat and did nothing, feeling rather sleepy. Soon Twiddle pointed away in the distance, and said that he could see Feefo coming home from market.

Down the hill they went and hid in the bracken at the bottom, meaning to jump out at the gnome when he came walking by.

Feefo had a lot to carry. He had the two frying-pans, and nice big ones they were, too – he had nine tin buckets and nine tin spades – and a fine red waste-paper basket for himself. They were all very awkward to carry and when he reached the top of Breezy Hill he stopped to have a rest.

He sat down and mopped his head. Then he suddenly caught sight of a small yellow button lying not far off. He picked it up.

'Father Bun has been here,' he said to himself. 'He's been sitting down over there. Dear me, the grass is very flattened just there. He must have had some others with him.'

He poked about and found a red match, which he looked at very closely.

'Now who uses red matches?' he thought. 'Let me see – yes, Mr. Twiddle does. He's been here too, and not so long ago, either. And here's a handkerchief left behind. It's got a name on it – Tickles. Ho, so *he's* been here too. That means that Apple was here as well, because they do everything together. Now why should Twiddle, Apple, Tickles and Bun all come up here on this hill today and sit here together?'

He sat down and thought. Then he got up and looked on every side of the hill, shading his eyes with his hand.

'They're nowhere to be seen,' he said. 'That's funny. Are they hiding somewhere? And if they *are* hiding, why should they do such a funny thing?'

Then Feefo suddenly guessed that Twiddle, Tickles, Apple and Bun were keeping a look-out for him, and meant to jump on him and take away the things he had bought. And he sat down and grinned to himself. He would go down the hill all right – but he didn't think they would jump on him. Ho, ho!

Feefo got some string out of his pocket and tied the tin spades in a row together. He slung them over his left shoulder. Then he strung the handles of the tin buckets together and slung these over his right shoulder. Then he put the red waste-paper basket firmly on his head and took the frying-pans up, one in each hand. How strange he looked!

'Now here we go!' he said to himself with a big grin on his cheeky face. He began to run down the hill, and as he ran he shouted at the top of his voice.

'Ho, ho, ho! Make way for Hanky-Panky, the Snorting Bing-Bong with his clinking, clanking, clonking Fire-eaters! Ho, ho, ho, here I come, Hanky-Panky, snorting and snuffling, the great and dangerous Bing-Bong!'

As he ran and bounded in the air, all the nine tin buckets clanged together and all the tin spades crashed on one another, making a simply fearful din. The red waste-paper basket jumped up and down as Feefo leapt in the air, and all the time he banged his two frying-pans together with a terrible crashing noise.

Goodness, what a fearful sight he looked, and what an awful noise he made! How the spades crashed and smashed together, how the buckets clanked and clinked, and as for the two frying-pans they sounded so terrifying that everyone thought the end of the world had come!

'Ho, ho, ho! Make way for Hanky-Panky, the

Snorting Bing-Bong with his clinking, clanking, clonking Fire-eaters! Ho, ho, ho! here I come, Hanky-Panky, snorting and snuffling, the great and dangerous BING-BONG!'

When Twiddle, Bun, Tickles and Apple heard this terrible noise and saw this awful creature tearing down the hill with a great red hat on his head, banging and clanking, with long strings of things crashing behind him, they fell over one another with fright.

'Get out of his way, quick! Get out of his way!' they cried to one another, and they fell over each other's legs in their hurry. Poor Twiddle had fallen asleep whilst he was waiting, and he awoke to see the terrifying creature racing down the hill not far from him. He was so frightened that his legs bent under him when he tried to run, and he fell, bumping his nose on the ground.

Feefo the gnome was enjoying himself very much. On and on he ran, shouting and jumping high into the air, all the tin buckets and spades flying out behind him, making more noise than ever, banging the two frying-pans in front of him, trying not to laugh at the sight of the four scrambling gnomes in front of him, struggling their hardest to get out of his way.

He passed them at a run, leaping his highest,

whilst they dived into the bracken and hid, trembling and shaking. Then, when he had left them well behind him, Feefo sank down on the ground and began to laugh. The tears came into his eyes and ran down his long nose to the ground, where they made a big puddle.

How he laughed! He rolled on the ground and roared till his sides ached. Then he sat up and wiped his eyes.

'Dear, dear me,' he said. 'What a joke that was! I shall never laugh so much again. Ho, ho! Make

way for Hanky-Panky, the Snorting Bing-Bong!'

He got to his feet, took the basket off his head and went peacefully home. He gave his wife and children their presents and they were delighted. Then he lighted his pipe and went to lean over his front gate, waiting for Twiddle, Bun, Tickles and Apple to come home.

At last they came, looking white and scared, turning round to look behind them every now and again.

'Hallo!' called Feefo. 'What's the matter?'

'Oh, Feefo, didn't you see the Snorting Bing-Bong with his clinking, clanking, clonking Fire-eaters?' cried Twiddle. 'He came tearing down Breezy Hill not so long ago.'

'Yes, it was Hanky-Panky, snorting and snuffling, the great and dangerous Bing-Bong,' said Bun, trembling. 'He trod on my toe when he passed and it has swelled up to twice its size.'

'He's a fearful person,' said Apple. 'Didn't you see him, Feefo? He's twice as big as you are, and wears an enormous red hat.'

'Oh, yes, I know Bing-Bong,' said Feefo. 'He's a great friend of mine. I know him as well as I know myself, and I'm very fond of him. I know why he came, too.'

'Why?' asked Twiddle, in surprise.

'He came because he knew that there were enemies waiting for me round the corner,' said Feefo solemnly. 'He came to eat them up. Fancy that! No wonder you were frightened when you met him.'

Twiddle, Tickles, Bun and Apple looked very guilty, indeed. Could it really be that the Bing-Bong had known of their plan to jump on Feefo that afternoon? Ooh, what an escape they had had!

'Where is he now?' asked Apple fearfully.

'He's here,' said Feefo. 'Would you like to see him?'

'OOOOOOOOOOH!' shouted Twiddle, Bun, Apple and Tickles in a great fright, and they took to their heels and ran away as fast as ever they could. And that rascally Feefo ran indoors and banged his two frying-pans together to make them go faster!

Well, well! He hasn't a single enemy now, and I'm sure I don't wonder at it!

Adventures of the Sailor Doll

Once there was a sailor doll, and he lived in Janet's nursery. She was very fond of him, and he went everywhere with her. He was such a smart doll, with a blue velvet uniform and a nice sailor collar and round hat. He had a pink, smiling face, and was the most cheerful person you can imagine!

And then one day a dreadful thing happened to him. A puppy came into the garden where Janet was playing, and began to romp about. Janet was frightened and fled indoors. She left her sailor doll behind her on the grass! Oh, dear, what a pity!

The puppy saw the doll smiling up at him, and he picked it up in his teeth. He threw the doll into the air. The sailor stopped smiling, for he was frightened.

The doll came down on the grass. The puppy picked him up again and began to nibble him. He nibbled his hat and made a hole. He nibbled his sailor collar and tore it. He nibbled a shoe and got it off.

And then he did a really *dreadful* thing. He chewed one of the sailor's arms off! He bit it right off, and there it lay on the grass beside the poor scared doll.

Then there came a whistling, and the puppy's master came along. The puppy heard the whistling, ran to the gate, and darted out to his master. Off he went down the road, galloping along, leaving behind him the poor chewed sailor.

Well, Janet's mother very soon came out to clear up her little girl's toys, and she saw the sailor doll lying on the grass with his arm beside him. She was very sorry. She picked him up and looked at him.

'I'm afraid you're no more use,' she said. 'You'll have to go into the dust-bin, sailor. You are all chewed, and you have lost an arm.'

She put him on the seat and went on collecting the other toys. The sailor doll was so horrified at hearing he would have to go into the dust-bin that he lay and shivered. Then, seeing that Janet's mother was not looking, he quietly picked up his chewed arm, put it into his pocket, jumped down from the seat, and slipped away into the bushes. *He* wasn't going to be put into the dust-bin! Not he!

Janet's mother was surprised to find he had gone; but it was getting dark, so she went in with the other toys and didn't bother any more about the sailor. As soon as she had gone the sailor slipped out of the bushes and ran down the garden path. He went into the field at the end of the garden and walked over the grass.

He didn't know where he was going. He was just running away from the dust-bin. He went on and on, and soon the moon came up and lighted everything clearly. Still he walked on. He met a hedgehog ambling along looking for beetles, and a mole with a long snout, and heard two mice quarrelling in the hedges. Still he went on – and

at last he could go no further. He was really quite tired out. He had come to a little stream, and being a sailor doll he loved the sound of water.

'I think I'll settle down here for the night,' thought the sailor. 'I can go on in the morning. I think I am far enough away from that dust-bin now.'

So he crept under a dock leaf and lay down. Soon the moon went behind a great cloud, and it began to rain. A goblin crept under the dock leaf to shelter and, finding the sailor there, pushed him away. So the rain poured down on the poor sailor doll and soaked him through. He was so tired he didn't wake up till the morning – and then what a shock he had!

His sailor suit had shrunk in the rain and was now far too small for him. His hat had shrunk too, and looked very silly perched right on top of his head. His trouser legs were up to his knees, and his coat would no longer meet. He really looked dreadful.

He walked out into the sunshine, and how he sneezed, for he had caught a cold in the rain:

'A-tishoo! A-tishoo!'

'Hallo, hallo!' said a small voice, and the sailor doll saw an elf peeping at him. 'What's the matter with *you*? You look a bit of a scarecrow! What are you?'

'I am supposed to be a sailor doll,' said the sailor humbly. 'I know I look dreadful now.'

'Well, you've got a bad cold,' said the elf. 'Come into this rabbit-hole and I'll make a fire and dry you.'

The doll followed the elf, and to his enormous surprise he saw that down the rabbit-hole was a small door, neatly fitted into the side of the burrow. The elf opened the door, and inside was a cosy room with a fire laid ready for lighting. Soon it was crackling away cheerfully. The doll dried his clothes and felt more cheerful, especially when the elf brought him some hot lemonade and some ginger biscuits. Aha! This was good!

'Now you must get on to my sofa and have a good rest,' said the elf kindly. 'You can stay here all day in the warmth, if you like.'

So he did; and when the night came, the elf said he might sleep there too.

'I am going to a boating party,' she said. 'It's being held on the stream. So you can sleep here all night, if you like. I shan't be back till dawn.'

'A boating party!' said the sailor doll, excited. 'Oh, can't I come?'

'No, it would be better for you to stay here in the warm and get rid of your cold,' said the elf.

She put on a cape and ran out. The doll wished he knew what a boating party was like. He had never been to one. He opened the door and went into the rabbit-hole to see if he could hear any merry shouts and screams from the boating party. At first he heard laughter and shouts – and then he heard a great crying:

'Oh! Oh! You horrid frogs! Go away! You are spoiling our party!'

Then there came a sound of splashing and screaming. Whatever could be happening?

The doll ran out into the moonlight – and he

saw a strange sight. The elves had many little silver boats on the stream, and a great crowd of green frogs had popped up to sink the little boats.

One after another they were pulled under by the mischievous frogs. The elves flew out of the boats as soon as they began to sink, but they were most unhappy because they had lost their pretty boats, and the party was spoilt.

The sailor doll ran to the bank in anger. 'How dare you do such a thing, frogs?' he cried. 'I will go and tell the ducks to come here and eat you!'

The frogs swam off in fright. But not a single boat was left!

'A-tishoo!' said the sailor doll. 'I *am* sorry I didn't come before!'

'Our party is spoilt!' wept the little elves. 'We have no more boats – and oh, we were having *such* fun!'

A bright idea came into the sailor doll's head.

'I say,' he said, 'I know how to make boats out of paper. They float very well too. I used to watch Janet making them. If you can get me some paper, I could tell you how to make them.'

The elves gave a shout of delight and ran off. Soon they came back with all sorts of pieces of paper, and they placed them in front of the doll.

'I wish I could make the boats for you,' he said, 'but, you see, I have only one arm, so I can't. But I will tell you how to do it. Now – fold your paper in half to begin with.'

The elves all did as he said, and soon there were dozens of dear little paper boats all ready to float on the river. Lovely!

The elves launched them, and presently another boating party was going on. The frogs didn't dare to appear this time, so everything went off merrily.

In the middle of the party a big ship with silver sails came floating down the stream.

'Look! Look! The Fairy King and Queen are sailing to-night, too!' shouted the elves in glee.

'Let us float round them in our paper boats and give them a hearty cheer!'

So they did; and the King and Queen were *most* astonished to see such a fleet of boats appearing round their ship, full of cheering elves.

'Go to the bank and anchor there,' the King commanded. So the ship was headed for the bank and very soon it was anchored there, and the elves went on board to bow and curtsy to their majesties.

'Who has taught you how to make these lovely boats?' asked the Queen, in surprise. 'I have never seen any like them before!'

'The sailor doll did,' said the little elf who had helped the doll. She told the King all about the boating party spoilt by the frogs, and how the doll had taught them to make paper boats.

'Bring him here!' commanded the King. But the sailor doll was shy and didn't want to go before their majesties.

'I am all dirty and wet, and my suit is too small for me,' he said. 'Besides, I have lost an arm, and I am ashamed of having only one. Also, I have a bad cold, and I should not like to give it to the King or Queen. A-tishoo!'

So the elf told the King what the doll had said, and the King nodded his head.

'See that the doll is given a new suit,' he said, 'and do what you can about his arm, elf. Then send him to me at the palace. I want to speak to him about something very important.'

The elf took the surprised sailor doll back to her cosy home in the burrow. She looked him up and down and pursed up her tiny mouth.

'You'll have to have a new suit altogether,' she said. 'It wouldn't be any good patching up the one you have on. I can get you a new hat made too. The only thing that worries me is your arm. I don't know how I can get you one to match your own.'

'Oh, I've got my old one in my pocket,' said the sailor doll, and he pulled out his chewed arm.

'Oh, splendid!' said the elf. 'Now look here, sailor, just take off all your old clothes, whilst I go to fetch little Stitchaway the Pixie to measure you for a new suit. You can put on my dressing-gown. Sit by the fire and drink some more hot lemon. Your cold seems better already.'

She went out. The doll took off his old, dirty suit, put on the elf's little dressing-gown, and sat down by the fire. He was very happy. Things seemed to be turning out all right, after all.

Soon the elf came back with a small pixie who was all hung about with pin-cushions, scissors, and needle-books. With her she carried a great bunch of bluebells.

'Good-day, sailor,' she said. 'I shall have to make your suit of bluebells. I hope you won't mind, but that is the only blue I have at the moment. Now, stand up, and let me measure you.'

It didn't take long to measure the sailor. No sooner was this done than two more pixies appeared. One was a shoemaker, and he soon fitted a pair of fine black boots on the sailor and took away his old ones. Then the other pixie, who was a hatter, and wore about twenty different hats piled on his head, tried them all on the sailor, and found a little round one that fitted him exactly. It had a blue feather in it, but the elf said that it looked very nice, so the sailor left it in.

'Now where's your arm?' said the elf. The doll took his arm from the shelf where he had put it whilst he was being measured. The elf fitted it neatly into his shoulder, said a few magic words, and let go. The arm was as good as ever! The doll could use it just as well as he could use the other one. He was so delighted!

In two days' time the dressmaker elf came back with the grandest blue sailor suit of bluebells that you can imagine! When the sailor dressed himself in it, he did feel smart. The elf looked at him in admiration.

'You look like the captain of a ship,' she said. 'Now come along to the palace, and we'll see what the King wants.'

Well, what *do* you suppose His Majesty wanted? The captain of his fairy fleet was old, and was going to leave the sea and live in a little cottage with his wife. The King wanted another captain – and that was why he had sent for the sailor doll.

'Will you be my new captain?' he asked him. 'You look so cheerful, always smiling – and the way you sent off those wicked frogs, and taught the elves how to make new boats, was wonderful. I'd very much like you to be my new captain.'

'Oh, Your Majesty, it's too good to be true!' cried the doll, blushing all over his smiling face. 'I promise you I will do my very best.'

'Very well. You are my captain, then!' said the King. 'Now come and have tea with the Queen and our children. They are all longing to know how to make paper boats.'

And now the sailor doll is very important indeed, and everyone in Fairyland salutes him when he goes by. You should see him commanding his ship too! You would never think he was once a poor chewed doll who was nearly put in a dust-bin!

Clickety-Clack

There was once a gnome called Clickety-Clack, though nobody knew why. He lived at the top of a very long field in a nice little toadstool house. He was so vain that nobody liked him at all, not even Kindheart the fairy, who liked almost everyone.

Clickety-Clack boasted terribly. He said he could do anything, and most people believed him. He said he was cleverer than witches or wizards, and he didn't think there was anyone in the world who was so powerful as he was.

One day quite a lot of people were outside Clickety-Clack's house. He sold fresh honey, and they had come to buy some and to have a chat with one another. Clickety-Clack was pleased to see so many pennies ready for honey, and he began to boast, as usual.

'I shall be richer than anybody in the kingdom soon,' he said. 'I've got heaps of gold hidden away.'

'It's better to be good than rich,' said Kindheart.

'It's better to be healthy than wealthy!' said Twiddles the brownie. 'You don't look at all well, Clickety-Clack. You're a thin, skinny creature, you are! I'd be sorry to be you, for all you think yourself so clever and strong!'

Clickety-Clack felt very angry.

'I'm thin because I wish to be thin!' he said. 'If I wanted to be fat, like you, Twiddles, I could make myself plump to-morrow!'

'Ooh, story-teller!' said Chipperdee the squirrel. 'Nobody can do that!'

'*I* can do anything!' said Clickety-Clack. 'I can tell you anything, too!'

'All right, then, tell us what those big birds are

318

that have been flying about high up in the air lately,' said Dimity the elf.

'No, make one come down, and we'll all see it,' said Twiddles. 'Look, there's one ever so high up.'

He pointed up into the sky. What he saw was an aeroplane, but he didn't know it. He thought it was some strange bird that groaned as it flew.

Clickety-Clack was fairly caught! How could he do such a thing as make that bird come down? Why, he didn't even know enough magic to make a cloud come down, and that was a thing that the youngest fairy knew.

There was nothing for it but to be bold and pretend he could make the bird come down. So he drew a circle round himself, clapped his hands three times, jumped head-overheels twice and then bawled out a long string of words that didn't mean anything at all.

And just at that very moment the airman decided to land! He saw the long field stretching out below, and as he was running out of petrol, he decided to come down.

He began to go round and round in circles, getting lower each time. The little group below watched the aeroplane in amazement. What a strange bird! How big! What a noise it made!

Twiddles began to feel frightened. It seemed as if the great monster was going to come right on top of them. Chipperdee the squirrel trembled, for he had never heard such a fearsome noise in his life.

'It's got two eyes underneath!' cried Kindheart in fright. 'Look – they're red, white and blue! Ooh, tell the nasty thing to go back into the sky, Clickety-Clack!'

'I can't! I can't!' wept Clickety-Clack in terror, his knees shaking beneath him.

'You *can*!' said Twiddles. 'You made it come down, so you can make it go up again!'

Down came the aeroplane, lower and lower. It seemed to Clickety-Clack that it was going to knock the chimney off his house. He could bear it no longer. He jumped out of the circle he had made and raced away as fast as his legs could carry him. Down the lane he went, and into the wood. He scuttled down a rabbit-hole and lay at the bottom with his nose in the earth, shaking from head to foot.

'Oh, why did I say I could get it down?' he wailed. 'How could I know it would really come? I didn't think it would! Oh, the horrid big bird! It will eat us all up, I'm sure it will!'

All day long Clickety-Clack lay in the rabbit-hole, not daring to move. When night came he ventured out again, and crept back to the long field. He looked up and down – but the strange monster was gone.

'Clickety-Clack!' suddenly cried a voice, making him jump two feet into the air. 'Why did you run away? Oh, Clickety-Clack, we *do* think you are clever! We didn't really believe you could do all the things you said you could – we thought you were boasting – but we know that you can, now!'

Chipperdee the squirrel came leaping down to

Clickety-Clack, and soon Twiddles, Dimity and Kindheart came up too.

'That strange monster landed on our field,' said Twiddles, 'but no sooner did it land than it went up again, and disappeared. Do you know why?'

Clickety-Clack didn't – but the airman could have told him; for no sooner did he touch ground than he discovered he had more petrol than he thought, so off he went again. He didn't see Chipperdee the squirrel, Twiddles the brownie, Dimity the elf, or Kindheart the fairy.

They all thought Clickety-Clack was wonderful to have brought the strange bird down, as he had said he would. They couldn't understand why the gnome didn't boast about it as he generally did. But Clickety-Clack had learnt his lesson. He wasn't going to boast any more, not he! He was going to be very careful indeed what he said or did in the future.

'I'm not going to have any more monsters coming down from the sky!' he thought. 'I'll not be vain or conceited any more. People will think much less of me – but that can't be helped.'

But the funny thing was that everyone thought much *more* of Clickety-Clack when he became humble and modest. They liked him very much, and often had happy evenings with him in his little toadstool cottage. But as soon as anyone began to talk about the strange bird, Clickety-Clack would get red, and not have a word to say for himself. Nobody could guess why – but I can, can't you?

The Enchanted Bone

There was once a greedy tabby cat called Whiskers. He was a dreadful thief, and no one dared to leave anything on the table in case he jumped up and got it. If he found the larder door open, he would slip inside – and then there would be no chicken, no meat, no pie left on the shelves, you may be sure.

Now one day Whiskers went to visit his cousin in Pixieland. His cousin was a wonderfully clever cat, black as soot, with great green eyes and a tail as long as a monkey's. He belonged to a witch and helped her with her spells. He was always pleased to see Whiskers and gave him a saucer of cream.

One day he told Whiskers about a marvellous magic bone that the witch owned.

'Do you know, Whiskers,' said the black cat, 'that bone is so magic that if you put it on a plate and say:

'Bone, please multiply yourself,
And give me meat to fill my shelf' –

it will at once make more and more and more bones, and you can get the most delicious soup all for nothing!'

Whiskers' eyes nearly fell out of his head with surprise. What a bone! If only he had one like that! He would always be able to have a fine meal then.

'Where does the witch keep that bone?' he asked.

'In the cupboard over there,' said the black cat, 'but it's always locked.'

Whiskers had a good look at the cupboard. Yes, it certainly was locked. There was no doubt about that.

But, do you know, the next time that Whiskers

went to visit his cousin, that cupboard door was open! Yes, it really was! And what was more, both the witch and her black cat were away!

'Well, well, well!' said Whiskers in delight. 'Here's a chance for me. I'll borrow that bone this morning and make myself a fine collection of bones out of it, and then bring it back again before the witch and my cousin come back.'

He slipped into the cupboard. He jumped up on to the shelf. He saw the magic bone there, and taking it in his mouth he jumped down. Then out of the kitchen he went at top speed, the big enchanted bone in his mouth.

He ran home. He took the bone into the back garden and set it down on an old enamel plate, belonging to Spot the dog. And then Whiskers said the magic spell:

> 'Bone, please multiply yourself,
> And give me meat to fill my shelf!'

The bone began to work. My goodness, you should have seen it! It was really marvellous. A big bone grew out of one end and fell on to the plate. A joint of meat grew out of the other end and fell right *off* the plate. Whiskers stared in the greatest surprise and delight. What a feast he would have! Oh, what a feast!

The bone went on throwing out more bones and more joints. Soon the back garden smelt of meat, and Spot the dog woke up in surprise. He sat up. Meat! Bones! Where could they be? He raced over to Whiskers and stared at the meat and the bones in astonishment. Then he pounced on a bone.

'It's mine! It's mine! Drop it, Spot!' hissed Whiskers. But Spot wouldn't. He crunched up the bone and then started on a joint of meat.

The next-door dog sniffed the meat and came running in at the gate. The two dogs next door but one smelt it too and tore in, yelping happily. Whiskers didn't like strange dogs. He hissed and spat. But they took no notice of him and began to eat all the meat and bones.

That was too much for Whiskers. He wasn't going to have all his magic wasted like that. He caught up the enchanted bone and ran off with it. But it wouldn't stop growing bones and meat, and soon half the dogs in the town were after Whiskers in delight.

Whiskers was frightened almost out of his life. He took one look round at the dogs and fled on and on. He didn't dare to drop the magic bone, for he knew it would be eaten if he did – and then what would the witch say?

He ran right round the town and back again. He came to his own house once more. The door was open. Whiskers ran inside and jumped up on to the table.

'Get down, Whiskers, get down!' shouted the cook, and she stared in astonishment – for into her kitchen poured dozens of dogs – black dogs, white dogs, brown dogs, spotted dogs, little ones and big ones, nice ones and nasty ones!

'Shoo! Shoo!' cried the cook, taking up a broom and hitting the dogs. But they jumped over the broom and leapt on to the table after Whiskers and the magic bone. Whiskers mewed in fright and jumped up on to the top shelf of the dresser. The dogs jumped too – and crash, smash, crash, smash, down went cups and saucers, dishes and plates. The cook yelled in rage and smacked dogs right and left with the broom – but more and more came in!

Then the cook saw that there was only one way of getting rid of them. She picked up the bones and meat that seemed everywhere – on the floor and the table and the dresser – and threw them out into the street as fast as she could. Out went all the dogs after them! Soon the kitchen was empty and the

cook slammed the door. She glared at Whiskers and took up her broom again.

'What do you mean by stealing all that meat and bringing it home?' she said. 'Take that, you bad cat – and that!'

Thwack, smack! Poor Whiskers got a dreadful spanking. He squealed and leapt out of the window, still with the magic bone in his mouth. He tore off with it to the witch's house – no dogs following this time because they were all busy in the street, gobbling up the meat and the bones that the cook had thrown out for them.

The witch was at home. So was the black cat. And how they glared at Whiskers when he came in with the stolen bone. The witch took hold of him and gave him a good whipping. As for the black cat, he flew at Whiskers and scratched him down the nose.

'Never come here again,' he mewed. 'You deserve to be well punished.'

'I have been punished,' mewed poor Whiskers. 'I shall never steal again – not even the hind leg of a kipper!'

He never did – and as for bones, he wouldn't go near them, no matter how nice they smelt! Poor old Whiskers!

Fiddle-de-dee, the Foolish Brownie

Fiddle-de-dee was a young brownie. He lived with his mother in Pudding Cottage, and was very lazy indeed. He simply wouldn't do a thing, though his mother had far more than she could do.

'Now look here, Fiddle-de-dee,' she said one day. 'You really must help me. Your aunt and uncle are coming to tea, and I want some nice fresh muffins. You must go to the baker's and buy twelve.'

So Fiddle-de-dee set off. He bought twelve muffins at the baker's and then started off home. On the way back he felt tired, so he jumped into a bus. At the next stop so many people got in that some had to stand.

'May I sit on your knee?' another brownie asked Fiddle-de-dee.

'Certainly,' said Fiddle-de-dee – but he had the bag of muffins on his knee, and he wondered what to do with them. He slipped them underneath him, and then pulled the brownie down on to his knee. When the end of the ride came, the other brownie thanked him and they both got off the bus. The bag of muffins looked very strange.

How cross Fiddle-de-dee's mother was when she saw them!

'You stupid, silly fellow!' she cried. 'You've been sitting on them!'

'Well, I had to put them somewhere,' said Fiddle-de-dee. 'If *I* hadn't sat on them the other brownie would have, for he sat on my knee. And as he was a lot heavier than I am, I thought it would be better if *I* sat on them!'

'You didn't think that you were *both* sitting on them, then?' asked his mother. 'Now, listen, Fiddle-de-dee – the next time I send you out you must think what you're doing. You should have asked the baker to lend you a tray, and then you should have walked home with the muffins on your head like the muffin man.'

'I see,' said Fiddle-de-dee, and determined to do better next time.

Now two days later his mother thought it would be nice to have some ice-cream, for the day was hot. So she gave Fiddle-de-dee a shilling and told him to fetch some from the ice-cream shop. He set off, and bought a nice lot. It was in a cardboard box.

He had just left the shop when he remembered how he bad been scolded about the muffins.

'Mother said I ought to have brought them home on my head,' he said. 'Well, I forgot to borrow a tray this time, but I'm sure I can balance this box on my head all right.'

So he popped the box of ice-cream on his head, and walked home with it. But the sun was tremendously hot that day and beat down on Fiddle-de-dee all the way home. The ice-cream soon melted and began to run out of the corners of the box. It ran down Fiddle-de-dee's hair and trickled down his neck.

'Ooh!' said Fiddle-de-dee in surprise. 'I do feel

nice and cold. It isn't such a hot day after all. I'm not nearly so hot now.'

The ice-cream went on trickling down his head and neck all the way home. When his mother saw him she gave a cry of dismay.

'Fiddle-de-dee!' she cried. 'Whatever are you doing with the ice-cream, carrying it on your head like that in the hot sun! Oh, how foolish you are! It is all melted now, and you are in a terrible mess! You should have wrapped a damp cloth round the box, and covered it with your coat to keep it cool.'

'Oh,' said Fiddle-de-dee. 'Well, how was I to know that? I'll do better next time.'

The next day his mother heard that a fine goose was for sale, and she determined to buy it and keep it for Christmas-time.

'I'll fatten it up,' she said, 'and when Christmas comes it will make us a good Christmas dinner.'

So she sent Fiddle-de-dee to get it. He bought it from the farmer, and set off with the goose. But he hadn't gone very far before he remembered how his mother had scolded him about the ice-cream.

'She said I ought to have wrapped it in a damp cloth and carried it home under my coat,' he said. 'Well, I must try to take the goose home as she said.'

Hanging on a near-by clothes-line was a tablecloth belonging to Mother Wimple. Fiddle-de-dee took it down and soaked it in a pond. Then he wrapped the struggling, angry goose in it, and tried to put it under his coat. But the bird was big and strong, and it was all Fiddle-de-dee could do to hold it.

By the time he reached home his coat and shirt were rent and torn by the goose in its struggles to escape. The table-cloth was in rags, and Fiddle-de-dee was all hot and bothered.

'Oh my, oh my!' groaned his mother, when she saw him. 'What *have* you been doing with Mother Wimple's lovely new tablecloth? And just look at your clothes, Fiddle-de-dee! They're only fit for the dustbin now! And the poor goose is half dead with fright!'

'I tried to do as you said,' said Fiddle-de-dee, 'but the goose didn't like being wrapped up in a damp cloth, Mother.'

'You stupid, foolish boy,' said his mother. 'Can't a goose walk? You should have tied a string round its leg and let it follow behind you!'

'I see,' said Fiddle-de-dee, and made up his mind to do better next time.

A week later his mother wanted him to fetch the

joint of meat from the butcher's, so he set off. He took the leg of mutton from the man, and turned to go home. Then he remembered how angry his mother had been with him last time he had gone on an errand for her, and he tried to think how he should take the meat home.

'Mother said last time I ought to have tied a string to the goose's leg and let it follow behind me!' he thought. 'Well, this mutton's got a leg, so I'll tie some string to it.'

He found a piece of string in his pocket and carefully tied it to the leg of mutton. Then he threw it behind him, and set off home, dragging the meat after him.

He hadn't gone far when half the dogs and cats in the neighbourhood smelt the meat and came running after it. Fiddle-de-dee turned round and saw them all. He became frightened and started to run. All the dogs and cats ran too!

He tore home, the meat bumping up and down behind him. He raced in through the kitchen door – and all the cats and dogs came too, snarling, growling and fighting over the leg of mutton!

'Oh, good gracious, oh, my goodness!' cried his mother. 'Whatever will you do next? What made you bring these creatures home with you? Oh dear, oh dear, look at that meat! You surely haven't dragged it home on a piece of string!'

'Well, that's what you told me to do with the goose, Mother,' said Fiddle-de-dee.

'Yes, but a leg of mutton isn't a goose!' cried his mother, in a temper, and she boxed Fiddle-de-dee's ears. Then she picked up a broom, and shooed the dogs and cats away.

'Shoo, shoo, shoo!' she shouted. 'Shoo, you cats, shoo, you dogs!'

When all the animals had gone away she turned to scold Fiddle-de-dee – but he wasn't there. He had gone to put himself to bed! He thought that would be the safest place for him that day, and he was quite right!

The Elephant and the Snail

Once upon a time a great elephant went roaming with the herd in the forest. As he went between the trees, pulling down leaves and fruit to eat, a snail fell off a nearby bush, and went rolling to where the elephant stood.

It was a fine snail, with a big, curly shell, brightly coloured in yellow and brown. It rolled underneath the great foot of the elephant. The big beast felt it rolling there, and lifted his foot to see what it was.

When he saw that it was only a small snail, the elephant put down his foot again, meaning to crush the snail – but the tiny creature spoke earnestly to the elephant:

'Don't crush me! Put down your foot to one side and let me crawl away in safety. I have never done you any harm, so have mercy on me, great elephant.'

The elephant was not cruel. He moved his

enormous foot away and looked at the yellow and brown snail.

'Well, go in peace,' he said. 'I will not harm you.'

'You are a kind creature,' said the snail gratefully, moving away. 'One day I may be able to save your life for you in return.'

The elephant trumpeted loudly with laughter. 'How could a creature like you ever do anything for *me*?' he bellowed. 'You think too much of yourself, snail!'

The snail said no more, but slid away as fast as he could for fear the elephant should change his mind and step on him. He hid in the bushes until the herd had gone by. All small creatures feared the heavy tread of the elephants.

The weeks went by. Hunters came to the wood – men who wished to capture the elephants and set them to work. They built a big enclosure of strong fences with a wide entrance.

'Now,' they said to one another, 'we know where the herd is. We will surround it and drive it gradually to our enclosure. The elephants will all go inside – and then they will find they cannot get out. They will be caught!'

So the next day the hunters went out to surround the herd. But the elephants were very wary and they had moved off, all except three who were separated from the herd. They were caught, for they ran when they heard the hunters coming, and very soon they had lumbered into the big ring of fencing, and were prisoners.

The three elephants trumpeted in rage. They knew they were caught. They tried to rush out of the gateway – but now the big gate had been closed, and there was no way out. The elephants pushed against the fence, but it was too strong to break down, even when the three of them pushed together. A fence like that would need a whole herd to push it down!

The elephants bellowed with anger, but they could do nothing. One of them was the elephant who had let the snail go free, but he had forgotten all about the little creature by now.

But the snail had not forgotten. When it heard the bellowing of the elephants, it crawled from its hiding-place nearby, and glided up to the top of the fence. On the other side stood the elephant the snail knew so well!

'Friend,' said the snail. 'Why do you roar so loudly?'

'Because I am caught,' said the elephant sulkily. 'I cannot get away from here.'

'Can I help you?' asked the snail.

The elephant laughed. 'Of course not!' he said. 'What can a snail like you do, I should like to know? Can you break down this fence? Can you open the gate? No – you are a worthless little snail, and can do nothing!'

'Can your friends help you?' asked the snail.

'Yes, if they were here,' said the elephant. 'But they do not know where I am. If the whole herd were here they could easily knock down this fence. But before they come wandering by this

way again I and the other two elephants here will be taken away.'

'I think I *can* help you,' said the snail. 'I know I crawl very slowly, but if you would tell me where to find your friends, I might be able to get to them in time for them to come here and break down the fence for you.'

The elephant stared at the yellow and brown snail in surprise. 'You are kind, snail,' he said. 'But you are such a slowcoach that it would take you weeks to crawl to my friends.'

'I will try,' said the snail. So the elephant told him where he thought the rest of the herd would be, and the little snail crawled down the fence again and made his way through the forest grass.

Certainly the snail was a slowcoach, but he did not rest for a moment. He kept a sharp look-out for birds, and went on his way steadily. He glided along all night, leaving a silvery trail behind him. He slid along all day, and all the next night too. He was very tired by the middle of the second day; but to his delight he thought he heard the sound of elephants' feet thudding along not far off. He crawled up a tree and waited. Perhaps the herd was coming that way.

It was! As the leader passed the tree on which

the snail hung, the little creature called to him:

'Great elephant! I have a message for you.'

'Tell me,' said the elephant.

'Three of your friends are caught in a big ring of fences,' said the snail. 'They cannot break the fence down. But if you take the whole herd there, you can break it down between you.'

The leader of the elephants spoke to the herd, and they listened, their eyes wise and bright.

'We will come where you lead,' they said.

'Snail, crawl on to my head, so that you can tell me the way,' said the leader of the elephants. He pressed close to the tree, and the snail dropped to his head. He clung there, and the elephant moved off.

'Who would have thought that I would ride on an elephant at the head of a herd?' thought the little snail, astonished. He told the elephant the way to go, and to his surprise they arrived near the fencing before nightfall.

'When it is dark,' said the leader, 'we will all go to one part of the fence. We will run against it with all our might and break it down. Keep close by me, and when I trumpet once, charge with me. Snail, crawl down from my head, for you may get hurt. You have been a good friend to us to-day.'

The snail crawled down and glided to a thick bush. It waited there in excitement. Before long there came the sound of a trumpeting noise – and the herd of elephants charged together at the great fence.

It went down as if it were made of cardboard. The herd turned and fled, and with them went the three elephants who had been captured, overjoyed at being free again.

The hunters were astonished. 'Now, who could have told the herd about the captured elephants?' they cried. 'How did the herd know where they were?'

'I could answer your questions,' thought the yellow and brown snail. 'But I won't! It is good to help a friend!'

The elephant was grateful to the little snail. 'I am sorry I laughed at you,' he said. 'I did not guess, when I gave you your life, that a little thing like you could help *me*.'

'Little things are very useful sometimes,' said the snail as he glided away.

The Invisible Gnome

There was once a gnome called Too-Much. He was called Too-Much because he was very fat, so there was too much of him. He was very greedy, very sly, and not at all to be trusted.

Now one day he stole a hat belonging to a witch. When he put it on – hey presto, he couldn't be seen! Marvellous! The hat was rather small, but that didn't matter – as soon as he wore it Too-Much disappeared – and then, think of the tricks he could get up to!

'I'll use this hat to get myself as many cakes, pies, and apples as I like,' thought Too-Much gleefully. 'My word, what a time I'll have!'

He clapped on the hat and went off down the street. Nobody could see him. How he chuckled! He went to Dame Biscuit's cake-shop and looked in at the window.

'Currant buns! Doughnuts with jam! Gingerbread

fingers! Oooooh! Here I go!' And into the shop he went. His quick fingers took three currant buns, two doughnuts, and six gingerbread fingers. Then out he went. Dame Biscuit was most amazed when she saw the cakes disappearing, and she cried out in rage. 'Hi! Come back, cakes!' She could see them travelling through the air, but she couldn't see who was taking them!

But of course the cakes didn't come back. They soon disappeared down Too-Much's throat. Then he went to the pie-shop, and Mister Crusty saw, to his great surprise, three large pies rise into the air and go out of the door. He took a stick and ran after them – but it wasn't long before they went the same way as the cakes.

'This is fine!' said Too-Much in delight. 'What a splendid way of getting what I want! Now for a drink!'

He stopped outside the lemonade-shop and looked into the window. Then in he went and took a glass from the counter. The shopkeeper shouted in fear when he saw the glass dipping itself into the jar of lemonade. It came out full, tilted itself up, and out fell the lemonade – and disappeared entirely!

'Oooh! Magic! Bad magic!' yelled the shopkeeper, and ran out into the street, calling people to come and see. But Too-Much slipped out with him and went towards the market-place.

He didn't want anything more to eat and drink for a while, so he amused himself by taking all the farmers' hats off, one by one, and throwing them into the horse-trough.

What an uproar there was in the market! Soon there was a free fight going on, for each farmer thought another had knocked off his hat.

Suddenly a bell rang, and everyone stood still. On the steps of the Town Hall stood Bron, the chief gnome of the town.

'What's all this?' he roared. 'You should be ashamed of yourselves.'

Too-Much skipped up the steps unseen, took off the chief gnome's hat, and threw it neatly on to the roof of the Town Hall. Bron gaped in astonishment, and everyone roared with laughter.

'It's an invisible gnome!' cried the farmers. 'We shall have to catch him, or he will plague the life out of us.'

But how? Ah, that was the question.

Too-Much, still wearing the witch-hat, stole sweets, pears, and apples next. Soon the whole town wanted to catch him – and once they very nearly did. Too-Much trod in a puddle – and suddenly the marks of wet feet appeared on the pavement, though there seemed to be nobody walking there.

'There he is!' cried everyone, and ran after the trail of wet foot-marks. Too-Much, glancing round, saw the townsfolk after him and ran for his life. He tore into the nearest house, which happened to be Mother Twitchet's, and found himself in her parlour. The townsfolk rushed after him, much to Mother Twitchet's surprise and anger, for she was having a nap.

'Shut all the doors,' cried Bron, the chief gnome. 'He's in here somewhere.'

So all the doors were shut. Then Bron made everyone sit down on the floor whilst he went round the room, his hands stretched out as if he were playing Blind Man's Buff. But Too-Much found it easy to slip away, for he could see Bron all the time.

'What are we to do?' groaned Bron. 'Someone else try now!'

So the others tried to find Too-Much, but no one could. By this time it was evening, and Mother Twitchet said they must go and leave her in peace.

'But that sly gnome is somewhere about your parlour,' said Bron. 'You don't want him here all night, do you, snoozing by your fire?'

'Don't you worry – *I* can find him all right,' said

Dame Twitchet. 'You come here in the morning, Bron, and you'll find I've got him for you. It takes a cleverer gnome than this invisible one to get the better of old Mother Twitchet.'

'You boast too much,' said Bron crossly. 'See you keep your word, or I'll have something to say to you to-morrow.'

He held the door a very little open, and all the gnomes slipped out. Bron made sure that the invisible gnome did not slip out too, then he went. The door was locked on the outside, and Mother Twitchet was left alone.

'Are you going to show yourself, or shall I make you?' said Mother Twitchet. Too-Much said nothing, but just grinned to himself. Mother Twitchet went to a drawer and took out a little yellow box full of sneezing powder. It was a favourite snuff of hers, very strong indeed. She first wrapped a handkerchief round her nose so that she would not smell it herself, then she took pinches of the powder between finger and thumb and scattered them all over the room.

Too-Much was hiding behind the sofa. As soon as a pinch of snuff flew there, it tickled his nose terribly. He got out his handkerchief and buried his face in it – but the mischief was done.

'A-TISHOO!' he said. 'A-TISHOO! A-TISHOO!'

His head jerked as he sneezed, and off flew his tight witch-hat. Mother Twitchet ran to the sofa as soon as she heard the first sneeze and snatched up the fallen hat. Then she dragged Too-Much out – and, my word, the spanking she gave him! How he howled! How he yelled!

She tied him up to her mangle – and there he was next day when Bron peeped in at the door. Oh, clever Mother Twitchet!

Mr. Grumpygroo's Hat

Mr. Grumpygroo was the crossest old man in the whole of Tweedle village. No one had ever seen him smile, or heard him laugh. He was so mean that he saved all his crumbs and made them into a pudding instead of giving them to the birds.

Of course, as you can guess, no one liked him. No one smiled at old Grumpygroo, or said good morning. They frowned at him, or scowled, for no village likes to have such a crosspatch living in it. Grumpygroo didn't seem to mind. He lived all alone in his tumble-down cottage, and made friends with no one.

But he was very lonely. He often wished the children would smile at him as they smiled at the Balloon woman and Mr. Sooty, the Sweep. But they never did, and old Grumpygroo vowed and declared he wouldn't be the first to smile at anyone, not he!

Every day he went walking through the village with his old green scarf round his neck, and his old top-hat on his head; and he might have gone on scowling and frowning for ever, if something strange hadn't happened.

One morning he went into the hall to fetch his scarf and his hat. It was rather a dark day, and old Grumpygroo could hardly see. He felt about for his scarf, and tied it round his neck. Then he groped about for his hat.

There was a lamp, unlighted, standing in the hall on the chest where Grumpygroo usually stood his hat. On it was a lamp-shade made of yellow silk with a fringe of coloured beads. By mistake Mr. Grumpygroo took up the shade instead of his hat. It was so dark that he didn't see the mistake he had made, and he put the lamp-shade on his head! It felt rather like his top-hat, so he didn't notice any difference; and out he walked into the street wearing a bright yellow lamp-shade instead of his old hat.

He looked very funny indeed, for all the beads shook as he walked. Just as he went out of his gate, the clouds fled, the sun came out and all the birds began to sing. It was a perfectly lovely spring day.

Even old Mr. Grumpygroo felt a little bit glad, and he half wished he had a friend who would smile at him. But he knew nobody would, so he set his face into a scowl, and went down the street.

The first person he met was the jolly Balloon woman carrying her load of balloons. As soon as she saw the yellow lamp-shade on Mr. Grumpygroo's head, she smiled, for he looked so very funny.

Grumpygroo thought she was smiling at him, for of course he didn't know what he had on his head, and he was most surprised. He didn't smile back, but went on his way, puzzled to know why the Balloon woman should have looked so friendly

355

for the first time in twenty years.

The next person he met was Mr. Sooty, the village sweep. Mr. Sooty loved a joke, and when he saw the lamp-shade perched on old Grumpygroo's head, he grinned very broadly indeed, and showed all his beautiful white teeth.

Mr. Grumpygroo blinked in surprise. The sweep usually called out something rude after him, and certainly he had never smiled at him before. Could it be the fine spring morning that was making people so friendly?

'I shall smile back at the very next person who smiles at me,' said Grumpygroo to himself, feeling quite excited. 'If people are going to be friendly, I don't mind being nice too.'

Round the corner he met Straws the farmer riding on his old horse. As soon as the farmer caught sight of the lamp-shade, he smiled so widely that his mouth almost reached his ears.

And Grumpygroo smiled back! Straws nearly fell off his horse with astonishment, for no one had ever seen such a thing before! He ambled on, lost in surprise, and Grumpygroo went on his way with a funny warm feeling round his heart.

'I've smiled again!' he said to himself. 'I've forgotten how nice it was. I hope someone else smiles at me,

for I wouldn't mind doing it a second time.'

Four little children came running up the street. As soon as they saw Grumpygroo with the yellow lamp-shade on his head, they smiled and laughed in delight.

Grumpygroo was so pleased. He smiled too, and the ice round his heart melted a little bit more. The children laughed merrily and one of them put her hand in his, for she thought Grumpygroo had put the lamp-shade on to amuse her.

Something funny happened inside Grumpygroo. He wanted to sing and dance. He wanted to give pennies away and hug someone. It was lovely to have people so friendly towards him. He put his hand in his pocket, and brought out four bright pennies. He gave one to each child, and they kissed him and ran to the sweet-shop to spend their money, waving and laughing as they went.

Mr. Grumpygroo rubbed his hands in delight. It was lovely to be smiled at and kissed. He would show the people of Tweedle village what a fine, generous person he was, now that they were being so nice to him!

The next person he met was Mr. Crumbs, the baker. Grumpygroo smiled at him before Mr. Crumbs had time to smile first. The baker was so surprised that he nearly dropped the load of new-made cakes he was carrying. Then he saw Grumpygroo's lamp-shade hat, and he gave a deep chuckle. Grumpygroo was delighted to see him so friendly.

'Good morning,' he said to Crumbs. 'It's a wonderful day, isn't it?'

The baker nodded his head and laughed again.

'Yes,' he said; 'and that's a wonderful hat you're wearing, Mr. Grumpygroo.'

Grumpygroo went on, very much pleased.

'What a nice fellow to admire my old top-hat,' he thought. 'Dear, dear me, and I always thought

the people of Tweedle village were so unpleasant.
That just shows how mistaken I can be!'

He smiled at everyone he met, and everyone
smiled back, wondering why Grumpygroo wore
such a funny thing on his head. The children loved
it, and the old man gave away so many pennies
that he had to change a shilling into twelve more,
or he wouldn't have had enough.

By the time he reached home again, he was
quite a different man. He smiled and hummed a
little tune, and he even did a little jig when he got
into his front garden. He was so happy to think
that people had been friendly to him.

'It shows I can't be so grumpy and cross as
they thought I was,' he said to himself. 'Well, well,
I'll show them what a fine man I am. I'll give a
grand party, and invite everyone in the village to it.
Whatever will they say to that!'

He walked into his hall, and was just going to
take off his hat when he saw himself in the glass.
He stood and stared in surprise and dismay –
whatever *had* he got on his head!

'Oh my, oh my, it's the lamp-shade!' he groaned,
and he took it off. 'Fancy going out in that! And oh
dear! Everyone smiled at the lamp-shade, because
it looked so funny – they didn't smile at *me*!'

How upset Grumpygroo was! He sat down in his armchair and thought about it, and after a while he became very much ashamed of himself.

'How dreadful to have to wear a lamp-shade on my head before people will smile at me!' he groaned. 'I must be a most unpleasant old man. Well, well! I don't see why I shouldn't have my party. Perhaps the village folk will learn to smile at me for myself if I am nice to them. I'll send out those invitations at once!'

He did – and wasn't everybody surprised!

'Fancy old Grumpygroo giving a party!' they

said. 'Something must have happened to make him nicer! Do you remember how funny he looked yesterday when he wore that lamp-shade?'

The party was a great success, and soon old Grumpygroo had heaps of friends. Nobody could imagine what had changed the old fellow and made him so nice, nor could anyone understand why he kept his old yellow lamp-shade so carefully, long after it was dirty and torn.

But Grumpygroo knew why! It had brought him smiles and plenty of friends – but he wasn't going to tell anyone that – not he!

The Fairy and the Policeman

One night a fairy wandered into the nursery, where the toys were all talking and playing together. They were delighted to see her, and begged her to tell them all about herself.

'Well, I live under the white lilac bush in the garden,' she said. 'But, you know, I'm afraid I shall soon have to move.'

'Why?' asked the toys in surprise.

'Because,' said the fairy with a shiver, 'a great fat frog has come to live there. I don't mind frogs a bit usually, but this one likes to cuddle close to me, and he *is* so cold and clammy! When I move away from him he gets angry. I am so afraid that he will bring his brothers and sisters there too, and if they all cuddle up to me for warmth I'm sure I shall die!'

'Dear me,' said the toy policeman, in a shocked voice. 'But, you know, my dear little fairy, frogs have no right to go to the place you have made

362

your home. That is trespassing, and isn't allowed.'

'Well, how can I prevent them?' said the fairy. 'They are much stronger than I am.'

'Look,' said the toy policeman, taking a whistle from his pocket. 'Here is a police whistle. Take it home with you to the lilac bush. If those frogs do come, blow it loudly and I will come to your help.'

'Oh, thank you,' said the fairy, and she slipped the whistle into her pocket. Off she went, out of the window, waving merrily to the toys.

And the very next night, just as the toys were playing 'Here we go round the Mulberry Bush,' they heard the police whistle being blown very loudly indeed.

'The fairy is whistling for help!' cried the policeman, and he jumped out of the window. He ran to the white lilac bush, and underneath he saw such a strange sight.

There were seven yellow and green frogs, all crowding round the poor little fairy, and she was *so* frightened. The policeman drew his truncheon, and began to smack the frogs smartly. Smack! Smack! They squeaked and croaked in pain and began to hop away.

The fairy threw her arms round the brave policeman's neck and hugged him.

'Come back to the nursery with me,' begged the toy policeman. 'You'll be safe there. I'm afraid the frogs might come back again when you are asleep.'

So the fairy went back to the nursery with the policeman, and all the toys welcomed her. She played games with them and had a perfectly lovely time. When they were hungry they went to the little toy sweet-shop and bought some peppermint rock. It was great fun!

'I do wish I could live here with you,' said the fairy. 'It's so jolly.'

'Well, why can't you?' asked the policeman. 'There's plenty of room in the toy cupboard. We can hide you right at the back.'

So that night the fairy slept in the toy cupboard with all the other toys – and what do you think? Early the next morning Gwen, the little girl who lived in the nursery, went to the cupboard and began to pull all the toys out. Oh, how the fairy trembled!

'Keep quite still and pretend you are a toy doll,' whispered the policeman. So she did.

'Oh, oh! Here's a beautiful fairy doll!' cried Gwen, suddenly seeing the fairy. 'Where did she come from? Oh, Mummy, look!'

She pulled out the doll and showed it to her

mother. The fairy kept so still and made herself so stiff that she really did look just like a fairy doll.

'Isn't she beautiful?' cried the little girl. 'Where did she come from, Mummy?'

'Well, really, I don't know,' said Mummy, surprised. 'I've never seen her before. It's the nicest toy you have, Gwen.'

Gwen played with the fairy doll all day long and loved her very much. The fairy was delighted, and when night came and all the toys came alive once more, she danced round the nursery in joy.

'I shall be a toy now instead of a fairy,' she cried. 'I shall live with you in the cupboard and be happy.'

'Hurrah!' shouted the toys. 'What fun!'

The fairy is still there, and Gwen is very fond of her. Wouldn't she be surprised if she knew that her doll is really a fairy?

The Little Red Squirrel

Once upon a time Leslie and Gladys went to look for nuts. They hunted in the hazel hedges, but not a single nut could they find. They looked for the bigger hazel trees, but even there they could only find two or three nuts.

'We shall never get our basket full,' said Gladys. 'I wonder where the best nuts are? The children we saw coming home from nutting last week had hundreds of nuts.'

'Well, perhaps that's why we can't find any,' said Leslie. 'They've picked them all.'

'Listen!' said Gladys, stopping. 'There are some other children in the woods this morning.'

'Let's see if they know any good nut trees,' said Leslie. So the two children ran between the trees and came to where three boys were.

And what do you suppose they were doing? You will never guess, because it was so horrid.

They had found a little red squirrel up an oak tree and they were throwing stones at it! Wasn't it unkind? The oak tree was standing quite alone with no other trees near it, so that the little squirrel couldn't jump to another tree and escape that way. It did not dare to run down the trunk of the oak tree, for it was afraid it would be hit.

So there it sat up in the tree, looking as frightened as could be! When Gladys and Leslie saw what was happening they were very angry and upset. They rushed up to the boys and shouted to them:

'Stop! Stop! You mustn't do that! That is very cruel!'

368

But the boys only laughed. So what do you think Leslie did? He climbed quickly up the tree, and then said, 'Now throw stones if you like! And if you hit *me* my sister will tell the keeper of the wood, and you will all get into trouble!'

Well, the boys did not dare to throw stones when Leslie was in the tree, so they stopped, and very soon went away. Leslie slid down the tree. Gladys hugged him.

'That was a brave thing to do, Leslie,' she said. 'The boys might have gone on throwing stones and hit you hard.'

The red squirrel peered down at the two children. It had a dear little face with big black eyes. Its tail was very bushy. It made a little chattering noise and came bounding down the tree to Gladys and Leslie.

'Oh, it's quite tame,' said Gladys, pleased. The squirrel bounded to their basket and looked inside. Gladys wondered if it wanted a nut, so she held one of her few nuts out to the little creature. But it did not take it. Instead it ran off between some bushes. Then it stopped and looked back at the children and made a chattering noise again.

'Look!' said Gladys. 'I believe it wants us to follow it, Leslie! Come on!'

They ran after the squirrel. It went on again and took them down a tiny path made by rabbits. The children followed; and then they suddenly saw what the red squirrel was leading them to!

He knew where the best nuts were to be found! He ran to a group of hazel trees that no one had been to – and dear me, you should have seen the nuts on their branches! There were dozens and dozens – big, ripe, and so pretty in their green cloaks.

'Oooh!' cried Leslie. 'Look! We can get a basketful in no time.'

And so they did. They pulled the ripe nuts down by the handful, and soon their basket was overflowing. The children turned to thank the little red squirrel. It was sitting up in a nearby tree, watching them out of its big bright eyes, its bushy tail curled upright behind it.

'Thank you, little red squirrel,' cried the children. 'It was kind of you to show us where these fine nut trees grew.'

The squirrel made a funny little noise that sounded like 'Don't mention it!' and bounded off into the trees. The children went home – and on the way whom did they see but the three unkind boys!

'Look!' cried the boys, pointing to Leslie's full basket. 'Look. What lovely nuts! Where did you get them from?'

'That's our secret,' said Leslie. 'The little red squirrel you were teasing took us to some wonderful nut trees. If you had been kind to him he might have shown them to you too. You ought to be ashamed of treating a pretty little creature so cruelly!'

The boys said no more. They ran off – but I expect they wished they had been kind too, don't you?

The Little Walking House

If it hadn't been for Puppy-Dog Pincher the adventure would never have happened. Jill and Norman were taking him for a walk in Cuckoo Wood, and he was mad with joy. He tore here, there and everywhere, barking and jumping for all he was worth.

The children laughed at him, especially when he tumbled head over heels and rolled over and over on the grass. He was such a fat, roly-poly puppy, and they loved him very much.

Then something happened. Pincher dived under a bramble bush, and came out with something in his mouth. It was a string of small sausages!

'Now wherever could he have got those from?' said Jill, in surprise. She soon knew, for out from under the bush ran a little fellow dressed in red and yellow, with a pointed cap on his head. He wasn't much taller than the puppy, but he had a very big voice.

'You bad dog!' he shouted. 'You've stolen the sausages I bought for dinner! Bring them back at once or I'll turn you into a mouse!'

Pincher took no notice. He galloped about with the sausages, enjoying himself very much. Then he sat down to eat them! That was too much for the small man. He rushed at Pincher and struck him on the nose with a tiny silver stick. At the same time he shouted out a string of words so strange that Jill and Norman felt quite frightened. They knew they were magic words,

although they had never heard any before.

And then, before their eyes Pincher began to grow small! He grew smaller and smaller and smaller and smaller, and at last he was as tiny as a mouse. In fact, he *was* a mouse, though he didn't know it! He couldn't think what had happened to him. He scampered up to Jill and Norman, barking in a funny little mouse-like squeak.

The children were dreadfully upset. They picked up the tiny mouse and stroked him. Then they looked for the little man to ask him if he would please change Pincher back to a dog again.

But he had gone. Not a sign of him or his sausages was to be seen. Norman crawled under the bramble bush, but there was nothing there but dead leaves.

'Oh, Jill, whatever shall we do?' he said. 'We can't take Pincher home like this. Nobody would believe he was Pincher, and he might easily be caught by a cat.'

Jill began to cry. She did so love Pincher, and it was dreadful to think he was only a mouse now, not a jolly, romping puppy-dog.

'That must have been a gnome or a brownie,' she said, wiping her eyes. 'Well, Norman, I'm not going home with Pincher like that. Let's go farther into the wood and see if we meet any more little folk. If there's one here, there must be others. We'll ask them for help if we meet them.'

So they went on down the little winding path. Norman carried Pincher in his pocket, for there was plenty of room there for the little dog, now that he was only a mouse.

After they had gone a good way they saw the strangest little house. It had two legs underneath it, and it stood with its back to the children. Norman caught hold of Jill's arm and pointed to it in amazement. They had never seen a house with legs before.

'Oh!' cried Jill, stopping in surprise. 'It's got legs!'

The house gave a jump when it heard Jill's voice, and then, oh goodness me, it ran off! Yes, it really did! You should have seen its little legs twinkling as it scurried away between the trees. The children were too astonished to run after the house. They stood and stared.

'This is a funny part of Cuckoo Wood,' said Norman. 'I say, Jill! Look! There are some more of those houses with legs!'

Jill looked. Sure enough, in a little clearing stood about six more of the houses. Each of them had a pair of legs underneath, and shoes on their big feet. They stood about, sometimes moving a step or two, and even stood on one leg now and again, which made the house they belonged to look very lopsided.

Jill and Norman walked towards the funny houses – but dear me, as soon as they were seen those houses took to their heels and ran off as fast as ever they could! The children ran after them, but they couldn't run fast enough.

They were just going to give up when they saw one of the houses stop. It went on again, but it limped badly.

'We could catch that one!' said Jill. 'Come on, Norman!'

They ran on and in a few minutes they had caught up the limping house. Just as they got near it the door opened and a pixie looked out. She was very lovely, for her curly golden hair was as fine as spider's thread, and her wings shone like dragonfly wings.

'What's the matter, little house?' they heard her say. 'Why are you limping?'

Then she saw the children and she stared at them in surprise.

'Oh, so that's why the houses ran off!' she said. 'They saw you coming! Could you help me, please, children? I think my house has a stone in one of its shoes, and I'm not strong enough to get it out all by myself.'

Jill and Norman were only too ready to help. Norman held up one side of the house whilst the house put up one of its feet to have its big shoe off. The pixie and Jill found a big stone in the shoe, and after they had shaken it out they put on the shoe again. The little house made a creaking noise that sounded just like 'Thank you!'

'What a funny house you've got!' said Jill to the pixie.

'What's funny about it?' asked the pixie in surprise, shaking back her long curly hair. 'It's just the same as all my friends' houses.'

'But it's got legs!' said Norman. 'Where we come from, houses don't have legs at all. They just stand square on the ground and never move at all, once they are built.'

'They sound silly sort of houses,' said the pixie. 'Suppose an enemy came? Why, your house couldn't run away! Mine's a much better house than yours.'

'Oh, much better,' agreed Jill. 'I only wish I lived in a house like this. It would be lovely. You'd go to sleep at night and wake up in a different place in the morning, because the house might wander miles away.'

'I say, pixie, I wonder if you could help us!' suddenly said Norman. He took the little mouse out of his pocket. 'Look! This was our puppy-dog not long ago and a nasty little man changed him into a mouse. Could you change him back into a dog again?'

'Oh no,' said the pixie. 'You want very strong magic for that. I only know one person who's got the right magic for your mouse, and that's High-Hat the Giant.'

'Where does he live?' asked Jill eagerly.

'Miles away from here,' said the pixie. 'You have to go to the Rainbow's End, and then fly up to Cloud-Castle just half-way up the rainbow.'

'Goodness, we couldn't possibly go there,' said Jill. 'We haven't wings like you, Pixie.'

'Well, Dumpy the gnome lives near the Rainbow's End,' said the pixie. 'He keeps pigs that fly, you know, so he might lend you two of them. But I don't know if High-Hat the Giant will help you, even if you go to him. He's a funny-tempered fellow, and if he's in a bad humour he won't do anything for anybody.'

'Well, we might try,' said Norman. 'Which is the way to the Rainbow's End?'

'It depends where there's a rainbow to-day,' said the pixie. 'I know! I'll get my house to take you there. It always knows the way to anywhere. Come inside and we'll start. You helped me to get the stone out of my house's shoe, and I'd like to help you in return.'

The children went inside the house, feeling

most excited. Norman had Pincher the mouse safely in his pocket. Pincher kept barking in his squeaky voice, for he couldn't understand how it was that Jill and Norman had grown so big! He didn't know that it was himself that had grown small.

The pixie shut the door, and told the children to sit down. It was a funny house inside, more like a carriage than a house, for a bench ran all round the wall. A table stood in the middle of the room and on it were some dishes and cups. In a corner a kettle boiled on a stove, and a big grandfather clock ticked in another corner.

The clock had two feet underneath it, like the house, and it gave the children quite a fright when it suddenly walked out from its corner, had a look at them and then walked back.

'Don't take any notice of it,' said the pixie. 'It hasn't any manners, that old clock. Would you like a cup of cocoa and some daffodil biscuits?'

'Oooh yes, please,' said both the children at once, wondering whatever daffodil biscuits were. The pixie made a big jug of cocoa and put some funny yellow biscuits on a plate, the shape of a daffodil trumpet. They tasted delicious, and as for the cocoa, it was lovely – not a bit like ordinary cocoa, but more like chocolate and lemonade mixed together. The children did enjoy their funny meal.

Before the pixie made the cocoa she spoke to her house. 'Take us to the Rainbow's End,' she said. 'And be as quick as you can.'

To the children's great delight the house began to run. They felt as if they were on the sea, or on the elephant's back at the Zoo, for the house rocked from side to side as it scampered along. Jill looked out of the window. They were soon out of the wood, and came to a town.

'Norman, look! There are hundreds of fairy

folk here!' cried Jill, in excitement. So there were – crowds of them, going about shopping, talking and wheeling funny prams with the dearest baby fairies inside. The grandfather clock walked out of its corner to the window too, and trod on Jill's toe. It certainly had no manners, that clock.

They passed right through the town and went up a hill where little blue sheep were grazing. Looking after them was a little girl exactly like Bopeep. The pixie said yes, it really was Bopeep. That was where she lived. It was a most exciting journey, and the children were very sorry when they saw a great rainbow in the distance. They knew they were coming to the end of their journey in the walking house.

The little house stopped when it came to one end of the rainbow. The children stepped outside. There was the rainbow, glittering marvellously. It was very, very wide, far wider than a road and the colours were almost too bright to look at.

'Now High-Hat the Giant lives halfway up,' said the pixie, pointing. 'Come along, I'll take you to Dumpy the gnome, and see if he has a couple of pigs to spare you.'

She took them to a squat little house not far from the rainbow. Outside was a big yard and in

it were a crowd of very clean pigs, bright pink and shining. Each of them had pink wings on his back, so they looked very strange to Jill and Norman.

'Hie, Dumpy, are you at home?' cried the pixie. The door of the house flew open and a fat gnome with twinkling eyes peeped out.

'Yes, I'm at home,' he said. 'What can I do for you?'

'These children want to fly to High-Hat's,' said the pixie. 'But they haven't wings. Could you lend them two of your pigs?'

'Yes, if they'll promise to be kind to them,' said Dumpy. 'The last time I lent out my pigs someone whipped them and all the curl came out of their tails.'

'Oh, these children helped me to take a stone out of my house's shoe,' said the pixie, 'so I know they're kind. You can trust them. Which pigs can they have, Dumpy?'

'This one and that one,' said the fat little gnome, and he drove two plump pigs towards the children. 'Catch hold of their tails, children, and jump on. Hold on to their collars, and, whatever you do, speak kindly to them or the curl will come out of their tails.'

Jill and Norman caught hold of the curly tails of the two pigs and jumped on. The pigs' backs were rather slippery, but they managed to stay on. Suddenly the fat little animals rose into the air, flapped their pink wings and flew up the shining rainbow. It was such a funny feeling. The pigs talked to one another in little squeals, and the children were careful to pat them kindly in case the curl came out of their tails.

In ten minutes they came to a towering castle, set right in the middle of the rainbow. It was

wreathed in clouds at the top, and was made of a
strange black stone that reflected all the rainbow
colours in a very lovely manner. It
didn't *seem* a real castle, but it
felt real enough when the
children touched it. They
jumped off the pigs'
backs and patted
them gratefully.

'Stay here, dear
little pigs, till we
come out again,'
said Norman. Then
he and Jill climbed
up the long flight of
shining black steps

to the door of the castle. There was a big knocker on it shaped like a ship. Norman knocked. The noise went echoing through the sky just like thunder, and quite frightened the two children.

'Come in!' called a deep voice from inside the castle. Norman pushed open the door and went in. He found himself in a great high room full of a pale silvery light that looked like moonlight. Sitting at a table, frowning hard, was a giant.

He was very, very big, so big that Jill wondered if he could possibly stand upright in the high room. He was sucking a pencil and looking crossly at a book in front of him.

'Good morning,' said Norman politely.

'It isn't a good morning at all,' said the giant snappily. 'It's a bad morning. One of the very worst. I can't get these sums right again.'

'Well, bad morning, then,' said Jill. 'We've come to ask your help.'

'I'm not helping anyone to-day,' growled the giant. 'I tell you I can't get these sums right. Go away.'

'We *must* get his help,' whispered Norman to Jill. 'We'll keep on trying.'

'What sums are they?' Jill asked the giant. To her great surprise High-Hat suddenly picked her up in his great hand and set her by him on the table. When she had got over her fright Jill looked at the giant's book.

She nearly laughed out loud when she saw the sums that were puzzling the giant. This was one of them: 'If two hens, four dogs and one giant went for a walk together, how many legs would you see?'

'I'll tell you the answer to that,' she said. 'It's twenty-two!'

The giant turned to the end of the book and looked. 'Yes!' he said in astonishment. 'You're right! But how did you know that? Do another sum, please.'

Jill did all the sums. They were very easy indeed. The giant wrote down the answers in enormous figures, and then sucked his pencil whilst Jill thought of the next one.

When they were all finished Norman thought it was time to ask for help again.

'Could you help us now?' he asked. 'We've helped *you*, you know.'

'I tell you, this is one of my bad mornings,' said the giant crossly. 'I never help people on a bad morning. Please go away, and shut the door after you.'

Jill and Norman stared at him in despair. What a nasty giant he was, after all the help they had given him too! It really was too bad.

'I don't believe you know any magic at all!' said Jill. 'You're just a fraud! Why, you couldn't even do easy sums!'

The giant frowned till the children could scarcely see his big saucer-like blue eyes. Then he jumped up in a rage and hit his head hard against the ceiling. He sat down again.

'For saying a rude thing like that I will punish you!' he growled, in a thunderous voice. 'Now listen! You can sit there all the year long and ask me to do one thing after another so that I can show you my power – and the first time you can't think of anything I'll turn you into ladybirds!'

Goodness! Jill and Norman turned quite pale. But in a trice Norman took the little brown mouse out of his pocket and showed it to the giant.

'You couldn't possibly turn this mouse into a puppy-dog, I'm sure!' he cried.

The giant gave a snort and banged his hand on the table. 'Homminy, tinkabooroyillabee, juteray, bong!' he cried, and as soon as the magic words were said, hey presto, the little mouse grew bigger and bigger and bigger, and there was Puppy-dog Pincher again, as large as life, and full of joy at being able to run and jump again. But the giant left the children no time to be glad.

'Next thing, please!' he cried.

'Go to the moon and back!' cried Jill suddenly. In a trice High-Hat had vanished completely.

'Quick, he's gone to the moon!' cried Jill. 'Come on, Norman, we'll escape before he comes back!'

Out of the castle door they ran, Pincher scampering after them. The two pigs were patiently waiting outside on the rainbow at the bottom of the castle steps. Jill and Norman jumped on their backs, Norman carrying the puppy in his arms. Then quickly the flying pigs rose into the air and flew back to the end of the rainbow.

Just as they got there they heard a tremendous noise far up in the air.

'It's the giant, come back from the moon!' said Jill. 'Goodness, what a noise he's making! It sounds like a thunderstorm.'

The pixie came running to meet them.

'Is that High-Hat making all that noise?' she asked, looking frightened. 'Give the pigs back to Dumpy, and climb into my house again with me. The next thing that happens will be High-Hat sliding down the rainbow after you, and we'd better be gone before he arrives. He'll be in a dreadful temper!'

The pigs were given back to the twinkling gnome, and then the children climbed into the walking

house with the pixie and Pincher. Off they went at a great rate, far faster than before. Pincher couldn't understand it. He began to bark and that annoyed the grandfather clock very much. It suddenly came out of its corner and boxed Pincher's ears.

'I'm so sorry,' said the pixie. 'It's a very bad-mannered clock. I only keep it because it's been in my family for so many years. By the way, where do you want to go to?'

'Oh, home, please!' begged the children.

'Right!' said the pixie. Just as she said that there came the sound of a most tremendous BUMP, and the whole earth shook and shivered.

'There! That's the giant slid down the rainbow!' said the pixie. 'I knew he would bump himself.'

The house went on and on. When it came to a sunshiny stretch of road it skipped as if it were happy.

'Here you are!' suddenly cried the pixie, opening her door. And sure enough, there they were! They were in their very own garden at home!

The children jumped out and turned to call Pincher, who was barking in excitement. The grandfather clock suddenly ran out of its corner and smacked him as he went.

'Oh dear, I'm so sorry!' cried the pixie. 'It hasn't any manners at all, I'm afraid. Well, see you another day! Good-bye, good-bye!'

The little house ran off, and the children watched it go. What an adventure they had had! And thank goodness Pincher wasn't a mouse any longer, but a jolly, jumping puppy-dog!

'Come on, Pincher!' cried Norman. 'Come and tell Mother all about your great adventure!'

Off they went and, dear me, Mother *was* surprised to hear their strange and exciting story!

Sly-One's Puzzle

Sly-One, the brownie, took up his basket of eggs and butter and set off through the woods to Mother Twinkle's cottage. As he went, he counted the steps he took, for, like you, he sometimes counted things like that, just for fun. When he got to Mother Twinkle's cottage he knocked at the door and gave her the butter.

'It is exactly seven thousand steps from my door to yours,' he told her. 'Would you think it was so far? It took me eighty minutes to get here.'

Then off he went to call on Mister Snips with the eggs. He counted his steps again, just for fun, and to his very great astonishment he found it was exactly seven thousand again, from Mother Twinkle's to Mister Snips's. He looked at his watch and found that it had taken him eighty minutes, as before. Most extraordinary!

Then he turned his steps homeward, and once

again he counted them – and what do you think? It was seven thousand steps from Mister Snips's door to Sly-One's own little cottage. 'So the distance between each place must be the same,' thought Sly-One. 'This is very strange. When I go out to tea this afternoon I will tell the others.'

So that afternoon Sly-One looked round the tea-table and told his little story – but he thought he would puzzle everyone, so this is how he told it:

'Listen to me. This morning I went to Mother Twinkle's, and I walked seven thousand steps, and it took me eighty minutes. Then I walked from there to Mister Snips's and I took seven thousand steps again in eighty minutes. And then I walked home, and again I took seven thousand steps – but whatever do you suppose? – I took *an hour and twenty minutes* that time. Why do you think that was?'

'Don't be silly, Sly-One,' said Gobo. 'If you took the same number of steps you couldn't have taken an hour and twenty minutes. But perhaps you walked more slowly because you were tired.'

'No, I wasn't tired,' said Sly-One. 'I walked just the same pace – really I did.'

'Very puzzling!' said Tubby, frowning. 'Well, you must have stopped to talk to someone.'

'No, I didn't,' said Sly-One. 'I didn't meet anyone at all. I just went on steadily.'

'Now, just think a minute!' said Burly. 'Didn't you stop to do up your shoe-lace, or pick up your handkerchief, or gather a few flowers?'

'No,' said Sly-One, 'I didn't do any of those things.'

'Well, you must have made a mistake, then,' said Gobo. 'It couldn't have taken you *an hour and twenty minutes* to go exactly the same distance. Your watch must have told you wrong.'

'My watch keeps perfect time,' said Sly-One with a grin. 'Do you mean to tell me that not one of you clever brownies can tell me what I want to know? Really, I didn't think you were so stupid!'

'It's *you* who are stupid!' said Gobo. 'You can't have taken an hour and twenty minutes that third time. You must have taken eighty minutes as you did the first two times.'

'Well,' said Sly-One, 'I did! Eighty minutes *is* an hour and twenty minutes, isn't it? Ho, ho, ho! What a joke! I wonder how many people could see through my puzzle at once!'

Well, children, did *you*?

Mr. Widdle on the Train

Once a month Mr. Widdle went to see his old mother. He walked to the station, caught the train that went at ten o'clock, spent the day with the old lady, and then came home by the four o'clock train.

And very often when he came home he looked as white as Mrs. Widdle's front doorstep, and could hardly eat any tea at all. Then Mrs. Widdle would shake her head and say: 'Really, Mister Widdle, you are no good on a train journey. It does upset you so!'

'I know why it upsets me,' said Mister Widdle one day. 'I always feel ill when I sit with my *back* to the engine. Now the other day I sat *facing* the engine and I was quite all right. Isn't that strange?'

'But, Widdle dear,' said Mrs. Widdle, 'if that is all that is wrong with you when you travel, we can soon put that right.'

'How?' asked Mr. Widdle in surprise.

'Why, whenever you get into a carriage and find you are sitting with your back to the engine, you must just lean forward to the person in the opposite seat and say: "Madam (or Sir, if it's a man), I wonder if you will be so kind as to change places with me, as I always feel ill if I sit with my back to the engine." Then you will change seats and be quite all right.'

'Oh, but I couldn't say all that to a stranger,' said Mister Widdle, who was a very shy man.

'Oh yes you can if you practise it,' said Mrs. Widdle. 'Now pretend I am the person opposite, Widdle dear, and say that speech to me.'

So Mister Widdle practised saying it till he knew it off by heart. He felt very pleased. Now he would always be able to change places with anyone, and could sit facing the engine and never feel ill. How splendid!

When the day came for him to go to see his old mother, he set off happily, but alas! when he arrived home again that night he looked just as white as ever, and so ill that Mrs. Widdle bundled him into bed at once.

'I *am* disappointed in you, Widdle,' she said. 'I did think you would say that speech you practised.'

'Well, my dear,' said Mister Widdle, 'it was quite

all right when I caught the train at ten o'clock. I got into the carriage and sat down. I began to feel ill because I had my back to the engine, and so I leaned over to the little boy opposite and said: "I wonder if you'd be so kind as to change places with me, as I always feel ill if I sit with my back to the engine." And the nice little chap raised his cap and said: "Certainly, sir, I don't mind at all." So we changed places, and I felt as well as could be.'

'Well, go on,' said Mrs. Widdle. 'What happened coming home? Did you sit with your back to the engine then?'

'Yes,' said Mister Widdle.

'But, Widdle, you are foolish!' cried Mrs. Widdle crossly. 'Why didn't you change places with the person opposite you again?'

'I am *not* foolish!' said Mister Widdle, his nose in the air. 'I *would* have changed places – but there was nobody there to change places with!'

Then, to Mister Widdle's surprise, Mrs. Widdle began to laugh and laugh and laugh. 'Oh!' she said, wiping her tears away, 'you are even more foolish than I thought you were!'

Poor Mister Widdle couldn't *think* why. Can you?

Who Stole the Crown?

The King of Pixieland had two crowns. One was a summer crown, made of gold, light and easy to wear. The other was also made of gold, but it had a warm winter lining of red velvet, for the pixie King suffered from cold ears.

In the winter-time, when the King wore his warm crown, the summer crown was placed in a safe place, locked up in a box in the middle of a hollow tree. Nobody knew where it was except the King himself, and Pointy, the keeper of the crown.

One wintry day, when Pointy went to get out the summer crown to give it a polish-up, he found it was gone! Goodness, what a state he was in! He looked up and down the hollow tree, he ran all round it in the thick snow – for it was a bitterly cold winter's day and snowing hard – and he looked everywhere he could think of. But it was no use; the crown was gone.

'Oh, oh, oh, it's gone!' cried Pointy, in a great way. 'It's been stolen! Who did it? Who did it?'

He ran to the King and told him. The King sent his soldiers to hunt through the wood, but all in vain. The golden crown was gone.

'What shall I do when summer comes?' wondered the King. 'I can't wear *this* heavy crown – and I can't afford to buy another. Dear me, this is very annoying. I wonder who could have found my crown and stolen it. If I knew the thief I could go and search his house and see if the crown was there.'

'Your Majesty,' said Pointy, suddenly, 'you have heard of Little-cap, the pixie, I expect? Well, folk say he is very clever indeed. Shall we ask him to come here and find out the thief for us? He boasts that he can solve any mystery, so maybe he can help us.'

'Send for him at once,' ordered the King. So Little-cap was sent for, and he came. He was a funny little pixie. The King looked at him and wondered if he even knew that twice times two were four, he was so little and so babyish.

He was dressed in a yellow tunic with green buttons, and on his head was a funny little cap of yellow, with bells all round it. They tinkled whenever Little-cap thought hard, and were silent when he wasn't thinking about anything much.

Little-cap took off his hat when he came before the King, for it was not polite to keep it on. He bowed very low and went red with excitement.

'I hear you can solve mysteries,' said the King.

'Well, I have tried to,' said Little-cap. 'Most mysteries are easy to solve if you think about them hard enough. Have *you* a mystery for me to solve?'

'Yes,' said the King, and he told Little-cap about his stolen crown. The pixie listened without saying a word.

'Now,' said the King, when the tale was told, 'can you find out who stole my crown?'

'Yes, I think so,' said the pixie, smiling all over his babyish face. 'I just want to know a few things first.'

'Ask any question you like,' said the King.

Little-cap put on his hat and thought hard. All the bells rang loudly.

'First,' said Little-cap, 'please tell me the names of all who live in the wood where you kept your crown.'

Pointy stepped forward and told the pixie all who lived in the wood.

'There is Prickles, the hedgehog,' he said. 'There is Bushy, the squirrel. There is Dozy, the dormouse, and Sly-one, the snake. There is Crawler, the toad, and Hopper, the frog, who lives in the pond in the middle of the wood. And there is Floppy, the rabbit, too, of course, and all the little folk as well. But they had all gone to a party that day and the wood was empty of them. So you can rule out any of the little folk. It was one of the four-footed creatures – but which one?'

'It's a puzzle,' said the King, sighing.

Little-cap thought again, and all the bells on his hat jingled merrily.

'One more question,' he said. 'What sort of a day was it when the crown was stolen?'

'Oh, the weather was terribly bad,' said the King, shivering. 'I remember the day well because my ears were cold even under my red velvet crown. It was snowing hard and there was a bitter wind. That was why we couldn't see any footprints, you see – because the snow was falling and had covered up any marks.'

'I see, I see,' said Little-cap, and he put his head down upon his chest. Once more the bells on his hat rang loudly and cheerfully.

'It's a terrible puzzle, isn't it?' said the King. 'I'm afraid it's too deep a mystery for you, Little-cap.'

'Not at all,' said the pixie, raising his head and looking at the King with a smile. 'It's easy. I was only just wondering why the thief took your crown, because it would look so silly on him.'

'What! Do you know who the thief was?' cried the King, in astonishment.

'Oh yes,' said Little-cap. 'Of course I do.'

'But how do you know?' asked the King, only half believing him. 'Why, you haven't even been to look at the tree or the wood or anything!'

'I don't need to,' said Little-cap, getting up from his seat. 'Why, Your Majesty, if you thought for a few moments about what you have just told me, *you* would know who was the thief, too.'

'Well, who *is* the thief?' asked the King, impatiently.

'Floppy, the rabbit,' said Little-cap. 'Send your soldiers to look through his burrow. The crown will be there.'

Pointy at once sent off six soldiers to Floppy's burrow. The rabbit was sitting just inside and when he saw the soldiers, his nose began to woffle up and down in fright.

'W-w-w-w-what do you w-w-w-want?' he said.

'We've come to search your burrow,' said the Captain. 'See, here is a note from the King to give us permission.'

He showed the frightened rabbit the King's scribbled order and Floppy shook from whiskers to tail.

'We've come to find the crown you stole from the hollow tree,' said the Captain. 'If you'll tell us where you've put it, we needn't turn your burrow upside-down.'

Then the rabbit began to cry loudly, and woffled his nose so fast that the soldiers could hardly see it.

'It's in my b-b-b-b-bedroom!' stammered the rabbit, miserably, weeping big tears down his whiskers. 'I'll go and get it.'

'No, you won't,' said the Captain, catching hold of the rabbit firmly. 'I know you rabbits – you're in at one hole and out at the other before anyone can wink an eye! Yes, you'd just whip up the crown and run off before anyone could stop you! You stay here and I'll send a couple of soldiers to your bedroom.'

Two soldiers went down the burrow. They soon came to the big hole where the rabbit slept. It was lined with dry grass and leaves and was a cosy, warm place. Under the leaves was the crown! Yes, really, there it was, dazzling bright, the King's beautiful summer crown.

The rabbit and the crown were both taken to the King. He was delighted to see his crown, and he frowned angrily at the wicked rabbit.

'Take him to the castle and lock him up underground,' he ordered.

'Oh no,' said Little-cap, the pixie. 'Don't do that! Put him in the highest tower!'

'Why?' asked the King, in astonishment.

'Because rabbits love to be underground,' answered Little-cap. 'Floppy will simply dig a tunnel and escape! But put him in a high tower and he'll be safe!'

So the rabbit was marched off to a high tower. Then the King turned to Little-cap and begged him to explain how he had solved the mystery in such a short time.

'Well,' said the pixie, with a laugh, 'I knew it was Floppy, because the rabbit was the only one of those seven creatures out that day.'

'How do you know that?' asked the King. 'How

do you know it wasn't Dozy, the dormouse, or Sly-one, the snake?'

'Because the dormouse sleeps hard all the winter through and never wakes, and the snake sleeps too, curled up with his brothers in the tree at the edge of the wood,' said Little-cap. 'Dormice and snakes are never about in the winter.'

'Well, what about Hopper, the frog?' said the King.

'The frog always sleeps in the pond during the winter,' said the pixie. 'It was frozen over that day, so it couldn't have been Hopper, even if he had woken up.'

'Why couldn't it have been Crawler, the toad?' asked Pointy.

'The toad crawls under a stone and goes to sleep in the cold weather,' said Little-cap, smiling. 'He never wakes up till the spring-time. All toads and frogs sleep the winter through.'

'Well, Bushy, the squirrel, and Prickles, the hedgehog, don't sleep all the winter through,' said the King. 'It might have been them, mightn't it? Bushy is often out on a sunny winter's day, looking for the nuts he hid in the autumn – and as for Prickles, I've sometimes met him snuffling about the ditches on a warm night in winter!'

'Quite right,' said Little-cap, nodding his head. 'Quite right – but you will remember, Your Majesty, that Pointy said it was bad weather with a bitter wind when the crown was stolen, and both squirrels and hedgehogs curl themselves up tighter than ever and sleep deeply in weather like that. So it couldn't have been them.'

'Well,' said the King, thinking hard, 'well, that only leaves Floppy the rabbit.'

'Exactly,' said the pixie, with a grin. 'That's just what I thought! And I was right! It's quite easy to solve a mystery when you think hard enough, isn't it, Your Majesty!'

And off he went, humming a little tune, while all the bells on his hat tinkled and rang.

'Well, well!' said the King. 'We might have been just as clever as Little-cap, if we'd thought!'

'But we *didn't* think!' said Pointy.

'Tell Me My Name!'

The Hoppetty Gnome lived in a little cottage all by himself. He kept no dog and no cat, but outside in the garden lived a fat, freckled thrush who sang to Hoppetty each morning and evening to thank him for the crumbs he put out.

Hoppetty was very fond of this thrush. She was a pretty bird, and the songs she sang were very lovely.

> *'The sky is blue, blue!*
> *And all day through, through,*
> *I sing to you, you!'*

That was the thrush's favourite song, and Hoppetty knew it by heart.

Now one day a dreadful thing happened. Hoppetty was trotting through the wood, going home after his shopping, when out pounced a big black goblin and caught hold of him. He put little

Hoppetty into a sack and ran off with the struggling gnome over hill and meadow until he came to the tall hill on the top of which he lived. Then he emptied Hoppetty out of his sack, and told him he was to be his cook.

'I am very fond of cakes with jam inside,' said the grinning goblin, 'and I love chocolate fingers sprinkled with nut. I have heard that you are a clever cake-maker. Make me these things.'

Poor Hoppetty! How he had to work! The goblin really had a most enormous appetite, and as he ate nothing but jam cakes and chocolate fingers, Hoppetty was busy all day long at the oven, baking, baking. He was always hot and always tired. He wondered and wondered who this strange goblin was, and one day he asked him.

'Who are you, Master?' he said.

'Oho! Wouldn't you like to know?' said the goblin, putting six chocolate fingers into his mouth at once. 'Well, Hoppetty, if you could guess my name, I'd let you go. But you never will!'

Hoppetty sighed. He was sure he never *would* guess the goblin's name. Goblins had such strange names. Nobody ever came to the house, no letters were pushed through the letter-box, and Hoppetty was never allowed to go out. So how could he possibly find out the goblin's name? He tried a few guesses.

'Is your name Thingumebob?'

'Ho, ho, ho! No, no, no!'

'Is it Mankypetoddle?'

'Ho, ho, ho! No, no, no!'

'Well, is it Tiddleywinks?'

'Ho, ho, ho! No, no, no!'

Then Hoppetty sighed and set to work to make more jam cakes, for the goblin had eaten twenty-two for breakfast, and the larder was getting empty.

The goblin went out and banged the door. He locked it too, and went down the path. Hoppetty knew he couldn't get out. He had tried before. The windows opened two inches, and no more. The door he couldn't open at all. He was indeed a prisoner. He sighed again and set to work quickly.

And then he heard something that made his heart leap. It was a bird singing sweetly.

> *'The sky is blue, blue!*
> *And all day through, through,*
> *I sing to you, you!'*

It was his thrush! Hoppetty rushed to the window and looked out of the open crack. There was the pretty freckled bird, sitting in a nearby tree.

'Thrush!' cried Hoppetty. 'I'm here! Oh, you dear creature, have you been going about singing and looking for me? Did you miss your crumbs? I'm a prisoner here. I can only get away if I find out the name of the goblin who keeps me here.'

Just then the goblin came back, and the gnome rushed to his baking once more. The thrush sang sweetly outside for a few minutes and then flew away.

The bird was unhappy. It loved little Hoppetty.

The gnome had been so kind to her, and had loved her singing so very much. If only the thrush could find out the name of the goblin. But how?

The bird made up her mind to watch the goblin and see where he went. So the next day she followed him when he left the cottage, flying from tree to tree as the goblin went on his way. At last he came to another cottage, and, to the thrush's surprise, the door was opened by a black cat with bright green eyes.

'A witch cat!' thought the thrush. 'I wonder if she knows the goblin's name. I dare not ask her, for if I go too near she will spring at me.'

The goblin stayed a little while and then went away. The thrush was about to follow, when the cat brought out a spinning-wheel and set it in the sunshine by the door. She sat down and began to spin her wool.

And as she spun, she sang a strange song.

> *'First of eel, and second of hen,*
> *And after that the fourth of wren.*
> *Third of lean and first of meat,*
> *Second of leg and third of feet.*
> *Fifth of strong and second of pail,*
> *Fourth of hammer and third of nail.*

Sixth of button and third of coat,
First of me and second of boat.
When you've played this curious game,
You may perchance have found his name!'

The cat sang this over and over again, and the thrush listened hard. Soon she knew it by heart and at once flew off to the goblin's cottage. She put her head on one side and looked in at the window. Hoppetty was setting the table for the goblin and was talking to him.

'Is your name Twisty-tail?'

'Ho, ho, ho! No, no, no!' roared the goblin.

'Well, is it Twisty-nose?'

'Ho, ho, ho! No, no, no! And don't you be rude!' snapped the goblin.

'Well, is it Pointed-ears?' asked poor Hoppetty.

'Ho, ho, ho! No, no, no! Give me some more jam cakes!' ordered the goblin.

The next day the thrush waited until the goblin had gone out, and then she began to sing sweetly.

Hoppetty knew that it was his own thrush singing, and he went to the window and listened – but what a peculiar song the bird was whistling! The thrush sang the cat's song over and over again – and suddenly Hoppetty guessed that it was trying to

tell him how to find the goblin's name. He frowned
and thought hard. Yes – he thought he could!

He fetched a pencil and a piece of paper and sat

down. The thrush flew to the window-sill and sang the song slowly. Hoppetty put down the words and then he began to work out the puzzle in great excitement.

'The first of eel – that's E. The second of hen – that's E too. The fourth of wren – that's N. The third of lean – A. The first of meat – M. Second of leg – another E. Third of feet – E again! Fifth of strong, that's N. Second of pail – A. Fourth of hammer – M. Third of nail – I. Sixth of button – N. Third of coat – A. First of me – M, and second of coat – O! Now what do all these letters spell?'

He wrote the letters out in a word, and looked at it – Eena-Meena-Mina-Mo!

'So that's the goblin's name!' cried the gnome in excitement. 'Oh, I would never, never have thought of that!'

The thrush flew off in a hurry, for she heard the goblin returning. He strode into his cottage and scowled when he saw the gnome sitting down writing instead of baking.

'What's all this?' he roared.

'Is your name Tabby-cat?' asked the gnome, with a grin.

'Ho, ho, ho! No, no, no!' cried the goblin. 'Get to your work.'

'Is it – is it – Wibbly-Wobbly?' asked the gnome, pretending to be frightened.

'Ho, ho, ho! No, no, no!' shouted the goblin in a rage. 'Where are my jam cakes?'

'Is it – can it be – Eena-Meena-Mina-Mo?' cried the gnome suddenly.

The goblin stared at Hoppetty and turned pale. 'How do you know that?' he asked, in a frightened whisper. 'No one knows it! No one! Now you have found out my secret name! Oh! Oh! Go, you horrid creature! I am afraid of you! What will you find out next?'

He flung the door wide open, and Hoppetty ran out gladly, shouting:

> *'Eena, Meena, Mina, Mo,*
> *Catch a goblin by his toe;*
> *If he squeals, let him go,*
> *Eena, Meena, Mina, Mo!'*

He skipped all the way home – and there, sitting on his garden gate, was his friend the thrush. You can guess that Hoppetty gave her a fine meal of crumbs, and told her all about how angry and frightened the goblin was!

'I shall bake you a cake for yourself every time I have a baking day,' he promised. And he did – but, as you can guess, he never again made a jam cake or a chocolate finger!

Gooseberry Whiskers

There was once a rascally gnome who sold fine paint-brushes to the fairies. No brushes were half as good as his, for the hairs in them were so fine and strong. 'Where do you get them from?' asked the elves one day. But the gnome wouldn't tell them.

'It's a secret,' he said. 'Perhaps I make them out of moonbeams drawn out long and thin, and snipped off in short pieces!'

'You don't!' cried the elves. 'Oh *do* tell us your secret!'

But he never would – and the reason was that he was afraid to. He got the hairs from sleeping caterpillars, and such a thing was not allowed in Fairyland, as you may guess. Many caterpillars were covered with soft fine hairs, and by pulling a few from this one and a few from that, the little gnome soon had enough for a new brush.

One spring-cleaning time there was a great

demand for his brushes. All through May the elves came to buy from him and the gnome could hardly find enough caterpillars to pull hairs from!

He began to pull more than a few hairs from each. Once he took quite a handful, and the caterpillar woke up with a squeak.

Another furry caterpillar woke up one morning to find that he was quite bald. He hadn't a single hair left and he shivered with cold.

When the Queen passed by the stopped in surprise.

'But who could have taken your hairs away?' she asked the caterpillar. 'No one would do such a naughty thing.'

'Please, Your Majesty, someone must have done it last night,' said the caterpillar.

'And half *my* coat is gone too!' said another.

'And about thirty of my finest hairs have disappeared as well!' cried a third.

'This must be looked into,' said the Queen, sternly.

She called to her guards and spoke to them. 'Twelve of you must remain here to look after these caterpillars,' she commanded. 'You can hide under the hedge, and watch for the thief. Catch him and punish him well.'

The caterpillars crawled to their leaves. Now at

last they would be safe! The twelve guards looked about for good hiding-places, and then played a game of snap until night-time, for they felt sure there would be no sign of the thief until darkness fell. The caterpillars were so interested in the game that they called 'Snap!' when they shouldn't, and made the guards quite cross.

'Don't interfere,' said the captain. 'We are playing, not you. You eat your juicy leaves, and don't disturb us or we will leave you to the robber!'

When night came the soldiers squeezed

themselves into their hiding-places and kept watch. The night was dark, and it was difficult for them to see an inch in front of their noses. Just the night for a robber to come!

Time went on. No thief. Ten o'clock came, eleven o'clock. Still no thief. The guards began to yawn. Surely the robber would not come now.

But at that very moment the little gnome was out on his rounds, looking for furry caterpillars. He was hunting under the leaves, down the stalks, on the ground, and everywhere. He didn't know that anyone was lying in wait for him.

He was very silent. His feet made no sound as he crept along, and he didn't even rustle a leaf.

'Where are all the caterpillars to-night?' he thought. 'I can't seem to find any!'

From bush to bush he went, feeling along the leaves, and at last he really did find a large furry caterpillar, peacefully sleeping.

'Good!' thought the gnome. 'This one has a fine crop of hairs! I can make a fine brush from them.'

He grabbed a big handful from the back of the sleeping caterpillar, and pulled hard. The caterpillar woke up with a loud squeak. 'Eee, eee, eee!' it cried.

At once all the guards sprang up and shouted loudly. 'The robber, the robber!'

The gnome fled away in terror, holding all the hairs in his hand. The guards ran after him, and went crashing through the woods into the palace gardens. Up and down the paths they went, searching for the thief. Where was he? Where had he gone?

The little gnome had found a prickly hiding-place under a big gooseberry bush. He crouched there in fright, wondering what would happen to him if he was found. In his hand he still held the caterpillar hairs. Whatever could he do with them?

'The guards mustn't find them in my hand,' he thought. 'And I daren't throw them away, for they are sure to be found. What *can* I do?'

He put out his hand and felt about. He touched two or three big fat gooseberries – and then an idea came to him. He would stick the hairs on them, for surely no one would think of looking on the fruit for caterpillar hairs!

In a trice he was sticking the hairs on the green smooth surface of the gooseberries. He made them all hairy and whiskery, and just as he had finished, somebody came down the path near-by, and flashed a lantern on to him.

'Here's someone!' they cried. 'Here's the thief! Quick, come and get him!'

The gnome was dragged out and searched. No hairs were found on him, but in his pocket were two brushes that he had forgotten about – and they were made of caterpillar hairs!

'Spank him, spank him well!' cried the captain. 'That will teach him not to steal! Then turn him out of Fairyland for ever!'

So the gnome was spanked very hard, and taken to the gates of Fairyland. They were shut behind him, and out he went, weeping bitterly.

No one has heard of him since – but from

that day to this gooseberries have always grown whiskers. If you don't believe me, go and look for yourself!

The Mean Old Man

Once upon a time there was a mean old man who wouldn't pay his bills. He owed Dame Rustle a lot of money for his newspapers. He owed Mr. Pork shillings and shillings for his meat. Mother Cluck sent him in a bill for milk and eggs time after time, but it was never paid. Really, it was dreadful!

One day they all put their heads together and laid a little plan. They bought a come-back spell from Witch Heyho and took bits of it back to their shops.

And the next day, when Dame Rustle gave a newspaper to old Mister Mean, she tucked a bit of the come-back spell into it. When Mr. Pork sold him a string of sausages, he tucked a come-back spell into them too, and when Mother Cluck let Mister Mean have a basket of new-laid eggs she carefully put a come-back spell at the bottom.

Well, old Mister Mean set off home, carrying

the basket of eggs, the sausages in paper, and the morning newspaper. But before he had got very far a curious thing happened. The come-back spell began to work!

It worked on the newspaper first. The paper grew small legs and tried to get away from under Mister Mean's arm! Mister Mean could not think why it kept slipping. He kept pushing it back under his arm – but still that newspaper wriggled and wriggled and at last it fell to the ground. No sooner did it feel its feet there than it tore off down the pavement as fast as it could go, running back to Dame Rustle's!

'Gracious!' said Mister Mean in surprise. 'How the wind is taking that paper along, to be sure.'

Well, the next thing that happened was most annoying to Mister Mean. The come-back spell began to work in the sausages, and they wriggled out of their paper wrapping, which fell to the ground. Mister Mean stopped to pick it up – and, hey presto! that string of sausages leapt to the ground and tore off on tiny legs as fast as could be. All the dogs in the street barked to see them rushing along like a large brown caterpillar – but they knew better than to touch sausages with a come-back spell in them.

'Jumping pigs!' said Mister Mean in the greatest alarm. 'Now, what's the meaning of that? Look at those sausages! Do they think they are in for a race or what? Something funny is about this morning – or else I'm dreaming!'

He pinched himself hard to see if he was dreaming – but the pinch hurt so much that he knew he was wide awake. So on he went again, wondering what could be the matter with everything.

'Anyhow, the eggs are all right,' he said, looking down at them. But even as he spoke the come-back spell began to work in them, too. One by one those eggs grew chicken-legs and climbed up to the rim of the basket, ready to jump out!

'Oh no, you don't!' said Mister Mean, grabbing

431

at the top egg. 'No jumping about like that, eggs, or you will get broken.'

But the eggs took no notice of Mister Mean. One by one they jumped out of the basket and tore back to Mother Cluck's as fast as they could. It was a most astonishing sight to see.

Mister Mean was furious. 'There's some spell at work,' he cried. 'Someone's playing a trick on me!'

'Perhaps, Mister Mean,' said Mrs. Twinkle-toes, who was just nearby, 'perhaps you haven't paid for those things. They have gone back to be sold to someone who *will* pay for them.'

Mister Mean went home in a rage. He wasn't going to pay his bills till he wanted to. Nobody could make him take his money out of the bank if he didn't mean to!

But, oh dear! what a life he led the next few days! His new that jumped clean off his head and hurried back to the hatter's. His new shoes wriggled off his feet and ran back to the shoe shop with such a clatter that everyone turned to see what was making the noise – and of course they saw old Mister Mean standing in his stockinged feet looking as wild as could be – and, dear me, he had such a big hole in one toe.

Even the bananas he bought hopped out of

the bag they were in and galloped back to the greengrocer's. Soon the people of the town followed Mister Mean when he did his shopping, so that they could see the strange sight of everything racing back to the shops afterwards.

Well, Mister Mean knew there was nothing else to be done but to pay his bills. So he took some money out of the bank and paid them all, every one. Then his goods stopped behaving in such an unusual manner and stayed in their bags and baskets till he got home.

And you may be sure they will behave all right just so long as he pays his bills – but as the shopkeepers still have some of the come-back spell left, they will play old Mister Mean some more tricks if he begins to be mean again.

Witch Heyho still has plenty of come-back spells to sell, so if you know of anyone who needs one, just send a message to her!

The Nice Juicy Carrot

In the field at the back of the farm lived three grey donkeys. They were called Neddy, Biddy, and Hee-Haw. Sometimes the farmer put one into the harness belonging to a small carriage, and his

little daughter drove out for a ride. But usually the donkeys didn't have much to do, and they very often quarrelled.

One day Neddy found a large juicy carrot in the ditch, and he was most excited about it. In fact, he was so excited that instead of keeping quiet about it and nibbling it till it was gone, he raised his head and cried: 'Eeyore! Eeyore! Eeyore!'

Just like that.

Well, of course, the other two donkeys came running up to see what was the matter, and they saw the nice juicy carrot too. And they wanted to eat it.

But Neddy put his thick little body in the way and said: 'No, that's my carrot.'

Biddy tried to scrape the carrot near her with her foot.

'It's *my* carrot!' she said.

'I'm the hungriest, so it's *my* carrot!' said Hee-Haw, and he tried to push the others away.

Then Neddy saw that he would not be allowed to eat it in peace, and he thought of a plan to decide which donkey should have the carrot. 'Let us see who can bray the loudest,' he said.

So they began. First Neddy brayed.

'Eeyore, eeyore, eeyore!' he cried, and a little

sandy rabbit running not far off was so astonished at the loud noise that he came near to see what it was all about.

Then Biddy brayed. 'Eeyore, Eeyore, Eeyore!' she cried, and the watching rabbit thought it a very ugly noise.

Then Hee-Haw brayed, and dear me, his voice was so loud that a hedgehog not far off was frightened almost out of his life, and curled himself up into a tight ball.

'EEYORE, EEYORE, EEYORE!' roared Hee-Haw. The listening rabbit thought that donkeys had terrible voices. Then, dear me, the rabbit caught sight of that nice juicy carrot lying just nearby in the ditch. How his nose woffled when he saw it!

He crept out from his hiding-place and the three donkeys saw him.

'Look! There is a rabbit!' cried Hee-Haw. 'He shall tell us which brayed the loudest just now. Then we shall know who wins the carrot!'

So they called to the rabbit to judge between them. But the bunny was very artful. He didn't want to see the carrot eaten by a donkey. So he looked wisely at the three grey animals and shook his head.

'There wasn't much to choose between your

braying,' he said. 'Why don't you have a race? Then you could easily tell who should have the carrot.'

'That's a good idea,' said the donkeys. 'Where shall we race to, rabbit?'

'Oh, all round the field and back again to where I sit,' answered the wily rabbit. 'Now, are you ready? One, two, three, off!'

Away went the three donkeys at top speed. Round the field they went at a gallop, much to the astonishment of the farmer's wife. They panted and puffed, kicking up their heels in fine style, each trying to get ahead of the other.

They all arrived back at the starting-place at the same moment. But each donkey thought it had won.

'I've won!' said Neddy.

'No, I'm first!' brayed Biddy.

'The carrot's mine!' roared Hee-Haw.

'Let's ask the rabbit who's won,' said Neddy. 'He'll know.'

So they called to the rabbit – but there was no answer. They called again, and still they had no reply. Then they looked for the carrot.

It was gone!

The Dandelion Clock

Once upon a time there was a fine dandelion plant that lived in a field. It put up many flowers – but one after another they were eaten by the brown horses that slept in the field each night.

At last the dandelion plant put up a golden flower bigger and finer than any before. The horses did not eat it, for they had found some very juicy grass at the other end of the field, and they did not visit the hedge where the dandelion lived. So the flower grew tall.

The bees came to it. So did many little flies. The flower lasted for five whole days, and then it closed its pretty petals and hid its head in its green leaves. It stayed hidden there for a few days, and then once more it straightened out its long stalk, which had grown even taller. And lo and behold, the dandelion's golden head had turned white! All the gold had gone.

'You do look different,' said a little copper beetle, hurrying by.

'My head is full of seed now, precious seed!' said the dandelion. 'I have thirty-one seeds to send away on the wind – and that means, little beetle, thirty-one new dandelion plants!'

'Wonderful!' said the beetle, and ran down a hole.

The dandelion head fluffed itself out into a beautiful clock. You should have seen it! It was round and white and soft, like a full, silvery moon. It stood there shining softly in the hedge, waiting for the wind to come and puff all the seeds away.

But before the wind came someone else came – and that was a little girl. She saw the dandelion clock there and she squealed in delight.

'What a beautiful clock! I must blow it to tell the time!' So she picked the clock and began to puff.

'One o'clock! Two o'clock! Three o'clock! Oh! The fluff is all gone. It's three o'clock!'

The little girl threw away the stalk and went dancing away. And what happened to all the seeds?

A pretty goldfinch came by and saw them blowing away, all the thirty-one. He twittered to his companions, and the flock came flying down. 'Dandelion seeds!' sang the goldfinch. 'Take them, brothers! We have feasted on thistledown to-day, and now here are some dandelion seeds.'

They ate all they could see – twenty of them! Then off they flew. Now there were only eleven of the seeds left. 'Never mind!' sighed the plant, and it rustled its leaves together. 'That will be eleven new plants some day.'

The eleven seeds flew off. Each tiny seed had a little parachute to help it to fly. They swung through the air, enjoying the sunshine and the wind. Two flew down to earth to look for a resting-place, but a little mouse was there and he caught them. He ate the seeds and then carried the fluff to his nest to make it cosy. So now there were only nine left.

The nine seeds flew on and on, over the fields and hedges. Three floated downwards – and a tiny pixie caught them and sewed them on to her pointed cap. They made a lovely trimming and she was very pleased with it.

Now there were only six seeds, and they floated high on the wind. Two flew into a squirrel's hole and caught on the bark of the tree. The squirrel saw them and licked them off. Down his throat they went, and that left only four – four little dandelion seeds, adventuring through the air, blown up and down and round about by all the autumn breezes!

One fell to earth and was eaten by a brown
sparrow. Another fell down a chimney and was
burnt in the fire. Now there were only two left.

They floated onwards. One came to a pond and fell there. A fish saw it floating on the water, its little parachute looking like wings – and the fish thought the seed was a fly, and snapped at it. That was the end of that little seed. Only one was left. It flew for a long while, soaring up high, and then sinking down low.

And at last it rested on the ground, a tiny, tired seed, its parachute falling to bits. It lay there, not moving, for there was now no wind at all. It was just outside a worm-hole. That night the worm came out of its hole and wriggled about on the grass. When it went back again it glided over the dandelion seed, and the tiny seed stuck to the worm's slimy body. It went into the hole with the worm.

And there it grew! Yes – it really did! It put out a little root. It put out a tiny green shoot – and when the spring came, there was a small dandelion plant growing out of the worm-hole!

'Now, how did that dandelion get there?' wondered the little girl in whose garden the worm-hole was. 'I like dandelions. I shall let it grow and give me some golden flowers.'

So the dandelion grew, and was happy and content in the warm spring sunshine and soft rain.

And before long it had seven fine white clocks, all ready to be puffed.

The little girl puffed them – and off went the seed. I wonder if any will fall in your garden? Perhaps they will – and you will see a tiny plant growing up, and find golden flowers, as round as pennies, shining in the sun!

King Bom's Ice-Cream

King Bom was a perfect nuisance. He was a very stupid fellow, but he thought he was clever, so he was always interfering in everything and making muddles. People got very tired of him, especially his wife, Queen Prylla, who often used to long to box his ears. But she didn't dare to in case Bom ordered her head to be cut off.

That was one of his very stupid habits. He would say 'Off with his head!' at any time, and, although he might be very sorry the next day, by that time, of course, it was too late to change his mind.

One day King Bom went to a meeting of his councillors, and upset all their plans. No matter what they proposed to do he wanted something different. In the end all the councillors walked out in a huff, and the King roared, 'Off with their heads!'

'You can't do that,' said the Queen quickly. 'The

people will rise against you if you do, and put you off the throne.'

'Off with *their* heads then!' roared the King, losing his temper even more.

'Don't be silly,' said the Queen sharply. 'If you cut off everybody's head you won't have any people to rule over and you won't like that!'

The King stared so fiercely at Queen Prylla that she quite thought he would say 'Off with her head!' too. So she went up to him and patted his hand. 'It's very hot,' she said. 'Let's go and have an ice – a strawberry one with vanilla all round.'

Now if there was one thing that the King liked more than another, it was an ice. He was always in a good temper when he was eating ices, and he ate a great many. So he stopped frowning, took the Queen's arm, and went down the High Street to the ice-cream shop.

That night the councillors came to the Queen and warned her that if King Bom interfered any more they would put him on the non-stop train to Topsy-Turvy Land, and that would be the end of *him*.

'Your Majesty, we are very sorry,' said the chief councillor to the Queen, 'we are devoted to *you* – and if you liked to stay behind and rule us whilst

the King goes to Topsy-Turvy Land we shall be delighted.'

'Oh, dear me, no, I couldn't do that,' said the Queen. 'I should have to go with the King if he went. If I didn't he would do all sorts of dreadful things – put his socks on inside out and try to eat his egg with a fork instead of a spoon. Things like that. I couldn't stay behind and rule you.'

'Well, we don't know who else to have,' said the chief councillor. 'There's nobody quite so clever as you are, Queen Prylla. Just think about it, will you?'

Off they went and left the poor Queen in a great way. It would be dreadful to have to leave the Palace and go off to Topsy-Turvy Land – especially as she had only just finished making her new strawberry jam. It would be a pity to leave that before she had tasted it properly.

Queen Prylla sat and thought hard. She was fond of King Bom, for all his stupid ways, and she wanted him to be happy – but *she* wanted to be happy too, and she wanted the people to be happy as well. It was all very difficult.

'Bom would be perfectly happy if only he could sit all day eating ices!' she thought. And then a great idea flashed into her head! Perhaps she could find a way out of her difficulty, after all!

She put on a dark cloak and ran down to the ice-cream shop. It was kept by two brownies. They were most surprised to see the Queen.

'Listen,' she said to them. 'Tomorrow is the King's birthday, as you know. Now I want you to make a very, very special ice indeed – one that he will think is the most deliciout ice he has ever eaten. Put all the loveliest things you know into it – silver moonlight, a butterfly's blue shadow, the heart of a crocus – and flavour it with strawberry, because that is his favourite.'

'Oh, certainly, Your Majesty!' said the brownies, bowing. 'We will do our very best.'

'Bring it up to me at eleven o'clock in the morning,' said the Queen. 'Don't forget.'

Off she went – and this time she disappeared into a tiny cottage at the very end of the village. Here lived Mrs. Wrinkle, a witch who had long since retired from business, and had taken up knitting.

She was pleased to see the Queen, and when she heard that she wanted a wishing-spell she was only too delighted to give her one. She still had a few left in a tin in the kitchen.

'Here's quite a good one,' she said to the Queen, handing her a very small object indeed. 'This will melt if you put it into a cake, for instance.'

'Ah, that will do nicely,' said the Queen, and she slipped it into her bag. 'Thank you so much. Now pray get on with your knitting, Mrs. Wrinkle, and don't mention to anyone that I've been here.'

The next day, at eleven o'clock, the ice-cream brownies arrived with the ice. It was magnificent. It was all colours of the rainbow and it glittered and shone in a most gorgeous way. It really looked far too good to eat.

The Queen took it and thanked them. Then she

went quickly into the pantry with it, and slipped into the very middle of it the wishing-spell she had got from Mrs. Wrinkle.

The King had been very stupid that morning. He had sent for his councillors and given them all a good scolding, so that they fumed and raged. They went out of the Palace and came back with a large ticket.

The Queen caught sight of it as she came out of the pantry with the ice.

'Goodness!' she said, nearly dropping the ice, 'is that a ticket to Topsy-Turvy Land?'

'Yes, and it isn't a return-ticket, either!' said the chief councillor angrily.

'Wait a minute!' begged the Queen. 'Wait a minute! Don't be in such a hurry! I've got an idea to put everything right. Just let me try it, before you go in and give the King that ticket.'

'All right,' said the councillor gruffly. 'But don't be long, Your Majesty.'

The Queen hurried into the King's study. Bom sat there looking as black as a thunder-cloud.

'Look, Bom, dear!' said Queen Prylla, going up to him. 'Here's a most delicious birthday ice, specially made for you by the ice-cream brownies.'

'I don't want it,' said Bom, peevishly.

'Oh, yes you do!' said the Queen, setting it down in front of him.

'Oh, no I don't,' said Bom, pushing it away.

'Then I'll give it to the cat,' said the Queen. 'Puss, puss, puss, where are you? Come along, here's a lovely ice for you!'

'Don't give my ice to that wretched cat!' said the King crossly.

'But you said you didn't want it,' said the artful Queen. 'Puss, puss!'

'Well, I *do* want it!' cried Bom in a temper, and he took up the spoon and began to eat the ice.

It really was a marvellous ice. I couldn't tell you all that was in it, but it tasted like sunshine and snow, and made the King feel better than he had done for days.

'This is a very good ice,' he said, when he was

half-way through. 'It's perfectly delicious. The best I've ever eaten!'

The Queen watched him finish up the ice greedily. She knew that he must have eaten the little wishing-spell inside it and she was anxiously waiting for him to say what he usually said at the end of a specially nice ice.

He said it. He finished up the last spoonful, laid down the spoon, leaned back in his chair, gave a huge sigh and said, 'How I wish I could eat that ice all over again!'

Immediately his wish was granted. The ice appeared before him just as it had done when he first saw it, and in great glee he took up his spoon once more.

'Now he's off!' thought the Queen in delight. 'He'll wish the wish again when he comes to the end, and eat yet another ice – and then wish the wish again. Well, he's happy for the day. Now I'll go and tell the councillors.'

Off she went and told them what she had done.

The councillors peeped in at the King gobbling up his birthday ice. He came to the end and sighed, 'How I wish I could eat that ice all over again!' And immediately the ice reappeared, and he began to eat it greedily.

The councillors began to laugh. They thought it was funny. The Queen laughed too. The King heard them, but instead of shouting 'Off with their heads!' he simply waved his spoon at them and went on with his ice.

'You're a clever woman, Your Majesty!' said the chief councillor. 'We'll take this ticket to the station and get back the money for it this very minute. You shall rule us from to-day!'

Off they went, and the Queen sank down into a chair, quite exhausted. Things had really been a little too exciting the last few days. Then she heard a contented voice from the study, 'How I wish I could eat that ice all over again!'

And, so people say, King Bom is still eating ices to this very day!

The Cat, the Mouse, and the Fox

Once upon a time a cat walked into a trap. Click! The catch of the cage sprang down, and the cat was caught. She mewed pitifully, and a little mouse heard her and came running.

'Press back the spring, little mouse,' begged the cat. 'Set me free, I pray you!'

'No,' said the mouse. 'You would eat me!'

'I give you my word that I would do no such thing,' said the cat. So the little mouse pressed

back the spring and out from the cage leapt the cat. She pounced at once on the mouse, and the tiny creature squeaked in fright. 'You promised not to eat me if I did you a kindness.'

'You were foolish to believe me,' said the cat scornfully. The mouse squeaked again, and a fox who was running by paused and listened. 'What is the matter?' he asked. The mouse, with many squeaks, told him all that had happened. The fox winked at the mouse, put on a most innocent look, and turned to the cat.

'Let me get this tale right,' he said. 'The mouse was in the trap, Cat—'

'No,' said the cat, '*I* was in the trap.'

'Sorry,' said the fox. 'Well, *you*, Cat, were in the trap, and I came running by—'

'No, no!' cried the cat impatiently. 'The *mouse* came running by.'

'Of course,' said the fox, 'the trap was in the cat and the mouse came—'

'Stupid creature!' cried the cat angrily. 'Of course the trap was not in me! I tell you *I* was in the trap.'

'Pardon, pardon!' said the fox humbly. 'Do let me get it right. Now – you were in the mouse and the trap came running by—'

'Listen!' cried the cat in a rage. 'Have you no

ears or understanding? I was in the trap and the *mouse* came running by–'

The cat almost flew at the fox, she was in such a rage at his stupidity. Her tail swung from side to side, and she spat rudely at the innocent-looking fox opposite to her.

'Who would think anyone could be so stupid?' she hissed. 'And you are supposed to be so sharp, Fox! Never have I met anyone so slow and dense. Listen! *I* was in the trap and the *mouse* came running by. Surely that is easy to understand!'

'Quite easy,' said the fox, blinking his sharp eyes. 'I've got it this time, Cat. The trap was in the mouse and–'

The cat stared at the fox as if she could not believe her ears. Could anyone be so stupid? She spat again and then glared in a fury. 'I will *show* you what happened,' she said. 'Then perhaps you will understand at last, you very stupid fox!'

She jumped into the trap and looked out through the bars at the fox. 'See,' she said, 'I was in the trap like this, and the mouse came running by.'

'I see *now*,' said the fox, and he snapped down the spring. 'Thank you, Cat, for being so patient! The mouse will *not* set you free this time. To be ungrateful to a friend is a hateful thing – think it

457

over in peace and quiet, for you will be a long time in the trap.'

Then, leaving the cat in the cage, the fox and the mouse went off together. 'You will see, friend Mouse,' said the fox with a grin, 'that I am not half so stupid as I appear. Good-day to you, and good luck!'

The Bed That Took a Walk

The pixie Miggle was always late for everything. If he went to catch a train he had to run all the way and then he would miss it. If he went to catch a bus it had always gone round the corner before he got there.

'It's just as easy to be early as to be late,' said his friends. 'Why don't you get up a bit sooner, then you would be in time for everything?'

'Well, I'm so sleepy in the mornings,' said Miggle. My wife comes and calls me, but I go off to sleep again. I really am a very tired person in the morning.'

'Lazy, he means!' said his friends to one another. 'Never in time for anything! It's shocking. One day he will be very sorry.'

In the month of June the King and Queen of the pixies were coming to visit Apple Tree Town, where Miggle and his friends lived. The pixies were very excited.

459

'I shall get a new coat,' said Jinky.

'I shall buy a new feather for my hat,' said Twinkle.

'I shall have new red shoes,' said Flitter.

'And I shall buy a whole new suit, a new hat and feathers, and new shoes and buckles with the money I have saved up,' said Miggle. 'I shall be very grand indeed!'

'You'll never be in time to see the King and Queen!' said Jinky, with a laugh.

'Indeed I shall,' said Miggle. 'I shall be up before any of you that day.'

Well, the day before the King and Queen came, Miggle was very busy trying on his new things. The coat didn't quite fit so he asked his wife to alter it. She stayed up very late trying to make it right.

It was about midnight when Miggle got to bed. How he yawned! 'Wake me up at seven o'clock' he said. 'Don't forget.'

Mrs Miggle was tired. 'I shall call you three times, and then, if you don't get up, I shan't call you any more,' she said. 'I have to call myself – nobody calls *me* – and I am tired tonight, so I shall not be very patient with you tomorrow if you don't get up when I call you.'

'You *do* sound cross,' said Miggle, and got into

bed. He fell fast asleep, and it seemed no time at all before he felt Mrs Miggle shouting in his ear, and shaking him.

'Miggle! It's seven o'clock. Miggle get up!'

'All right,' said Miggle, and turned over to go to sleep again. In five minutes time Mrs Miggle shook him again, and once more he woke up, and went to sleep again.

'This is the third time I've called you,' said Mrs Miggle, 10 minutes later, in a cross voice. 'And it's the last time. If you don't get up now, I shan't call you any more.'

'Right,' said Miggle. 'Just getting up, my dear.' But he didn't. He went to sleep again. Plenty of time to get up and dress and go and see the King and Queen!

Mrs Miggle kept her word. She didn't call Miggle again. She got dressed in her best frock and went to meet the King and Queen. Miggle slept on soundly, not hearing the footsteps going down the road, as all the pixies hurried by to meet the royal pair.

Miggle's bed creaked to wake him. It shook a little, but Miggle didn't stir. The bed was cross. It thought Miggle stayed too long in it. It knew how upset Miggle would be when he woke up and found that the King and Queen had gone.

461

So it thought it would take Miggle to the Town Hall, where the King and Queen would be, and perhaps he would wake up there.

The bed walked on its four legs to the door. It squeezed itself through, for it was a narrow bed. It trotted down the street, clickity-clack, clickity-clack.

Miggle didn't wake. He had a lovely dream that he was in a boat that went gently up and down on the sea, and said 'clickity-clack' all the time.

'Gracious! Look, isn't that Miggle asleep on that bed?' cried Jinky, with a squeal of laughter. 'The bed is wide awake, but Miggle isn't – so the bed is taking him to the Town Hall!'

'Clickity-clack, clickity-clack,' went the four legs of the bed. Miggle gave a little snore. He was warm and cosy and comfy, and as fast asleep as ever.

The bed made its way into the Town Hall just as the King and Queen came on to the stage to speak to their people. The pixies jumped to their feet and cheered loudly.

The bed jumped up and down in joy, because it was enjoying the treat too. Miggle woke up when he heard the cheering, and felt the bumping of the bed. He sat up and looked round in the greatest surprise.

'Ha ha, ho ho, look at Miggle,' shouted everyone,

and the King and Queen had to smile too. Miggle was full of horror and shame! What had happened! Had his silly bed brought him to the Town Hall? Oh dear, and he was in his pyjamas too, instead of in his lovely new clothes!

Miggle could have wept with shame. Mrs Miggle saw him and went over to him. 'Really Miggle! To think you've come to see the King and Queen in bed, not even dressed! I'm ashamed of you! What *can* you be thinking of?'

Miggle slid down into bed and pulled the clothes over his head. Mrs Miggle pulled them off.

'Now you get up and bow properly to His Majesty the King and Her Majesty the Queen,' she said.

'What, in my pyjamas?' said poor Miggle.

'Well, if you've come in pyjamas, you'll have to bow in them,' said Mrs Miggle. So Miggle had to stand up on the bed in his pyjamas and bow to the King and Queen. How they laughed!

'What a funny man!' said the Queen. 'Does he often do things like this?'

Miggle didn't know what to do. He lay down again and ordered the bed to go home. But the bed wasn't a dog, to be ordered here and there. It wanted to stay and see the fun.

So Miggle had to jump out and run all the way home in his pyjamas. 'How dreadful, how dreadful!' he kept thinking, as he ran. 'I can't bear it! I'd better put on all my fine clothes, and go back and let the King and Queen see how grand I really am!'

So he did – but alas, when he got back to the Town Hall, the King and Queen had just gone. Everyone was coming away, pleased and excited. Miggle's bed trotted with them, 'clickity-clack.'

'Hallo, Miggle? Going to ride home asleep in bed?' cried his friends. 'Oh, how you made the King and Queen laugh! It was the funniest sight we've ever seen.'

Miggle frowned and didn't say a word. His bed tried to walk close to him, but he wouldn't let it. Horrid bed! 'I'll never be late again!' thought Miggle. 'Never, never, never!'

But he will. It's not so easy to get out of a bad habit. Won't it be funny if his bed walks off with him again?

Brownie's Magic

One night the snow came. It fell quietly all night through, and in the morning, what a surprise for everyone! The hills were covered with snow. The trees were white. The bushes were hidden, and the whole world looked strange and magical.

Bobbo the brownie looked out of his cave in the hillside. The path down to the little village was hidden now. The path that ran over the top of the hill had gone too.

'Snow everywhere,' said Bobbo. 'Beautiful white snow! How I love it! I wish I had watched it falling last night, like big white goose feathers.'

He saw someone coming up the hill, and he waved to him.

'Ah!' he said, 'there is my clever cousin, Brownie Bright-Eyes. I wonder what he was brought to show me today. He is always bringing me wonderful things.'

Brownie Bright-Eyes walked up the hill in the

snow, making deep footprints as he came, for he carried something large and heavy.

'What have you got there?' said Bobbo, when Bright-Eyes at last came to his cave. 'You are always bringing me something strange and wonderful to see, Bright-Eyes.'

'I have made a marvellous mirror,' panted Bright-Eyes, bringing the shining glass into the cave. 'I do think I am clever, Bobbo. I made this magic mirror myself. I think I must be the cleverest brownie in the world.'

'Don't boast,' said Bobbo. 'I don't like you when you boast.'

'I am not boasting!' cried Bright-Eyes crossly. 'Wait till you do something clever yourself, and then scold me for boasting. It's a pity you don't use your own brains.'

'I do,' said Bobbo. 'But you are always so full of your own wonderful doings that you never listen to me when I want to tell you something.'

'I don't expect you would have anything half so wonderful to tell me as I have to tell you,' said Bright-Eyes. 'Now – just look at this mirror.'

Bobbo looked at it. It was a strange mirror, because it didn't reflect what was in front of it. It was just dark, with a kind of mist moving in the glass. Bobbo could see that it was very magic.

'I can't see anything,' said Bobbo.

'No, you can't – but if you want to know where anyone is – Tippy the brownie for instance – the mirror will show you!'

'What do you mean?' asked Bobbo, astonished.

'Now look,' said Bright-Eyes. He stroked the shining mirror softly. 'Mirror, mirror, show me where Tippy the brownie is!'

And at once a strange thing happened. The mist in the glass slowly cleared away – and there was Tippy the brownie, sitting in a bus. The mirror showed him quite clearly.

'Isn't that wonderful?' said Bright-Eyes. 'You couldn't possibly have told me where Tippy was, without the help of the mirror, could you?'

'Yes, I could,' said Bobbo. 'I knew he was in the bus.'

'You didn't!' said Bright-Eyes.

'I did,' said Bobbo.

'Then you must have seen Tippy this morning,' said Bright-Eyes.

'I haven't,' said Bobbo. '*You* found out where he was by using your magic mirror, but I, Bright-Eyes, I found out by using my brains! So I am cleverer than you.'

Bright-Eyes didn't like that. He always wanted to be the cleverest person anywhere. He frowned at Bobbo.

'I expect it was just a guess on your part that Tippy was in the bus,' he said. 'Now – can you tell me where Jinky is – you know, the pixie who lives down the hill?'

'Yes,' said Bobbo at once. 'He's gone up the hill to see his aunt, who lives over the top.'

Bright-Eyes rubbed the mirror softly. 'Mirror, mirror show me where Jinky is!' he said. And at once the mirror showed him a pixie, sitting in a chair, talking to a plump old lady. It was Jinky, talking to his aunt!

'There you are, you see – I was right,' said Bobbo, pleased. 'I am cleverer than your mirror. It uses magic – but I use my brains. I can tell you a lot of things that *you* could only get to know through your magic mirror – but which *I* know by using my very good brains. Ha, ha!'

'What can you tell me?' asked Bright-Eyes.

'I can tell you that Red-Coat the fox passed by here in the night, although I did not see or hear him,' said Bobbo. 'I can tell you that six rabbits played in the snow down the hill this morning. I can tell you that Mother Jane's ducks left the frozen pond today and went to her garden to be fed.'

'You must have seen them all. That's easy,' said Bright-Eyes.

'I tell you, I have not seen anything or anyone today except you,' said Bobbo. 'I know all this by using my brains.'

'What else do you know?' asked Bright-Eyes, thinking that Bobbo must really be cleverer than he thought.

'I know that the sparrows flew down to peck crumbs that Mother Jane scattered for them,' said Bobbo. 'I know that Crek-Crek the moorhen took a walk by the side of the pond. I know that Mother Jane's cat ran away from Tippy's dog this morning. And I know that Tippy's cow wandered from its shed, and then went back to it.'

Bright-Eyes stared at Bobbo in wonder. 'You are very clever to know all this, if you did not see anyone,' he said. 'I shall ask my magic mirror if what you say is true!'

He stroked the glass and asked it many things – and each time the glass showed him that what Bobbo said was true! There was the cat chasing the dog. There was the moorhen walking over the snow. There was Tippy's cow wandering all about!

'Please tell me your magic,' said Bright-Eyes to

Bobbo. 'It must be very good magic to tell you all these things.'

'Well – come outside and I will show you how I know them all,' said Bobbo, beginning to laugh. They went outside, and Bobbo pointed to the crisp white snow. There were many marks and prints in it as clear as could be.

'Look,' said Bobbo, pointing to some small footprints that showed little pointed toes. 'Tippy always wears pointed shoes – and do you see how deep his footprints are? That shows that he was running. Why was he running? To catch the bus! That's how I knew where he was, without having seen him.'

'How did you know about Jinky going to see his aunt?' asked Bright-Eyes.

Bobbo pointed to some very big footprints. 'Those are Jinky's marks,' he said 'He has enormous feet. The footprints are going up the hill, and the only person Jinky goes to see over the top is his aunt. So I knew where Jinky was!'

'Very clever,' said Bright-Eyes.

'And I knew that Red-Coat the fox had passed in the night because there are *his* footprints,' said Bobbo, pointing to a set of rather dog-like marks that showed the print of claws very clearly. 'I knew it was Red-Coat because I saw the mark his tail made here and there behind his hind feet – see it?'

'Bright-Eyes saw the mark of the fox's tail in the snow, and the line of footprints too. Bobbo took Bright-Eyes farther down the hill. He showed him the rabbit-prints – little marks for the front feet and longer, bigger ones for the strong hind feet. He showed him where Mother Jane's ducks had walked from the pond to her garden.

'You can see they were ducks because they have left behind them the mark of their webbed feet,' he said. 'And you can see where the sparrows fed because they have left little prints in pairs – they hop, you see, they don't walk or run – so their prints are always in pairs.'

'And there are the moorhen's marks,' said Bright-Eyes. 'He has big feet rather like the old hen at home, although he is a waterbird. But he runs on land as well as swims on water, so he doesn't have webbed feet. Look how he puts them one in front of the other, Bobbo, so the footprints are in a straight line!'

'And there are the marks made by Tippy's cow,' said Bobbo. 'You can tell each hoofmark quite well. And Mother Jane's cat ran *here* – look at the neat little marks. And Tippy's dog ran *here* – you can tell the difference, because the cat puts her claws in when she runs, so they don't show in her footprints, but the dog doesn't – so his *do* show!'

'Bobbo, you are very, very clever,' said Bright-Eyes. 'You are cleverer than I am. It is better to use your eyes and your brains, than to use a magic mirror! I think you are the cleverest brownie in the world!'

Would you like to be as clever as Bobbo? Well, go out into the snow, when it comes, and read the footprints you find there! You will soon know quite a lot.

Dame Lucky's Umbrella

Dame Lucky had a nice yellow umbrella that she liked very much. It had a strange handle. It was in the shape of a bird's head, and very nice to hold.

Dame Lucky had been given it for her last birthday. Her brother had given it to her. 'Now don't go lending this to anyone,' he said. 'You're such a kindly, generous soul that you will lend anything to anyone. But this is such a nice umbrella that I shall be very sad if you lose it.'

'I won't lose it' said Dame Lucky. 'I shall be very, very careful with it. It's the nicest one I've ever had.'

She used it two or three times in the rain and was very pleased with it because it opened out big and wide and kept every spot of rain from her clothes.

Then the summer came and there was no rain to bother about for weeks. Dame Lucky put her umbrella safely away in her wardrobe.

One morning in September her friend, Mother Lucy, came to see her. 'Well, well, this *is* a surprise,' said Dame Lucky. 'You've been so ill that I never thought you'd be allowed to come all this way to see me!'

'Oh, I'm much better,' said Mother Lucy. 'I mustn't stay long, though, because I have to get on to my sister's for lunch. She's expecting me in half an hour.'

But when Mother Lucy got up to go she looked at the sky in dismay. 'Oh, goodness – it's just going to pour with rain. Here are the first drops. I haven't brought an umbrella with me and I shall get soaked.'

'Dear me, you mustn't get wet after being so ill,' said Dame Lucky at once. 'You wait a moment. I'll get my new umbrella. But don't lose it, Lucy, because it's the only one I have and it's very precious.'

'Thank you. You're a kind soul,' said Mother Lucy. Dame Lucky fetched the yellow umbrella and put it up for her. Then off went Mother Lucy to her sister's, quite dry in the pouring rain.

She had a nice lunch at her sister's – and, will you believe it, when she left she quite forgot to take Dame Lucky's umbrella with her, because it had stopped raining and the sun was shining.

So there it stood in the umbrella-stand, whilst

Mother Hannah waved goodbye to her sister Lucy.

In a little while it began to pour with rain again. Old Mr Kindly had come to call on Mother Hannah without an umbrella and he asked her to lend him one when he was ready to go home.

'You may take any of the umbrellas in the stand,' said Mother Hannah. 'There are plenty there.'

So what did Mr Kindly do but choose the yellow umbrella with the bird-handle, the one that belonged to Dame Lucky! Off he went with it, thinking what a fine one it was and how well it kept the rain off.

When he got home his little grand-daughter was

there, waiting for him. 'Oh, Granddad! Can you lend me an umbrella?' she cried. 'I've come out without my mackintosh and Mummy will be cross if I go home wet.'

'Yes, certainly,' said Mr Kindly. 'Take this one. I borrowed it from Mother Hannah. You can take it back to her tomorrow.'

Off went Little Corinne, the huge umbrella almost hiding her. Her mother was out when she got in, so she stood the umbrella in the hall-stand and went upstairs to take off her things.

Her brother ran down the stairs as she was about to go up. 'Hallo, Corinne! Is it raining? Blow, I'll have to take an umbrella, then!'

And, of course, he took Dame Lucky's, putting it up as soon as he got out of doors. Off he went, whistling in the rain, to his friend's house.

He put the umbrella in the hall-stand and went to find Jacko, his friend. Soon they were fitting together their railway lines, and when Pip said goodbye to Jacko he quite forgot about the umbrella because the sun was now shining again.

So there it stayed in Jacko's house all night. His Great-aunt Priscilla saw it there the next morning and was surprised because she hadn't seen it before. Nobody knew who owned it. What a peculiar thing!

Now, two days later, Dame Lucky put on her things to go out shopping and visiting. She looked up at the sky as she stepped out of her front door.

'Dear me – it looks like rain!' she said. 'I must take my umbrella.'

But it wasn't in the hall-stand. And it wasn't in the wardrobe in her bedroom, either. How strange! Where could it be?'

'I must have lent it to somebody,' said Dame Lucky. 'I've forgotten who, though. Oh dear, I do hope I haven't lost it for good!'

She set out to do her shopping. It didn't rain whilst she was at the market. 'Perhaps it won't rain at all,' thought Dame Lucky. 'I'll visit my old friend Priscilla on my way back.'

She met Jacko on the way. 'Is your Great-aunt Priscilla at home?' she asked him.

'Oh, yes,' said Jacko. 'She was only saying today that she wished she could see you. You go in and see her, Dame Lucky. You might just get there before the rain comes.'

She went on to the house where her friend Priscilla lived. She just got there before the rain fell. Dame Priscilla was very pleased to see her.

Soon they were sitting talking over cups of cocoa.

'Well, I must go,' said Dame Lucky at last. 'Oh dear – look at the rain! And I don't have an umbrella!'

'What! Have you lost yours?' asked Priscilla. 'How unlucky! Well, I'll lend you one.'

She took Dame Lucky to the hall-stand and Dame Lucky looked at the two or three umbrellas standing there. She gave a cry.

'Why! Where did *this* one come from? It's mine, I do declare! Look at the bird-handle! Priscilla, however did it come here?'

'Nobody knows,' said Dame Priscilla in astonishment. 'Is it really yours? Then *how* did it get here? It has been here for the last two days!'

'Waiting for me, then, I expect,' said Dame Lucky happily. 'Isn't that a bit of luck, Priscilla? I shan't need to borrow one from you. I'll just take my *own* umbrella! Goodbye!'

Off she went under the great yellow umbrella, very pleased to have it again. And whom should she meet on her way home but her brother, the very one who had given her the umbrella!

'Hallo, hallo!' he cried. 'I see you still have your umbrella! I *would* have been cross if you'd lost it. Let me share it with you!'

So they walked home together under the big yellow umbrella – and to this day Dame Lucky doesn't know how it came to be standing in Dame Priscilla's hall-stand, waiting for her.

He Wouldn't Take the Trouble

Oh-Dear, the Brownie, was cross.

'I ordered two new tyres for my old bicycle ages ago,' he said, 'and they haven't come yet! So I have to walk to the village and back each day, instead of riding. It's such a nuisance.'

'It won't hurt you,' said a friend Feefo. 'Don't make such a fuss, Oh-Dear! Everything is so much trouble to you, and you sigh and groan too much.'

Feefo was right. Oh-Dear did make a fuss about everything. If his chimney smoked and needed sweeping he almost cried with rage – though if he had had it swept as soon as it began to smoke, his rooms wouldn't have got so black.

If his hens didn't lay eggs as often as they should, he shouted angrily at them – but if only he had bothered to feed them properly at the right times, he would have got all the eggs he wanted.

Now he was angry because his new bicycle

tyres hadn't come. It was really most annoying.

The next day he walked down into the village again to ask at the post-office if his tyres had come. But they hadn't. 'They might arrive by the next post,' said the little postmistress. 'If they do, I will send them by the carrier.'

'Pooh – you always say that – and they never do come!' said Oh-Dear rudely. He walked out of the shop. It was his day for going to see his old aunt Chuckle. He didn't like her very much because she laughed at him – but if he didn't go to see her she didn't send him the cakes and pies he liked so much.

Oh-Dear walked in at his aunt's gate. He didn't bother to shut it, so it banged to and fro in the wind and his aunt sent him out to latch it.

'You just don't take the trouble to do anything,' she said. 'You don't bother to shine your shoes each morning – just look at them – and you don't trouble to post the letters I give you to post – and you don't even take the trouble to say thank-you for my pies and cakes. You are so lazy, Oh-Dear!'

'Oh dear!' said Oh-Dear, sulking. 'Don't scold me again. You are always scolding me.'

'Well, you always need it,' said his aunt, and laughed at his sulking face. 'Now cheer up, Oh-

Dear – I've a little bit of good news for you.'

'What is it?' said Oh-Dear.

'I've heard from my friend, Mr Give-a-Lot, and he is having a party tomorrow,' said Aunt Chuckle. 'He said that if you like to go, he will be very pleased. So go, Oh-Dear, because you love parties, and you know that Mr Give-a-Lot always has a lovely tea, and everyone goes away with a nice present.'

'Oh!' said Oh-Dear, pleased – but then his face grew gloomy. 'I can't go. It's too far to walk. No bus goes to Mr Give-a-Lot's – and I haven't got my new bicycle tyres so I can't ride there. Oh dear, oh dear, oh dear – isn't that just my luck?'

'Well – never mind,' said Aunt Chuckle. 'I should have thought you could walk there – but if it's too far, it's a pity. Cheer up. Look in the oven and you'll see a pie there.'

Oh-Dear stayed with his aunt till after tea. Then he set out to walk home. It was quite a long way. He groaned.

'Oh dear! It will be dark before I get home. Oh dear! What a pity I can't go to that party tomorrow. Oh dear, why isn't there a bus at this time to take me home?'

He went down the hill. A cart passed him and bumped over a hole in the road. Something fell out of the cart and rolled to the side of the road.

'Hi, hi!' shouted Oh-Dear, but the driver didn't hear him. 'Now look at that!' said Oh-Dear, crossly. 'I suppose I ought to carry the parcel down the road and catch the cart up – or take it to the police-station.'

He picked up the parcel. It was too dark to see the name and address on it, but it was very heavy and awkward to carry.

'I can't be bothered to go after the cart or carry this all the way to the police-station!' said Oh-Dear to himself. 'I really can't.' And what's more I won't. Somebody else can have the trouble of taking it along!'

He threw the parcel down at the side of the road and went on his way. He wasn't going to take the trouble of finding out who it belonged to, or of handing it over safely. There the parcel lay all night, and all the next morning, for no one came by that way for a long time.

About three o'clock Cherry the pixie came along. She saw the parcel and picked it up. 'Oh!', she said, 'This must have been dropped by the carrier's cart yesterday. Somebody didn't get their parcel. I wonder who it was.'

She looked at the name and address on it.

'Master Oh-Dear, the Pixie,' she read. 'Lemon Cottage, Breezy Corner. Oh, it must be the bicycle tyres that Oh-Dear has been expecting for so long. Well – the parcel is very heavy, but I'll carry it to him myself.'

So the kind little pixie took it along to Oh-Dear's cottage and gave it to him. 'I found it lying in the road,' she said. 'It must have dropped off the carrier's cart last night.'

'Yes, I saw it,' said Oh-Dear, 'but I wasn't going to be bothered to carry it all the way after the cart.'

'But Oh-Dear – it's for you,' said Cherry, in surprise. 'I suppose it was too dark for you to see

the name on it. It's your very own parcel – I expect it's the tyres you wanted.'

'Gracious! It is!' said Oh-Dear, in excitement. 'Perhaps I can go to Mr Give-a-Lot's party after all.'

He tore off the paper and took off the lid of a big cardboard box. Inside were all the things he had ordered for his bicycle – two new tyres, a pump, a basket and a lamp.

Oh-Dear rushed to put them on his bicycle. He forgot to thank Cherry for her kindness. He worked hard at fitting on his tyres, but it was very very difficult.

At last he had them on – but when he looked at the clock, it was half-past six! Too late to go to the party now!

'Oh dear, isn't that just my bad luck!' wailed Oh-Dear. 'Why didn't you bring me the parcel earlier, Cherry?'

'Why didn't you take the trouble to see to it yourself last night, when you saw it in the road!' said Cherry. 'Bad luck, indeed – nothing of the sort. It's what you deserve! You won't bother yourself about anything, you just won't take the trouble – and now you've punished yourself, and a VERY GOOD THING TOO!'

She went out and banged the door. Oh-Dear sat

down and cried. Why did he always have such bad luck, why, why, why?

Well, I could tell him the reason why, just as Cherry did, couldn't you?

Muddle's Mistake

There was once a brownie called Muddle. I expect you can guess why he had that name. He was always making muddles! He did make silly ones.

Once his mistress, the Princess of Toadstool Town, asked him to take a note to someone who lived in a fir tree. But Muddle came back saying that he couldn't find a tree with fur on at all!

Another time she asked him to get her a snapdragon and he said he didn't mind fetching a dragon, but he didn't want to get one that snapped.

So, you see, he was always making muddles. And one day he made a very big muddle. The Princess always said he would.

'You just don't use your eyes, Muddle,' she would say. 'You go through the world without looking hard at things, without listening well with your ears, without using your brains. You are a real muddler!'

Now once the Princess was asked to a party given by the Prince of Midnight Town. She was very excited.

'I shall go,' she told Muddle. 'You see, this prince gives really wonderful midnight parties, and he lights them by hanging glow-worms all over the place. It's really lovely!'

'Shall I go with you?' asked Muddle. I expect you will need someone to look after you on your way to the party, because it will be dark.'

'I think I shall fly there on a moth,' said the Princess. 'That will be nice. You get me a nice big moth, and you shall drive me.'

'Very well, Your Highness,' said Muddle, and he went off to get a moth. He hunted here and he hunted there, and at last he found a beautiful white-winged creature.

'Ah!' he said, 'just the right moth for the Princess. I must get it to come with me. I will put it into a beautiful cage, and feed it on sugar and honey, so that it will stay with me until the night of the party.'

So he spoke to the lovely creature. 'Will you come home with me White-Wings? I will give you sugar and honey. You shall stay with me until next week, when you may take the Princess of Toadstool Town to a party.'

'I should like that,' said White-Wings. 'I love parties. Get on my back, brownie and tell me which way to go to your home.'

Muddle was pleased. He got on to White-Wings' back, and they rose high in the air. It was fun. They were soon at Muddle's house, which was a sturdy little toadstool, with a little green door in the stalk, and windows in the head.

'Shall I put you in a cage, or just tie you up, White-Wings?' asked Muddle. White-Wings didn't want to be put into a cage. So Muddle took a length of spider thread and tied her up to his toadstool. He brought her honey, and she put out her long tongue and sucked it up. Muddle watched her.

'What a wonderful tongue you have!' he said. 'It is a bit like an elephant's trunk! I like the way you coil it up so neatly when you have finished your meal.'

'It is long because I like to put it deep down into flowers, and suck up the hidden nectar,' said White-Wings. 'Sometimes the flowers hide their nectar so deep that only a very long tongue like mine can reach it.'

Muddle told the Princess that he had found a very beautiful moth to take her to the midnight party. The Princess was pleased. 'Well, I am glad you haven't made a muddle about *that*!' she said. 'Bring White-Wings to me at twenty minutes to midnight and we will fly off. Make some reins of spider thread, and you shall drive.'

Muddle was so pleased to be going to the party too. It was a great treat for him. He had a new blue suit made, with silver buttons, and a blue cap with a silver knob at the top. He looked very grand.

When the night came, Muddle went out to White-Wings. The lovely insect was fast asleep. 'Wake up,' said Muddle. 'It is time to go to the party.'

White-Wings opened her eyes. She saw that it was quite dark. She shut her eyes again. 'Don't be silly Muddle,' she said. 'It is night-time. I am not going to fly in the dark.'

'Whatever do you mean?' asked Muddle in surprise. 'It is a midnight party! You *must* fly in the dark!'

'I never fly at night, never, never, never,' said White-Wings. 'Go away and let me sleep.'

'But moths always fly at night!' cried Muddle. 'I know a few fly in the day-time as well – but most of them fly at night. Come along, White-Wings. The Princess is waiting.'

'Muddle, what is all this talk about moths?'

asked White-Wings in surprise. 'I am not a moth. I am a BUTTERFLY!'

Muddle lifted up his lantern and stared in the greatest surprise at White-Wings. 'A b-b-b-butterfly!' he stammered. 'Oh no – don't say that! No, no, say you are a moth!'

'Muddle, sometimes I think you are a very silly person,' said the butterfly crossly. 'Don't you know a butterfly from a moth? Have you lived all this time in the world, and seen hundreds of butterflies and moths, and never once noticed how different they are?'

'I thought you were a moth,' said Muddle, and he began to cry, because he knew that the Princess would be very angry with him. 'Please be a moth just for tonight and let me drive you to the midnight party.'

'No,' said White-Wings. 'I am a butterfly and I don't fly at night. If I were you, I'd go and find a moth now, and see if you can get one that will take you.'

'But how shall I know if I am talking to a moth or a butterfly?' said Muddle, still crying. 'I might make a mistake again.'

'Now listen,' said the butterfly. 'It is quite easy to tell which is which. Do you see the way I hold my wings? I put them neatly back to back, like this, so that I show only the underparts.'

The white butterfly put her wings back to back. 'Now,' she said, 'a moth never holds her wings like that. She puts them flat on her back – like this; or she wraps her body round with them – like this; or she just lets them droop – like this. But she certainly doesn't put them back to back.'

'I'll remember that,' said poor Muddle.

'Then,' said the butterfly, 'have a look at my body, will you, Muddle? Do you see how it is nipped in, in the middle? Well, you must have a look at the bodies of moths, and you will see that they are not nipped in, like mine. They are usually fat and thick.'

'I will be sure to look,' promised Muddle.

'And now here is a very important thing,' said the butterfly, waving her two feelers under Muddle's nose. 'A *most* important thing! Look at my feelers. What do you notice about them?'

'I see that they are thickened at the end,' said Muddle. 'They have a sort of knob there.'

'Quite right,' said White-Wings. 'Now, Muddle, just remember this – a moth *never* has a knob or a club at the end of his feelers, never! He may have feelers that are feathery, or feelers that are just threads – but he will never have knobs on them like mine. You can always tell a butterfly or moth at once, by just looking at their feelers.'

'Thank you, White-Wings,' said Muddle, feeling very small. 'All I knew was that butterflies flew in the day-time, and moths mostly flew at night. I didn't think of anything else.'

'Now go off at once and see if you can find a moth to take you and the Princess to the party,' said White-Wings. 'I'm sleepy.'

Well, off went poor Muddle. He looked here and he looked there. He came across a beautiful peacock butterfly, but he saw that it held its wings back to back as it rested, and that its feelers had thick ends. So he knew it wasn't a moth.

He found another white butterfly like White-Wings. He found a little blue butterfly, but its feelers had knobs on the end, so he knew that wasn't a moth, either.

Then he saw a pretty moth that shone yellow in the light of his lantern. It spread its wings flat. Its feelers were like threads, and had no knob at the tips. It *must* be a moth. It left the leaf it was resting on and fluttered round Muddle's head.

'Are you a moth?' asked Muddle.

'Of course!' said the moth. 'My name is Brimmy and I am a brimstone moth. Do you want me?'

'Oh *yes!*' said Muddle. 'Will you come with me at once, please, and let me drive you to the midnight party, with the Princess of Toadstool Town on your back?'

'Oh, I'd love that,' said the moth, and flew off with Muddle at once. The Princess was cross because they were late, and Muddle did not like to tell her why.

They went to the party and they had a lovely time. Muddle set White-Wings free the next day and gave her a little pot of honey to take away.

'You have taught me a lot,' he said. 'I shall use my eyes in future, White-Wings!'

Now let's have a game of Pretend! I am the Princess of Toadstool Town and you are just yourself. Please go out and see if you can find a moth to take me to a party! If you point out a butterfly to me instead, do you know what I shall call you?

I shall call you 'Muddle' of course!

Silky and the Snail

Silky was a pixie. She lived under a hawthorn hedge, and often talked to the birds and animals that passed by her house.

One day a big snail came crawling slowly by. Silky had never seen a snail, and at first she was quite afraid. Then she ran up to the snail, and touched his hard shell.

'How clever you are!' she said. 'You carry your house about with you! Why do you do that?'

'Well, you see,' said the snail, 'I have a very soft body that many birds and other creatures like to eat – so I grow a shell to protect it.'

'What a good idea,' said the pixie. 'Can you put your body right inside your shell, snail?'

'Watch me!' said the snail, and he curled his soft body up quickly into his shell. There was nothing of him to be seen except his spiral shell.

'Very clever,' said the pixie. 'Come out again,

please, snail. I want to talk to you.'

The snail put his head out and then more of his body. He had four feelers on his head, and the pixie looked at them.

'Haven't you any eyes?' she said. 'I can't see your eyes, snail.'

'Oh, I keep them at the top of my longer pair of feelers,' said the snail. 'Can't you see them? Right at the top, pixie – little black things.'

'Oh yes, I can see there now,' said the pixie. 'What a funny place to keep your eyes, snail! Why do you keep them there?'

'Well, it's rather nice to have my eyes high up on feelers I can move about here and there,' said the snail. 'Wouldn't *you* like eyes on the ends of movable feelers, pixie? Think what a lot you could see!'

'I should be afraid that they would get hurt, if I had them at the end of feelers,' said Silky.

'Oh no!' said the snail, and he did such a funny thing. He rolled his eyes down inside his feelers, and the pixie stared in surprise.

'Oh, you can roll your eyes down your feelers, just as I pull the toe of my stocking inside out!' she said. 'Sometimes I put my hand inside my stocking, catch hold of the toe, and pull it down inside the stocking, to turn it inside out – and you do the same with your eyes!'

'Yes, I do,' said the snail. 'It's rather a good idea, don't you think so?'

'Oh, very good,' said Silky. 'Where's your mouth? Is that it, under your feelers?'

'Yes,' said the snail, and he opened it to show the pixie. She looked at it closely.

'Have you any teeth?' she said. 'I have a lot.'

'So have I,' said the snail 'I have about fourteen thousand.'

Silky stared. 'You shouldn't tell silly stories like that,' she said.

'I'm not telling silly stories,' said the snail. 'I'll show you my teeth.'

He put out a long, narrow tongue, and Silky laughed. 'Don't tell me that you grow teeth on your *tongue*,' she said.

'Well, I do,' said the snail. 'Just look at my tongue, pixie. Can't you see the tiny teeth there, hundreds and hundreds of them?'

'Oh yes,' said the pixie in surprise. 'I can. They are so tiny, snail, and they all point backwards. It's like a tooth-ribbon, your tongue. How do you eat with your teeth?'

'I use my tongue like a file,' said the snail.

'I'll show you.'

He went to a lettuce, put out his tongue, and began to rasp away at a leaf. In a moment he had eaten quite a big piece.

'Well, you really *are* a strange creature,' said Silky. She looked closely at the snail, and noticed a strange little hole opening and shutting in the top of his neck.

'What's that slit for, in your neck?' she asked. 'And why does it keep opening and shutting?'

'Oh, that's my breathing-hole,' said the snail. 'Didn't you guess that? Every time that hole opens and shuts, I breathe.'

'Why don't you breathe with your mouth, as I do?' asked Silky.

'All soft-bodied creatures like myself, that have no bones at all, breathe through our bodies,' said the snail. 'Now, if you will excuse me, I must get into my shell. I can see the big thrush coming.'

He put his body back into his shell and stayed quite still. The thrush passed by without noticing him. The pixie went into her house, and came out with a tin of polish and a duster.

'Snail, I am going to polish up your shell for you,' she said. 'I shall make you look so nice. Everyone will say how beautiful you are!'

'Oh thank you,' said the snail, and he stayed quite still whilst Silky put polish on her cloth and then rubbed his shell hard.

'I rather like that,' he said.

'Well, come every day and I'll give you a good rubbing with my duster,' promised the pixie.

So, very soon, the two became good friends, and the snail always came by the pixie's house for a chat whenever he was near.

One day Silky was sad. She showed the snail a necklace of bright-blue beads – but it was broken, for the clasp was lost.

'I wanted to wear this at a party tomorrow,' said Silky. 'But I can't get anyone to mend it for me.'

'I know someone who will,' said the snail. 'He is a great friend of mine. He lives in a tiny house the fifth stone to the left of the old stone wall, and the fifteenth up. There's a hole there, and Mendy lives in it, doing all kinds of jobs for everyone.'

'I would never find the way,' said Silky. 'I know I'd get lost.'

'Well, I will take the necklace for you tonight,' said the snail. 'But I know Mendy will take a little time to do it, so you would have to fetch it yourself some time tomorrow.'

'But I should get lost!' said Silky.

'I will see that you don't,' said the snail. 'I will take the necklace to Mendy, give it to him, and come straight back here. And behind me I will leave a silvery trail for you to follow!'

'Oh, snail, you *are* kind and clever!' said Silky, delighted. She hung the beads over the snail's feelers, and he set off towards the old wall he knew so well. It was a long way for him to go, because he travelled very slowly.

It was a dry evening and the soft body of the snail did not get along as easily as on a wet night. So he sent out some slime to help his body along, and then he glided forwards more easily.

The slimy trail dried behind him, and left a beautiful silvery path, easy to see. The snail went up the wall to the hole where old Mendy the brownie lived, and gave him the broken necklace.

'It will be ready at noon tomorrow,' said Mendy. 'Thank you,' said the snail, and went home again, very slowly, leaving behind him a second silvery trail, running by the first.

Silky was asleep, so he didn't wake her, but he told her next morning that her necklace would be ready at noon.

'And you *can't* get lost,' he said, 'because I have left two silvery paths for you to follow. It doesn't matter which you walk on – either of them will lead you to Mendy.'

So Silky set off on one of the silvery paths, and it led her to the old wall, up it, and into Mendy's little house. Her necklace was mended, so she put it on ready for the party. She was very pleased indeed.

'Thank you,' she said. 'Now I know the way to your house, I'll bring some other things for you to mend, Mendy!'

She went to find her friend, the snail. 'Thank you for leaving me such a lovely silvery path,' she said. 'I do think you are clever!'

I expect you would like to see the snail's silvery path too, wouldn't you? Well, go round your garden any summer's morning – you are sure to see the snail's night-time trail of silver gleaming in the sunshine here and there.

The Train That Went to Fairyland

Once, when Fred was playing with his railway train in the garden, a very strange thing happened.

Fred had just wound up his engine, fastened the carriages to it and sent them off on the lines, when he heard a small, high voice.

'That's it, look! That's what I was telling you about!'

Fred looked round in surprise. At first he saw no one, then, standing by a daisy, he saw a tiny fellow dressed in a railway guard's uniform, but he had little wings poking out from the back of his coat! He was talking to another tiny fellow, who was dressed like a porter. They were neither of them any taller than the nearest daisy.

'Hallo!' said Fred, in surprise. 'Who are you and what do you want?'

'Listen,' said the tiny guard. 'Will you lend us your train just for a little while, to go to Goblin Town and back? You see, the chief goblin is taking a train from Toadstool Town and our engine has broken down. We can't get enough magic in time to mend it – the chief goblin is getting awfully angry.'

'Lend you my train?' said Fred, in the greatest astonishment and delight. 'Of course I will, but you must promise me something first.'

'What?' asked the little guard.

'You must make me small and let *me* drive the train,' said Fred.

'All right,' said the guard. 'But you won't have an accident, will you?'

'Of course, not,' said Fred. 'I know how to drive my own train!'

'Shut your eyes and keep still a minute,' said the guard. Fred did as he was told, and the little guard sang out a string of very strange words. And when Fred opened his eyes again, what a surprise for him! He was as small as the tiny guard and porter.

'This is fun!' said Fred, getting into the cab. 'Come on. Will the engine run all right without lines, do you suppose?'

'Oh, we've got enough magic to make those as we go along,' said the little guard, and at once some lines spread before them running right down the garden to the hedge at the bottom. It was very strange and exciting.

'Well, off we go!' said Fred. 'I suppose the engine has only got to follow the lines, and it will be all right!'

He pulled down the little handle that started the train, and off they went! The guard and the porter had climbed into the cab of the engine too, so it seemed rather crowded. But nobody minded that, of course.

The lines spread before them in a most magical manner as the train ran over them, down the garden, through a hole in the hedge, and then goodness me, down a dark rabbit hole!

'Hallo, hallo!' said Fred in surprise. 'Wherever are we going?'

'It's all right,' said the little guard. 'This will take us to Toadstool Town. We come up at the other side of the hill.'

The engine ran through the winding rabbit holes, and once or twice met a rabbit who looked very scared indeed. Then it came up into the open air again, and there was Toadstool Town!

'I should have known it was without being told,' said Fred, who looked round him in delight as they passed tiny houses made out of the toadstools growing everywhere. 'Hallo, we're running into a station!'

So they were. It was Toadstool Station. Standing on another line was the train belonging to the little guard. The engine-driver and stoker were trying their hardest to rub enough magic into the wheels to start it, but it just wouldn't go!

On the platform was a fat, important-looking goblin, stamping up and down.

'Never heard of such a thing!' he kept saying, in a loud and angry voice. 'Never in my life! Keeping me waiting like this! Another minute and I'll turn the train into a caterpillar, and the driver and stoker into two leaves for it to feed on!'

'What a horrid fellow!' whispered Fred. The guard ran to the goblin and bowed low. 'Please, your Highness, we've got another train to take you home. Will you get in?'

'About time something was done!' said the goblin, crossly. 'I never heard of such a thing in my life, keeping me waiting like this!'

He got into one of the carriages. He had to get in through the roof, because the doors were only pretend ones that wouldn't open. The little guard slid the roof open and then shut it again over the angry goblin.

'Start up the train again quickly!' he cried. So Fred pulled down the handle again and the little clockwork train set off to Goblin Town. It passed through many little stations with strange names, and the little folk waiting there stared in the greatest surprise to see such an unusual train.

Fred was as proud and pleased as could be! He drove that engine as if he had driven engines all his life. He wished and wished he could make it whistle. But it only had a pretend whistle. Fred wished the funnel would smoke, too, but of course, it didn't!

Suddenly the train slowed down and stopped. 'Good gracious! What's the matter?' said the little guard, who was still in the engine-cab with Fred. 'Don't say your train is going to break down, too? The goblin certainly will turn us all into something unpleasant if it does!'

The goblin saw that the train had stopped. He slid back the roof of his carriage and popped his angry face out.

'What's the matter? Has this train broken down, too?'

Fred had jumped down from the cab and had gone to turn the key that wound up the engine. It had run down, and no wonder, for it had come a long, long way! It was surprising that it hadn't needed winding up before.

The goblin stared in astonishment at the key in Fred's hand. He had never seen a key to wind up an engine before. He got crosser than ever.

'What are you getting down from the engine for? Surely you are not going to pick flowers or do a bit of shopping? Get back at once!'

But Fred had had enough of the cross goblin. He slid the roof back so that the goblin couldn't open it again.

'Now you be quiet,' said Fred. 'The pixies and elves may be frightened of you, but *I'm* not! Here I've come along with my train to help you and all you do is to yell at me and be most impolite. I don't like you. I'll take you to Goblin Town with pleasure, and leave you there with even greater pleasure, but while we are on the way you will please keep quiet and behave.'

Well! The little guard and porter nearly fell out of the cab with horror and astonishment when they heard Fred speaking like that to the chief goblin! But Fred only grinned, and wound up the engine quickly.

There wasn't a sound from the goblin. Not a sound. He wasn't used to being spoken to like that. He thought Fred must be a great and mighty wizard to dare to speak so angrily to him. He was frightened. He sat in his roofed-in carriage and didn't say a word.

The train went on to Goblin Town and stopped. Fred got down, slid back the roof of the goblin's carriage and told him to get out.

The goblin climbed out quickly, looking quite scared.

'What do you say for being brought here in my train?' said Fred, catching hold of the goblin's arm tightly.

'Oh, th-th-thank you,' stammered the goblin.

'I should think so!' said Fred. 'I never heard of such a thing, not thanking anyone for a kindness. You go home and learn some manners, goblin.'

'Yes, yes, I will, thank you, sir,' said the chief goblin, and ran away as fast as he could. Everyone at the station stared in amazement.

'However did you dare to talk to him like that?' said the little guard in surprise. 'Do you know, that is the first time in his life he has ever said, 'Thank you'! What a wonderful boy you are!'

'Not at all,' said Fred, getting back into the engine-cab. 'That's the only way to talk to rude people. Didn't you know? Now then, back home we go, to my own garden!'

And back home they went, past all the funny little

stations to Toadstool Town, down into the rabbit-burrows and out into the field, through the hedge and up the garden, back to where they started.

'Shut your eyes and we'll make you your own size again,' said the little guard. In a moment Fred was very large indeed and his train now looked very small to him!

'What would you like for a reward?' said the little guard. 'Shall I give your train a real whistle, and real smoke in its tunnel? Would you like that?'

'Rather!' said Fred. And from that very day his clockwork engine could whistle and smoke exactly like a real one.

The Cat That Was Forgotten

Once there was a big black cat called Sootikin. He lived with the Jones family, and he killed all the mice that came to eat their crumbs.

Sootikin was a fine cat. His eyes were as green as cucumbers, and his whiskers were as white as snow. He was always purring, and he loved to be petted.

But the Jones family didn't pet him very much. Jane and Ronnie Jones were not very fond of animals, and Mrs Jones often shouted at him because he mewed round her feet when she was cooking fish.

Next door lived a boy called Billy. He loved Sootikin. He thought he was the finest cat in the world, and he was always looking out for him to stroke him.

'I wish Sootikin was mine, Mummy,' he said to his mother. 'I wish we had a cat.'

But his mother didn't like cats or dogs in the

house, though she often said she liked Sootikin, and wished he would come and kill the mice in her larder.

Now one day the Jones family were very excited. They called over the fence to Billy.

'We're going away for a whole month to the seaside, to our Granny's. Aren't we lucky?'

'Yes,' said Billy, who had never even seen the sea. 'How I wish I was going with you!'

'We're catching the ten o'clock, train,' said Hilda. 'We'll send you a postcard.'

All the Jones family got into a taxi-cab at half-past nine and went off to the station. Billy felt lonely. He liked hearing the children next door shouting and laughing. Now for a whole month their house would be empty.

'I suppose they've taken dear old Sootikin too,' he thought.

But they hadn't, because, to Billy's great surprise, the big black cat suddenly sprang on to the top of the wall, and curled himself up in the sun. 'Mummy. The Joneses haven't taken Sootikin,' said Billy. 'Isn't that funny?'

'Oh, I expect they have arranged with a friend of theirs to come and feed him every day,' said Mummy. 'That is what people usually do when they

have animals they leave behind. Maybe someone will come along with bread and milk or a bit of fish each day.'

Sootikin wondered where his family had gone. They hadn't even said good-bye to him. He went to the kitchen door after a bit and mewed to get in. But nobody opened the door. He went to see if he could find an open window, but they were all shut.

All that day Sootikin felt lonely, but he felt sure his family would come back in the evening. Then he could go indoors, have his milk, and jump into his own basket.

But his family didn't come back. Sootikin began

to feel very hungry. There were no mice to catch, because he had caught them all. He wished he could have something to eat.

He had to sleep outside that night because he couldn't get into his house. It rained, and although Sootikin was under a bush, he got very wet. He sneezed.

He felt sad. His family had gone. They had forgotten him. They hadn't left him any food. They hadn't remembered that he had nowhere to sleep. They didn't love him at all. They were unkind.

He was very hungry the next day and the next. He found an old kipper bone and ate that. He chewed up an old crust.

When the fourth day came, he was thin and his coat looked rough and untidy. He had a cold. He didn't feel at all well, but he still felt hungry.

He thought of Billy, the boy next door. He had always been kind to him. Perhaps he would give him something to eat.

So Sootikin jumped over the wall to find Billy. He was in the garden, digging. Sootikin mewed.

Billy turned round. At first he hardly knew Sootikin, for the poor cat was so thin and his coat was no longer silky and smooth.

'Why – is it *you*, Sootikin!' cried Billy, and he

bent down to stroke the cat. 'Poor, poor thing – you look so thin and hungry. Has no one been feeding you?'

Sootikin mewed to say that no one had fed him, he was lonely and sad, and please could he have something to eat.

Billy understood, and ran to his mother. 'Mummy,' he cried, 'poor old Sootikin is half-starved. Look at him – all skin and bone. Oh, Mummy, can I give him something to eat?'

'Poor creature!' said his mother, putting down a plate of fish scraps and milk. 'Here you are, Sootikin. He's got a cold too, Billy – he must have slept out in the rain at night.'

'Mummy, could he sleep in our kitchen till his cold is better?' said Billy. His mother nodded. She was kind and she didn't like to think that Sootikin had been forgotten like that.

Sootikin was glad. He ate a good meal and felt better. He washed himself and made his fur silkier. Then he jumped into a box that Billy had found for him, and went fast asleep.

He slept all night in the kitchen. He had a good meal the next day, and he slept the next night in the kitchen too – but not *all* night! No – he heard the mice in the larder, and he went to see what they were up to. Sootikin knew that mice were not allowed in larders.

Sootikin killed three big mice and one little one. He left them in a row to show Billy's mother what he had done. She was very pleased when she saw the mice.

'Mummy, that's Sootikin's way of saying thank you for our kindness,' said Billy, stroking the big cat, who purred loudly. 'Oh, Mummy, I do love Sootikin. I do wish he was my cat.'

'Well, the Joneses will want him as soon as they come back,' said his mother. 'You must make the most of him whilst they are away. I do think it was unkind of them to forget all about him like this.'

But do you know, when the Jones family came back, Sootikin wouldn't live with them any more. He simply wouldn't. Every time Billy put him over the wall, he came back again.

'He just won't live with us,' said Jane. 'Silly cat. He doesn't know his own home.'

'Well – you didn't seem to know your own cat – you forgot all about him,' said Billy. 'You don't deserve a cat like Sootikin. I hope he *does* live with us, and not you!'

Sootikin did. He had quite made up his mind

about that. He never went into the Joneses' garden or house again but kept close to Billy.

'A cat can't help loving people who are kind,' purred Sootikin. 'I'm *your* cat now, Billy, and you're my little boy!'

The Dog Who Wanted a Home

There was once a dog who wanted a home. He had had a bad master, who was unkind to him, and he had run away because he was so unhappy.

'I shall find a new master, or perhaps a mistress,' said the dog to himself. 'I want someone who will love me. I want someone to love and to care for.'

But nobody seemed to want a dog, nobody at all. It was very sad. The dog ran here and he ran there, but either there was already a dog in the houses he went to, or the people there didn't want a dog.

He talked to his friend, the cat, about it. 'What am I to do?' he said. 'I must have a home. I cannot run about wild, with no food, and only the puddles to drink from.'

'Dogs and cats need homes,' said the cat, licking herself as she sat on top of the wall. 'I don't know of anyone who wants a dog. It's a pity you are not a cat.'

'Why?' asked the dog.

'Because I know a poor, blind old lady who badly wants a cat,' said the cat. 'She is lonely, and she wants a nice, cosy cat she can have in her lap.'

'Perhaps she would have a dog instead,' said the dog. 'If she is blind, I could help her, couldn't I? I could take her safely across the roads, and guard her house at night. A cat couldn't do that.'

'Well, she says she wants a cat, not a dog,' said the cat. Then she stopped licking herself and looked closely at the dog.

'I have an idea!' she said. 'You have a very silky coat for a dog, and a very long tail. I wonder whether you could *pretend* to be a cat!

'The poor old lady is blind and she wouldn't know.'

'I shouldn't like to deceive anyone,' said the dog.

'No, that wouldn't be nice,' said the cat. 'But after all, a dog *would* be better for the old lady, and when she got used to you, you could tell her you were a dog, and ask her to forgive you for pretending.'

'And by that time she might be so fond of me that she wouldn't mind keeping me!' said the dog joyfully. 'Yes – that is quite a good idea of yours, cat.'

'I will give you a few hints about cats,' said the

cat. 'Don't bark, whatever you do, because, as you know, cats mew. If you bark you will give yourself away. And do try and purr a little.'

The dog tried – but what came from his throat was more of a growl than a purr. The cat laughed.

'That's really enough to make a cat laugh!' she said. 'Well, perhaps with a little practice you may get better. And another thing to remember is – put your claws in when you walk, so that you walk softly, like me, and don't make a clattering sound.'

The dog looked at his paws. The big, blunt claws stuck out, and he could not move them back into his paws, as the cat could. 'I must try to practise that too,' he said.

'Good-bye,' said the cat. 'I wish you luck. She is a dear old lady and will be very kind to you.'

The dog ran off to the old lady's house. She was sitting in her kitchen, knitting. The dog ran up to her, and pressed against her, as he had seen cats do. The old lady put down her hand and stroked him.

'So someone has sent me a cat!' she said. 'How kind! Puss, puss, puss, do you want some milk?'

She got up and put down a saucer of milk. The dog was pleased. He lapped it up noisily. 'Dear me, what a noise you make!' said the old lady in surprise. 'You must be a very hungry cat! Come on to my knee.'

The dog jumped up on to the old lady's knee. She stroked his silky coat, and felt his long tail. He tried his very best to purr. He made a very funny noise.

'You must have got a cold, Puss,' said the old lady. 'That's a funny purr you have! Now, go to sleep.'

The dog fell asleep. He liked being in the old lady's warm lap. He felt loved and happy. If only she went on thinking that he was a cat.

When he woke up, the old lady spoke to him. 'Puss, I want you to lie in the kitchen to-night and catch the mice that come. You will be very useful to me if you can do that.'

The dog was not good at catching mice. He was not quiet and sly like the cat. But he made up his mind to try. He did try, very hard, but as soon as he jumped up when he saw a mouse, the little animal heard his claws clattering on the floor, and fled away.

So in the morning there were no dead mice for the old lady to find. She was quite nice about it and stroked the dog gently.

'Never mind, Puss,' she said. 'You can try again tonight.'

The old lady was so kind and gentle that the dog longed with all his heart to catch mice for her, or to do anything to please her. He trotted after her all day long, as she went about her work. It was wonderful what she could do without being able to see.

'The only thing I can't do with safety is to go out and see my grand-children,' she told the dog. 'You see, I have to cross two roads to get to their house, and I am always afraid of being knocked over by something I can't see.'

The dog nearly said, 'Woof, woof, I will help you,' and just remembered in time that cats never bark.

The old lady was puzzled that day. Every time the dog ran across the floor she put her head on one side and listened.

'Your paws make such a noise,' she said. 'Surely you put your sharp claws in as you run, Puss? It sounds as if you are making quite a noise with them.'

So the dog was, because he couldn't help it. He couldn't put his claws in, like a cat. No dog can.

Then another thing puzzled the old lady. She put some milk on her finger for the dog to lick. The dog put out his pink tongue and licked the milk away.

'Well!' said the old lady, surprised. 'What a strange tongue you have, Puss! All the other cats have had very rough, scraping tongues but you have a very smooth one!'

'Oh dear!' thought the dog. 'This is quite true. Dogs have smooth tongues, and cats have rough ones. I remember an old cat licking me once, and I noticed how rough her tongue was – almost as if it was covered by tiny hooks!'

'I'll give you a nice meaty bone, Puss,' said the old lady at tea-time. 'You can scrape the meat off it with your tongue, and when you have taken away the meat, we will give the bone to the next-door dog to crunch. Cats cannot crunch bones, but dogs can!'

The dog was delighted to see the lovely, meaty bone. He lay down and began to lick it with his tongue, as cats do. But his tongue was not rough, and he could not get the meat off the bone.

It was sad. He was hungry and longed to crunch up the bone. He sniffed at it. He licked it again. Then he got it into his mouth and gave it a bite with his hard, strong dog's teeth, that were so different from the teeth of cats!

The bone made a noise as he crunched it up. The old lady was surprised. 'Well, I never heard a cat crunch up a big bone before!' she said. 'You must have strong teeth, Puss!'

She put on her hat and coat. 'I am going out,' she said. 'I shall try to get to the house where my grand-children live. Maybe someone will help me across the road. Keep house for me whilst I am gone, Puss.'

The dog did not like to see the blind old lady going out alone. He ran after her. When she came to the road she had to cross, he stood in front of her, making her wait until a bicycle had gone by. Then he gently tugged at her dress to show her that it was safe to go across.

The old lady was delighted. She bent down to stroke the dog. 'Puss, you are the cleverest cat in the world!' she said.

But dear me, when the old lady reached her grand-children safely, what a surprise for her! They ran out to greet her, all shouting the same thing.

'Granny! You've got a dog! Oh, what a nice one!'

And so at last the secret was out. 'No wonder I was so puzzled!' said the old lady, stooping to pat the dog. He barked a little, and licked her hand, wagging his tail hard.

'That's right!' said the old lady. 'Don't pretend to be a cat any more! Bark, and lick my hand and wag your tail! I'll have you instead of a cat. You're a kind little animal, and you'll help me across the road, won't you?'

'Woof, woof, woof!' said the dog joyfully, and ran off to tell the cat that he had found a home at last.

Freckles for a Thrush

An elf once came to the garden where the thrush lived. He was a clever little elf, and the thrush used to love to watch him at work.

He painted the tips of the daisy-petals bright crimson and spots on the ladybirds. He even painted the blackbird's beak a bright orange-gold for him in the spring.

The thrush was rather tiresome. He was always asking questions, always poking his beak here and there, always upsetting pots of paint.

The elf got angry with him. 'Look here, you big clumsy bird, don't come near me any more!' he said. 'I'm going to be very busy just now, painting mauve and green on the starling's feathers. If you keep disturbing me I shall get the colours wrong.'

But the thrush couldn't leave the little painter alone. He always had to peep and see what he was doing. Then one day he spied a worm just by the elf and darted at it. He pulled it up and upset half a dozen paint pots at once.

The colours all ran together on the grass, and the elf groaned.

'Look there! Half my colours wasted! That blue was for the blue-tit's cap – and that yellow was for the celandines in spring. I detest you, thrush. Go away!'

'I don't see why you should waste your lovely colours on stupid birds like the starling and the blue-tit,' said the thrush. "They have nice feathers already. What about *me*? I am a dull brown bird with no colour at all, not even a bright beak! Won't you paint *me*, elfin painter – that would be a kind and sensible thing to do.'

'I don't want to be kind and sensible to you,' said the elf. 'I don't like you. Go away!'

'Yes, but elf, I do think you might spare me a little of your . . .' began the tiresome thrush again, and trod on the painter's biggest brush and broke it.

'*Now* look what you've done!' shouted the elf, in a rage, and he shook the brush he was using at the thrush. A shower of brown drops of paint flew all over the front of the surprised thrush, and stuck there.

'Oh – you've splashed my chest with your brown

paint!' said the thrush crossly. 'I shall complain to the head-brownie in the wood. He will punish you!'

He flew off – but the head-brownie only laughed. 'It serves you right, anyhow!' he said. 'And why complain, thrush? Didn't you want your coat to be made brighter? Well, I think your freckled breast is very, very pretty. Go and look at yourself in the pond.'

The thrush went and looked into the water. Yes! He looked fine with his speckly, freckly breast. He liked it enormously. He flew back to thank the elfin painter, but he had collected his pots and gone off in a temper.

I like the freckles on the thrush, too. Do you? You might go and look at him. He's very proud of his freckles now.

He's a Horrid Dog

'There's a dear little puppy next door,' said Mummy to Alice. 'I saw him this morning. You'll love him, Alice.'

'I'll look out for him as I go to school,' said Alice. So she did, and she soon saw him, running round the next-door garden. The gate was shut, so he couldn't get out. Alice peeped over the top, and he rushed up and licked her on the nose.

'Don't,' said Alice, who didn't know that licking was a dog's way of kissing. She went off down the street, her satchel over her back, and her ball in her hand. She was not allowed to bounce it in the road, in case it went too near cars and she ran after it. She wanted to play with it at break.

Suddenly there came the sound of scampering feet, and after her tore the puppy! He had managed to jump over the gate, and wanted to catch her up. He had smelt the ball in her hand.

A ball. How that puppy loved a ball! His mistress often threw one for him, and he loved to scamper after it and get it into his mouth. A ball was the greatest fun in the world!

He jumped up at the surprised little girl. He knocked the ball right out of her hand! It went rolling along the pavement, and Alice gave a cry of alarm.

'Naughty dog! You'll make me lose my ball!'

The puppy pounced on it, threw it into the air, caught it again, and then danced all round Alice as if to say, 'Catch me if you can! I have your ball!'

But he wouldn't let Alice catch him, or get her ball, either. He ran off as soon as she tried to grab him. 'You're a horrid, horrid dog!' said Alice, almost in tears. 'I don't like you a bit. Give me my ball! You'll make me late for school.'

But the puppy was having such a lovely game that he couldn't possibly let Alice catch him. So, in the end, she had to go to school without her ball. She was late and the teacher scolded her.

'It wasn't my fault,' said Alice. 'It was the fault of the dog next door. He's a horrid dog. He took my ball away from me and wouldn't give it back.'

The puppy was waiting for her to come home, and as soon as he saw her he rushed out and put the ball at her feet. Really, he wanted her to play with him, and throw the ball for him to fetch. Alice wasn't doing that!

She picked up her ball and looked at it. The puppy had chewed it a little, and it wasn't such a nice-looking ball as before. Alice was very cross. She stamped her foot at the puppy and made him jump. 'Bad dog! Horrid dog! I don't like you! Go home!'

'Why, Alice!' said her mother's voice in surprise. 'I thought you'd love the puppy!'

'I don't. He's a horrid dog! I shan't play with him or take any notice of him at all,' said Alice. 'He's unkind and mean.'

And, do you know, she wouldn't pat him or talk to him, no matter how often he came rushing up to her. He was surprised and sad. Usually everyone made a fuss of him, for he really was a dear little fellow, with a tail that never stopped wagging.

Now, one afternoon Alice was going out to tea. She put on her best blue frock, socks and shoes, and a new hat with a blue ribbon round. It suited Alice beautifully.

'That's the prettiest hat you've ever had,' said Mummy, and kissed her goodbye. 'Hold it on tightly round the corner, because it's very windy today.'

Alice set off. The puppy came to meet her as usual, and as usual she took no notice of him at all. He trotted behind her, his tail down. What a funny little girl this was! Why didn't she give him a pat? The puppy couldn't understand it at all.

At the corner the wind blew very hard. Off went Alice's beautiful new hat. It flew into the road and rolled over and over and over, all the way back home. Alice gave a real squeal. 'Oh! My new hat! Oh, dear!'

The puppy saw the hat rolling along and he tore after it, barking. Was this a new game? Had the little girl thrown her hat for him to play with?

He was almost run over by a car. Then a bicycle just missed him. The hat rolled in and out of the traffic, and the puppy scampered after it. He caught the hat at last and was just going to toss it into the air and catch it again when he heard Alice's voice, 'Bring it here! Puppy, bring it here. It's my best hat!'

Ah! He knew the words 'bring it here!' He tore back to Alice at once and dropped the hat at her feet, his tail wagging hard. He looked up at the little girl with shining eyes and his pink tongue hung out of his mouth.

Alice picked up the hat. It wasn't damaged at all. She dusted it a little, and then put it on. She looked down at the puppy. 'Thank you,' she said. 'That was kind of you, especially as we weren't friends. But we will be now!'

'Woof!' said the puppy, and to Alice's surprise he put out his paw. Did he want to shake hands? He did! This was his newest trick and he was proud of it. Alice felt sure he was trying to say, 'Yes, we'll be friends! Shake hands!'

So they shook hands solemnly, and the puppy went all the way to her aunt's with Alice, waited for her, and then went all the way home. And she asked him in to play with her in her garden.

'But I thought you said he was a horrid dog?' said Mummy, in surprise.

'I made a mistake,' said Alice. 'I was the horrid one, Mummy – but now we're *both* nice!'

Hoppitty-Skip and Crawl-About

Hoppity-Skip was a frog. He could jump very high in the air, because his hind legs were long and strong.

One day he leapt high, and came down plop – but not on the ground! He had jumped on to the back of a toad!

'Crrr-oak!' said the toad crossly. 'Look where you are going!'

'Oh, I'm sorry,' said the frog, jumping off the toad's back quickly. 'You are so like a clod of earth that I didn't see you.'

'I suppose I am,' said the toad. 'It is a good idea to hide from enemies by looking exactly like the ground. Where are you going?'

'I am going to the pond,' said the frog. 'I think it is time I found a wife and had some eggs laid in the pond.'

'I shall soon be doing the same,' said the toad. 'I always go to the pond at the bottom of this field.'

'Oh, that's a long way away,' said the frog. 'I go to the little pond near by.'

'Don't go there this year,' said the toad. 'There are ducks on it.'

'Well, I will come to your pond, then,' said the frog.

In a short time the frog had found a mate, and she had laid her eggs in a big mass of jelly in the pond. The toad, too, had eggs, but they were not in a mass – they were in a doublestring of jelly, wound in and out of the water-weeds.

'My eggs rise up to the surface where the sun can warm them,' said the frog. 'Look – you can see the tiny black specks wriggling in the jelly. They are tadpoles already.'

Soon there were both frog and toad tadpoles in the pond. They wriggled about and had a lovely time.

'Let us leave the pond now,' said the frog to the toad. 'I am tired of all these wriggling tadpoles. We will go and find a nice damp place somewhere in a ditch.'

So they left the warm pond and made their way to a ditch the toad knew. The frog went by leaps and bounds, but the toad didn't. He either crawled, or did some funny little hops that made the frog laugh.

'Why don't you leap along like me?' he said. 'You're so slow.'

'I am not made like you,' said the toad. 'I am heavier and my legs are shorter. Anyway, why do you leap along so quickly? It is a hot day. Go slowly.'

'I can't help jumping,' said the frog. 'And besides, Crawl-About, my high leaps are very useful to me sometimes, when enemies are near.'

'I don't believe it,' said Crawl-About. 'It is much wiser to crouch on the ground and pretend to be a clod of earth, as I do.'

Just then a rat came by and saw the frog and the toad. The toad sank to the earth and seemed to vanish, he was so like the soil. The rat pounced on the frog – but at once the little creature rose high in the air, and the rat ran back, startled. By the time he had come back again to find the frog, Hoppitty-Skip had vanished into some long grass.

He waited until the rat had gone. Then he looked for his friend. He could not see him at all – and then suddenly he saw the toad's beautiful coppery eyes looking at him near by. He was still crouching on the ground, so like it that the frog could only make out his shining eyes.

'Well, did you see how I startled the rat?' asked

the frog in delight. 'Didn't I make him jump? I just had time to vanish into the long grass.'

'Well, your way of dealing with enemies is good for you, and mine is good for me,' said the toad, beginning to crawl again. 'We all have our different ways, Hoppitty-Skip. Mine is to crouch down and keep still, yours is to jump. I have another way of getting the better of an enemy too.'

'What's that?' asked the frog. But the toad had no breath to tell him.

They found a good place in a ditch. The long grass was damp there, and both the creatures liked that. They did not like dryness. They sat and waited for food to come to them. The toad fell asleep.

The frog had a lovely time. A big bluebottle fly came along and perched on a leaf just above the frog's head. Out flicked his tongue – and the fly was gone! The frog blinked his eyes and swallowed.

He waited for another fly to come. But the next thing that came along was a fat green caterpillar, arching its back as it crawled.

Out flicked the frog's tongue – and the surprised caterpillar disappeared down the frog's throat.

'I say!' said a little mouse near by. 'I say, Hoppitty-Skip – how do you manage to catch flies and grubs so easily? You must have a very long tongue!'

'I've a very clever sort of tongue,' said the frog, and he flicked it out to show the mouse. 'Look, it's fastened to the front of my mouth, instead of the back, as yours is. So I can flick it out much farther!'

He flicked it out again and hit the mouse on the nose with it. 'Don't,' said the mouse. 'Your tongue feels sticky. Look – there's another fly!'

A big fly was buzzing just above their heads. The frog flicked out his long tongue, and flicked it back again. The fly was stuck on the end of his tongue, and went down his throat! 'Most delicious,' said the frog. 'It's a very great pity old Crawl-About sleeps all the day – he misses such a lot of good meals!'

Crawl-About woke up at night. He gave a croak and set out on a walk. 'Where are you going?' called the frog, who wanted to sleep. 'You'll lose your way in the dark.'

'No, I shan't,' said the toad. 'I never do. I always know my way back easily. I am off to find a few slugs, a score or so of beetles, and maybe even a baby mouse if I can get one. I'll be back by the morning.'

Sure enough, he was back in his place by the morning, though he had crawled and hopped quite a long way in the night. He told Hoppitty-Skip that he had had a very good time, and eaten so many

things that all he wanted to do now was to sleep.

'You are not really very good company,' said the frog. 'You like to sleep all day and wander off at night. Well, well – all the more flies for me, I suppose!'

The frog's body was smooth and fresh-looking. The toad's was pimply and dark, much drier than the frog's. The frog thought he had much the nicer body of the two, and he was glad he had quick legs and a high bound. It was fun to be in the field in that hot summer weather. It was always moist in the ditch.

One day the rat came back again. The frog gave a great leap and got away. The toad crouched down flat as before. But the rat saw him and pounced fiercely on him.

'Now he'll be eaten!' said Hoppitty-Skip, in fright. 'Oh, what a pity he hasn't a good high jump as I have, then he could get away quickly.'

But the toad had yet another way in which he could get rid of an enemy. From his pimply body he sent out some nasty-smelling, nasty-tasting stuff. The rat got a taste of it and drew back, his mouth open in disgust.

'Eat me if you like,' croaked the toad, 'but I shall be the most horrible-tasting meal you have ever had! I may even poison you. Lick me, rat – taste me! Do you still think you would like me for a meal?'

The rat fled, still with his mouth wide open. He couldn't bear the horrible taste on his tongue. Oh, he would never, never pounce on a toad again!

'Are you there, Hoppitty-Skip?' asked Crawl-About. 'Don't look so frightened. I am quite all right. Your trick of leaping is very good – but my trick of hiding, and of sending out nasty-tasting stuff all over my back, is even better!'

Soon the cold days came. 'I must get back to the pond,' said the frog. 'Come with me, Crawl-About. Come and sleep in the mud with me. We shall be safe there all through the winter.'

'I might,' said the toad sleepily. 'Go and have a look at the pond and see if it is very crowded.'

The frog went, and soon came hopping back. The toad was under a big stone. The frog peeped beneath it.

'Come to the pond,' he said. 'There is plenty of room. I have found two good places in the mud at the bottom.'

But there was no answer. The toad had already gone to sleep for the winter! Nothing would wake him. He slept soundly under his stone, looking like a dark piece of earth.

'Well, there's no waking him,' said Hoppitty-Skip. 'Good-bye, Crawl-About. I'm off to sleep in the pond. See you again in the spring!'

And off he hopped to sleep the cold days and nights away, tucked into the mud at the bottom of the pond. You won't be able to see him in the winter – but you might find Crawl-About. Don't disturb him, will you.

The Lamb Without a Mother

Ellen was staying at her uncle's farm. She liked being there, because there were so many nice things to do. She could feed the hens. She could take milk in a pail to the new calf. She could ride on Blackie, the old farm-horse.

It was winter-time, so it was not such fun as in the summer-time. But there was one great excitement – and that was the coming of the new lambs!

Ellen loved the baby lambs. The old shepherd lived in his hut on the hillside near the sheep, so that he could look after them when their lambs were born. Ellen often used to go and talk to him.

'Ah, it's a busy time with me,' said the old shepherd. 'Sometimes many lambs are born the same night, and there are many babies to see to. You come and look at these two – a sweet pair they are!'

Ellen peeped into a little fold and saw a big mother-sheep there, with two tiny lambs beside her. Each of them had black noses, and they were butting them against their mother.

'I love them,' said Ellen. 'What do you feed them on, shepherd?'

'Oh, the mother feeds them,' said the shepherd with a laugh. 'Didn't you know, missy? Ah, yes, the lambs suck their mother's milk, and that's what makes them frisky and strong.'

'What a good idea,' said Ellen, and she watched the tiny lambs drinking their mother's milk. 'Aren't they hungry, shepherd!'

'Little creatures always are,' said the shepherd. 'They have to grow big, you see, so they want a lot of food to build up their growing bodies. Birds bring grubs to their little ones, caterpillars eat the leaves of plants, young fish find their own food – and lambs drink their mother's milk.'

One day, when Ellen went to see the old shepherd, she found him looking sad. 'One of the mother-sheep has died' he said. 'And she has left this little lamb behind her.'

'Oh dear – and it has no mother to get milk from!' said Ellen sadly. 'Will it die too?'

'I am going to see if another mother-sheep will take it,' said the shepherd. 'Maybe she will. She has only one lamb.'

So he gave the tiny lamb to another sheep. But she butted it away angrily.

'Isn't she unkind?' said Ellen, almost in tears. 'She's got one lamb of her own, and surely she wouldn't mind having another. Most of the sheep have two.'

'She isn't really unkind,' said the shepherd. 'She doesn't know the strange smell of this little lamb, so she doesn't like it. Well, well – she won't have it, that's plain!'

'What will you do?' asked Ellen.

'It will have to be fed from a baby's bottle,' said the shepherd. 'I shall put milk into a bottle, put a teat on it, and let the lamb suck. Then it will live.'

Ellen stared at him in surprise. 'Can you really feed a lamb out of a baby's bottle?' she said. 'Oh, shepherd, please may I watch you?'

'Of course,' said the shepherd. He took out a glass bottle from his shed. He washed it, and then put some warm milk into it. He fitted a large teat on the end, and went to where he had left the tiny lamb.

He smeared the teat with milk and pushed it against the lamb's black nose. The tiny creature sniffed at it and then put out its tongue and licked it.

'It likes the taste!' said Ellen in excitement. 'Oh, lamb, do drink the milk!'

The lamb opened his mouth and took hold of the milky teat. He sucked – for that is a thing that all lambs, all calves, all babies know how to do. He sucked hard.

The milk came through the teat and went into his mouth. The lamb sucked and sucked. He was hungry. The milk was nice. He sucked until he had nearly finished the bottle.

Ellen watched him in delight. 'Please, please do let me hold the bottle whilst he finishes the few last drops,' she begged the shepherd. So he gave her the bottle to hold.

Ellen loved feeding the tiny lamb. She liked feeling him pulling hard at the bottle. He finished every drop of the milk, and licked the teat. Then he gave a sigh of happiness, as if to say, 'That was really nice!'

'He'll do all right,' said the shepherd, taking the empty bottle. 'The pity is – I've no time to bottle-feed lambs just now.'

'Shepherd – let me do it, then!' cried Ellen. 'I know Uncle will let me. Can I go and ask him?'

The shepherd nodded, and Ellen sped off down the hill to where her uncle was working in the fields.

'Uncle! There's a lamb without a mother, so it hasn't any mother's milk to drink! The shepherd

says it must be fed from a baby's bottle. Can I feed it for him every day, please, Uncle?'

'If you like,' said her uncle. 'It will need to be fed many times a day, Ellen, so you mustn't forget. You had better let the shepherd bring it down into the farmhouse garden for you. It can live there, and you can easily feed it from a bottle then, without climbing the hill every time.'

Ellen ran to tell the shepherd. 'You needn't carry it down for me,' she said. 'I can carry the little thing myself.'

So she carried the little warm creature down to the garden. She shut the gate carefully so that it could not get out. It seemed to like being there, and frisked round happily.

Ellen fed it when it was hungry. Her aunt put milk into the baby's bottle, and Ellen went to take it to the lamb. He soon knew her and ran to meet her. How he sucked the milk from the bottle! He almost pulled it out of Ellen's hand sometimes!

He grew well. He had a tight, woolly coat to keep him warm, and a long wriggling tail. He could jump and spring about cleverly. Ellen often played with him in the garden, and they loved one another very much.

He grew quite fat and tubby. Ellen looked at

him one day and said, 'You are almost like a little sheep. Don't grow into a sheep, little lamb. Sheep never play. They just eat grass all day long, and say "Baa-baa-baa".'

The lamb could bleat in his little high voice. Sometimes he would bleat for Ellen to bring him a bottle of milk. 'Maa-maaa-maa!' he would say.

But soon there came a time when he did not need to drink milk any more. He could eat grass. He nibbled at it and liked it. Ellen watched him eating it, and was afraid that soon he would have to leave the garden and go into the big field with the others.

'Then you will forget about me, and won't come running to meet me any more,' she said sadly.

One day the big sheep were sheared. The farmyard was full of their bleating, for they did not like their warm, thick woolly coats being cut away from them.

Ellen watched the shearing. 'What a lot of wool!' she said. I suppose that will be washed, and woven, and made into warm clothes. How useful the sheep are to us.'

The lamb was not sheared. He was allowed to keep his coat that year. 'It is not thick enough for shearing,' said the shepherd. 'The lambs keep their coats. They will be very thick next year. And now, I think your lamb must come and live in the field. He is old enough to be with the others, now that you have quite finished feeding him by bottle.'

Ellen was sad. She took the little lamb from the farmhouse garden to the field. She opened the gate and let him through. He stood quite still and stared at all the sheep and lambs there.

Then a small lamb came up to him. 'Come and play "Jump-high, jump-low" with us,' he said. 'It's such fun.'

The little lamb frisked off in delight. 'He has forgotten me already,' said Ellen.

But he hadn't. Whenever the little girl goes by the field, the lamb comes running up to the hedge, bleating. He pushes his nose through, and Ellen pats him. And I expect that he will always remember his little friend, and run happily to greet her, don't you?

Moo-ooo-ooo!

Once upon a time there was a little girl called Lucy. She lived in a big town, and every year she went to the seaside.

But one year she went to stay in the country instead. Her mother sent her to stay with her Aunt Mary on a big farm.

'You will have such a lovely time, Lucy,' said her mother. 'You will have chickens and ducks round you, big sheep in the fields, and perhaps Aunt Mary will let you ride on one of the big horses.'

'Will there be cows?' asked Lucy.

'Oh yes,' said her mother. 'Lovely big red and white cows that say "Mooo-ooo-ooo!" You will like them, Lucy.'

'I shan't,' said Lucy. 'I'm afraid of cows.'

'Silly girl,' said her mother. 'There's no need to be afraid of cows. They won't hurt you.'

'They might toss me with their big horns,' said Lucy

'Of course they won't,' said her mother. 'Cows are gentle animals. You will like them.'

But Lucy didn't like them. As soon as she was down at the farm, she began to look out for cows. She saw some in a field – and oh dear, as she walked by the field, one of the cows put its head over the hedge and mooed loudly.

'Mooo-ooo-ooo!' it said. It did make poor Lucy jump. She ran home crying, and her aunt was sorry.

'Darling, the cows won't hurt you,' she said. 'They are our friends. They give us lots of nice things, really they do.'

'They don't give *me* anything,' sobbed Lucy. 'At least, they only give me nasty things. That cow gave me a horrid fright.'

'Well, come with me and feed the hens,' said Aunt Mary. Lucy dried her eyes and went with her aunt.

When she came back again it was eleven o'clock. Her aunt went to the larder and brought out a bun. Then she poured some rich yellow milk into a blue cup.

'A present from the cow,' she said to Lucy. 'Drink it up and see how nice it is. The cow gave it to me this morning, and I put it in a jug for you.'

Lucy tasted the milk. It was simply lovely. 'It's much nicer than my milk at home,' she said. 'Did the cow really give it to me?'

'Yes, it came from the cow,' said Aunt Mary. 'As soon as you stop being afraid of my dear old cows, I want you to come with me and see me milk them. You will like to hear the milk splashing into the pail. It is a lovely sound.'

When dinner-time came, there was an apple pie for pudding. Lucy was glad.

'It's one of my favourite puddings,' she said. 'Is there any custard, Auntie?'

'No,' said her aunt. 'But the cow sent you this instead. You will like it.'

Aunt Mary put a little blue jug of cream down beside Lucy's plate. 'Pour it out over your pie yourself,' she said. 'It is all for you. Have it all and enjoy it. Isn't the cow kind?'

Lucy poured out the cream over her pie. It was thick and yellow and tasted very good.

In the afternoon she went out to play, but she didn't go near the field where the cows were. 'If I do they will shout "Moo-ooo-ooo" at me again,' she said to herself.

When tea-time came Lucy was hungry. She was glad to hear the tea-bell and ran indoors. There was a loaf of crusty new bread on the table, and beside it was a white dish full of golden-yellow butter. There was a pot of strawberry jam, and some buns. Lucy thought it was a lovely tea.

'What lovely golden butter!' she said. 'Can I spread it on my piece of bread myself Auntie? Mother lets me at home.'

'Yes, you can,' said Aunt Mary. 'It's a present from the cow again.'

'*Is* it?' said Lucy, surprised. 'I didn't know butter came from the cow.'

'Well, we make it from the cream that we get from the milk that the cow gives us,' said Aunt Mary. 'So it is really a present from the cow, too, you see.'

'Oh,' said Lucy, spreading her bread with the rich yellow butter. 'The cow *does* give us a lot of things, doesn't it?'

Lucy met the cows that evening as they walked to their milking-place. One mooed rather loudly and she ran away again. She told her aunt about it at supper-time.

'That nasty horrid cow mooed loudly at me again,' she said. 'I don't like cows. They are horrid things.'

'Dear me, I'm sorry,' said Aunt Mary, as she set down Lucy's supper in front of her. 'I suppose you won't want to eat another present from the cow, then?'

'Does this lovely cheese come from the cow too?' cried Lucy, in great surprise. 'Oh, Aunt Mary – I didn't know that! Milk – and cream and butter – and cheese! Well, really, what a nice animal!'

Lucy ate her bread and butter and cheese. She had some stewed apple and cream, and she drank a glass of milk. What a number of things came from the cow! She thought about it quite a lot.

'Auntie,' she said the next day, 'I think I am wrong to be silly about cows. But I can't help it. Do you think if I got used to baby cows first, I would grow to like grown-up cows?'

'I am sure you would,' said Aunt Mary. 'That is a very good idea! We have some calves, and you shall help me to feed them today. You shall see me feed a little newborn calf. You will like that.'

'Do calves grow into cows?' asked Lucy, trotting after her aunt.

'Oh yes, always,' said Aunt Mary. 'Now look, here is our very youngest baby. We must teach her to suck milk. We cannot let her suck her mother's milk – that big cow over there – because we want all *her* milk to sell; so we must feed her out of a pail.'

The baby calf was very sweet. She was rather

wobbly on her long legs, and she had the softest brown eyes that Lucy had ever seen. She sniffed at Lucy's hand and then began to suck it.

'Oh – she's very hungry, Auntie,' said Lucy. 'She's trying to suck my hand.'

It wasn't long before Aunt Mary had a pail of milk ready for the calf. 'Now watch me teach her to drink,' she said.

She dipped her fingers in the milk and held them out to the calf. The calf sniffed the milk and then licked it eagerly, trying to take Aunt Mary's hand into her mouth. She dipped her fingers in the pail of milk again, and once more the calf licked the milk off.

The next time Aunt Mary did not hold her fingers out so far. She held them in the pail. The calf put her head in the pail, and followed her fingers down. Aunt Mary put them right into the milk as soon as the calf began to suck them.

Then the little creature found that she was sucking up a great deal of milk! She still nuzzled around Aunt Mary's fingers, but she couldn't help taking in some of the milk in the pail, for her mouth was in it!

'That's a clever way of teaching her to drink milk,' said Lucy, delighted. 'Let me put *my* fingers in, Aunt Mary. I want to do it too.'

So Aunt Mary held the pail whilst Lucy dipped her fingers in, and let the calf suck them. Then slowly the little girl put them nearer to the milk, until once again the calf was drinking in the pail!

'She will soon learn,' said Aunt Mary. 'You can help me to feed the little thing three times a day, if you like, dear.'

So for the next week or two Lucy helped to feed the little calf. She loved her, and then one day she found that she was no longer afraid of cows!

'I can't be afraid of you when I love your little calf so much,' she told the big red and white cow. 'The little calf will grow up to be just like you, and she will give me presents like you do – milk and cream and butter and cheese. Thank you, cow. I'm sorry I ever said you were horrid. I like you now, big red cow, and one day I'll help to milk you!'

'Moo-ooo-ooo!' said the cow, pleased. 'Moo-ooo-oooo!'

Old Ugly the Water Grub

Once upon a time there was an ugly grub that lived in a little pond.

At first it was only small, but as time went on it grew. It had a long body, with many joints, and six legs on which it could crawl about in the mud.

The other creatures in the pond thought it was very ugly indeed. 'Look at it!' said the pretty little stickleback. 'I'd be ashamed of myself if I was as ugly as that!'

'I don't like its face,' said a water-snail with a nicely-curved shell. 'There's something wrong with its face.'

'Let's call it Ugly,' said a cheeky tadpole. 'Old Ugly! There goes Old Ugly! Hi, Old Ugly! What's wrong with your face?'

The grub did not like being called names. It could not help being ugly. Nor could it help its enormous appetite. It was always hungry.

The water-snail sometimes crawled near to where Old Ugly lay in the mud. 'Hallo, Old Ugly!' it would say. 'Would you like me for your dinner? Well, you can't have me, because I can always pop back into my shell-house if you come too near. What's the matter with your face, Old Ugly?'

Certainly the grub had a curious face. The water-snail used to watch him, and see it change.

Sometimes the grub would lie quietly in the water – and then perhaps a cheeky tadpole would swim too near him.

At once a strange thing happened to his face. The lower part of it seemed to fall away – and out would shoot a kind of claw that caught hold of the tadpole. The claw put the little creature to the grub's mouth – and that was the end of him.

Then the grub would fold up this curious claw, and put it by his face, so that it seemed part of it. The water-snail was very curious about it.

'Show me how it works,' he asked the grub. 'No – I'm not coming too near you – and I'm only going to put my head out just a little, in case you think of taking hold of it. Now – show me how that funny claw-thing works.'

The grub showed him. It was very clever the way he could fold it up below his face, so that it looked like part of it. It was on a hinge, and could be folded or unfolded just as he liked. 'It's a good idea,' said the water-snail. 'You are really rather a lazy creature, aren't you, Old Ugly – you like to lie about in the mud, and wait for your dinner to come to you. You don't like rushing about after it, like the water-beetle does. So that claw-thing is useful to you.'

'Very useful,' said the grub. 'I can just lie here and wait – and then shoot out my claw – like this!'

The water-snail shot his head in just in time. 'Don't play any tricks with *me*, Old Ugly,' he said. 'I tell you, I've got a hard shell. You could never eat me.'

The other creatures in the pond were very careful not to go too near the grub. When they saw his face looking up out of the mud, they swam away quickly.

'That dreadful face!' said a gnat grub. 'It is horrid the way it seems to fall to pieces when that lower part, the claw, shoots out. It really gives me a fright. There he is – look! Hallo, Old Ugly!'

'Don't call me that,' said the grub. 'It hurts me. I can't help being what I am. It is not my fault that I am ugly.'

But nobody called him anything else. Nobody

liked him. The snails teased him. The stickleback said that he would tear him to bits with his three spines if he went near his little nest of eggs. The tadpoles gathered round him at a safe distance and called him all the rude names they knew. And they knew a good many, for they were cheeky little things.

Even the frogs hated the grub. 'He snapped at my leg today,' said one. 'I didn't see him in the mud down there, and swam too near. Out shot that claw of his and gave my leg quite a nip.'

'Let's turn him out of the pond,' said the stickleback. 'We don't want him here. He is ugly and greedy and fierce. If we all get together, we can turn him out.'

So the stickleback, the frog, the two big black water-beetles, the tadpoles, the water-spider, the gnat grub, and the water-snails all swam or crawled to where Old Ugly was hiding in the mud, and called to him, 'We don't want you in the pond!'

'Go away from here or I will tear you with my spines!'

'Leave our pond, or we will chase you round and round it till you are tired out!'

Old Ugly's face fell apart, and he shot out his long claw in anger. 'How can I go away? There is nowhere for me to go to. I can't leave this pond. It is my home.'

'You must leave it by to-morrow or we will bite you,' said one of the water-beetles, the very fierce one.

'Yes, you must, or I shall rip you with my spines,' said the stickleback, and he went scarlet with rage.

Well, of course, there was nowhere that the ugly grub could go. He could not breathe out of the water. He could not catch his dinner except in the pond.

He was sad and frightened. Next day the other creatures came to him again. The stickleback rushed at him and nearly pricked him with his spines. The fierce water-beetle tried to bite his tail.

'Go away!' cried the water-creatures. 'Go away, Old Ugly.'

Old Ugly felt ill. There was the stem of a water-plant near by and he began to crawl up it.

'Leave me alone,' he said. 'I feel ill.'

The water-snail crawled after him. The stickleback tried to spear him with his spines. The grub went on up the stem, and at last came to the top of the water. He crawled right out of the water, and stayed there on the stem, still feeling strange.

'Has he gone?' cried the tadpoles. 'Has he gone?'

'He's out of the water,' said the water-snail. Then he stared hard at the grub. 'I don't think he feels very well,' he said. 'He looks a bit strange.'

The grub stood still on the stem, and waited. He didn't know what he was waiting for, but he knew that something was going to happen. He felt very strange.

Then, quite suddenly, the skin began to split across his head. The water-snail saw it and called down to the creatures below:

'His skin has split! He really is ill! Something strange is happening to Old Ugly.'

Something strange certainly *was* happening to the ugly grub. The skin split down his back too. Out from the top part came a head – a new head – a head with big brilliant eyes! The water-snail nearly fell from his leaf with astonishment.

'He's got a new head,' he said. 'And my goodness, he's got a new body too! His skin is splitting down his back. I can see his new body beneath.'

'Is it as ugly as his old one?' asked a tadpole.

'No – it's beautiful – it's wonderful!' said the snail, watching patiently. And, indeed, it *was* wonderful. As time went on, the grub was able to wriggle completely out of his old skin.

He was no longer an ugly grub. He was a most

beautiful dragonfly! His body gleamed bright green and blue – and what a long body it was! He had four wings, big, shining ones that quivered in the sun. He had wonderful eyes. He had six rather weak legs and a strong jaw.

'The ugly grub has changed into a dragonfly!' said the water-snail. 'Oh, what a strange thing to see! Dragonfly, what has happened?'

'I don't know!' said the dragonfly, glad to feel his wings drying in the sun. 'I don't know! I only know that for a long, long time I was an ugly grub in the pond – but that now I have wings, and I shall live in the air! Oh, what a wonderful time I shall have!'

When his wings were ready, the dragonfly darted high in the air on them, his blue and green body almost as bright as the kingfisher's feathers. He flew off, looking for insects to catch in his strong jaws. Snap – he caught a fly!

'What a beautiful creature!' said a little mouse in surprise, as the dragonfly whizzed past. 'Hi, Beauty, Beauty, Beautiful! Where are you going?'

'Are you talking to *me*?' said the dragonfly in surprise. 'I've always been called Old Ugly before!'

'You are lovely, lovely, *lovely*!' said the mouse. 'Stay and talk to me, do!'

But the dragonfly was off again, darting through

the air on strong wings, as happy as a swallow.

'What a strange life I have had!' he hummed to himself. 'This is the nicest part. How happy I am, how happy I am!'

Maybe you will see him darting down the lane or over the pond. Look out for him, won't you, for he is one of the loveliest insects.

Acknowledgements

All efforts have been made to seek necessary permissions. The stories in this publication first appeared in the following publications:

'Winkle-Pip Walks Out' first appeared in *Sunny Stories for Little Folks*, No. 135, 1932.

'Trit-Trot The Pony' first appeared in *Enid Blyton's Sunny Stories*, No. 297, 1943.

'The Magic Walking Stick' first appeared in *Sunny Stories for Little Folk*, No. 152, 1932.

'The Snoozy Gnome' first appeared in *Sunny Stories for Little Folk*, No. 248, 1936.

'The Three Strange Travellers' first appeared in *Sunny Stories for Little Folks*, No. 165, 1933.

'The Secret Cave' first appeared in *Sunny Stories for Little Folks*, No. 61, 1929.

'The Proud Little Dog' first appeared in *My Second Enid Blyton Book*, Latimer House, 1953.

'The Little Bully' first appeared in *Teachers World*, Nos. 1677-1678, 1935.

'The Six Little Motor Cars' first appeared in *Enid Blyton's Sunny Stories*, No. 303, 1943.

'The Unkind Children' first appeared in *Enid Blyton's Sunny Stories*, No. 301, 1943.

'The Little Paper Folk' first appeared in *Sunny Stories for Little Folks*, No. 174, 1933.

'The Tiresome Poker' first appeared in two separate parts in *Enid Blyton's Sunny Stories*, No. 280 and No. 281, 1942.

'The Enchanted Table' first appeared in *Sunny Stories for Little Folks*, No. 152, 1932.

'The Boy Who Boasted' first appeared in *Enid Blyon's Sunny Stories*, No. 294, 1943.

'The Disagreeable Monkey' first appeared in *Sunny Stories for Little Folks*, No. 169, 1933.

'The Golden Enchanter' first appeared in *Sunny Stories for Little Folks*, No. 146, 1932.

'The Wizard's Umbrella' first appeared in *Sunny Stories for Little Folks*, No. 202, 1934.

'The Little Singing Kettle' first appeared as 'The Humpy Goblin's Kettle' in *Sunny Stories for Little Folks*, No. 187, 1934.

'The Little Brown Duck' first appeared in *Enid Blyton's Sunny Stories*, No. 32, 1937.

'The Pixie Who Killed the Moon' first appeared in *Sunny Stories for Little Folks*, No. 16, 1927.

'Old Bufo the Toad' first appeared in *Sunny Stories*, No. 8, 1937.

'The Boy Who Pulled Tails' first appeared in *Sunny Stories for Little Folks*, No. 189, 1934.

'The Tale of Mr. Spectacles' first appeared in *Teachers World*, Nos. 1719-1720, 1936.

'The Goblin's Pie' first appeared in *Sunny Stories for Little Folks*, No. 162, 1933.

'Feefo Goes to Market' first appeared in *Sunny Stories for Little Folks*, No. 190, 1934.

'Adventures of the Sailor Doll' first appeared in *Enid Blyton's Sunny Stories*, No. 6, 1937.

'Clickety-Clack' first appeared in *Sunny Stories for Little Folks*, No. 90, 1930.

'The Enchanted Bone' first appeared in *Sunny Stories*, No. 35, 1937.

'Fiddle-dee-dee, The Foolish Brownie' first appeared in *Sunny Stories for Little Folks*, No. 103, 1930.

'The Elephant and the Snail' first appeared in *Sunny Stories*, No. 31,

1937.

'The Invisible Gnome' first appeared in *Teachers World*, Nos. 1747-1748, 1936.

'Mr. Grumpygroo's Hat' first appeared in *Sunny Stories for Little Folks*, No. 88, 1930.

'The Fairy and the Policeman' first appeared in *Sunny Stories for Little Folks*, No. 147, 1932.

'The Little Red Squirrel' first appeared in *Sunny Stories*, No. 33, 1937.

'The Little Walking House' first appeared as 'The House With Six Legs' in *Sunny Stories for Little Folks*, No. 190, 1934.

'Sly-One's Puzzle' first appeared in *Teachers World*, No. 1722, 1936.

'Mr. Widdle on the Train' first appeared in *Teachers World*, No. 1735, 1936.

'Who Stole the Crown?' first appeared in *Sunny Stories for Little Folks*, no. 103, 1930.

'"Tell Me My Name!"' first appeared in *Sunny Stories*, No. 8, 1937.

'Gooseberry Whiskers' first appeared in *Sunny Stories for Little Folks*, No. 92, 1930.

'The Mean Old Man' first appeared in *Sunny Stories*, No. 35, 1937.

'The Nice Juicy Carrot' first appeared in *Sunny Stories for Little Folks*, No. 171, 1933.

'The Dandelion Clock' first appeared in *Sunny Stories*, No. 34, 1937.

'King Bom's Ice Cream' first appeared in *Sunny Stories for Little Folks*, No. 188, 1934.

'The Cat, the Mouse and the Fox' first appeared in *Teachers World*, No. 1706, 1936.

'The Bed that Took a Walk' first appeared in *The Enid Blyton Pennant Readers (No. 15)*, Macmillan, 1950.

'Brownie's Magic' first appeared in *The Enid Blyton Nature Readers (No. 1)*, Macmillan, 1945.

'Dame Lucky's Umbrella' first appeared in *Sunny Stories*, No. 424, 1948.

'He Wouldn't Take the Trouble' first appeared in *The Enid Blyton Pennant Readers (No. 28)*, Macmillan, 1950.

'Muddle's Mistake' first appeared in *The Enid Blyton Nature Readers (No. 11)*, Macmillan, 1945.

'Silky and the Snail' first appeared in *The Enid Blyton Nature Readers*

(No. 5), Macmillan, 1945.

'The Train that Went to Fairyland' first appeared in *Sunny Stories*, No. 330, 1944.

'The Cat That Was Forgotten' first appeared in *The Enid Blyton Pennant Readers (No. 6)*, Macmillan, 1950.

'The Dog Who Wanted a Home' first appeared in *The Enid Blyton Nature Readers (No. 3)*, Macmillan, 1945.

'Freckles for a Thrush' first appeared in *Sunday Mail*, No. 1890, 1944.

'He's a Horrid Dog' first appeared in *Sunny Stories*, No. 411, 1947.

'Hoppitty-Skip and Crawl-About' first appeared in *The Enid Blyton Nature Readers (No. 25)*, Macmillan, 1945.

'The Lamb Without a Mother' first appeared in *The Enid Blyton Nature Readers (No. 7)*, Macmillan, 1945.

'Moo-ooo-ooo' first appeared in *The Enid Blyton Nature Readers (No. 10)*, Macmillan, 1945.

'Old Ugly the Water Grub' first appeared in *The Enid Blyton Nature Readers (No. 10)*, Macmillan, 1945.